The Golden Secret of Kri Koro

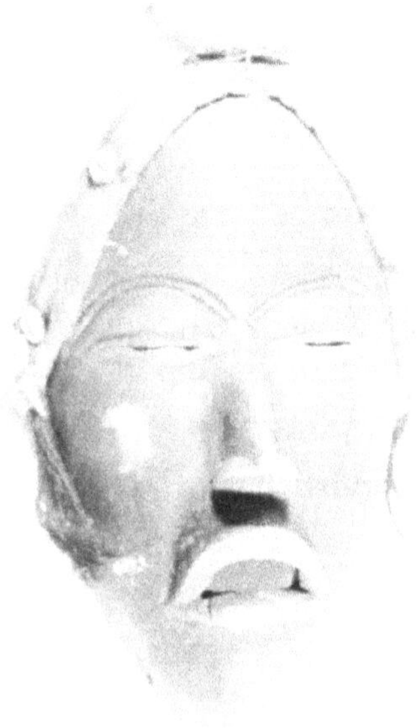

by

Stephen Belcher

The characters and events in this book are fictitious. Any similarity to real persons, living or dead, is coincidental and not intended by the author.

Back Cover design by MiblArt & Trisha Lewis

Cover Photos taken by author.

Back Jacket Photo taken by David Conrad

PHOTOS AVAILABLE on Author's FaceBook Page for full in-color enjoyment. These photos were taken by the author unless otherwise noted.
https://www.facebook.com/stephen.belcher.7370/

Edits & Layout & Publishing via Van Velzer Press
ISBN: 978-1-954253-06-3

Printed in the United States of America

Van Velzer Press
Americana with a Twist

VanVelzerPress.com

DEDICATION

The first debt is to relatives. My father's career in the Foreign Service exposed me to countries and cultures that have enriched my appreciation of our human world; my mother's enthusiasm and interest in all those countries and her encouragement of reading set me on my course. The second debt is to my father's sisters, Jane Belcher and Barbara Mericle; an inheritance due to their Depression-conditioned frugality allowed me the time to write this book.

The second, and principal debt, is to the wide community of Africanists that over many generations have documented the traditions and narratives that I have borrowed to construct this book. The extent of their work is poorly appreciated: it was published in specialized journals and in many languages, and so remains invisible to a general public. Special recognition goes to my colleagues in the Mande Studies Association whose research covers the geographic area presented in this novel. I have learned much from them over the years (and any mistakes are due to my misunderstanding). In the matter of oral tradition, special recognition should go to David Conrad who has been a guide, a dear friend, and an inspiration in his dedication to recording and disseminating the oral traditions of the peoples of the Manden.

This community should be extended to include the many people I have met in my travels in Africa who welcomed me, and from whom I learned histories and perspectives.

Finally, I would like to thank Trish Lewis for her enthusiasm for the project and the quality of the work she has done in transforming a manuscript to a book.

PART I

Mortars and Pestles: 1980
in the streets of Jenne, Mali

CHAPTER 1

I LEFT MY VILLAGE when my father was murdered. He had just started the noon meal under the dense shade of a mango tree at the center of our large family compound. To his right sat his younger brother, my uncle. Nearby were two cousins, sons of the uncle, waiting for the signal from their elders to join them at the bowl. Across the courtyard, I stood talking to my mother about work in her garden patch.

My uncle's first wife had just placed the bowl before the men. The younger brother naturally deferred to his elder. So my father ate first, molding a ball of *to* (pounded millet paste) and dipping it into the sauce at the center of the bowl. He was just raising a second ball of to to his mouth when his body went into a spasm. I looked from my father's eyes—suddenly glazed, slightly bulging, and empty—to my uncle's face and saw on his lips the flicker of a triumphant smile. On my father's mouth I saw a wisp of foam. His head bowed down, the first movement in the slow collapse of his body. I understood immediately that my uncle had poisoned my father. Control of the family lands passed from older to younger brother, and my uncle was envious.

Before I could decide what to do, my mother settled the matter. She was sitting on a small stool before her hut and had seen what I saw. She reached out, took my hand, stared up into my eyes, and quietly ordered, "Fly! Do not look back. Go now!"

"But..." I began to protest, numbed by shock and then worrying what would become of her.

"This is not your affair," she cut me short. "Do not waste time in talk if you wish to live. Go now."

So I ran. I took nothing. I had little enough to bring: perhaps my best *dloki*, a handful of *cowries*, some food. My wealth was in my kin, and I had just lost them. I turned from my mother, circled her hut, and then began to run between compounds, through cooking spaces and passageways until I came to the women's garden plots that surrounded our village. I raced through these without thought following the first trail I saw leading into the bush. I didn't choose my path; it chose me.

The path led east, over the dry *marigot* that flooded during the rainy season. I crossed the streambed without thinking. Beyond the watercourse, other paths branched off to outlying fields farmed by the men. I kept to the central way, the quickest escape from the village. My feet took me beyond the fields into the bush; the domain of hunters and wild beasts. The path became a narrow track, hard to follow.

I ran, my eyes now fixed on the ground before me, willing a path into being before my feet. They avoided the small termite mounds that rose mushroom-shaped from the earth, the thorny bushes, the occasional acacia with low-hanging branches. I thought only of placing my feet one before the other on what trail I could see—other thoughts, struggling to be recognized, were too painful.

My course was interrupted. One foot caught! I fell flat, my body spread on the hard, hot soil. I pulled my palms under my shoulders and began to raise myself, the momentum of my panic broken by surprise at the fall.

"*Bamana-kè,*" a voice addressed me.

I looked up at a large termite mound, the sort that rises out of the low scrub into massive halls with buttressed bastions and towering spires. To this day I don't believe it was on my path until I fell. Sitting above me, on a ledge between the spires, was a small reddish figure.

"Rise, *Bamana-kè*. We must talk."

"My life is in danger," I said. "My uncle and cousins..."

"They will not harm you," said the figure.

It was elusive to my sight: a small, vaguely human shape seated between the ocher towers as though the termites had built it a throne. Its skin was red, darker than the red of fresh blood, and glistened. The eyes...I could not see them. The face vanished in a haze. I could see hands, with long fingers, and feet which seemed to point backwards. I had the impression of wrinkles and age.

"*Bamana-kè,*" said the being. "I require your help."

I considered. This being was certainly a *wokòlò.* I had never before directly encountered a spirit of the bush. Such meetings were the privilege of diviners and hunters. From what I had heard, its magical powers should allow it to do anything it wished. Such beings rarely appeared to the uninitiated, although it was accepted that great hunters could find them and had probably reached some bargain with them to allow success in the chase.

"*N'koro,* how can a human help a master of the bush?"

"That is something you will see in time," answered the spirit. "I wish to set your feet upon a path. You have lost your heritage, you have lost your village. I take from you your *jamu.* Without your family name, you are now such a man as I need."

He spoke the truth. My uncle had poisoned my father—I

had seen the admission on his face. He did it because my father was the senior of the clan and controlled the family lands. My uncle had numerous sons; he had long envied my father his authority. My father's death would make him the clan head, his claim strengthened by his many sons' arms.

"N'koro, I will help you as I can," I told him. Refusal was impossible. Humans are powerless against the spirits.

The spirit nodded, acknowledging my agreement. "You will find your path before you, although I cannot tell you its length. I will give you the sight to perceive other signs. Be patient, and remember your engagement. Now follow the path you see." The red skin shimmered and flashed in the sunlight; my eyes shut before the glare. When I opened them, the spirit had vanished. Before me, the beaten clay suggested a path around the termite mound. I followed it.

This path led down to a copse of trees where water collected in the rainy season. I walked now, my urgency cooled by the encounter with the *wokòlò*. Curiously, I could see no prints or marks of passage in the dust, but the line of the trail was clear and luminous, almost bright enough to limn the overhanging grasses and leaves with backlit edges.

As I left the copse, I heard the murmur of voices and soon I met their source: a salt caravan was halted in the shade. Some thirty or forty men stood, sat, or reclined before me, all aligned along the path. The carriers had laid aside their loads: the broad slabs of rocksalt wrapped in leaves against any destructive rain or moisture.

At the head of the caravan, to my right, I observed a cluster of activity. The master, as I presumed from his robe (white despite the dust) stood over two men who were ministering to a third lying limp against the grass. Even from where I stood it was clear that death rather than exhaustion or fatigue had come to their patient. Their efforts were futile.

"No pulse, no breath," said the man who knelt to the left of the corpse. "He is gone."

"That serpent was from Shaitan!" cried the caravan master. "Why did it strike him?" And then he turned to the others who were watching. "Tiemoko!" he called. "Are you not from his village? Did you not come together when I was gathering porters?"

"*Ah-ah,*" answered Tiemoko, who was seated not far away and who had been watching the attempt to save the victim. "We came together."

"Did he leave a family? Who must be told of his passing?"

"He was no elder," said Tiemoko drily. "Many were glad when he left the village. Few will care he is gone."

"What was his faith?"

"He was a Bamana of the village. I do not know if he had joined a cult."

"Then we shall bury him here and let others worry about the rites. On our return, you shall carry the news to his family."

"*Ah-ah,*" answered Tiemoko again, clearly meaning 'maybe, but unlikely.'

The master then saw me.

"And who are you?" he demanded without any of the usual greetings.

"A wanderer," I answered, then added as a precaution, "I am a free man. I flee no master."

"A wanderer who comes to my caravan just as a man has died, just as a load has lost its bearer, just as a slithering servant of demons has ended a human life by striking from the bushes...Are you a servant of God or of the Devil? What brings you to us?"

As he spoke, I examined him, as he me. He was of middle height and age. His face showed lines. I felt, somehow, that his cheeks were more used to smiles than his brow was to frowns. But now his face showed anger and pain at loss of life.

"I cannot speak for our meeting," I answered cautiously. "My feet have been set upon a path."

After a moment of scrutiny he declared, "There is something of the jinns about you. Allah does nothing by chance, and here you arrive just as a man dies...It seems a sign." He looked down to the men who had been trying to revive the corpse. One I recognized from his cap as a Bamana; the other I could not place immediately. "Can we trust this man? Is he from Shaitan, like that deadly *bida*?"

"*Eh,* Diawara!" said the Bamana. "How can we know the worth of a stranger?"

The second was more optimistic. "He is a man, not a serpent nor a jinn. The questions are, will he work? And can he carry a load?"

"I can carry a load," I answered immediately. "If you have work, my back is strong."

"We shall test that," said Diawara. I understood that I would join the caravan. "First, we must deal with these mortal remains. Tiemoko! Are special rites required?"

"Put him in the earth," answered Tiemoko. "You say that Shaitan has taken him; I think it was Miniamba, the *subaga muso* who takes the form of a serpent across the path to kill those who have been doomed. He had reasons to leave his village. Bury him and place a stone over his remains."

My ears echoed to no real sound and my eyes blinked. Hovering over the corpse, I saw a spirit, a pallid double of the dead man. It pointed distinctly to a calabash hanging at the belt of one of the porters and then gestured directions.

"Not a stone." I was surprised to hear myself speak, the words coming from some flash of understanding. "We must lay him with his head to the south and his face turned to the east. Over his head, bury a calabash with a hole in the bottom and the spout above the ground."

Diawara and his two captains turned to me in doubt.

"And we must make an offering of *dolo*," I added. *Dolo*, a bitter millet beer, figured prominently in all the burial rites of my village. Later I had occasion to explain to Diawara: the essence of *dolo* links different states of being. The beer calmed the departed spirit. The dead man's *nyama*, his vital power, was released and could depart the body. The calabash served as a channel. It was unlikely that any kinsman would find this burial spot, but it was important to leave the possibility.

"Are you a *soma*?" asked Tiemoko.

"No, I am no *soma*, but those are the rites if you wish his spirit to leave you in peace," I answered.

Diawara and his captains exchanged glances and then nodded. Men began digging with *dabaw* (hoes) and we laid the body to rest. Diawara looked away while a small calabash of *dolo* appeared and was poured onto the grave. For a moment, we all stood silent. Then Diawara considered the sun and its position in the western sky.

"We shall move on," he ordered. "I see no reason to linger here. We shall stop at the time of *fitiri*." Then he turned to me. "You said you were ready to work. There is a load of salt to carry. Are you willing?"

"Indeed," I answered.

The dead man's load was there: a slab of rocksalt wrapped

in leaves. I was handed his head pad, fallen when the serpent struck. I raised the salt over my head and settled it on the pad; the other bearers watched to see if I had balanced it properly. So did Diawara. I realized that I carried great wealth. Surely this load of salt would buy several head of cattle...I learned later that such a bar of salt traded for a slave, or even two if the exchange was made far from the desert.

Wealth, and also weight. I was accustomed to the labor of fields, clearing scrub and tilling earth, wielding the *daba* and the axe, but not to the task of carrying a load on my head. In our world, that was women's work. I thought of the line of girls who would soon—as the sun settled in the west—return from the spring above the village with their pots of water on their heads. Some would sing. Once I heard one calling:

Water is sweet,
Water is clear,
Water is heavy!

Path be sweet,
Path be clear,
Path be short!

That song, and that girl swaying along the path, were lovely. My new load was not so sweet. I bore the burden of a dead man, and behind me I had left another corpse. Yet I was now on the path of the *wokòlò*. My father's death had become a distant reality. In our villages fathers and sons are rarely close until later in life: the father's attention is divided among several wives and their offspring; death comes too often to the very young. Sons must turn to their fathers for assistance in finding a bride, in obtaining fields, and fathers yield their wealth only grudgingly, for they too, are often considering another bride. The truest family bond lies in the mother's hut: *badenya,* we call it, the love nurtured by a mother for her children. Now even thoughts of my mother were numbed. The *wokòlò* had taken my family name, my *jamu*. I was lost and alone. But the spirit said my feet were set upon a path. I could only hope to find my way.

The next day was long. We set off in the cool of the early morning, just after the birds began their chatter. We stopped for water and food, resting in the hottest hours and continuing until the time of the evening prayer when Diawara called a halt. I was aching from the muscles behind my ears—where had those come from?—to the tendons at my ankles. Salt is sharp, salt is bright, salt is heavy! I rubbed my neck.

"*Bamana-kè,*" said the man who had followed me in line and who once steadied me just as I was slipping on a patch of loose sand. He held out a small pot of paste. From the smell I recognized it as *karité,* a cream which the women of our village sometimes acquired in neighboring markets. They bought it as a cake wrapped in leaves.

"Rub it in," he said, and stretched out his leg, showing where he, too, had smeared and smoothed the paste over his skin. I nodded thanks and dipped my fingers to the pot. We sat and watched as women, whom I had not noticed before, prepared our dinner: dishes of *to* and some meat sauce that must have been left over from the noon meal.

Diawara and several other men were performing their evening prayers. I understood that they were Muslims. No Muslims lived in our village; we had been spared the Fula horsemen who spread their faith at the edge of a sword, but Muslim traders occasionally passed through. These men passed a gourd of water from hand to hand, rinsing face and hands and bare feet, and then they faced the east, away from the setting sun that glowed red through the trees. Diawara stood in front of the small group and muttered words I couldn't understand:

"La'illa ila 'illahi wa Muhamad rasul il-lahi, al-hamdu l'illahi." He and his fellows bowed and muttered more words, and bowed again. Then they knelt upon the ground and spoke in unison as they bowed their heads to the dirt. Their shadows spread before them over the ground.

"Remember," said my companion, "when they do this on the road, we can rest. But in the morning, they will wake us before dawn."

"Where are we bound?"

"To the *worodugu* and the town of Minignan. There Diawara sells his salt and buys kola nuts, and perhaps ivory, to take back north to Bougouni."

I had no idea where Minignan or Bougouni might be. The world was a much larger place than it had seemed from the shade of my father's mango tree.

Rock Salt:
Harbor of Mopti, Mali in 1980

CHAPTER II

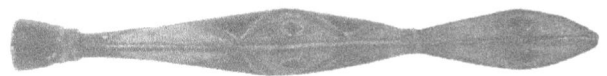

SO MY FEET WERE set blindly upon their dusty red paths across our entrancing and perplexing world. I was numbed in spirit. As days and miles passed, I began to recover. Unattached to family or lineage or place, I began to discover new skills that I attributed to the gift of the *wokòlò*. I also remembered that I owed them a debt of service and wondered how it would be acquitted: this is the story I now share. But it was some years before the occasion for the service arose. I will not tell all my travels until that time, but this first trip under Diawara deserves an account, if only because towards its end I met the partner who would show me what I must do. It was also my initiation into the greater world beyond my village, the start of my education.

I had two teachers on those first steps of my road: first, Boloba, my companion of the muscle-soothing *karité* paste, and then Diawara himself, the caravan leader. Diawara was at first quite suspicious of me; he associated me with lethal serpents and death. He recognized that I had an inexplicable link with numinous powers; this perception led to caution rather than trust.

Boloba held no such concerns. He was moved by innate kindness, or perhaps by some odd sense of kinship. He believed my village (guessing, for I never named it to him) lay close to his own home. Of all the saltporters he was the most sensitive to individual behaviors and concerns. He listened, he learned, and then, sometimes, he would do what he could. He had a soft and kindly voice that did indeed reflect his character.

At any rate, he took me as his charge. On the first night he found me a sleeping cloth to keep off mosquitoes and other biting insects. The dead man, whose salt I carried, had been buried in his cloth for want of a shroud. On the second night Boloba again offered the *karité* paste to soothe my aches. Over the next days he acquainted me with the rhythms and routines of the caravan. He led me to get my ration of food from the women who accompanied our caravan and helped me to cajole extra snacks—a piece of boiled cassava, a strip of sugar cane. And he told me about our companions along the line, teaching me names—nicknames most often, for we did not discuss origins. None of the bearers were slaves (or captives, as they are sometimes called) but still social rank or origin was not mentioned. I later learned that in past days the caravans would have been almost twice the size: slaves bearing salt who would be sold, along with the salt, at the various waystations of the route, and an equal number of armed guards to enforce discipline and prevent escape. But the recent turmoil of Samori's wars and the new rules that had come with the *nasrani* changed the situation. Merchants could find unattached, hungry men to bear the loads. Many porters now made a round trip, delivering salt to the forest zones in the south and then carrying the delicate kola nuts north to the savannas. The return trip moved at a quicker pace to ensure the kola nuts could be sold while fresh.

This was Boloba's second trip with Diawara. He hoped to earn enough for a bride price; he was the fourth son in a family of strained means. For those who worked with Diawara, payment meant a share in the profits at the end of the voyage unless one chose to leave the caravan early. This did happen. Several bearers had been marched north as captives of Samori's *sofas*, and so they now used the caravan to return to their villages.

For several days we marched through a familiar landscape where I knew the trees and the bush. Then our surroundings changed. The trees grew thicker, larger, and massive. Passing under them we entered a world of daytime darkness. Their branches laced over our heads; our path twisted around their great trunks, some as large around as the huts of my father's compound. I welcomed the cool shade, but later I shivered in unease. We were not alone in this forest. Not that we saw animals. The forest was silent around us, nor did we see people. But with that trace of mental echo of the spirit world, I knew that in these woods immaterial beings surrounded us. They were not now concerned with us—our passage was too fleeting. Rather, most seemed to follow the massively slow time-sense of the great trees. They measured the span of the branches, the fall of the seeds. Some, I think, called to the fruitbats whose lumbering and clumsy flight was at least something I recognized; they emerged in the evening, at much the same time as Diawara called a stop for the evening prayer: the *fitiri* that also marked the end of a day's march.

The forest also brought us dangers. One morning, the column caught up with Djime Koita, who normally walked ahead out of sight. He was standing, his right hand raised, staring at a metal blade sunk in the center of the path. The hilt stood up from the ground. I learned later it was a cutlass, a steel blade traded up from the coast and the *nasrani* world beyond.

"*Ah-ah,*" said Diawara when he saw what had stopped Koita.

"Shall we pass?"

"Who do you think has left this?"

"Many of Samori's *sofa*s have not returned to farming. But there may also have been trouble in Kong, or among the Baule." The *sofa*s were the warriors of the army of Samori Toure; even in my village we had heard how he conquered lands, fought the *nasrani*, and was at last defeated.

Diawara turned and looked back over his caravan. Clearly, he was weighing human strength and will, the value of his goods, the threat of this unseen brigand, and perhaps also the distance to the nearest established community where we might find shelter—if it was not they who had set this sign in the path.

"I will not risk conflict," decided Diawara. "We will leave half a salt bar and march on. If they require more, I am sure we shall learn of it."

We passed without incident. In the next village, I saw Diawara and Koita discussing the matter with the town ruler (I never learned his title or what territory he claimed to rule). What they learned seemed to satisfy them that the path of caution, yielding the salt, had been safest: there were in fact large groups of brigands hiding in the forest. We engaged a guide from that village, a man who wore a tattered brown hunter's shirt on which numerous amulets had been sewn. He was armed with a bow, arrows, and a slim bladed spear as well as a heavy knife.

Diawara was wise to hire him. He slipped ahead of the column and of Koita, vanishing quickly into the dark shadows of the trees. Two hours later we came upon him standing in the path, motioning us all to silence. We were not chattering—men with a bar of salt upon their heads save their breath—but there was some noise. We paused, and the hunter explained the danger to Diawara: further on, where the path dipped into a vale, was a small herd of elephants. They were watering themselves and feeding on the reeds.

This news was both exciting and frightening. Elephants were at one time common in my region. They raided our crops. They could be frightened away by loud noises, and so small boys, who delight in such production, would be set to guard the fields. But elephants can also kill: we heard of a man torn in half by a charging elephant. Recently, elephants had become rare. The greatest threat to our crops came from the rooting warthogs and plundering baboons. I had never seen an elephant.

This herd had several calves; it was clearly best not to alarm them. Diawara and the hunter discussed paths. The hunter's descriptions of alternate routes through the forest did not satisfy Diawara, so he decided we would stop early for the midday meal and hope the elephants would move on as we ate. Naturally, we all talked about the elephants. The hunter told us that elephants were indeed fewer in number, but that this small herd continued in the region. People said this small herd was formed after a village maiden married a king of the elephants who transformed her people into beings of his kind. Because of this kinship, through marriage and blood, the villages in the area did not hunt the elephants, nor did they allow others to hunt them, and so the herd survived.

* * *

Diawara became less wary of me after an incident involving a spirit path. He clearly associated me with the death of my predecessor and with snakes (and his book taught him that snakes were evil). He had not yet decided whether my arrival was due to evil magic or to the divine will that he acknowledged many times each day.

We were approaching a village through the dark forest. We could see light from farmed clearings to one side—when I again felt the echoing silence of the *wokòlò* in my ears. I half-expected to see another termite mound. Instead, I saw a glow ahead of us, a glimmering trail through the forest that crossed our path. Along the trail walked spirits of various forms. I didn't recognize any of the shapes. These were not the horned *chi-wara* of our harvest dances, nor the hyena-headed *komo,* nor the lions and buffalo and fish of other festivals. Nor did they resemble the red, knock-kneed *wokòlò* who had set me on my path. One or two were conical, like huge bundles of millet stalks stood on end, their heads deformed by bulbous eyes and dangling snouts. Several had tusks or horns or mandibles about their mouth-parts. A few had the heads of birds with long and fearsome beaks, like the storks that devastate the shallows of the rain-ponds. One was two-headed and walked on all fours. Several hopped, but not lightly like mice; they were squat and broad-faced and their glowing skin was mottled with livid spots like toads. One was a stinking spirit, its form vague in a fog of repulsive aromatic particles. Some had the spindly legs of insects, others the jointed limbs of goats or gazelles; a few walked on two legs like men. They were not substantial. Looking at them, I had the sense of seeing through reflections on water into some different world which had attained some congruence with our own, so that the spirits occupied space in both worlds. They were luminous, yet not bright. Somehow, through their light, I sensed colors we humans cannot see:

textured brightnesses, warmths, and coolnesses.

Nothing in their bearing gave any clue to their purpose save their steady and regular pace, the even spacing between individual spirits, and their attention to the path before them. Still, I had little doubt that an intrusion on this path would be disastrous to any mortal.

Geladio Paté, Diawara's second captain, was leading the column and had almost reached the trail. Unawares, he was about to step in front of a large, round four-legged spirit (later, I recognized the shape as that of a hippopotamus), and I was sure he would suffer.

"Stop!" I cried as loudly as I could. Fortunately he did, turning to see what caused this most unusual interruption. "There is a spirit path across our trail," I explained. "The spirits are moving along it, we cannot cross it now. Unless," I added, for Geladio was glaring at me, "you wish to accompany the spirits to their destination."

Geladio turned away from me impatiently, clearly planning to proceed.

"No!" I protested. "The spirits are passing! You must not cross their trail."

"Geladio!" Diawara's voice stopped him. Diawara turned back to me. "What do you see?"

"A path crosses our own, traced in light," I told him. "Along it I see a procession of spirits. They are walking, they show their power ..." I paused. "It would be death or madness to cross the path at this moment."

Diawara's eyes moved from me back to to Geladio. "Paté, wait!" he ordered. "We all know that this is a forest of spirits. Let us be cautious. *Bamana-kè*, tell us when the path is clear."

I moved up to stand beside Geladio. I gazed east, the

direction from which the spirits were coming: a glow still moved along the unseen trail as small and shapeless entities swarmed in the wake of the larger, more definite shapes. Finally the glow vanished and the glimmer of the spirit path faded.

"We may pass," I said to Diawara who nodded to Paté.

We spent that night in a village. I found no one to ask about the spirits that dwelled there or why they might march.

The day after we crossed the spirit path, Diawara called me over at noontime and indicated that I should join him and the captains at his meal. When the bowl was empty and we had washed our hands he sat back and looked at me. "*Bamana-kè,*" he began. "When you joined us I said you had something of the jinns about you. Now you have warned us about spirit trails. Can you tell me how you came by this knowledge?"

An explanation required family history that I couldn't give. In suppressing shock at my father's death, I had not erased my memories. But when I tried to talk of them, my tongue was stilled. I stammered a few times, trying instead to tell of the encounter with the *wokòlò*. I failed and bowed my head.

Diawara waited until I stopped my stammering. "The spirits have claimed you, and forbid your speech," he stated, as a deduction. "We shall trust that it is for no evil end, for you have helped us. Do you know what your purpose may be?"

Again, I bowed my head.

"You walk in ignorance of your purpose, yet you have been of service to us." He paused in thought. "I am grateful. I presume you have been sent to us. Not to learn the skill of carrying salt, which any beast might do, but to learn about the world of men outside your village. Am I correct that you have never traveled?"

"*Tinye don,*" I confessed. (It was true.)

"You know nothing of the lands from which the salt you carry has come or the people and towns through which it has passed. You believe, perhaps, that your village lies close to the spot where the earth was created."

"I could not say," I answered. That was a mystery for the cults of the village, not something with which young men were concerned.

"I will not ask you of your village's *boliw*. Nor will I tell you of Islam, although you should know that it is the one true faith, perfected through the succession of prophets from Abraham to Mohammed, the Messenger of God, praise be upon him. But you should know something of the histories of the men among whom you will now travel."

My head bowed in acknowledgement of his words.

"We live in a time of change. This is true of all times: change is the marker of human life. No day is exactly like a past day; no man can relive his youth. But these days have brought greater and different changes, not those of natural cycles but the meetings of different worlds. Two or three generations ago the Tukolor Laji Umaru came through the Manding and the Kaarta and Segou like a blazing meteor. He was from our world. He rose in the Futa Toro that lies beyond the kingdom of Bondu. The Tukolor are Fula, and there are many such around us. Paté, who accompanies us, is a Fula. The Fula live in Massina north of Djenne, they live in the Futa Jallon, and you will see them herding cattle wherever their beasts may live and feed. Laji Umaru stayed in the north of the Sahel: the land between the sandy empty desert and the dark forest. Laji Umaru conquered many lands, but died in violence, and his sons...have disputed his heritage.

"In the last generation, twenty years ago, Samori Toure

conquered the lands south of that zone, from the savanna to the forest. He was a Maninka from the west. It is said that in his youth he was a brigand, a trader, and that later he sought wisdom. He killed his own son, whom he had sent to see the *nasrani* in their own country. The son returned from that voyage and told his father that the *nasrani* were too powerful and could not be resisted. For such a cowardly statement, his father ordered him buried alive. Samori's brother, Keme Brema, let himself die in battle because he had offended his elder. Samori was cruel, but Umar was a child of this land. Shall we compare him to Mari Jata Keita who gave us the empire of Mali, or to the Kante upstart from whom Sunjata took the kingdom?"

I nodded eager to hear more.

"Now Samori has been conquered by the *nasrani* he was at last forced to fight, and these *nasrani* have come into our world. They are something new. Their speech is different, their skin is different, they have no understanding of kinship or other relations. They are not part of our old world. The changes they bring may change our world completely. But you must never forget that you are a child of *your* land. I say this not as a Muslim, but as a Diawara, a Soninke, a member of a people that has seen history flow by and remembers it.

"You, Bamana, entrust your histories to your *jeliw*, except in the great houses where the elders recall the details that the *jeliw* dare not speak out loud. Can you tell me the history of your village?"

Abashed, I shook my head. This again was one of those topics that did not concern the *kamalen* (young men). At that age, we learned to work and to keep an eye out for pretty girls when they were free. It was when we were granted fields to cultivate and established a family that men began to learn the background to the rights and obligations that determined the opportunities.

"What crops do you grow? What do you sell?"

"We grow millet and vegetables; some grow tobacco."

"Do men leave your village to trade?"

"A few. They take tobacco or our woven grass mats or perhaps hides and smoked bushmeat."

He considered me. "You know your village. You know nothing of the great web of trade that links our lands and carries goods from one people to another: salt from the desert to the forests, the kola nuts from the forest to the desert, gold when it can be found, the ivory of elephants, the cloth of the weavers, and also the lives of men who have become slaves. This web has persisted through wars and invasions and famines and droughts, over centuries, and it has linked all those it has touched.

"I trade salt from the desert, brought on camels across the ever-moving and barren sands, and then shipped on boats on rivers to further markets. From the river, my porters carry it into the forest regions where it is needed. There I exchange it for kola nuts. I would prefer to find gold or ivory, as once I could. Whatever I buy, I bring north where the kola nut doesn't grow but is highly valued. Gold is welcome everywhere. Commerce of this sort is considered the most worthy occupation by people of my faith, the Jakhanke. We follow the school of Laji Sumare who interpreted the faith for us. We imitate the Prophet of Islam, may peace be upon him, who started in life as a merchant in the lands around Mecca. We find what people need and provide it to them, and from our work and their desires we gain our profit."

"Are you then Arab?" I asked, finally venturing a question.

"No, although some of my people claim descent from an Arab ancestor. The Jakhanke are Soninke in origin. Once the Soninke were kings in these lands." He paused and looked down. "*A kamane no rini, a wo dangini*, sings the *gesere*—what you would call a *jeli*, a *griot*. This world comes into being and it will pass. Other worlds will come, filled with confusion and strife, and so it has been for the Soninke. Our kingdom of Wagadu fell. Soninke leaders later established other realms—Dama Ngile in Nioro, for instance—but the day of the Soninke is past. After the fall of Wagadu, the Maninka arose, under Mari Jata who is also called Sogolon Jata, and they ruled the lands through which we now pass. The Maninka fell, the Songhay rose. The Songhay kings fell before the rifles of the Moroccans. The Moroccans could not settle their rule, and left chaos over the lands. The Bamana of Segou and Kaarta came to power and fought each other, and everyone else. They were known for treachery. Their kingdoms collapsed before the fury of the Tukolor of Laji Umaru. He died. Samori rose to power, and now he has fallen. He was defeated by *nasrani* who are also called *fransawi*. Now these French are here. Who knows what shall come next?

"Still, many need salt and others desire kola, and so there is a place for our work."

Later I asked him about Wagadu, so he explained further.

"Our ancestor Dinga traveled and found a spring of water. He struggled there with the spirit of the waters—a female spirit. He overpowered her and took her daughters to wife. They bore him sons. One of them was a spirit child, and he returned in serpent form into the waters. Dinga traveled to other lands, far from the waters of his wives. As he grew old, two of his sons competed for his powers. The oldest son should have inherited his father's magical materials, but it was the younger who took them: he was aided by an old servant to whom he had shown kindness, while the elder showed him contempt. The younger—Jabe Cisse, his name was—impersonated the older brother before his half-blind father, and so acquired his father's magics. But after that he feared his brother's anger and so he fled. After much wandering he came to the land of his grandmother and encountered his half-brother, who had the form of a great serpent, living in the waters under the earth. There Jabe Cisse established his kingdom. He and his step-brother came to an arrangement: the serpent would bless the land with gold, and the new king would make an annual offering of the land's best wealth: its most beautiful daughter and a noble horse."

Diawara sighed. "It seems a small price to pay for prosperity and wealth, and in many places you will find people who kill each other for far less. But such a balance is unsteady and unsure, and indeed it came to an end. One year, the maiden who was chosen had an admirer—I cannot say a lover, for she was pure and noble. But Mamadi Sefa Dekhote, the halting of speech, determined that he would save the woman he desired, and he rode out with a sharp bright sword on the day she was to be offered. He cut off the head of the serpent as it rose from the well to consume the maiden. The head flew into the air and vanished… but before doing so it cursed the land and promised famine, drought and an end to the gold that had been the wealth of Wagadu.

"The Soninke escaped destruction. The mother of Mamadi lived near the river, the great Joliba. She had storehouses of food, and so she fed the people during the time of the drought. But the city of Wagadu was abandoned and the Soninke began to wander. We are now a dispersed people, with no home to call our own. But we Diakhanke have found the true faith, and I believe that this was the will of our Lord."

"What was the maiden's name?" I asked. As he told the story, a tingle came to me, not quite the unheard echo of *wokòlò* sight, but still a perception out of the ordinary. Diawara looked at me and chuckled.

"Assya," he answered. "A Béréte by her lineage. But that story did not end happily. The hero carried off the maiden, but she refused him. She had wanted to give herself for her people, and she did not love him. He punished her. Her fate is unknown."

Bissandougou, Guinea: 2005
Bissandougou was the capital of Samori Toure, who ruled a state covering parts of Mali and Guinea until he was overthrown by the French

CHAPTER III

I CAME TO KNOW the guards escorting our caravan somewhat better than other bearers, although I'm sure that Boloba knew more of everyone than I. After Diawara showed me favor, they warmed to me and included me in mealtime conversations. Naturally, I eventually asked them how they joined the caravan. They had nothing to hide about their origins, so they talked. Perhaps it was the truth.

Geladio Paté was a Fula—one of those Fula, he claimed, that 'when you twist his neck, milk spurts out,' although in our travels together I never heard him longing for the Fula staple of soured milk. He preferred *dolo,* millet beer. The cattle-herding Fula are known all across all the bright savanna north of the great forests, and almost every Bamana village has a Fula in residence to care for the herds in which wealth is invested. "I am a peaceful man," he said, by contrast to his great-grandfather, Hama the Red. That great-grandfather lived in the time of the strife between the Bamana of Segou and the Fula of Massina. This man was accounted a notable warrior. "In one day," said Paté, "he destroyed three villages along the Joliba River." Hama the Red earned the song *Saïgalare,* a tune played only for heroes, from the spirits. Paté's grandfather, Geladio, moved away from Massina after the rise of the Muslim Cheikou Amadou. The grandfather and Cheikou Amadou disagreed over the freedoms allowed to women. Cheikou Amadou wished to limit those freedoms. He also insisted that the Fula give up drinking *dolo* and singing heroic songs. Paté's grandfather felt such demands went too far. They undermined *pulaaku*, the quality of being a Fula. Our Paté clearly understood this to mean nobility, self-possession, innate superiority, self-restraint, irresistible charm (towards women, who should be free) and these qualities were either created or reinforced through beer and heroic songs. *Pulaaku* also involved an intimate knowledge of the herding of cattle and small livestock such as goats and sheep, but Paté rarely raised that theme.

Cattle brought him west from the town of Wuro-Geladio (named for the grandfather who went into exile), an enclave of Fula among the Zarma and Hausa along a far stretch of the Joliba. Driving one herd and then another as they moved with the seasons, he crossed the plains of the Mossi lands. He learned weapon skills along the way, protecting the herds. Wild beasts threatened the herds: hyenas, occasionally lions. Too often, the threat was human. Old alliances and agreements had been effaced by recent troubles. The pasturage, paid for in milk and manure, was often challenged. So Geladio learned the skills needed to defend his herd.

Otherwise, he claimed, the pastoral life was wonderful. "The peace, *Bamana-kè*," he said, "the calm of the plains, the slow movement of cattle through brush, the soughing of the wind over grass and leaf. At such times you might think yourself in the pastures of Ilo-Dadie, in those golden-green meadows that lie between the sun and the silvery moon along the watered plains of the stars." With daybreak came movement; the cattle woke and went in search of fodder, and then during the heat of the day cattle and men would seek any shade they might find. "We filled those hours with thought and with music. Every group had a fluteplayer who could call up the voice of the wind and wrap it around our speech. Many herders were poets and they would embed the rhythms of the cattle's hooves in the cadences of their poems calling upon the many-colored cattle—tawny and dun, red and russet, black- or white-faced, yellow and bronze. They sang to the heifers and the cows, to the steers and the bulls, and they sang also to their fellow men." He paused and then intoned:

"*Kerewel, Kuungunngel,*
Dondingel, Jamalel
Baawaral, Kogolal, Toodal, Daakal
That was how we named them:
Dapple-belly, Proud-hump
Winghorn and Colored-coat,
Goosefeathers, Prow-horn, Black-withers, White-neck!"

"Did you sing?" I asked. Koita snorted.

"No," said Paté. "My lineage leaves the making of music and songs to the *maabube,* whom you Bamana call *jeli.* The men of my line hear the songs of others, and may earn a song themselves through valor, but they do not sing or play the flute." After an amused pause, he added, "Among the Fula, only a *maabo* plays the *hoddu,* but the flute has no rules. I might have learned it, but I thought more of swords. Among our group was a flute player gifted by the spirits—he could play anything. His tunes could set our feet dancing. Even the cows would trot when he played a certain air. He could rouse our anger or calm it. His strains were solace to our grief when some sorrow struck us—most often, when we lost a cow."

"Did that happen often?"

"No, but any loss was a great sorrow. Cattle are beautiful and sweet animals, although they can also be dangerous and fierce. But they are also stupid: getting mired in the mud, getting lost, eating grasses that are poison, tripping and spraining their legs…when they don't break them. They require care and love, but they reward it. His music served as a thread for our love of the herd. I think he had a tune for every cow, and I think some of them knew their own music.

"But the life can be hard." He nodded. "The Fula are thin because there is little to eat in the bush, and no time for cooking. We ate only at night when we returned to the camp kept by the wife of the herd leader. All day watching the herds, and then through the night—the time of greatest risk from hyenas and other beasts, and also when skillful thieves might come. And the biting insects... Still, any Fula feels deep fulfillment and pride when herding cattle."

Koita broke in. "Many people suffer hardships in the bush," he objected. "I've heard hunters complaining of their sufferings. Alone in the bush... "

Bala the hunter heard the word 'hunter' and joined us. "The hunter enjoys little respect," he admitted. "The hunter may bring the knowledge and the wealth of the bush into the village, but few thank him. Rather, mothers will pray that their sons should not become hunters to spare them the long hours of waiting and suffering in the bush, and the dangers of the wild beasts. Hunters are considered unclean, for they must often coat themselves with mud or skat to disguise their scent. In the bush no one bathes. Hunters must observe many strictures and abstinences to ensure success; the hunter's wife is often unhappy."

"But hunters help the villages," noted Koita.

"Indeed. A good hunter is a man of skill, knowledge, and foresight. He is not like the people of Fali-du who went out to kill a lion in their fields."

"What happened?" I asked enjoying this sharing of personal histories; their stories made these men more dear to my young mind.

"This lion was wounded and lying in the fields," said Bala. "They decided they could trap it under the framework for the roof of a hut and then despatch it in safety. If need be, they could also protect themselves by taking refuge under the framework. So they approached the lion carrying a conical frame of laths and struts. The lion rose to meet them; they tried to shelter under the frame, but the lion moved quickly enough to slip in as well! They were trapped with the lion and it ate them all." He chuckled. "Fools who face the creatures of the bush often meet such a fate. If there had been a brave man among them, the lion would have been quickly killed. In the old days, kings were often hunters and their test was to face a lion."

"*Tinye don*," agreed Koita. "Mari Jata was the greatest. The later kings of Segou were less admired."

Bala noddded. "The first Kulibali was a hunter."

"Is it since his time," asked Koita, "that they count the title *mogofaga*, killer of man, among the levels of hunting prowess?"

"That is too great for my mouth," demurred Bala. "True, there are levels of skill among hunters. Praise and titles come to the man who slays a noteworthy beast. But in my *ton* we do not recognize that title. Among us, the greatest is the *samafaga*, the slayer of elephants." He thought for a moment, calling on his memory. "Only one man in my *kafu* holds that title, and he is now old. Our elders argue whether the killer of the lion or the buffalo should take precedence. The days of Samori showed it was too easy to become a killer of men."

"Most of the *tonjon* of Segou might have taken the title of *mogofaga,*" agreed Geladio. "They were all killers and hunters of slaves."

"They hunted to the south," said Koita. "To the north they found only bullets and cold steel." We all looked at him. "North of Segou lies Kala, my land," he explained. "It is the land of heroes and warriors, where each noble's stable has steeds unmatched under the sun, where sons learn the skill of arms before they are circumcized, where the *griots* are hard-pressed to find new ways to praise the exploits of the warriors. We resisted Segou, we resisted Cheikou Amadou." He nodded to Geladio. "We fought off the Tuareg from the sands to the north and the riders from Kaarta and Segou to the south and west. Any one of our great warriors is worthy of an epic, and many are the tales preserved and retold. It is a land of living legends." He touched the sword at his side.

"My father had a good life," he continued. "He served a small *mansa* and was able to win cattle and gold in their raids, and so he acquired several wives and some good horses. Then he devoted himself to breeding horses. He earned greater wealth from horses than from his sword. The horses brought him slaves that increased his wealth. But he sometimes yearned for the days of companionship with his fellow warriors. In idle times he and his fellows sat before their lord's house—there was a *bolon,* an entrance chamber, at the gate and the warriors took turns to guard it. Most of the time they played games: *mpaari* and *sigi.* They drank beer and summoned singers...But times have changed. The *nasrani* have brought new weapons." He turned to me. "Does your village have walls?"

"No," I answered. "The elders decided that it would be

simpler to post guards and then to hide. We have little wealth."

"In most villages, wealth lies in strong arms and bodies. Walls of *banko* must be specially built to stand against horses, and now the *nasrani* can destroy them from a distance. Did you hear of the capture of Segou?" I shook my head.

"The *nasrani keletigi* brought guns, much greater than our muskets, and placed them across the river from the city. At leisure those guns fired shots that destroyed the walls and the buildings. The city surrendered quickly. Some of the Tukolor wished to continue resistance in the name of their faith, but most recognized the cause was lost. So we face a new era. Instead of sitting in a *bolon* playing *mpaari* with my comrades, I walk along shaded paths with my eyes alert for beasts and brigands."

Behind us in the darkening evening Diawara was finishing his evening prayer. "You alone we worship, and to You we turn for help. Guide us in the straight path..." We stopped our talk at that point, for the end of Diawara's evening prayer meant that the evening meal would be served.

Fula hat:
Photo taken at the market in Dienne, Mali, 1980

CHAPTER IV

WE ENTERED MANIGNAN BEFORE the noon meal. We came from the forest into fallow sunlit fields, and then saw the thatched peaks of the town roofs. Small boys who had been hunting lizards and birds in the stubble on the fields swarmed about us and screamed in delight at their cleverness, spotting a caravan with a noisy donkey in an open field. But I shouldn't mock; I was once one of them, greeting anything new with screeches.

Diawara had sent a messenger to alert his *jatigi* (the local host and agent) of our arrival; the messenger returned with a guide who showed us where to make camp on the western side of the town, away from the water and its pestilent insects. As we approached the buildings at the town's edge, the *jatigi* himself appeared. He was a Wattara with some relation to the ruling family of the kingdom of Kong, the great kingdom east of Manignan. I never learned why he left Kong.

As we circled the perimeter of the compounds, we passed an open blacksmith's shop. I was surprised to hear the blacksmith suddenly call out. "*Eh*! Pullo! where's your sister? I need a woman urgently!"

Geladio riposted, "*Numu-kè*, your fires are dead and your iron is cold and shapeless."

"No, no! I have something for her far better than that milk you are always drinking."

"Hit yourself in the groin with your hammer! That's where your wits are seated."

"*Eh*! Pullo! Cow-loving, chicken-necked, milk-sopped tatterdemalion! If you must bring the smell of sour milk to the village you should bring something sweet as well."

"I pity the village where you are smith! Do your tools last more than a day? Can they cut more than grass? No wonder the village needs sweetness."

I realized this was the *senankuya*, the joking relationship between smiths and Fula that requires them to insult and abuse each other upon meeting, but forbids any form of violence, no matter what the provocation. Many other groups have such a bond: within my own village the Magasuba and the Dumbuya treated each other the same way. I learned many interesting words from listening to them that I never dared repeat, although my cousins' behavior often tempted me. It was one of those given social rules that applied in our world.

I was surprised only to encounter this relationship so far into the forest. At that time, I thought it was something that existed only in my own village. Much later, I realized how useful it was where different groups lived together.

The smith then offered Geladio some palm wine from a calabash hanging from the roof in the back of the forge, pouring it into a coconut shell cup. Geladio took it and gulped it down. The two promised to meet later and that each would establish his personal, social and virile supremacy.

Manignan was the end of the trail for our caravan. Diawara planned to leave unsold salt with Wattara and to return north with kola nuts—*woro* as they are called. Because of them the forest area was known as *worodugu*. But his plans had to adjust to conditions. Wattara did not yet have enough kola nuts in store to match the agreed worth of the salt. It was uncertain how many porters might be available. Diawara began to consider other trading options. Then events within the town caused complications.

I happened to witness the event that upset the town's order. Diawara had me accompany him and Koita to the compound of the village chief. I carried a half bar of salt, the appropriate gift to a ruler who would also receive a reward from every one of the traders who came from the south to acquire salt. Wattara led us, threading between the high walls of family compounds where privacy was demanded and the open spaces of more relaxed households. The residence of the village chief, a Bagamoyo, was considerably more than a compound: it was surrounded by thick mud walls built in the zigzag pattern that had become common in the days of Samori's warfare, to resist assault by horses. The entrance was through a chamber, *bolon*, with thick wooden doors at either end. Outside the *bolon* sat armed guards playing *mpar.* I glanced at Koita. The guards nodded as Wattara approached. Before us lay a wide courtyard of pounded earth, well-swept and clean. To the back were buildings I presumed were living quarters; closer, on the right and left, were closed huts that must be storerooms or work areas of some kind.

A servant led us to a large mango tree with thick, cool shade, beneath which mats awaited us. Wattara, Diawara and Koita seated themselves. Koita motioned me towards the back of the space. I laid my half bar behind Diawara.

Another servant quickly brought drinks of water to the honored guests, ladling cupfuls from a *canari* I had not noticed in the dark shade. Soon the chief approached, but he seemed perturbed; he looked backwards at least once, and barked orders to someone we could not see. Then he tried to compose himself for his visitors. He was, of course, accompanied by a *jeli*, a spokesman who would be his voice if the situation required ceremony.

Greetings followed. Wattara introduced his visitors and explained who they were. It was clear that the chief and Diawara had met before, and the chief was pleased to recognize the acquaintance. He made a sign to the *jeli* who nodded to someone out of sight, and a young servant approached carrying a small brazier and the makings of tea: the pot, the small glasses, even some sprigs of mint.

The chief meanwhile addressed Diawara directly, asking about his travels. Diawara spoke of towns and rulers unknown to me. There had been changes; the capture of Samori had given opportunities to ambitious leaders.

"*Ah*, those are the ones who drank the *dege*," exclaimed the chief. *Dege* is a thin gruel of millet; it had become a token of submission in the days of Samori. A chief was invited to drink the *dege* in the presence of the *Almami*...or to die.

"He is gone and now they are free," answered Diawara. "They seek to reclaim power. But the *dege* weakened their authority; people question their courage. New leaders are rising. I fear a time of strife."

"I think not," replied the chief. "The *nasrani* come not only from the north, along the Joliba, but also from the great waters that lie south, beyond the forests. They forbid warfare."

"They may be better than the *fanga* of Segou," suggested Diawara. "The arrogance of the *tonjon* combined with the blindness of the Tukolor has made that region uncomfortable for traders, from what I hear. Our salt," and there was a half-nod behind him to indicate the gift I had carried, "came at a higher price than last year."

Later I learned what he was talking about. Just then their exchange was interrupted.

Shrieks burst out. A woman came running across the beaten earth courtyard towards the entryway, pursued by a man in bright yellow robes holding a musket. As she approached the *bolon* he raised the gun, aimed vaguely, and fired. Powder flashed in the pan…after a tiny delay the gun exploded. The man was thrown backwards. Pieces of the gun flew into the air and then fell, spinning and skittering over the hard clay. The woman threw up her arms and collapsed facedown at the entrance to the *bolon*.

At once, a crowd that had been following the shooter rushed forward to surround both figures. Women picked up the fallen victim, who seemed unharmed: she had fallen because of fear and shock at the explosion. The man, by some miracle, was also whole. He had powder marks on his cheek and a scrape on his temple, but the flying shards of metal missed him completely. Koita suggested later that he had committed a common mistake, closing his eyes and turning his head before firing. He added that locally-made powder was often unreliable. Some hunters still preferred arrows, but warriors had no choice.

This man was evidently not a warrior. His yellow clothing was rich, with embroidered trim, and he was fleshy, not lean with toil. He was a younger brother of the chief, by the same mother. He had been allowed to stay while the step-brothers, rivals for power, had been forced away. He had been a wrestler who was known for his violent temper and rash judgments.

The chief rose and made a gesture of regretful dismissal. We all rose with him. Diawara brought the half-bar of salt to the attention of the *jeli*, who nodded and summoned a servant to take it away.

Later in the day an older man approached the chief's residence. He was the father of the woman. He had come to express concern about the matter. A natural sentiment, but to challenge a chief is a daring thing, and in this case to ask a question was to challenge the chief. The warriors refused him entrance. He stood for a moment, nostrils flared, and then he turned away.

That night we heard drums and roars from the forest outside the village. Many voices of drums building to a thunder: the deep long-sounding tones of hollow, wooden slit-drums that spoke with the voice of the great trees through which we had marched; the high-pitched staccato of the *jenbe* drums that drive people to frenzies of dance and possession as well as talking drums, whose pitch varies in mimicry of the rise and fall of the tones of human speech. With the drum-roar came sounds I could not recognize: a whirring, now shrill and now low, continuous and somehow threatening.

Near me Boloba spoke. "They have called the *Komo*," he explained. I had heard of it, although my village was too small to house a cult. The *Komo* emerges in times of trouble to impose peace and order.

"The chief?"

"No. Did you not hear?" He told me of the old man's visit to the chief's compound. "This was no ordinary old man. He is the earthmaster of this town." I began to understand. The earthmaster represents the earliest inhabitants of a place, those who reached agreement with the spirits of the bush and the earth, determining where and how the humans might till their fields and what return they would make. The earthmaster was a priest; his family was usually prosperous, but never ruled.

Kings come and go, often quite quickly and bloodily, but the earthmasters abide, passing their secrets to their heirs and kin. When warriors ride into a town, they take control of the visible human wealth, but they have no knowledge of the hidden secrets of the land. They must bargain with the earthmaster if they wish their rule to last beyond a season or two.

All that night, the noise moved about the town. It sounded loudest when it came from the direction of the chief's residence, where it sounded longest—the spirit group marched twice around the extensive walls. We could not sleep. At dawn, they passed near us: apparently the spirit was returning to the bush.

First came young men, dancing about to the light of torches and wielding whips of leather. Their task was to clear the streets of all the uninitiated, those who might also be harmed by the presence of the spirit. Then came the talking drummers, leaping about while keeping up an incessant chatter marked by the cadences and tones of speech—some hymn or anthem, no doubt, that the people of Manignan would recognize through the pattern of tones, but that meant nothing to me. Their noise didn't drown out the sharp rolls of the *jenbe* drums whose rhythms impelled the dancers to ever more frenzied exertions. After them, the acolytes of the spirit danced before it with high vaults and whirls, occasionally stopping to add a thunder of stamping to the other pulses. I could feel the vibrations even at a distance.

The *Komo* came, and I caught my breath. I recognized, of course, that it was a man wearing a great wooden mask, his body hidden in a great loose garment of woven grass and fabric stretching from the shoulders down to the ground. The mask was a many-horned head of some beast with a great snout, its crocodile-jaws half open. Tusk-like spikes rose from the top of the snout. They were tipped with glittering metal. Darkened teeth filled the mouth opening. The head bowed and swayed from side to side as though sniffing out a trail. Slowly it moved, almost gliding over the earth. Then an unheard echo came into my ears. Over and through the mask and costume I perceived another being, a glowing figure above the masked dancer, anchored to the smaller human, yet far vaster and more menacing. This figure magnified the mask, enlarged its presence so that it towered over the walls and huts through which it passed. I sensed clearly the threat of violence and destruction.

They passed beyond my sight returning to the woods. Soon after, the drumming stopped. The usual noises of daily life returned. Donkeys brayed. Roosters realized that they should salute the dawn. Dogs raised their yips and yelps.

Most of us tried to go back to sleep.

The town was deserted the next day. The market stood empty. The women who sold milk or millet beer stayed home. The sounds of pounding pestles, screaming children, and squawking chickens occasionally broke the silence, yet few people left their compounds. No one came to the smith's forge. The potters sat by their stacks of earthenware, entertaining no purchasers. The calm was unnatural and disquieting.

That night the *Komo* returned…roaring through the empty streets. Again it circled the chief's compound, and again the drums there rose to a crescendo. Then their voices diminished and died out in the distance as the spirit returned to the forest.

Just after dawn the great tree-drums called an assembly. These drums were hollowed out from colossal tree trunks with slits along their length. They had no membranes or leather heads. They were considered too heavy to be moved. Wattara told us dispite their weight they had been moved some time before. They lay originally near the earthmaster's compound, sheltered by a thatch roof. Now they lay next to the chief's compound. Many in the town still considered this act an outrage.

This day not even vendors came to the market. Several age groups of *kamalen* spent the morning cleaning the open space; gathering up debris, spoiled merchandise and flattened fruit, and sweeping away all traces of animal passage. By noon the square was almost spotless. The *kamalen* received their lunch, delivered from the chief's compound: heaping bowls of *to* and meat-sauce, carried out by servants and placed on mats. They also received a good measure of *dolo* at the end of the meal.

As the noon-day heat abated slightly and the sun reached the tops of the trees around the square, men began to gather. Wattara invited Diawara to join him. Diawara told Koita and me to accompany him. We joined a stream of men heading towards the market; we sat at a judicious distance from the center, close enough to hear but not so close as to be intrusive. Wattara commented to Diawara as we walked that he had nothing to say about this matter, but that the chief's younger brother was known to be a fool.

I looked over the crowd, all older men. Most were dressed in African cloth, woven in strips and sewn into sheets. The local style was for a three-piece costume, including the hat, made of simple cotton. Some were dyed the ocher hue of clay. Others offered alternating stripes of blue and white, and a few sported robes of rarer colors: greens and yellows and some rich indigo. In one corner sat a concentration of robes made of *nasrani* cloth: smooth and sheer cotton printed with bright colors and vivid designs.

The square was already full when the earthmaster entered

unaccompanied. He stood alone waiting. Soon after, we heard the two *tabalé* drums that announced the chief. He came with an armed guard, his *jeli* walking before him.

The *jeli* waited until the chief was seated then raised his arms, a signal that he would speak. The murmur of expectant voices was hushed.

"The voice of the *Komo* has sounded," he called. His voice carried over the square easily reaching all ears. "Your chief, the Bagamoyo of great lineage, master of men, master of powder, master of iron, has heard the sound. He is concerned for his people. He thanks you for coming to this assembly, and trusts that your faithfulness will end the troubles. He asks that all present assure him of their good will for the town of Manignan. We live in a time of peril. Towns have been betrayed and fallen because of dissension. We must be wary of such tendencies among us; we must all be devoted to the welfare of our community! The chief now asks to learn what grievances may exist, that they may be settled." This, I realized, was the art of a political leader: to hide the real and well-known problem.

The crowd was silent. I had attended village meetings in my home. They were rare, for it was such a small village that any questions—almost always a grant of land—could usually be settled among the elders. Here the stakes were different because it was a question of authority against grievance. The obvious offense by the chief's brother would be weighed against advantages to be obtained from the chief. Some of this ceremony was similar, most particularly in its respect for seniors.

A very old man rose from the rows closest to the chief and turned to the corners of the market. "I greet the people of Manignan. I greet the people of the Gurodu quarter. I greet the people of Bawledu quarter. I greet the people of Filadu quarter. I greet the elders and their offspring. I thank the *kamalen* for their work in cleaning the square." His voice, surprisingly, was strong enough to carry clearly. "It is true that we live in a time of peril. But dangers can be of many kinds, and perhaps the greatest is that of ignorance. The first question we must address, without concern for blame or loyalty, is why the *Komo* felt called into Manignan. Its passage is a sign of *juguya*, some great unrighteousness. We must ask the cause. Rumors run around this town like chickens and goats, and should be trusted no more than the birds. I wish for this assembly to discover the truth and determine a remedy."

A second old man rose, still from the circles closest to the chief. Clearly, this was where the village notables were seated. He too greeted the neighborhoods of the town, then turned to the chief. "We no longer fear the *sofas* of the Almami. Our concern is for our commonwealth and our fellows. All know that two days ago there was a gunshot within our walls. This is a matter of concern. This town, as we all know, was born in a moment of harmony, when the Bagamoyo *bemba* encountered the Baule leader and they agreed to pool their resources. The Bagamoyo came from the Manding; they brought the wealth of trade and the exchange of goods. The Baule offered their mastery of the land. Their alliance was sealed by an exchange of daughters. Since that time we have prospered. We do not fight each other. So I ask the cause of the disturbance."

A man in *nasrani* robes rose and was recognized. "I greet the town; I greet the elders," he stated shortly. "As I understand it, we are gathered because there was a gunshot within a compound, but no one has shown a corpse. I do not believe so small a matter requires so many men. It is a waste of our time and effort. Shall we call an elephant because we have seen ants near our hut? No! Bring in the chickens! Let those who are most concerned discuss the matter and resolve it. It is not our concern."

Several men rose at this point. At a sign from the chief the *jeli* walked into the crowd and stood near another man also clothed in imported cotton.

"What my friend has said is true," started the man. "Much is being made of little here, and we should not waste our time. Our assemblies are intended for matters that involve all of us, not for family disputes."

The first elder stood up again. After some hesitation, and with a glance back at the chief, the *jeli* walked over to him.

"*N'dogo,*" began the elder, "you forget that this town should be as tight as a family, and that agreements must be respected. You claim this affair is a trivial concern and you wish to dismiss it. Others have heard of a serious offense against our customs, one that occurred within our town and did not come from the ignorance of strangers or the bloodthirstiness of bandits or the arrogance of a *sofa*. We wish to learn more of this matter and to resolve it in keeping with our town's customs."

The chief raised his staff; the *jeli* hastened back to the center of the circle. The chief spoke in a low voice and when he had finished the *jeli* stepped forward and began to declaim. "The Bagamoyo, master of men, master of powder, wishes you to learn the facts as he has learned them. It is true there was a gunshot in the town; it is true that no one was injured by the shot. The rifle was aimed at a wayward wife; the husband claims a conjugal privilege in this matter and asserts that the affair should be of no concern to the people of this town. The chief has heard the matter and agreed with the husband. The townsfolk need not concern themselves."

After this brief statement several men again rose. Diawara straightened his back, looking around the edges of the square. The *kamalen* who had cleaned it were still seated on benches or on mats against the walls. Many seemed somewhat the worse for the *dolo* with which their work had been rewarded. I could not understand his concern.

The jeli started with the *nasrani* cotton side of the crowd. They agreed strongly with the chief that a domestic dispute was not a municipal matter. "When a rooster cuffs a hen," they said, "the hen does not ask the lion for judgment."

"Indeed," added another in patterned indigo, "we should presume the husband had his reasons. Who among us wishes to encourage disobedience within our compounds? When you see flies buzzing, you may be sure there is some stink to draw them."

After this the jeli could no longer ignore an elder in brown cotton robes of local weave who had been standing patiently.

"We should remember," he began, "that flies are drawn to honey as well as to shit, and not draw conclusions from their buzzing. We must also remember that not every compound in this town is governed in the same way. Manignan is the child of two different parents—one who came from the savanna regions, and another who was born among the dense forests. We balance our double heritage and we have prospered in this manner. I must remind our brothers that the people of the forest value their women. We remain indebted to Queen Pokou who sacrificed her only child to preserve her people. We do not believe that wisdom resides only in manhood. Man and woman are a joint pair, each incomplete without the other. We have heard that a daughter of this town almost lost her life, not from a stranger or a brigand or from a wild beast or a bush-spirit, but from within her household. Such an action violates bonds that we hold sacred. A wife is not a captive, to be whipped or slain at will. Further we have heard that her father was turned away from the door when he came to learn of his daughter's state. As you have seen," the old man raised his staff and gestured in the direction from which the *Komo* spirit had come out of the forest, "such an action angers the spirits that protect this town."

Much further discussion followed this statement, for many wished their voices to be heard, even when they added little of substance. As the light began to fade, the chief rose and summoned his *jeli*. They spoke together briefly and then the *jeli* turned to the crowd.

"The *dugutigi*, the Bagamoyo,]master of men, master of iron, master of powder, has heard the voices and the wisdom of the town and thanks you for your efforts. The matter which has aroused your interest is a domestic matter, unworthy of so great a tumult. He shall meet with the principals to reach a settlement. Now you should return to your homes." The *jeli*'s voice was a trumpet, carrying the command across the square. The chief gestured, his drummers began to sound their deep *tabalas*. The chief's procession moved through the crowd. People moved quickly out of their way.

We returned to Wattara's compound. There, Wattara and Diawara settled on a stiff-reed mat and Wattara ordered tea.

Diawara broke the silence. "Will this satisfy the earthmaster?"

"It must. You had the same thought as mine," answered Wattara. Koita murmured. They looked at him, and then at me. I was completely lost.

Diawara began the explanation. "*Bamana-kè*, your world was made by the past actions of men. Your village has no chief.

But I have told you of the kings of Segou, the *famaw* who ruled with the power of their four spirits?"

I nodded. My village had paid tribute to Segou.

"When Monzon of Segou died, many years ago," explained Diawara, "he left many sons. Tiefolo was the eldest, but not the most ambitious. A younger brother, Da, wished to seize the throne. He was advised by his *jeli* who told him to make friends with the hatchetmen and spearmen of Segou. So he did. He ensured that they always had *diji* (mead) and the *jeli* ensured that they always knew their drink came from Da. The death of Monzon brought confusion. Monzon named no heir. Every prince advanced his claim. Da was loudest, but many preferred other candidates. Da summoned the elders to a meeting. Da also summoned the hatchetmen. At that meeting the hatchetmen went to work. No elders escaped. Da became the *Fama* of Segou."

I understood then why Diawara had looked at the *kamalen* lounging around the edges of the square. Had we really been under the threat of death by bludgeons to protect the power of the Bagamoyo chief? It was very hard to believe, yet it was also clear that those *dolo*-sodden minds could easily have been turned to violence. Diawara observed my enlightenment.

"Yes, I feared violence from the *kamalen*," he agreed. "But the stakes were not so high," he looked at Wattara for agreement, Wattara nodded, "and the chief chose conciliation. You heard the *jeli* call him a *dugutigi* not a *mansa*, and this word was a sign that the chief wished for peace in the village."

He looked at me and half-smiled. "The title makes the difference," he explained. "The kings of Segou were called *fama* because their rule was based on *fanga*, on force and violence. We do not call them *mansa*, which is the proper Maninka term for a king, because they didn't have the authority that comes with *mansaya*. They were called masters of men, masters of fire, masters of powder—like the Bagamoyo here in Manignan—but they were feared, not respected. *Mansaya* has become very rare in our world. That is why we remember the time of Mari Diata, even those of us who are not of Maninka stock. He was the greatest *mansa*, and he established the rules by which we have preserved our peace among peoples."

Wattara added, "In a town, many people can claim the title of *tigi*. The blacksmiths have a leader, the *numutigi*, as do the weavers and the leather workers and other craftsmen. The different quarters of our town each have their own ward leader. Bagamoyo chose to use a title that bound him to the people of the town."

"Even so," said Koita, "the *kamalen* were there, and they were drunk and they had clubs wrapped in bundles near their benches."

Photo taken at a magic display in Kankan, 2004

CHAPTER V

BEFORE THE CONFLICT OF powers was resolved, Diawara departed on an excursion. He decided he needed some higher value merchandise besides the kola nuts. He would venture into the forest, hoping for ivory and possibly gold. He and Wattara discussed possible destinations. They eventually decided on Gbedugu, a town several days to the southwest. Gbedugu lay near mountains in dense forest. Although the town had avoided destruction by Samori, it was not prosperous.

The first settlers came guided by the catfish oracle. It speaks for Faro, lord of waters. The settlers found a site at the foot of a mountain where great trees matched the marks foretold. Their leader consulted a diviner who told him to bring an albino girl and a nugget of the red gold found in the nearby streams. The leader did so. The diviner went into a trance. The girl and the gold nugget vanished into the earth. Later, others muttered and complained. They went to the leader and the diviner and demanded that this spell be undone. It was unclear if they were more worried about the girl or the gold. The diviner again went into a trance; the girl and the gold reappeared from the earth. Then the diviner spoke, "You people of Gbedugu! You have gone back on the word of your leader! You had no confidence in the powers I invoked. Your success will be limited. Your town will have food; your town will not be destroyed in war. Your lives will be content, but humble. You shall not be rich, you shall not have dominion; your sons will not become kings."

So there was doubt about any wealth to be found in Gbedugu. Still, it seemed the best choice: other towns nearby had been destroyed by Samori, or had untrustworthy chiefs, or lay too far from good hunting grounds.

Four men carried salt: Boloba, myself, and two slaves sent by Wattara. Koffi and Kouassi were also to serve as guides. Koita came armed with bow and spear. We set off early one morning, soon entering the dark-shadowed world of giant trees. We filed between their smooth trunks and ribbed roots. The path was clear. Little grew on the darkened ground.

"How can one tell the prayer times?!" complained Diawara, gazing at the leaves that completely blocked the sun. We had been on the march for most of the day, and we could tell from the gloom that the sun was setting. Diawara's complaint was the sign to halt and make camp. Diawara prayed while we gathered what firewood we could. Water was less of a problem; streams were common in the forest, protected from the thirsty sun by the thick canopy of leaves.

The morning brought a submarine glow of aquamarine light, and we resumed our march. Wattara estimated three days to Gbedugu. All that day we walked in shadow, our feet silent on the carpet of fallen and decaying leaves that filled the air with the scents of vegetative transfiguration.

Near the end of the day we came to a clearing where an ancient tree had finally collapsed, rotted from within or smitten by an erratic and devastating thunderbolt. We could see the sky; we could no longer see the earth, for around the toppled pillar of the tree a mass of shrubs and vines had exploded into green edifice that strove to fill the open space. There we stopped. The sight of the sky and the light were welcome, though at first blinding.

Koita moved on, seeking a stream for water. The rest of us waited; at a sign from Diawara we lowered our salt bars to the ground. We sat where we could see the sky and watch innumerable butterflies swarming around in the clearing.

Koita coughed, emerging from the darkness. He had encountered a hunter, a forest-dweller. The man was naked save for a light-colored penis sheath fastened to his groin by a thong; he carried a slender spear and a long knife hanging from his shoulder. In his left hand, raised for our appraisal, were a pair of cane rats held by their tails. He was far shorter than Koita, but slender and graceful, with a dark sheen to his skin.

Diawara had finished his prayers. He made a gesture of welcome, but spoke to Koita. "What is his language?" Before Koita could answer, Koffi stepped forward and greeted the hunter. The hunter smiled and answered a few words; Koffi spoke a different greeting, and the hunter nodded. As they spoke my ears tingled. I recognized that Koffi had spoken first in Guro and then in another language. Koffi then turned to us.

"He is a Donzomô," he explained. "They live in these forests in small groups and are rarely seen. We are the first travelers in several months, so he approached us."

"Thank him for us," said Diawara. "I ask if he will share his bushmeat?"

Before the translation was finished, the hunter's broad grin answered the question. As Koffi spoke, my ears were distinguishing words and suggesting meanings, and I understood that this was a gift of the *wokolo*. The hunter held out the rodents. Soon Kouassi had them skinned, gutted, skewered, and roasting over a small fire. While Kouassi tended the food,

Diawara turned to me and opened the wrappings on my salt bar. Koita handed him a sturdy iron saw blade. Diawara measured three fingers' widths from the end of the bar and began to saw, a few quick strokes to define his line and then cutting into the crystals. Soon, he had created a continuous groove in the bar. He collected the powdered salt on the leather flap below. Then he flipped the bar and struck the end sharply, breaking off a small block of salt—a *kokotla* Boloba called it—and placed it on a broad flat leaf with the salt powder. He offered the leaf to the hunter. The hunter's eyes widened. He licked his finger and dipped the dampened digit in the powder, taking only a trace which he tasted. "*Eeh,*" he sighed in satisfaction. Then he held out the leaf to Diawara, as though to return it. Diawara gently wrapped the leaf closed and then folded it into the man's hands.

"You have been generous with your food," said Diawara, "and we thank you. You have come with light to us in this forest of darkness and we are grateful." He glanced at Koffi, and the other man cleared his throat and then translated. I wondered if the hunter considered the forest a world of darkness; for me it seemed rather like a world below the waters, somehow outside the known human milieu. But a hunter would be at home in the dark, the sounds and the smells: birdcalls and buzzings, the redolent air filled with traces of fallen leaves turning to clay, fresher near the many small rills of water, the strange and sometimes luminescent fungi that grew on the damp trunks.

"Perhaps," added Diawara, "you can help us in another matter. We have come to trade salt for ivory—the tusks of elephants. Can you tell us if such merchandise is available here, and where it might be found?"

The hunter considered, then nodded. "There are fewer and

fewer elephants," he began, as Koffi translated. "They live to the west," he gestured towards a setting sun we could not see,"where there are no farmers. My people used to hunt them, when there were more of us and more elephants. There were enough of us to eat an entire elephant before the meat went bad. It was a great occasion, a feast to mark a lifetime. The hunters spend days brewing the ointments for their spears; they sharpen the points on stones, they test the shafts. Then they go at night, in the dark, silent, silent, between the trees; they follow a marked path to the place of the elephant herd. The elephants stand, swaying perhaps, clustered together. Who knows if they sleep or dream? They are still. The smell is strong and sweet and the hunters can draw near, step by careful step. The leader marks the chosen animal and takes the strongest spears—it is his job to place the weapons, and often he fails. In my grandfather's time our spearheads were made of stone. Many broke. Now we have iron spearheads, and they do not break so easily." Here he held up the slender spear he carried, whose fluted head broadened out from the point to a series of vicious barbs. "Still, it is dangerous work. Some men climb a tree and cast the spears from above. But the poison works best when the wound is made under the body. But the animal may turn and crush the hunter. If the blade is planted well, it stays in the hide and the poison works slowly upon the elephant. The other hunters follow the beast. Ever slower and weaker it walks, and often the other elephants may support it and some even bring it bunches of leaves to eat. Eventually it stops and stands, dazed, as the others mill anxiously about it. Finally it falls onto the knees of its forelegs, and then over onto its side. The rest of the herd move about, brushing it with their trunks, and then, admitting it is dead, they move on. Then we could move in. We sound drums to summon our kin and our friends, and we stay there feasting until the meat is gone. The skeletal carcass of the elephant stands over us, almost as large as one of your houses. And the tusks...the tusks bring wealth. One tusk always went to the man whose spear had pierced the hide, or to his family if he had not survived."

He spat on the ground. "Now the chiefs in the clearings outside the forest demand a tusk when we come to trade, so we are no longer so concerned with hunting elephants, although it is true a tusk will bring many spearheads and sharp knives and cloth. The chiefs now send their men into the forests, and this is why the elephants are becoming fewer and fewer. These men do not hunt for food. They dig great pits, and in the pits they place sharpened stakes pointing up, and they cover the pits with mats and earth. So an elephant falls and is impaled upon the stake. Then they come and cut out the tusks, and sometimes they will take the hide to make shields or whips, but they leave the meat to rot and the elephant is wasted. If the elephant is not dead when they come, they kill it with their thundersticks."

We stopped at this point to eat the bush rats, which had been roasted to flavorful succulence.

"There is a town," continued the hunter, pointing to the southwest, "one day's march from here. The chief there trades in elephant tusks. But I would ask you, is it only ivory you seek, or might some other goods serve as well?"

Diawara was frank. "I came from the north with many bearers to carry my salt. I will buy kola nuts to take back to the north. But on the return trip, I will not have so many bearers. I seek merchandise of greater worth and lesser weight to take back to the north, where I will, again, buy salt." The hunter nodded in understanding.

At the end of the next day, we came to Gbedugu. Koffi and Kouassi led us to the compound of Wattara's *jatigi*. He made us welcome showing us to a pleasantly shaded camping area at the side of his inner courtyard. After a first offer of fresh water, he offered drafts of palm-wine to those of us who would drink it, in cups of coconut shells. For Diawara, the abstinent Muslim, he ordered tea with mint. He was clearly accustomed to traders. We stored the salt bars in his granary.

The next day, Diawara gave us leave to visit the town with some cowries to spend. He and his host would visit the chief, and he needed no help to carry the two *kokotla*s of salt that were his offering.

Boloba and Koita stayed to watch over the salt. I went out with Vamisa, from the *jatigi*'s household, to see what I might. The town itself seemed reassuringly familiar in its basics: red earth walls around the compounds, dark brown thatch on the huts, the dark foliage of mango trees cropped to an even level above the ground by passing livestock. Women worked in the shade pounding foodstuffs in their mortars; chickens scuttled and scrabbled over the ground, hunting ants or loose grains. Small children toddled and screamed. Older children watched them or avoided their mothers, who might assign them tasks. The town had clearly been carved out of the forest, for on all sides huge trees rose beyond the edges of the gardens. To the west rose a mountain, capped by a light-colored rocky dome that allowed no hold for plants.

Still, the ambience of the town was different. Was it novelty? or might it be danger?

We crossed a vacant marketplace. It met every four days, explained Vamisa. We circled the girdling walls of the chief's compound. Beyond it, we encountered a wide clear space. At its center sat a strange white-painted building, outlandish in its form. The rest of the village presented an oscillation of intersecting curves and arcs from rounded compounds and huts. Here were straight lines, sharp angles, and an unyielding contour. It might almost have been lifted from some other place and planted there at the edge of the village: perhaps carried by great winds through the sky and then dropped, regardless of the destruction it might cause in its landing.

Vamisa glanced at it. "That is a church," he explained. "A man came from the south and said that he wished to speak of a new god. He made a gift to the chief, trade goods from the coast, and the chief granted him this land. His arrival has brought troubles to the town."

I asked what sort of troubles, as he was clearly waiting for a cue.

"Upstream was a mound where two great *karanaw* (monitor lizards) made their home. They were the embodiment of our ancestral spirits, the messengers of Tonba, the spirit of the mountain. We honored them... Have you heard of the problems when our town was founded? The question of the albino girl?" I nodded. "Our people saw the *karanaw* as a blessing, and believed that through them we could bring an end to the diviner's curse. People made offerings to them: eggs, occasionally a chicken if a woman wanted a child. But this southern man declared that the *karanaw* were emissaries from some evil god, and he took a matchet and went out one evening and killed them both. Most in the village believed he had committed a great crime and protested. The chief said that so far as he knew lizards were lizards." Vamisa frowned as he remembered. "He did make the man remove the heads that were placed on stakes in front of this church. There was much palaver, but no decision. The man began to teach. His followers became more numerous. Each received a white shirt at the entrance ritual, and later they also received trade goods: iron cooking pots, knives of excellent steel..."

"Where was the mound?" I asked, for something tingled and spoke to my uneasiness.

"Up near the spot where people draw water." Vamisa gestured beyond the white building.

He led the way, understanding that I was curious. We soon reached the stream, smooth and limpid over a sandy bed under the overlaced branches of the bordering trees. A good path led along the bank, far enough from the water to run straight, without curving around the massive tree trunks. I had still not come to terms with those trunks; I couldn't think of them as trees. Their boles were as wide around as the huts in my village, and many, many times taller; their branches wove shadows above my head. Within the shadows I sensed *nyama*, the life-force, channeled through many beings and now aroused: I sensed fear and anger building to malevolence.

We heard voices ahead so stepped aside. A line of girls bearing water on their heads was coming from the watering hole. They were a pleasant sight.

One caught my attention. Her face was beautiful: arched brows over bright eyes, a mouth of curved smiles, an almost dimpled chin. Unlike the others, she wore a blouse of light material over her top, and so her breasts were not visible. But they were clearly present, swaying with her movement and carrying the folds of the cloth with them as she walked. The girls were all of an age: nubile and glowing, and apparently they had been speaking of something amusing, for all of them were laughing. Most were wrapped in an African cloth, the banded cotton tight around their hips and bellies, reaching below the knees. The one in the blouse wore some sort of trade cloth with stripes.

With humorous greetings they walked on. As they passed, I realized that the beauty in the blouse had let some water spill down her back where it moistened her cloth: the material clung to the top of her palpable thigh, and one of the bands of color set off the line where the thigh became buttock, where the flesh swelled up and out. Then, with a step, the cloth stretched and the line disappeared, only to reappear with the next step when the fold and the curve were again defined...Vamisa woke me from my reverie and we continued up the path.

The burrow of the *karanaw* had been destroyed. It had been in a small hollow between two of the greatest trees where it caught the currents of *nyama* that I sensed, not attached to individual beings but imbuing something far greater. This forest was an entire living being, on a scale I couldn't conceive. Far greater than the tenuous water-hungry bush of my home. Each of the massive trees was an entire world, supporting plants upon its branches and upon the plants a population of insects, birds, frogs, worms...Somehow, this hollow had been a node, a channel for the various flows. Now that focus was destroyed. The forces moved in discordant motions.

I was now absorbed in a different sort of dream. I apologized to Vamisa. "This is painful to see. Truly, this was the heart of this place. Its destruction was a crime."

"You have almost seen the one who did it," commented Vamisa. "The girl in the blouse is the daughter of the man who killed the *karanaw*."

"She looked no different from the others," I answered. This was not quite true.

"I have heard that his father was a slave from this region. On the coast he was freed and began to follow the white men's religion. He found a wife of his own people. Their son had the idea of bringing their faith to his homeland. The father sends the trade goods which ensure a welcome to his son."

"Have white men come?"

"Not yet."

We drank from the stream—the water was cool and cleaned our throats. I realized how the air was filled with the smell of decayed vegetation and mold.

The next morning while Diawara still waited for word from the chief about trading possibilities, Vamisa and I again walked out. The market was open, largely populated by local women selling onions, yams, spices, and the inevitable dried fish. One or two had chickens, sulking and clucking in their reed-woven hutches. A few men offered smoked bush meat: monkeys, bush rats, portions of antilope. One trader had an assortment of cloths, steel knives, and metal cooking pots. We stopped and examined his wares. The cloths were the sort I had noticed swathed around a pair of lithe thighs the day before, and before that, less attractive on men, at the meeting in Manignan. The knives were short-bladed and dark with wooden handles. They resembled our local products but their edge, tested gently against my thumb, was clearly harder and sharper. The metal pots were large enough to hold the noon meal for an ordinary household.

Again we moved around the chief's walled compound. I noticed something unusual: bees were swarming over the top of one of the walls, crawling in a mosaic mass around some ill-defined center, humming with apian purpose. Occasionally dispatching scouts off to fly in direct lines away through the village.

I had observed bees before. A few of the farmers in my village had succeeded in housing swarms in hollow gourds or other containers to harvest the honey. Small boys of my age group made careful note of the hives' placement so we might attempt a raid, but only after dark. Some boys from the age group just older than mine had tried to do it once during the daylight hours, and of course they then had to wait until dark to emerge from the pond in which they had escaped the enraged bees. The farmer whose hive they had approached, he was known as Kumboro (the bee), laughed so hard when he saw them in the water, their heads just above the surface, that he fell down. My age group took note of this lesson. But we only tried to take honey once or twice; the combs were not so rich as we had hoped, and even in the dark some of the bees stung us.

These bees obeyed some different principle. I saw no sign of a hive. They swarmed and milled around, and they did not think of honey or nectar or whatever it is that bees feed upon.

Vamisa and I kept clear of them in case they decided to sting. We continued on toward the stream.

"*Eh*! Stranger!" the voice rang clear and low. I turned. It was the girl from the south, her mouth still curved to smiles, still in her blouse. I wondered why she used the word *luntan*, which is Maninka and not Dan, the local speech. Then she turned to Vamisa and spoke fluidly, extensively, and forcefully in Dan.

As she spoke, I observed her quite carefully, for she rewarded attention. Her bright white blouse—and I thought of that sudden white church—still swayed with the movement of the flesh behind it, her smile and eyes were bright as the sun, her cloth was tight around her hips. But behind her eyes I sensed a story and an ambition: she was the daughter of a man who had brought his family far from their home, filled with faith in a god who would protect and promote him. I knew nothing of their home country, nothing of the details of the faith that moved them. But I could see it granted assurance, if not arrogance, and also that it shut off the hearing of certain tones and nuances...I was probably wrong. Attractive young women have a self-confidence that allows them to ignore things they don't want to know, although I have never seen them fail to notice the interest of observers and (self-protection, no doubt) to assess it carefully.

Vamisa began to translate her harangue. She wanted to know who I was, why I was in the town, why I had come, what had brought me onto the path where we met the day before, why I had looked at her, what I thought I was doing, who I thought I was to look at her...and, eventually, what I thought of what I had seen.

I looked at Vamisa and he grinned back at me.

"I have come with a salt trader," I began. "I am a Bamana from a village..." I stopped. I could say nothing more about that. "We have come from Manignan. My friend and I were walking around the town when we met you." I paused and Vamisa translated quickly. She seemed to expect more.

"This is my first time in this town," I explained. "I find it pleasant. Is this the path you always take to the stream?" My feelings were more than mixed. She was a very pretty girl. For weeks I had not been thinking of girls. But something in her eyes, a hard narrowness, and something in her tone, an imperious expectancy, made me wary. I remembered that she was the daughter of the man who had slaughtered the guardian animals of the town.

"What is this salt trader?" she demanded. "Where have you

come from? Are you not servants of the warlords in the north?"

I told her where we were staying and Vamisa translated, although Vamisa could have given her the same information directly. If she really knew the town, she should already have guessed our *jatigi*. "We serve no one. We came to find ivory." I hesitated before saying that, but surely the more people who knew that Diawara would trade rocksalt for ivory, the better.

"What is your faith? Are you a Muslim?" she demanded.

"I am bound to no god," I answered, which was perhaps only partly true, for I felt an obligation to my *wokòlò*. But he didn't count as a god, certainly not in the terms used by this dynamic beauty.

"But you have come here to ogle the women," she accused me.

"I am here with my master to sell salt," I answered. "I looked at nothing that was not worth watching. Why are *you* in this town?"

"My father came to bring a new faith," she answered proudly. "We have been taught the truth about the world and he considers it his mission to share that truth. Come!" she said, "let me show you the new house of our god."

She seized my hand, a bold action for a girl in my village but certainly not unpleasant. She pulled me away from our path until the little white building came into sight.

But I could not approach it. The open ground around it had been swept so that it stood in an empty clearing. I could not step onto the earth where the marks of the brooms could be seen.

"Come!" she ordered, tugging on my hand, but I resisted. She had led me to a line I could not to cross. I felt no physical barrier, but I understood I stood at a threshold beyond which my world might, and probably would, change completely. The cause was her presence and her understanding of my actions; had she not been there to invest my steps with meaning, I knew I could have skipped around the clearing with abandon. Instead, I perceived paths of possibility: one step further, and this girl and I settled together, and that was an agreeable prospect. I would join her father in his beliefs and assist him with his efforts. I would have assented to the slaughter of the *karanaw*, to the denial of the village's history. This future had nothing at all to do with the world from which I had come. It would be a transformation, almost a death. I began then to perceive a problem that continues to perplex me: how we humans define the world we inhabit through our beliefs. This girl could never see a *wokòlò* or understand its messages. What then did she see that I could not?

She was filled with zeal. She wished me to join her—was it something I should undertake? I had run from my village, I was dead to them. What did I owe? To whom? I made an agreement with the *wokòlò*, but that was done almost without thinking. I still had no idea what task they wanted of me. That uncertainty marked the second path before me.

I was torn and wavered, but the answers were clear. I had assented to the request of the *wokòlò* who obeyed the same supernal authority that animated the slaughtered *varanaw*. I had already committed myself to opposition to the ambitions of this temptress and her father. It didn't occur to me that this might be a test (that thought came later). I was then simply torn between the enticement of the maiden, keenly aware of her charms, and a distrust of her motives and their consequences. I didn't like the sight of that angular building.

She pulled at my hand again. "Come!" she ordered. I understood the meaning, if not the words. "Let me show you our church, and then I shall take you to meet my father."

I pulled my hand free. "You are beautiful," I told her, "but I cannot go into your world." I turned and walked back to Diawara's host. I expected screaming behind me, but there was silence.

Photo taken in 1970 in Tanzania

CHAPTER VI

THE TOWN NO LONGER seemed hospitable. I had offended someone, probably someone with influence. I was also dazed, still trying to understand why I would (or could?) not enter the space around the white building. Feminine charms, paths of fate, promises...the decision was blurred.

I drank from the earthen jar (*canari*, a central feature of any household) kept in the shade near the entrance; it was filled every day by a slave girl. Then I sat near Diawara and his host, resting on a reed mat. I dozed. A breeze stirred the leaves above me and that sound became water rippling and then cloth swishing over arms and legs that were graceful and smooth and moved step by step, forward, back. The swish became a persistent and less pleasing sound, a droning buzz. I opened my eyes. A small cluster of bees sat on the trunk of the tree; most unusually they were motionless save for the beating of their wings, the cause of the sound that woke me. I stared, wondering what they were doing there. We had not been warned of a hive in the mango tree—and then my memory worked: I had seen such bees on the walls of the chief's house. Bees could serve as the eyes and even ears of sorcerers and I drew a conclusion: someone was observing Diawara and his host.

Should I warn them? They were doing nothing untoward that the bees might report. I had suspicions, but no idea who might have sent the bees. For some minutes I waited. The air was heavy under the tree. Then I slapped at my shin with a short exclamation. Diawara and his host turned, looking at me.

"I was stung!" I complained. "There are bees or wasps here."

"I have no hive," said our host. "The chief keeps a number of hives in the trees behind his compound. They are a defensive measure." Often, small villages that were too poor to build walls relied on thick and thorny hedges for protection in times of trouble, and they also kept hives as weapons to hurl at attackers. Angry bees will drive off many warriors and sting more accurately than arrows. I gestured and he saw the bees on the tree. His eyes paused on them for a moment.

"Come," he invited Diawara and me, and we rose and followed him behind a hut.

"The chief watches us with ill intent," he murmured. "Few traders come to Gbedugu. Salt is prized. We must stay alert, and tonight, we should move the salt to a different place. I have a small storage hut on the edge of the village where I keep yams and other crops as they come in from the fields."

"Leave one bar," said Diawara. "We shall cut it in half. If the chief finds half a bar he may be satisfied, and so at least you can save something."

We finished cutting and moved the remaining bars to an inconspicuous place at the back of the compound near the gate that opened onto the path toward the fields. A while later, Koita returned and slipped down next to us.

"There may be trouble," he said quietly. "The leader of this new faith visited the chief this afternoon. They spoke of devils and salt and again of devils and their powers. The leader fears the devils, and the chief desires the salt."

Diawara nodded. "I do not believe we can trade safely here." He spoke both to Koita and to his host. "We should leave this unfortunate town." He looked at his host. "Soonest is best, so tonight. Can you provide a guide to the forest path back to Manignan?" The host nodded. Diawara looked at Koita and me. "Then we shall prepare for a very early departure. Don't let your preparations be too obvious."

The last instruction was unnecessary; none of us had brought anything to speak of and we had almost no preparations to make. But we understood the need to make our actions seem ordinary.

After a short discussion with Diawara, Koita came to me. "We are leaving one bar of salt," he announced. "So one bearer can help serve as a guard. You have no weapons training, but you might serve. Are you willing?"

Life as a guard was more attractive than life as a bearer. "Yes," I answered firmly.

"Then we can teach you some simple things," said Koita. "You have no blade, but a staff can be effective, especially in the dark. We shall made do with wood." He produced a pair of pestles, staves some four feet long and three inches thick. In my village we knew the pestle as the woman's weapon. Almost every woman spent an hour a day hefting it as she pounded millet and other grains; also it was well known that the husband who chose a fight with his wife at the wrong time might get his skull cracked.

"You can do more than pound with this," he said, handing me one of the two pestles. I took it, stepped back, and then found myself on the ground: he had whirled his own stick around to knock my feet from under me.

"Remember," he observed. "If I had swung at your head,

you would have reacted instantly. But you did not notice the stick coming at your knees until too late."

I rose, unsteady.

"I caught your legs from behind," he added. "That is the direction they bend. What do you think would have happened if I had swung the stick the other way?" I considered the impact of the heavy staff on my shins and nodded.

He made me practice whirling the staff in all directions, with each hand. I fell over once, when my feet were not balanced and the staff pulled me too far. He laughed. Otherwise he did not seem displeased. We stopped our practice when the first fruit bat flew out of a nearby tree. This was an early sign of sunset.

We took a light supper at the usual time. Then when the fires died down to embers, Diawara gave the sign. We rose, moving to the back of the compound. Boloba and the others took up their loads of salt. I took my pestle; Koita took his spears and, after a moment's thought, another pestle. The town was silent around us, to our relief.

We were approaching the forest when we heard a tumult behind us: a mob of men rushing after us and shouting. Diawara hastened his pace towards the darkness below the trees.

Koita and I, as rear guard, waited at the edge of the fields until we saw torches. Their movement confirmed they were on our trail. Then we passed into the forest. Koita moved slowly, considering the path and the alignment of the trees. Soon he found a spot he liked: two of the large trees grew close together on either side of the path. He walked around each of the trees, and then explained his plan.

It turned out to be a quick and simple skirmish. We waited behind the trees until we heard the mob approaching. The leaders' torches lit the path before them showing their position. As they came between our two trees, we each stepped out swinging our staffs just below knee level. Two men fell. The backswings took down two more, probably with less damage. Then we swung somewhat higher, hitting men in the belly so they fell back against their fellows and knocked them down. Then we raced down the path after our companions. Behind us, at least six men lay in a welter of broken or bruised limbs and fallen torches. After a few hundred paces Koita took my arm and we paused to listen for sounds of pursuit. There were none.

We rejoined the others. Our progress was not entirely cheerful; this trading venture hadn't been successful and the dark of the woods was disheartening. But we had escaped danger and done some damage to our foes. I wondered what passion drove them to this attack—greed was not a good answer, for our salt was an ordinary commodity. I also wondered if I might continue as a guard. I had never tried to fight before, beyond boyhood fisticuffs. The excitement of the few seconds in which Koita and I stopped the mob lingered, lifting my feet and spirits. It didn't occur to me until much later that we were very lucky that the maneuver had come off so smoothly and effectively. Koita's comment on the event was, "Our reception in Gbedugu was very unusual. I have followed Diawara for several years, and I have only had to unsheathe my sword once. These spears have killed rats and snakes, not men."

The next morning, in the gloom before dawn, I heard Diawara pray. After the usual Arabic phrases he broke most unusually into Maninka: "May safety and security be granted to us and all the honest servants of God. Oh Lord of the world, who protected the Prophet [and here there was an Arabic phrase] as he traveled the sands of Arabia to trade, protect your servants who follow in his path."

* * *

We were perhaps midway between Gbedugu and Manignan when we heard whistles, clearly not bird calls. We recognized the sounds of many birds: the booming notes of hornbills, the chatter of parrots, the flutings of unseen songbirds. These shrill cries were human whistles, the sign of hunters around us. We wondered if we might be the prey. Worried, we continued until the path grew dim before us. Then we stopped and prepared to camp.

Donzomô emerged from the darkness beneath a tree as we were settling around the fire. He had no food in his hands this time. Diawara recognized and greeted him; they exchanged salutations, then sat near the fire. We had little food with us: some roasted yams and some jerky. Boloba acted as steward and served the food. Kouassi again served as interpreter.

"There was trouble in Gbedugu," observed Donzomô.

"There are newcomers who do not like Muslims or traders," answered Diarawa drily.

"You found no ivory."

"We still carry our salt," said Diawara.

"Might you be interested in this?" asked Donzomô. He held out his hand; on the palm was a pebble-sized globule, oddly shaped and glistening in the light of the fire. I didn't recognize it as gold; in my village, we never saw nuggets, and only the wives of the wealthiest farmers owned gold rings or other such finery. My mother had a pair of earrings, small and solid crescents.

Diawara carefully lifted the nugget and examined it. "Yes,"

he answered simply, and then, "but you must know that it's worth more than all the salt we have with us."

"Here and now," answered Donzomô, "its worth is what I am willing to trade it for. You have salt that we hunters require. But we cannot carry or store as much salt as you have with you."

Diawara chuckled. "You are not porters. You need your speed and agility to pursue the beasts in the bush. But you need not store the salt yourselves." He exchanged looks first with Kouassi and then with the hunter. "My *jatigi* in Manignan is Wattara. Can you come with us to Manignan?" The hunter nodded. "Then come, and there we shall weigh this gold. I shall leave its value in salt with Wattara. When you desire salt you need only go to him. If you desire to trade the salt for iron or other items, Wattara will help you."

I later wondered how sure this bargain might be. I mentioned my doubts to Boloba. He smiled his gentle smile. "Is gold so easy to find?" he asked. "Wattara will recognize that this hunter might bring him more gold. Therefore he will treat him fairly. Consider," he waved his hand at the forest, "how much searching would be needed to find a stone the size of that nugget."

In Manignan the arrangements with Wattara went smoothly. The nugget was weighed, admired, and not mentioned to the chief. Several bars of salt were set aside in Wattara's storehouse for the hunters; Donzomô inspected and counted them.

The storehouse was also filling up with bundles of kola nuts, the small red variety found in this region, carefully wrapped in leaves and moistened each day by a slave who used a whisk made from the tail of a cow to shake droplets of water over the leaves. The amount amazed me: at this time, one *kokotla* of salt brought something over six hundred nuts, and each salt bar counted around twelve *kokotla*. The neat, low array of salt bars had been replaced by a small mountain of green and odorous packets. I realized I would certainly be serving as a porter on this part of the trip, and that my load would be challenging: a weight of kolas equal to the weight of the salt I had carried would be a bulbous, cumbersome, and awkward load. It would be like balancing a mortar, bottom-side down, on top of a pestle.

Geladio had amusing news for us. The chief's brother, who fired his unreliable weapon in a fit of passion, was to live in the household of the earthmaster. In theory, he was to become an apprentice and learn the mysteries of that office. This involved an initiation, which might be uncomfortable, at the least. "They will coat him with honey and lay him over anthills," said a few. "They will starve him for days, and then beat him with scourges," said others. "He will have to learn Guro well enough to pass, and then serve in his father-in-law's fields," said yet others. But one or two voices suggested that if he won back his wife's affections—and none doubted that the two shared passion, since he had been moved to extreme, if ineffective and comical, violence—she might simply reveal her father's lore to him and allow him to take power. This had happened before, quite often.

One evening, a light rain fell. Diawara considered the skies and decided that he would wait no longer. He had enough kola on hand. Wattara would hold the unsold salt and trade it as he could. Soon the rains would start to fall heavily and make the paths impassable except to warthogs and other mud-loving creatures.

We marched out the next day. The kola nuts were packed in baskets lined with green leaves; the bottoms of the baskets were strengthened with slats of wood. Even so they were much harder to manage than the heavy but compact bars of salt. We also moved more slowly, for each morning and afternoon we had to leave time to open up the bundles, spread out the packets of leaves, and spray them with water. Also every day Diawara emptied a number of packets and inspected the nuts for rot and insect damage. The *manignan wooro* we carried, the kola of Manignan, did not fetch the best price, so quality mattered. The little red nuts were widely enjoyed for their taste, but other varieties were preferred for ceremonial functions. The opening of marriage negotiations, for instance, required ten large kolas. Still, if Diawara could get his load of nuts safely to the arid lands he would prosper.

So he urged speed. Our path north was not the same as our path south: he was making for Bougouni. Others would then carry the kola further north, while he returned to his family for farming activities of the imminent wet season.

We did not retrace the path that led near my village.

Water Pot Statuette
Owned by the Belcher Family

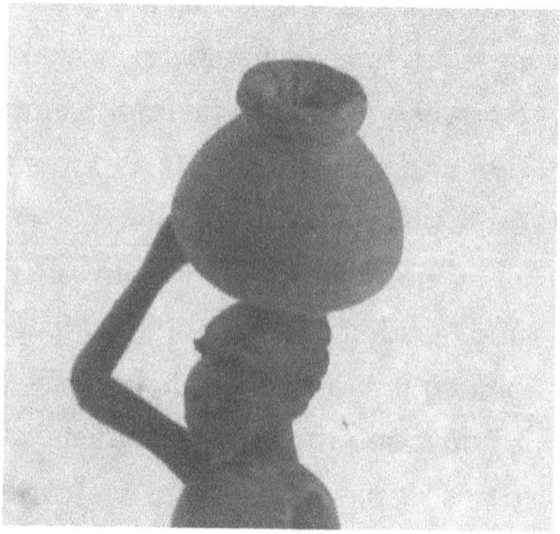

CHAPTER VII

WE WERE THREE DAYS march from Bougouni when Koita heard astonishing news.

We had stopped for the night. Somewhere, Koita encountered a *jeli* and heard his tidings. He rushed back with the *jeli* to share the news with Diawara: Kumi Josse Traore, the last great *keletigi* (war leader) of Beledugu, who had warred against the Koulibaly of Kaarta and the later Tukolor rulers of the marches of Segou, had been destroyed by the *nasrani*, the white men who had also defeated Samori.

To Koita, this meant the end of an era.

"He was the last of the *nganaw* (the heroes)," Koita explained. "He was fearless and arrogant. He never bothered to look behind himself, no matter what he heard. He rode as though he and the horse were one. He was the greatest warrior of his time in Beledugu, the land between Kaarta and Segou where warriors rise thick as the millet stalks in a watered field." He turned toward someone I had not noticed before. "Kabine, you tell the story."

"Kabine, *i ka kènè*?" Diawara greeted the *griot*. Kabine wore a tan shirt of African cotton with red and brown vertical stripes. His mouth had the marks of smiles, but now was shaped for serious matters. They exchanged greetings, then Diawara asked, "And you have fresh news from Beledugu?"

"*Ahuh,*" assented Kabine. "I was in the town of Kumi, I witnessed the fall."

"Will you tell us what happened?" asked Diawara. Certainly he was already assessing the gift he would have to make to the *jeli,* in kolas or some other commodity.

"It was the new *nasrani komanda,*" said Kabine. "The *nasrani* built a fort in Bamako during their wars with Samori. Since his fall they have been forcing the kinglets to obey them. Kumi Josse had so far resisted. The war rose from a question of women. The *nasrani komanda* sent a messenger to Kumi Josse to ask the number of slave women in his household.

"This *keletigi* had many women in his household! How could he not? He raids and captures villages and of course he keeps the pretty young ones around him until he finds reason to give them to his favored warriors. Older ones he keeps because they can cook and know their sauces, and some he keeps because they make pots. So he answered the *nasrani* that he had never counted his women but that they were part of the court of a king.

"The *nasrani* sent a soldier, a Wolof from the coast that come attached to the tails of the *nasrani.* He didn't send a *jeli,* a *griot,* a man of Traore's tradition, one who would have known how to couch the words to give the least offense. Kumi Josse was a Traore for whom dishonor is worse than death, a true slave of the shroud. No, the *nasrani* sent a stranger who knew nothing of the Beledugu, nothing of the Manding, nothing of *horonya,* but thought only that he was important because the *nasrani* had put a fine cloth coat upon him. So this Diop comes riding to the walls of Kumi. The warriors at the gates greet him, and he demands entrance. They consider whether they should shoot him there, or perhaps trim his ears, but decide to defer to their master. The Wolof enters. He speaks in the *franzawi nasrani* [French] speech, but he is hardly a master of the tongue. Kumi Josse has men of skill in his service, men who know the speech of others. One of them comes and answers this Diop. After some words they talk in Wolof.

"With hesitation, the man of Kumi leaves the soldier standing in the courtyard. He finds his master and informs him of the message. Kumi Josse reaches for his sword—surely he will send this messenger back to his master in pieces. But Kumi Josse considers and then orders the soldier brought before him. You must remember, the messenger was only a Wolof.

"The soldier comes and speaks. The servant of Kumi Josse translates and explains: the *nasrani komanda* says that women kept as slaves must be freed. The master of spears and iron, the master of the sword chuckles and tells the soldier that the women of his household are a personal matter in the town of Kumi, but that if the *nasrani komanda* desires a voluptuous bedmate he will be happy to send a skilled woman to bring him bliss.

"The Wolof listens. He looks around the courtyard. He is alone among many armed men. He says he will take the message to his *komanda*. He leaves.

"Some days later he returns, this time with a troop of other soldiers, *tirayé* [*tirailleurs*, soldiers of the French colonial army]. He demands entrance to the town without waiting for a guide. When the warriors at the gate refuse, he raises his hand. Two soldiers beside him raise their rifles and shoot. One warrior is wounded. These Wolof are not like our warriors in the Beledugu who can make one bullet count against three men. Even the Fula who live among us shoot better than they.

"Without a word to their master, the warriors around the

gates return the shots. Four of the *tirayé* fall dead. The others turn and flee, *perepereperepere*, back to their *komanda*. Kumi Josse hears the sounds and knows that trouble lies ahead, but he is a Traore, a *ngana*. He orders his warriors to prepare their horses and set up a camp outside of town. Then he calls his men of power and his diviners and set them to work to prepare *dalilu* to protect the town and bring trouble to his enemies. The diviners do their work; they call for this and that animal, for gum and blood and millet paste and powder; they chant their invocations, they call the spirits. Since the fall of Segou the four spirits that protected that town at a bloody price have wandered free: Makungoba, Binyejugu, Kontara, and Nangoloki. But Kumi Josse cannot provide the human sacrifice the diviners want: an albino dwarf. They settle for a white goat and a black goat and a red goat and spray the blood around the gates of the town.

"They do not know that the *nasrani komanda* relies not only on this Wolof in fine clothes. He also has a lieutenant, a Fula, but this Fula wears no uniform. He circles the town and comes in at the back. He finds the women's quarters and sees that they are lovely, even more beautiful than rumor reported. One among them, the finest, with the brightest eyes and the most graceful neck...She is Soninke, but she gives no name. She greets the Fula, for she understands his tongue and his purpose. They speak. The Fula warns them that the reign of Kumi Josse is ending. He tells them the power of the *nasrani* soldiers is greater than spears and swords, greater than heroes, greater than horses. The women listen but say very little.

"The Wolof and the soldiers return to the *komanda*. The *komanda* turns bright red, like a ripe mango, and orders an assault. The soldiers are given powder, food is stocked, and they prepare one of their cannons, the *nègè-da*. It is smaller than the cannon which Arsina [Gen. Archinard] used upon Segou. The soldiers march. It is five days from Bamako to Kumi; they move slowly because they have small carts drawn by donkeys and the carts often get stuck.

"When they come in sight of Kumi, they are attacked. The horsemen of Kumi Josse, like the *sofaw* of Samory, charge through the bush. They have been waiting where a marigot gives shelter.

"The *tirayé* fire, but many fall as the horsemen carve through the column. But the *nasrani komanda* has made his preparations: his cannon is ready, and he gives the order. The blast frightens the horses of Kumi; the riders are carried away. Their attack fails.

"The *nasrani komanda* and his men prepare an outpost: they build up low walls and plant palisades to stop the horses. They place their cannon with care. They fire upon the city: the ball goes high and falls near the market. The people run in terror to their houses and hide. The cannon fires again; this time it falls closer to the palace of Kumi Josse. The *nasrani* nods, gives orders. Another ball falls and destroys the *ce-bolon* in which Kumi Josse has placed the *dalilu* which his men of power had prepared.

"The *nasrani komanda* decides that he has done enough for the day. He will leave the town to stew overnight, like a simmering pot; the next day he is sure there will be no resistance. But he sends his Fula into the town again. The Fula goes in the dark like a gray cat, he finds the women. They give him their news. He continues on in the dark; he sees that Kumi Josse and his men are collecting their store of gunpowder. Death is better than dishonor! Surely they plan some action like that of Kansala when the king of Kaabu allowed the victorious Muslim

Fula to come into town and then exploded his powder, killing all. Word of that fall has spread.

"He returns to the women. He asks the women if they wish to die with the *keletigi*? These are not the *nyancho* princesses of Kaabu who threw themselves into a well rather than become slaves. These are women who served Kumi Jossi and his warriors, but they are not wives, they are not the mistresses of compounds. They have stayed within their quarters, but they have heard the sounds of the cannon, they have seen the effects of its balls. They listen to the Fula. The Soninké woman listens most carefully, and he sees she fully understands his purpose. He gives them instructions, and then he leaves the town."

Kabine paused to assess the listeners. His audience, including me, was caught in the story.

"In the morning, the *nasrani komanda* orders his column to march forward towards the town with their weapons ready. There is no resistance at the gates. No one is to be seen in the streets between the walls of *banko*. The soldiers advance. The Wolof leads them to Kumi Josse's palace.

"In the palace, Kumi Josse and his men await the arrival of the *tirayé*. Their horses would not carry them against the cannon; their *dalilu* have been destroyed; the millet beer has turned bitter in their mouths. They wait and they watch, and behind them stands a great pile of containers with the powder that Kumi Josse has stored. One warrior waits with his rifle aimed at this pile waiting for when Kumi Josse gives the order…when the *tirayé* and the *nasrani komanda* are within the walls, he will fire his bullet to cause great destruction. Few Fula returned from Kansala to Fuladugu and few *tirayé* will leave Kumi. Such is their hope.

"The *tirayé* come to the palace and surround it. Slowly,

slowly, step by step, they enter, waiting for the counter-attack which they are sure must come. But all is silent. Nothing moves. They come closer; Kumi Josse can hear them outside the hall in which he waits. He nods to the warrior. The warrior pulls his trigger; the shot resounds, the bullet strikes the powder. But the explosion fails. Some powder burns, but not enough. During the night, led by the Soninké woman, the concubines have come and poured water onto the containers, silently and invisibly. Surely they were helped by the spirits! Kumi Josse has been betrayed by women, as were Bassi of Samaniana and Douga of Kore!

"Kumi Josse Traore rises! Slave of the shroud! Death is better than dishonor! His horse has failed him, his rifle has failed him. He has nothing like *Tukulu-mukulu*, the spear that knew no pity, the spear of Tira Magan! He uses his sword: he carves his belly and falls bleeding to the ground. Around him, his warriors follow his example. They die slowly. Their blood seeps into the clay. At the door the *tirayé* gaze in horror.

"The *nasrani komanda* orders a burial outside the town for the fallen warriors; courage and death demand respect. He summons the elders of the clans, and this time he sends the word through a *griot*, a Diabate. The *nasrani komanda* announces that slaves are to be freed; slaves brought from other parts should be sent home. The Fula goes to the women's quarters and brings out all the women. They are to be returned to their families.

"And so Kumi has fallen." Kabine stopped, stepping slightly back.

After a moment of silence, Diawara, the highest-ranking listener, thanked him for his tidings. He paused, considering what gift should be made for this speech, but Koita forestalled him and reached out to take the *griot's* hands, no doubt with a gift. I caught a flash of silver as the hands parted. Even so, Diawara later arranged for a small basket of kola nuts to be delivered to Kabine.

We revisited this story at our next camp.

"Treachery!" exclaimed Koita. "It was always the mark of Segou. Do they not call it the town of the one thousand four hundred and forty-four *balanza* trees and the little twisted *balanza*, which signifies betrayal?"

"Do you think Josse was betrayed by the *boliw* of Segou?" asked Diawara. I observed him closely. Our travels had taught me that he was a remarkable man, not only for the knowledge he shared so freely with me. His concern for others and respect for the dignity of all had won my loyalty.

"It was a strategy of Segou that betrayed him," commented Geladio, the Fula. "Through women Segou conquered Samaniana and Dietekoro of Kaarta."

"In the Wasulu, they speak of the 'Fula coat of treachery,'" offered Boloba. "Surely the actions of this Fula serving the *nasrani* gave them the town."

"They were already defeated!" protested Geladio. "The Fula limited the damage; no doubt he had heard of the fall of Kansala."

"But he moved in the dark and led the women to act against their lords. Will you say that is a good action? Would those women have poured water on the powder without his incitement?"

"A Fula warrior," pronounced Geladio, with an edge to his voice, "has nothing to do with treachery. He faces his enemies and defeats them or dies."

"If the story is true," Diawara intervened, his tone

reminding all that a *jeli* will color his tale, "the agent of the *nasrani* performed his duty. The town was already lost. We *farafin* have no weapons that can match the cannon of the *nasrani*, and even our best rifles are barely as good as their worst. As Geladio has observed, he limited the damage. The women were not household slaves who count as part of a family; they were servants. No one can expect loyalty where trust and faith are not first given."

He paused.

"I too have heard of the 'Fula coat of treachery,'" he finally continued. "It is one of those accusations that people throw around. I wonder how it arose. The Fula care for their cattle, as we others for our fields and crops and merchandise. How can a cow betray a farmer? I believe the answer lies in our history.

"We of the Manding live in the shadow of Mari Diata who united the kingdoms. He defeated Sumaworo, the blacksmith magician; he gave us a rule based on laws and agreements. He united peoples and made them live together and reach an understanding. Because of his rule, I have a *jatigi* in Manignan. And some of us saw," he glanced around the circle of listeners, "what it is like to try to trade outside the world that Mari Diata united. There is no respect, no trust. That, I believe, is why Mari Diata fell. Few speak of his death. What I have heard is that he made an agreement with the Fula, and that later he broke the agreement. He prepared war against them and while crossing a river, the boundary of the land he had accorded them, his boat sank. He perished. Because he broke his word, he who most particularly should have remembered the importance of true faith.

"Do you know how he returned from exile to the Manding? He needed to cross the Joliba, the great river which he and his mother had crossed as they were fleeing the jealousy of his brother Dankaran Tuman. His mother had given silver bracelets to the chief of the Somono folk who control the ferries. On his return, Mari Diata stood on the river bank and raised his arms. He wore metal on his wrists. He clashed the metal and the sound rolled over the water. The Somono chieftain heard and understood: he remembered the present he had been given. He summoned his men and their boats. They brought the army of Mari Diata across to give battle to Sumaworo.

"My own people, the Soninke, in the days before we became Muslim, were settled through a debt acknowledged and repaid. When Jabe Cisse acquired his father's knowledge, by a trick, I admit, he wandered until he met an ancient vulture, a *duga*, and then a hyena, equally ancient, and they told him his father had made a pact with them. Jabe Cisse honored the engagement: he fed the two beasts, whitened with age, until they regained their strength, if not their youth, and they guided him to the land that would become Wagadu. There the Soninke prospered and were rich with gold."

He paused, and apparently decided not to recall the story of the fall of Wagadu.

"The Fula are not known for betrayals," he concluded, and nodded to Geladio.

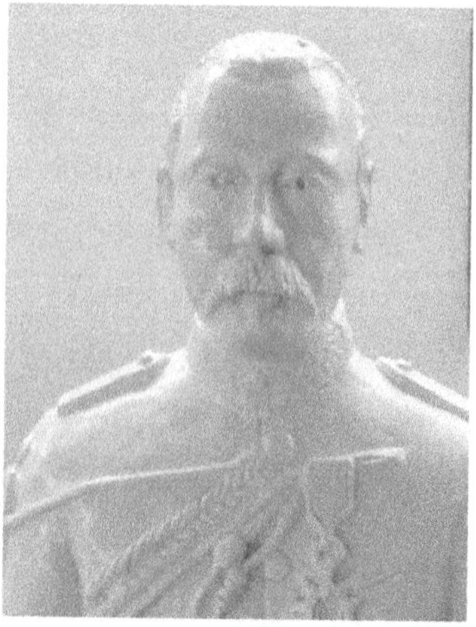

Bust of a French Colonial Officer
One of a series in the courtyard of the king of Mossou in Grand-Bassam, Côte d'Ivoire, 2014.

CHAPTER VIII

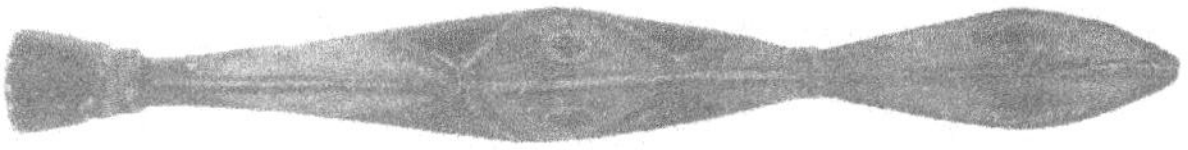

BOUGOUNI LIES NORTH OF a wide bend of the Baoule River. Our path brought us to the far side of the river about midday. We settled our loads in the shade. Diawara and Koita crossed the river to find the *jatigi*. Geladio bought food for us from a woman cooking near the river: *to* with a spicy fish sauce.

Diawara returned with his trading partner and two large boats. The partner, Niambele, a stout man with a pock-marked face, examined some of the kola nuts and nodded. We loaded the baskets into the boats. Unlike *pirogues* that are hollowed out from a single log, these were made of planks assembled on a framework of a keel and ribs fastened into place and then sewn together and carefully caulked. The crossing took two trips. Then the cargo was stowed in a well-guarded hut near the river; the partner planned to ship the kola nuts down the Bani River towards Jenne. The trip would require a portage from the Baoule to the Bani.

We arrived in a time of suspended action: two days before a great celebration: the fish festival that preceded the rainy season and the rising of the floodwaters, just before the start of a new season of crops.

The fish festival is perhaps the most joyous, and certainly the muddiest, of our annual celebrations in the Manding. It marks the *san yelema*, the turning of the year. It is the return of the waters that bring new life to the red earth, that revive the brown vegetation and start the growth of new crops. The waters come from the skies and flow over the earth to renew its life. In this cycle, the fish-festival marks the end of the old year in a specific way involving the recessional ponds that form after the rains. In their season, the river waters rise to cover the lands, creating vast but shallow stretches of silvered waters. As the waters recede, some ponds remain cut off from the rivers. By common agreement people do not fish those ponds during the dry season.

In my village, the pond dried out quickly. Before it vanished, the women and children of the village would swarm over the residual puddles, collecting the flapping fish. In Bougouni, close to a broad river, the pond was much greater and had lasted since the last rains. Now, before the new rains fell and raised the river waters to rejoin the ponds, the people gathered to harvest the fishy schools that had been increasing in the ponds through the year. The festival was also a tribute to Faro, the spirit of the waters, who took the form of a great catfish, like those that left the riverbeds during flood season to venture out over their newly expanded domain.

Bougouni was the largest town I had seen, twice the size of Manignan and many times the size of my village. It housed *horon* lords and wealthy traders who sponsored dance troupes and puppet-masquerades. The festival drew people from all over: the Buguni-denw, people born in Bougouni who had left because of marriage or trade or other circumstances, returning for the occasion; villagers from the surrounding region, not only from the farming slave villages but also the freemen and the artisans. Since the fall of Samori travel had become safer.

The next day we porters sat idle as Diawara and Niambele

examined the kola nuts more thoroughly and discussed their value in various markets. Niambele clearly wanted to ship the kolas downstream towards Djenne immediately, but he encountered resistance from his boatmen: they would not leave Bougouni on the eve of a major festival. I observed one dispute from a distance as Niambele argued with two boatmen, waving arms, stamping, stepping forward.

The confrontation was defused: a Somono boatman appeared with a group of strangers. By their dress they were Fula warriors: each carried a rifle slung across his back and a sword at his side, their shirts were studded with protective charms sewn at random.

Geladio greeted them in Fula with some reserve. Geladio's ancestors had difficulties with the Fula Muslims of Massina, as he had told us. These were not Massinanke, but *talibe*, followers of Laji Umaru of the Toro who had conquered Segou many years before, members of the Tijiani sect. They knew and cared nothing about the history of Massina.

The Somono led two to talk with Diawara and Niambele. They knew a Fula trader in the new *nasrani* town of Mopti, where the Bani met the Niger, who would give a very good price for fresh kola nuts. Niambele welcomed the thought of a new market and a new trading partner.

Two other Fula sat waiting. One was wild-eyed and unkempt; his hair was matted into thick braids and he muttered incessantly to himself. Geladio later explained this was the habit of some Tijiani: each initiate was given a *wyrd*, an individual prayer, by their master, and they repeated the prayers. This Fula occasionally broke into verse:

Huwa Umaru futiyyu ibnu saiduna
bi Sokna Adama, labbinado mo tunwataa!

Doftido yarli, ternomum kala pede fof
Diggandodum, newanidodum kala tikkatah

Geladio later explained that this was part of a long poem about Laji Umaru, calling him the leader one could not disobey and who calmed anger, and then comparing him to the sky ram, bright and powerful, whose clear voice called out, whose head had a black spot. This was, of course, one word, for the Fula have specific names for every coloring of an animal. I asked him how he knew this. He answered simply, "Any Fula worthy of the name knows the poetry of his language. A Fula may feel ecstasy at the sight of a well-fed herd of cattle, but the words of his language may also make him drunk!"

After the discussion the group of Fula and Diawara and a few others joined for the late-afternoon prayers.

The end of our trail led me to wonder what my future held. Would Diawara keep me as a porter?

The notion of release from his service was frightening. Among the Bamana, you worked with and for your family. If you were a *nyamakala,* you worked in your clan's craft: as a smith or a leather worker or a potter or, with talent, a *griot.* Most Bamana were farmers engaged in the hard labor of clearing fields, tilling thick clay soils with the *daba,* and praying for enough rain to make the crops feed the family until the next harvest. A few homeless men eked out an unhappy life around my village serving families that lacked manpower, but they were not respected. Often they were considered daft: if you asked them to hoe a field, you had to make sure they didn't dig a well.

That was my uncertain future. For the present, I was in a large town during a festival. Boloba again took care of me. He considered me a neighbor, for he said our villages were not distant. For him, arrival in Bougouni meant he would soon return home. We wandered through the town to the weavers' quarter. Their colorful warps stretched out for yards beyond their looms: blue and red and green ribbons of threads across the ochre tones of the earth. The weavers were mostly Fula, *maabube*, and they sang as they worked. We went down to the river and watched men working on boats: they used slender spikes of iron, heated red-hot, to burn holes through the wooden planks then carefully laced the planks with thin thongs of leather, wetted and stretched, and sealed the holes and the joints with gum and paste and pitch. I understood they were trying to finish their jobs before the celebrations.

In some places members of a *ton* (an age group) shooed us away. They were preparing their festival presentation in secret. An excitement lay upon the people of the town.

With my spirit-sight I occasionally caught glimmers of the spirits who were being summoned or invoked or embodied in artifacts of wood and cloth and metal and glass, or other more organic materials. We found places where animals had been slaughtered. Little pits had been dug to catch the blood as the throat was cut, and nearby lay the hooves of a goat or the paws of some bush-beast. Most, no doubt, were a dinner, but some may have been a sacrifice. Some pools of blood near the paws seemed darker to my non-human sight, as though the *nyama*, the life-force, had been concentrated and lingered still.

Despite the blood, the mood of the town was joyous and proud. Bougouni was pleased with itself and felt prosperous. The people of the town were proclaiming its worth.

The festival lasted over the three nights of the full moon. On the first day, there would be the preparatory dances and ceremonies; on the second, the people would go down to the pond for the fish festival, and then the third would be largely spent eating whatever fish might have been caught with dancing and continuing the good times late into the night. The moonlit nights would be filled with celebration. Diawara told his porters that they should stay for the festival (as they all planned to do anyway) and that he would settle with them afterwards.

The first day brought an unexpected spectacle. Boloba and I walked into the market to buy nuts and sugar cane as snacks. As we passed the cloth sellers, we encountered a thick crowd. Shoppers, passersby and even vendors had gathered to gape at a parade of beautiful and elegant women who were considering some cloths laid out for purchase. There were half-a-dozen, already adorned in fine shiny cloth woven of gold and indigo and vermilion red threads. They wore robes, where the women of Bougouni settled for their wrap-arounds and coarse cotton tops. These robes had been beaten and stiffened with gum-arabic and embroidered with gold or silver thread. A few went bareheaded, but their hair had been teased and oiled and braided into spikes and spirals and coils of great complexity. The others wrapped their heads with cloths to match or complement their robes, and each had her own distinctive style of tying the cloth, so that the ends fell by the ears or over the nape or rose into the air.

The dress proclaimed their wealth. Then I began to look at their faces as they moved around the rolled wheels of African cloth and the folded sheets of *nasrani* cotton. They were all young and beautiful. They were healthy and well-fed. Their cheeks glowed, their eyebrows had been carefully plucked, their lips were arched in fullness and glistened with moisture.

One stood out. My ordinary sight noted her beauty, but most important was the *wokòlò* sense, now whetted by wanderings among the believers in spirit cults and their rehearsals of summonings throughout Bougouni. Her features were finer than the other women's. She wore simpler robes, a pattern of horizontal blue and white stripes, and her head-cloth was a deep and entrancing indigo. She needed no adornment to proclaim her worth. Immediately, I recalled Diawara's story of the princess, the most beautiful of her people, appointed for sacrifice, saved against her will by a persistent lover. This woman embodied that role. In her I saw a rank, a social class, even a whole people with its history and sufferings, and deep within a grief for a loss.

She cast...not a shadow, but a presence, an extension of herself that suggested that she existed in many places at once, or that she was concentrating ages of time and motion into one place. She was no common mortal, discrete in space and time; she had seen times and places pass her by. Her presence recalled the mighty trees I had marveled at in the south, enduring and age-old.

I couldn't help staring in wonder. I was slow to notice how beautiful she was although beauty lay on her; visible and palpable, though mute. The lines and proportions of her face, the arch of her brows, the silken cheeks, the slender neck—I was lost in wonder, and not only because I was young and male.

A man beyond the women spoke: he wore a blue tunic, white pants, and a red fez: a soldier of the *nasrani*, a *tirayé*. Clearly, he was in charge of the women. He moved through the market and the women followed him. Their path led them past Boloba and myself.

As the timeless woman approached, I remembered the

name and spoke it aloud: "Assya! Assya Berete!" So Diawara had named the Soninke princess of Wagadu. I still wonder why I actually voiced the name. Was it intended as a compliment? Or had the *wokòlò* guided me?

She reacted immediately.

She stopped and stared at me. In all the crowd of faces, she knew immediately who had spoken and named her.

"*Bamana-kè*!" she demanded. "What did you call me?"

"I called you by the name of the lost princess of Wagadu, because surely you are as beautiful as she was."

I am sure she hesitated, but she replied quickly. "And how do you see a princess of the Wagadu among the captive women of the dead Kumi Josse?"

I hesitated. Her question led in many directions. It explained her presence. The *griot* named Sissoko had talked of the soldiers returning Kumi Josse's women to their homes. However the demeanor of the soldier didn't suggest that he was returning them to their homes. These paragons of varied beauty were a sampling of the blossoms that Kumi Josse had assembled and a source of profit for the soldier. But this woman was no ordinary concubine. Her vitality reinforced my sense of her persona; timeless and enduring. While she looked at me, the market and the crowd around us vanished. We stood alone.

I found an answer. "Because you are such a woman as would redeem a kingdom. And because you are far greater than Kumi Josse and his town." I had more to say, but she interrupted.

"Do you know the *full* story of that princess of Wagadu?" she demanded.

"She was to be sacrificed, and Mamadi the hard-of-speech killed the serpent," I answered. "She was chosen because– "

"Do you know what happened afterwards?" she insisted. She didn't wait for an answer. "He took her south. He was sure she would love him, since he had saved her life, but she refused. She had been chosen to serve her people through her death, not to satisfy the lust of some noble lout. She had accepted the sacrifice and went willingly. But his selfishness brought ruin upon the kingdom and the people. She refused his love. Do you know what happened then?"

I shook my head. Diawara had not continued the story.

"He set an enchantment upon her, a spell of love, but not for himself. He wished to shame her. She woke up one morning in the arms of his groom, smelling of straw and horse-manure. The groom was a slave from some land far to the south. She was a princess of the Wague. She tried to kill herself. She failed. She was bound to the spirit of the Bida serpent. Death refused her. She tried all sorts of means: the knife, the rope, poison, drowning...*muru y'a bana, tanba y'a bana, korte y'a bana*. All these methods failed her. She remained doomed to live with her shame, doomed to an unfulfilled purpose." She paused and fixed me with her eyes. "*Bamana-kè*, would you wish that upon me? Do you think I might share her fate?"

Her eyes showed traces of tears, recalling the fate of the lost princess. As I stared into them, I was lost. "I do not know your fate," I answered. "I could never wish any doom upon you; rather, I would carry for you any burden that would ease your path." As I spoke the words, I caught a glimmering of insight, that unheard echo, and I understood that my promised service to the spirits would be service to this woman.

She smiled suddenly. "A warrior would have offered to slay any foe. But it was slaughter that broke the bond. I think perhaps these times need men and women who will share their burden."

She was interrupted; the *nasrani* soldier was impatient at the delay.

"*Bamana-kè*, we shall meet again." She turned and was gone. Quite unwittingly, but with no doubts or hesitation, I had set my feet on whatever path might lead me back to her. I don't know if you can call it love after a three-minute conversation, but this woman owned me.

Boloba took my hand. "She is a fine woman," he agreed with my obvious thoughts, then led me away from the crowd.

We passed stalls offering beads and glassware, then found ourselves among the potters. Beyond them women offered sun-dried fish. We had come to the edge of the market, on the open path that circumscribed the vendors. Beyond us sat a number of Fula women with pots of sour milk; they were serving a party of warriors like the ones who had visited Niambele, Diawara's business partner, that morning.

Near the Fula women were some Maninka selling their *dolo*. We stopped to buy a cupful. The taste was richer than other millet beers I had tasted. I asked the woman how she made it.

"*Ah! Bamana-kè!*" she answered, her voice gathering power like a *jeli-muso* preparing to praise a rich patron, "it is the honey and the herbs and the *nyama* of the millet that you taste! My recipe is my own, and," her voice dropped, "it really is better than that of the other women here." I was sure that the other women selling *dolo* knew perfectly well what she was saying.

The ceremonies were about to begin.

Boloba and I had observed the members of the age group responsible for town order, the unmarried *kamalen*, hurrying about the town to keep rehearsals under control. It was impossible not to hear the various drum ensembles practicing and adjusting their pitches. And where drummers beat, the feet follow. Children in particular were laughing and dancing all around the town, practicing steps that as adults they would perform with more serious purpose.

Little pomp was involved. The people of the town massed around the edges of the pond.

Various notables in bright robes assembled and walked to the edge of the water. A man in a brown shirt—the *dugutigi*, the earthmaster—cried out some extended invocation (we were too far away to make out the words).

Somewhere out of sight an ox bellowed briefly as a heavy blade cut through its throat. Soon after a man brought a bowl of blood to the *dugutigi*, who again screamed out a prayer and then poured the blood into the waters at his feet. He had told Faro, the god of waters and bringer of fertility, that the town awaited his return and he had asked permission to harvest the fish of the pond. And the town, after this ritual, assumed consent.

The fishing of the pond would start the next day. But for now, the festival had begun!

Boat at Sunset
Photo taken in Mopti, Mali, in 1980

CHAPTER IX

THAT EVENING, BOLOBA AND I were free to wander the town after we enjoyed our share of a considerable meal (two roasted sheep) that Niambele provided for his large household and guests. As soon as we left the torch-lit space of the compound and set foot on the darkened street, I paused. Sound filled the air. The different quarters of the town and the various age groups had all prepared their own entertainments. Some were now in action: drum-ensembles and dancers in various open spaces.

Rehearsals for the morrow's pageants were not visible, although audible, and contributed to the polyphony.

The *bourdon,* a bass sound underlying all others, was drumming an almost constant pitch from all directions that somehow melded into a whole. Consciously or not, the drummers were all timed to the same tempo across different rhythms, and their staccato strokes from all the different performance venues overlapped to create a swelling continuum of sound.

Faint against the drums, heard only when we came close, came the rippling notes of a *balafon,* or sometimes two or three of them together, in courtyards where a *jeli* sang praises of a noble and evoked the royalty of old Mali. From other corners came the dull drone of a bull roarer swung in rehearsal to accompany the march of a masquerade. More and more persistently through the drums came the sound of horns and mirlitons, slightly dissonant, yet still more fluid and hypnotic than the drums.

Boloba paused, wondering what kept me. I realized I was hearing a symphony beyond Boloba's ears; I was tuned to the intent of the music and the response of the town and so heard what a *wokòlò* might hear. I took his hand and led him towards the sound of the horns. Somehow, I knew they marked the omphalos of the audible activity.

We passed the compound of the town chief and I paused, my heart leaping. Here a trio of balafons sounded out the traditional praises of the nobles. Two women singers embellished the time-worn phrases of the noble's *faasa*, epithets handed down through centuries with references to recent events and strong hints that generosity should be the mood of the moment.

The water from the spring is purest!
The water of the marigot comes from the spring,
It defers to the elder!

Ah! Keita! Nare Magan Konate!
Your ancestor took up the bow,
Your ancestor created *mansaya*,
You are the child of your *siya*,
Listen to the ancestors and rule this town!

Their music was not what stopped me. Near the chief I noticed a red fez, the headgear of the Fula soldier. Around him sat his beauties, and there was my timeless woman, attentive to the music, her face reflective as though she was judging this rendition against an endless series of artists. Then she looked up across the crowd. I would swear that our eyes met, that she knew I was there, watching and admiring her rather than the *jelimuso*. She smiled quickly, and then her eyes turned back to the singer.

Boloba and I moved on. On all sides we could hear the demanding beat of the *jenbe* drums calling feet to move, calling the minds above the feet to yield to the music. Before us sounded a more demanding call that reached beyond human ears. The spirits were summoned to attend the turning of the year.

Halfway across town we encountered the procession I had been seeking by intuition.

We saw torches held high and heard the music of horns—raucous, blaring and overpowering. Then we saw the masks marching in the midst of their human attendants: figures bristling with straw garments, long-legged and ungainly. The heads were beast-like figures, but not animals of the bush known to men. The jaws curved from the teeth back to globular eyes and pendulous ears.

Neither Boloba nor I noticed the heads first. Our eyes were drawn to priapic extrusions from their midriffs, enormous representations of masculine potency that bounced and swayed as the masked dancers advanced. I chuckled at the sight and relaxed; I had come to the core of the energy, the *nyama* I had sensed. These were the trickster clowns, those who disregarded the rules and opened the space for the new year. They embodied that vital force that explored all possibilities and broke molds, that animated the recombinants to create new generations. Their eerie and wind-born music, speaking of fire and air (unlike the drums, born of earth), were a clear call to the spirits. Their human escorts were dressed in black pantaloons, the naked chests criss-crossed with chains of cowrie shells and marked with daubs of red and white paint. The horns they sounded were of various types: the *buru ba,* one end carved into a human effigy and the other bulbous with some sort of gourd.

They provided the droning base against which the *dyoburu* traced their polyrhythmic counterpoints. Although the musicians seemed to be dancing as vigorously as the masks and their attendants, they somehow kept their breath. They maintained a steady output, a sonorous shield, for their sound overwhelmed other noises and isolated this procession from the other activities of the town. Their music was a melody whose rising and falling tones suggested the words of some paean, without ever quite making the meaning explicit.

Boloba and I followed the clown/dancers for a time, sharing in a calabash of beer that was passed around and dancing, on occasion, as our feet joined the rhythms of others. I found my attention sharply divided between the human mirth and what I sensed of the spirits. They were present, not as perceptible beings, but as traces of accumulating potential that grew in mass—airy nothings taking on the shape and preferred attributes of their owners: the eyes, the horns, the wings, the body shapes. They had been summoned by the charivari of the celebrations.

The moon was sinking when the course of these celebrants brought them near Niambele's compound and we left them. Within the compound almost everyone was asleep; Koita was keeping watch and greeted us quietly. We told him what we had seen and he laughed.

"In the south they have festivals where the clowns are

played by women," he said. "You would not believe how they treat their wooden *bangalas*."

The next day, an hour or two before noon, we followed the streams of people to the edge of the pond. Almost all were carrying some kind of net or trap or trident spear, and few had bothered with much clothing. Diawara was a visible exception in his plain white cotton robe, and we, his followers, were also normally clad. We were observers, not participants. But the *Buguni-denw*, male and female, sported little more than a loincloth and perhaps a straw hat. Children were mostly naked.

The pond was completely surrounded by an expectant mass of townsfolk waiting to begin the harvest. The chief and the water-priest stood visible on the land between the river and the pond; Niambele led us to a place near them.

On this day, the leader was the water-priest. I think he was Somono, of the boat-people. He wore a necklace of great hippopotamus teeth and was draped in fish nets; his belt must have been crocodile skin. He carried a great fishing spear: a bamboo shaft with a complex and vicious barbed iron head.

The priest turned away from the pond and walked toward the river. He screamed out an invocation of some kind. In response, from some cove hidden by reeds, boats appeared and glided smoothly down the river. The boats and the boatmen were concealed by scaffolding and coverings of cloth or straw draped around a platform. Each platform carried a masquerade representing some aspect of the water powers. The first bore the great animals of the water: hippos and crocodiles, whose wide mouths gaped at us while from somewhere the sound of bull roarers mimicked their bellows. Then came water spirits: mermaids and fish-headed men. Then finally a canoe with the representation of Faro as a massive whiskered catfish stretching the length of the boat, whose mouth yawned and whose tail waved gently from side to side, threatening to capsize the craft.

As this last boat moved on, a figure emerged from the far side of the catfish behind the tail. It whirled several times on the platform, and then darted across the water to the land. I could not see how it moved over the water. Its features were indistinct, blurred by motion or veiled by power. Its presence was strong: an old but energetic woman with a wiry body and a wrinkled face, thin hair, white with age. Once on the land, it whirled several more times and then vanished into the crowd. I looked around, wondering if others had been struck by its passage over the water, but most of the onlookers were calm, as though this was nothing unusual.

Beside me, Boloba stirred. He too had noted the figure. "It is Muso Koronin," he explained. "The little old woman who works with or against Faro. Some say that she taught farming to men."

When this water-borne procession passed, the priest turned away from the river and waded into the pond. Again, he called out prayers. He raised his spear and shook it. This was the signal. Behind him the great *tabala* drums of the chief sounded a quick, deep roll.

All around the pond the people of Bougouni rushed into the water and began fishing. Most had come with simple nets: large hoops of bamboo or palm spine supporting the net they dipped and lifted quickly to catch whatever they might. Some had conical fish-traps made of wicker which they planted in the shallow waters; they then reached down through the openings at the top to see what they might have caught. Many, more ambitious, had a larger net strung across two poles, scissored around their own bodies, seining the waters in front of them until they suddenly raised the poles and fish floppped down the netting into their hands. Everyone was equipped with a calabash to contain their catch.

I watched. I did not belong to Bougouni; I had no claim to their fish.

A grandmother with a hoop netted a mess of wriggling fry, poured into her calabash. Two small boys, working together, caught a medium size perch and brought it out, delighted and screaming shrilly. Further out a team of fishers tightened a circle which yielded the largest catch of the day: a catfish some three feet long. They immediately brought it to the *dugutigi,* who promised them some rich reward and handed the fish to the Somono river-folk beside him who immediately returned it to the waters of the river. The fish, I understood, was to lead the next year's crop into the pond when the waters had risen high enough.

As the *Bugini-denw* worked their way through the waters, a group of nubile girls wended their way around the edge, dancing and singing a hymn. Every third step they bowed down, swinging switches over the ground as though reaping the grass. They were moist but not muddy, glistening with the sweat of their effort in the heat, and shapely, young, and lovely. They were, clearly, the best the town could offer.

Boloba commented, "Even twenty years ago, at the end of the dance, one of them would be bound and thrown into the river. I wonder what offerings the Somono may have made by the light of the moon."

I watched them with the sense that another figure had joined their dance: the old woman of the river. Her shade darted through their line and back, sometimes leading them, sometimes falling behind, barely visible. They were clearly of the world of flesh, but their leader appeared to be purely a spirit.

After some two hours the harvest of the fishes was done. There might still have been something besides worms living and wriggling in the pond, but I doubted it. The people of Bougouni, as individuals and as groups, had removed everything: all the fish, all the frogs, a few small crocodiles, some newts (these elicited screams, for it was firmly believed that they were poisonous). No one had drowned as sometimes happened, usually when some old person fainted and slipped below the waters.

The people returned, washed the mud from their bodies, and set the fish they caught to cooking for the evening feast. Soon the beat of drums resumed as the various associations prepared for the pageant that would take place in the market square that evening.

Dancer
Fish Festival
in Guinea, 2005

CHAPTER X

AN HOUR BEFORE DUSK we followed Niambele and the others of his household to the market square, again moving among streams of the *Bugoni-denw*. Now they were dressed in festive finery: rich and colored cloth robes, glistening expanses of fabric, glinting gold and silver jewelry at necks and wrists and ears.

We went to the central market, the most important venue for the roving performers. The audience comprised the powerful, the wealthy, and the ambitious. Niambele wished to establish his presence among these notables.

The festivities began with presentations by the *flanton*, the age groups of the city: dancers who leapt and spun across the earthen ground with precise coordination, and then somersaulted away from the torch-lit central area into the dark; the drums died out and for a moment all was quiet. Then came the metallic rasping sound of *ngaringaw* with an assortment of whistles…a small party of hunters burst into the lighted area. They sang an incomprehensible hymn to Sanen and Kontron, deities of the hunt. They performed magic: swallowing and spitting fire, pulling strange objects from their hunting sacks, knotting ropes that untangled themselves without help and slithered away into the dark. After them came a youth association, the *n'tomo*, with a small band of *jenbe* and *dundun* drummers. The full moon rose over the low trees of the town and cast its pale light over the dance floor. Two beasts with raffia bodies and wooden face masks, the *waraba,* came prowling through the space, gamboling and scuffing at each other: friends but potential rivals. After them came the *muso koronin,* a conical construct of straw and cloth bedecked with streamers of cloth and feathers, above which a jointed head rose on top of a long, thin neck, like an ostrich. This figure lacked the power of the spirit that had darted from the boat; it was an homage, not an embodiment. It whirled, slowly and with more swaying because of the extended neck. Then a hyena, the stupid ogre of our stories, came foraging over the ground, snuffling and growling and tracking invisible traces to the edge of the crowd where it snapped and snarled at frightened children.

The *n'tomo* withdrew. Out of the dark came the sound of soft singing: the voices of young women. It was the party of dancers who had circled the pond that morning, emerging from the dark shadows beneath the trees and then coursing across the moonlit earth. All were silent, listening, yet the words were still inaudible. Only the lilt, the melody, the swell of their voices reached our ears, whispering of renewed life, the return of the waters, the burgeoning of a new season.

Once around the dance space they progressed, their numbers just enough to form a large circle. Their song grew somewhat louder, though still unintelligible. In their performance I sensed an aura that other groups had not possessed or projected. Through their dance and song these maidens echoed the spirit energies that were flowing over and around the town.

They were interrupted. With a rattle of *jenbe* drums and a fanfare of horns, the priapic clowns burst into the dance space, several of them vaulting over the dancing girls to land in the center space. There they leapt and contorted themselves for a few minutes, and then with undulating loins and bouncing codpieces they approached the girls who screamed, broke their formation, and darted into the darkness. After a few more leaps around the dance floor and with much suggestive thrusting of the hips, the clowns followed them into the darkness.

"This is disgusting!" came a voice from behind us. I turned and saw in the moonlight several of the Fula from Segou. The speaker was the man who had sat muttering. "This is the work of Shaitan! No Muslim should take part in such sinfulness!" The speaker's voice broke with passion and outrage. I couldn't tell at first to whom he was speaking, and then I realized that his words were addressed to Diawara, in his plain white robe, visible as a Muslim. The man continued in Fula, "*Dum baddo ummi, heldoyidi barkingomum, nyemtide golle, tubado koddo do daibataa.*" This was a line from the poem about Laji Umaru when he broke the fetishes of Segou.

Diawara understood the intent of the words. "*Ar-Rahman*, The Merciful One," he answered, "has laid down different rules for different peoples. This dance is the custom of this country..." Whatever else he had planned to say was lost. The man snapped: I could see it clearly. He had faith, and he now was responding to the great surges of non-human energies that filled the town in response to the passion and performance of the folk.

"No Muslim should defend such practices!" he screamed, and swept his sword out of its sheath. It glittered in the moonlight as he raised it over his head, and without knowing what I did or why, I hurled myself between him and Diawara, reaching for the hand that held the sword. It swept down as I rose, and it must have hit me for I saw no more of that fight.

I heard about it later. Koita and Geladio were there. They followed me in blocking the attack of the mad disciple of the Tijiani. The sword fell to the ground. Geladio quickly picked it up as the man staggered backwards. Then the madman turned to a companion and wrenched that man's sword from its scabbard. Around him, people stumbled in flight. Geladio simply smiled and said something in Fula causing the man to focus his anger on Geladio. The madman attacked with a slash; Geladio parried and spoke again, and then—this was Koita's description—with an elegant little twist of the blade sliced part of the man's belt away. The attacks were redoubled; Geladio met them all effortlessly, beating away the slashing attacks, deflecting the thrusts, and apparently expecting some intervention that did not come: he hoped, perhaps, for Koita or another to slip up behind and knock the madman on his head before the matter led to serious bloodshed. But no such assistance came. Geladio called out to Koita, "Must I do this then?"

Koita answered, "He is mad. You have no choice." Geladio shook his head sadly, and then with simple grace slipped forward and buried six inches of steel in the man's chest. He continued his forward movement after the lunge, so that he could wrap his arms around his victim. The dead madman was lowered gently to the ground rather than falling like a slaughtered ox.

The next day the village chief and elders decreed it was a fight in which one party attacked first with the intent to kill, and no blame could attach to Geladio whose actions were defensive. They told the man's companions they had no claim to compensation for his death, but rather might be liable for sanctions. The Fula muttered, but did not protest too loudly.

The man was apparently known for his passionate but limited understanding of his faith. The river-folk were not at all unhappy that a human life had been lost in the festivities for they counted it as an offering to the spirits of the water and the seasons.

I was unaware of all of this. When the blade hit my skull, I lost consciousness. I came from darkness to find myself floating in the silvery glow of moonlight, falling gently but irresistibly through layers of red light and yellow light within a blue fog. I had no body; I was simply a point of awareness in motion.

The fog turned greenish and space began to emerge. In the space I sensed spirits, akin to the *wokòlò*, yet different in kind: where mine had been red and hairy and warm, these were green and scaly and suggested, not cold, but coolness—refreshment, rather than a chill. They apparently perceived me, for their presences became more immediate, curious and increasingly interested. I had the feeling—it became physical—of beings swirling around me, brushing lightly and experimentally against my peculiar presence. It might have been a school of fish or freshly hatched flies that rise in a vortex, and that image reminded me of the little whirlwinds of dust that we understand to be spirits moving over the land. Perhaps, I thought, these are water spirits, and then came the further insight that on this night when the water spirits were invoked and summoned I might somehow have fallen into their world.

The touches became more frequent, and then definitely erotic. The beings exploring my presence assumed form. They were only partly green and scaly; their top halves were human and female, with full figures.

"He is young," came a thought.

"He is a *he*," came a giggling response.

"He is mortal," observed a third.

"*Weiawaha*!" sang yet another.

"Is he ours?"

"He is strong."

"But he must be stupid, to have fallen like that."

"But is he ours?"

"No," came a definite answer from a being of a vastly different kind. With that response the green fog cleared to show a vast cavern inhabited by all sorts of spirits. Faro the lord of waters was hosting all the guests who had been drawn by the human carnival.

My perception must have transposed the scene into human terms. I saw the great lord of the waters as a mature greenish king, seated with his queen and surrounded by courtiers, the lesser spirits of the waters taking the forms of water beasts and fish. On his right sat another spirit, a being glowing with inner fire, clearly a guest at this gathering: Shamharoush, lord of the Jinns of the Maghrib, more accustomed to mountain tops and dry desert sand than a river bottom. On either side sat spirits representing the various families and places of the region: the spirits of the wild and the bush, spirits of the fields, spirits of the hunt. In a row close to the head of the table sat spirits of the sky: the thunder gods frowning (they are never happy) and the various forms of rain: from the light and misty drizzle of a cool morning to the pounding and merciless downpours that can drown a village. There was the one-breasted woman, Wanzarbe Kasseye, who had become the wife of the Songhay water lord in far-distant stretches of the Joliba River. After her son came to empire she herself became a spirit, nurturing warriors among her people. There were Sanen and Kontron, the ever-changing patron spirits of the hunting guilds, accompanied by some of their followers in the form of hyenas, antilopes, lions, vultures, and a warthog. There, curiously, was Tyamabaa, the serpentine patron of the cattle-herders.

"How has this mortal come among us?" asked Faro; his voice had the penetrating timbre of a great bell.

From somewhere behind me, a small voice answered. "I think this is the mortal I recruited," said a *wokòlò*, hesitantly. "But I cannot tell why he has come into this gathering."

In an instant (I could sense the communications without being able to understand them) information was exchanged among Faro, the *wokòlò*, and others. I caught fragments: "...a thousand years...the debt is outstanding...Payment can be made...The woman has shown faith...He has been tested…"

Three sisters appeared, clearly kin to the water spirits, though not those who teased me. These were no nixies, all glamour to seduce men to their doom, but the stern guardians of a scant resource. They were accustomed to mortal form, but their essence was different and far older. They announced themselves without words: Jangana Boro, Katana Boro, and Sune Karo, daughters of Tenen Ngille, the spirit of the great well of Wagadu. Their claim was for a blood debt: the son of Jangana Boro had been slain and beheaded, and they required his lost head. They had delegated the *wokòlò* to find an agent; he had found me.

At this point, Faro's guest intervened. He had noted the wound on my head. Might the Jinn have a claim on a man struck by one of their faithful? Somehow Faro answered him, and then Faro turned to me.

"You are here, and I am clement," he said. "You have a *jatigi* in this world, although not one of great stature." And here the red *wokòlò*, already shrunken with the cold and damp, cowered in nervousness. "What might you desire?"

I thought of legends and heroes. I considered the water lord and his wife. "Should I ask to suckle from your wife's breast?" I asked, thinking of at least one man who founded a kingdom.

A gale of laughter washed through the hall. "No, my nameless man. This is no longer the time for founding kingdoms. Do not think you can rival the *nganaw* of old times."

"Then allow me to complete the task I have undertaken with this spirit," I answered, and added, "as best I can," for in the presence of the massed immortal spirits of nature I felt humbled.

"So be it," said Faro. "Is his service acceptable?" The three sisters bowed to him. He paused. "He has a hole in his head. Fix it before you send him back." Then he waved his hands and the scene faded. All went dark. I found myself lying on the ground not far from the corpse of the Fula disciple.

Koita was holding me. "He is alive," he announced, and then, with some surprise, "and I see no wound!"

"It healed," said a man standing next to him. "There was a wound across the top of his head—here…" and his fingers traced a line on my head. "But it vanished. You can still see his blood on the sand." And that was true.

Diawara examined me. "Wound or no wound, he has been hit on the head with a sword. Carry him back to the house of Niambele."

Boloba came to me the next morning. The festival was done. He was taking his earnings and returning to his village. He wished to make sure I was all right. He also had news that he raised quite delicately. "I have tidings," he said, "from our region. A man told me of a village in which an elder died of poison." I said nothing. "Some said he had been killed by his son, but others blamed his brother, who was known to be ambitious and hard." I listened; the world he evoked was now very far away. "At any rate, as was the custom, the surviving brother took his dead brother's widow as a wife, to care for her." At this thought I shuddered, for I remembered quite clearly what my mother thought of her brother-in-law.

"He was found dead, the next day," continued Boloba. "The widow vanished. They say she has gone to join the servants of Muso Koronin." At that I looked up and our eyes met. "I could tell yesterday that you saw more of Muso Koronin than the children of Bougouni, and so I thought you might wish to know this."

"Thank you," I answered. "It is interesting news."

"Until we share a path again, then," finished Boloba, and handed me a small packet. It was the last bit of his shea-paste, to ease the aches of the road.

Later that day Diawara called me to him. "You saved my life," he stated. He didn't ask why, but that was clearly his concern.

"You are my *siratigi.*" I answered slowly. The word means the leader of an expedition, the master of the path. It can apply to a merchant in a caravan, to the chief herder in a group of nomadic herders, or to a more spiritual leader: the *soma* who takes an apprentice, the hunter who trains a follower. "You took me, nameless and lost, and you have been my teacher. I could not stand by."

"*Bamana-kè,*" he said, and he reached forward. His finger lightly traced the line of the sabre blow that had vanished. "You came to me by the gift of God, and clearly you are protected in some way by the powers of these places. You are no Muslim, but you are honest and upright. I pray you may remain so. The powers that protect you do not seem to me the children of Iblis, the *shaitani* who bring evil into the hearts of men. I do not hesitate to believe that it is by the will of God, *ar-rahmani, ar-rahim,* that you have that protection. If you wish to stay in my service, you shall. I acknowledge a debt to you." He paused, thinking. "Still, you are now linked to the death of a Fula disciple of the Tijiani. I know nothing of the man's kin or connections. It may not be wise to bring you with us on the next trip east to fetch salt. Fortunately, there are other trade roads."

That is why, later that year after the rains, I found myself attached to a caravan carrying shea butter from Diawara's home on a long road that led west, up the hills to Kissidougou and then down the steep slopes of a jungly and verdant escarpment to the mangrove-infested coastal plains. It was several years before I returned from that excursion, but you need no account of that time.

Mami Wata image Mami Wata is a water-spirit, widespread across west Africa. Photo taken during a magic display in Kankan in 2004

PART II

Soninke House
Traditional house.
Photo taken in 1989 in Selibaby, Mauritania.

CHAPTER 1

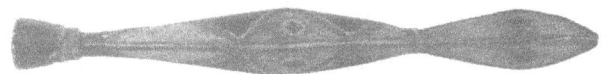

THE NEW AND STILL nervous *commandant de cercle* for Kri Koro stared out from his veranda over a patchwork of dense green foliage and the conical brown thatch of clustered roofs. His headquarters, the *campement*, sat on a hill. He was wondering how he could make this town a contributory affluent to the river of wealth that was supposed to flow from the new colonies of the western Sudan to the metropole of Paris.

Kri Koro was considered an old kingdom, honored by its neighbors but diminished from its former extent. Its wealth derived from...and there was a first problem. What were the resources in this town? It seemed self-sufficient in food, which was a relief; traveling from Saint Louis to Kayes and Medine and then south through the hills of the Manding, he had seen too many villages where crops failed and the inhabitants sat listless and gaunt, soon to die. In Kri Koro—was that really the town's name? He had heard variations: Kri Kunun, Kri Kolon, Kri Kunba. No matter, at least in this town the people appeared to be well-fed.

The traditional ruler was of the Condé lineage. Among the Maninka, inheritance went laterally or by seniority: the brothers of the senior branch of the ruling family would succeed each other until the time came to pass the power to the next generation. The eldest Condé, he knew, was incapacitated with age; the younger brother exercised power in the town.

Henri Dumont was new to the *Service colonial*. He had come from Berry in the heart of France, along a path through technical schools and ministerial offices to an assignment in the new territories of the French colonial empire. He was a civilian moving into areas governed, up to now, by military officers. His charge was to build institutions and to find the wealth to finance the development of these colonies. He was supported by a detachment of soldiers commanded by a Fula, Samba Ly, a well-recommended subaltern who apparently assisted greatly in the conquest of the interior regions and who now clearly aspired to rank outside the military.

Dumont was studying the local language, although it baffled him. Its grammar didn't respect the methods he had been taught in school: conjugation and agreement in gender and number. He was familiar with linguistic variations; the school French and the *langue du terroir*, although as a Berrichon, his speech was close to the national standard, unlike that in Brittany or Provence.

Maninka had no clearly defined verb 'to be,' although that was the starting point of the study of any language: *sum, es, est, sumus*... Those were familiar landmarks. But here... *n'ye ke ye*. I am a man. But the *'ye ... ye'* did not apply all the time. Sometimes you need *'ka.'* And the negatives ... *tè* or *man*, but how could you know when to use which?

Language was not his only worry. There were many diseases endemic in this region. The doctor who briefed him on his arrival in Saint Louis had been direct, brutal, and not optimistic. People in this region suffered from malaria, river blindness, typhoid, elephantiasis, yellow fever, schistosomiasis, guinea worm, leprosy, sleeping sickness, rabies, smallpox (comfort: he had been vaccinated), cholera, tetanus, dysentery, tuberculosis, yaws, goiters, various sexually transmitted diseases, all sorts of mental conditions...Not to mention the more familiar measles, chicken pox, mumps, whooping cough, catarrh, rubella, scarlet fever. He wondered suddenly whether there was a blue fever or a green fever—did diseases come in a spectrum? Were they were limited by the possible sickly hues of the body? If so, why no white or brown fevers? Why was there no gold fever? Surely that was a mental condition to be counted. Then his thoughts moved from colors to events: yes, there was a gold fever. Southern Africa, under British control, prospered thanks to the Kimberley gold mines. The far sides of the American continent swarmed with prospectors along some river…*Ah*! The Yukon.

He remembered his briefings. Gold was the commodity that fed medieval kingdoms in this part of Africa. One king brought so much gold to Cairo that it glutted the market. Might there be gold around Kri Koro?

* * *

In one of the huts below Dumont's veranda, Nyelle was serving gruel to her grandfather Cejan. He was the titular head of the Condé lineage in the town, eldest, but no longer capable. A seizure had struck his brain, paralyzing much of his body, although his mind remained lucid. Now his brother Gaoussou acted in his stead.

Cejan spent his days in his chamber, rarely taken outside. A small pot kept in a corner served his daily needs. Often Nyelle had to help and then clean him. His hands trembled and could not be trusted to bring food to his mouth. His clan cared for him, delegating the task down to the point of least resistance. Nyelle was the current attendant: one who had seen his decline as she grew towards womanhood. She was not put off by his bodily needs. As an older sister she had long been accustomed to caring for her siblings while her mother was busy with her garden or other chores. This meant washing snotty faces and wiping dirty bottoms. She didn't see Cejan's needs as greatly different from their's. She always brought a tuft of leaves to wipe his behind and rags for other cleansing.

Nyelle had always been fond of the old man. She remembered occasions when he came to her mother's hearth to watch her brood among his many grandchildren; he always had a small pot of honey that he doled out to the children as they lined up before him. He used a wooden spoon with a shallow bowl and a carved handle. She asked him once how he got the honey, and he had smiled. "The bees and I have a bond," he explained, but said no more. The children sometimes called him *kumboro-tigi*, the master of the bees. Now Nyelle brought her own spoon to her grandfather.

Nyelle was not yet concerned with cycles, although two years before she had begun the one that marked the break from childhood. She didn't yet know what changes that would bring, although she understood they would be profound. She had already observed changes in her body, some of which had been explained at her initiation. So she waited on their consequences. In the meantime, she served her *bemba* out of deference, out of affection, and as a duty ordered by her mother. She understood the duty. Elders were the creators, the origin from which people came, and if they were not accorded respect...the thread that linked one generation to another would be broken. For women it was fairly simple: in childhood you cared for your siblings and helped your mother; then you were married. Your children—for marriage without children was unthinkable—would help you in your tasks and build your status. You might pursue wealth of your own through gardening or brewing *dolo* or trade. A woman was fulfilled through the accomplishments and worth of her children. This debt was acknowledged: a famous son would be known by the name of his mother.

For men the stages might vary. Starting as barely human brats, they became *kamalen* after circumcision (the bloodletting that made them human). After hard work for their fathers, they could marry and establish their own household. All would age, like her grandfather. She lifted another spoonful of millet gruel to the mouth of Cejan Condé.

* * *

In a space between Nyelle and Henri Dumont, Ramata Diop considered her situation. She was nominally the spouse of Samba Ly, the highest-ranking *tirailleur* in the garrison of this new colonial outpost. The relationship had never been formalized, although it was long-standing and had covered many miles since a self-confident young woman crossed gazes with a young soldier in the town of Thiès in Senegal. She had been with him ever since. Samba Ly rose through the ranks; he was capable and ambitious. He attended carefully to the needs of the *nasrani* he served. She attended carefully to his needs, and later to those of the squadron of men who came under his command. She ensured a supply of food; she learned to sew and repair uniforms; she learned to inquire within a new community for the resources the troop would require.

Now Samba Ly was second in command under the

commandant. He didn't consider his position secure, for the interpreter might become the principal channel to the *commandant*'s authority and so receive the expected flow of gifts. All men seeking access to power came with something of value in their hands. Empty hands meant deaf ears. He intended to become the *commandant*'s trusted adviser.

Ramata's thoughts ran less on Samba's ambitions than on her domestic situation. Some years ago Samba had helped capture a town…what was its name? Kumi. She had never seen it; she stayed in Bamako when the column marched out. Samba returned from Kumi with a collection of women, the former bedmates of the fallen warlord. Most of the women had been disposed of, often quite profitably. But he had kept one, a Soninke woman of extraordinary beauty—even Ramata, jealous, had to admit that—and preternatural youthfulness and personal dynamism. So for several years Ramata had been part of a polygamous household. No bride-prices had ever been paid for either woman; no kola nuts exchanged, no praise-songs sung for the new brides. Instead, they followed the Fula in the fez as he astutely negotiated assignments and tasks with the *nasrani* officers. They shared him uneasily, so far as Ramata was concerned; he occasionally asked her to come to his bedchamber, but far more often she slept alone. She never talked with the Soninke woman.

The one consolation was that neither had borne him any children. Ramata had tried. She exhausted Samba at times with her demands, but no swelling of the belly ensued. She consulted healers and diviners. Their remedies didn't work. She hadn't tried the standard alternative, a change in partners. She belonged to Samba: the kindling spark that had brought them together those many years ago still glowed within her.

In Kri Koro, the atmosphere had changed. Samba thought he could use this assignment as a stepping stone to greater opportunity. He foresaw great things in his future. She could sense that his future didn't include the women of his past. So she looked out into the space of the town and wondered what she should do.

* * *

Many miles from Kri Koro, Marco Fernandes also considered plans. An American had arrived in Geba, an inland port of Portuguese Guinea. Accident brought them together. He saw possibilities in this accident. Possibilities were desirable, for Geba had become a backwater. No Portuguese shipped goods to Lisbon any more. The remaining Kristons formed an enclave, trying to define themselves as different and greater through their Christian faith and mixed ancestry in a world where Islam was spreading. But no wealth passed through Geba. The river port, once a gateway to the interior, was now a cul-de-sac, mainly because the overseas slave trade had ended. Other commodities from the interior which formerly passed through Geba—kola and indigo and hides and cattle and cloth and salt and foodstuffs and gums and pastes—now followed different paths to other markets.

Yet this American had arrived in Geba, bewildered and lost but determined. He thought he knew a path to gold. His grandfather had a story, and he had pursued it. He came to Geba, and the Kristons turned him away. He wandered and asked questions. He asked for the d'Almeidas, but they had never settled in Geba. Marco knew of them by reputation; they were the family in Ouidah, far away, who traded slaves to Brazil until the French arrived. The American claimed that his grandfather had bought slaves from a d'Almeida in Geba, and that one of the slaves had told a story about a throne of gold. Of course, slaves always told stories trying to escape their fate, trying to buy freedom or favorable treatment. How could the American believe this story? Yet he did.

Marco had met him several times now, usually at the *taberna* where Ma Maryam served sour beer and palm-wine and something she claimed was claret, along with grilled shrimp or chicken and roasted peanuts and corn. They talked; the American spoke poor Portuguese and a bit of French, and Marco had exercised his imagination wildly to bridge the gaps in their lexicons and worldviews. The American believed there was a treasure. Marco wanted to believe him, and to share in that treasure. Marco was the son of an unwed mother whose Portuguese father had long since returned to great Lisbon. He had none of the connections of other Kristons—the family relationships, the claims to land-ownership and to trading networks. To advance in the world, he must use his wits and seize any opportunities. The American might be such a chance.

But how to pursue it? The American spoke of a town in the interior—Kri Kuru, he said, the old kingdom by some mountain. Marco made inquiries. A woman, brought down from the interior and now the common-law wife of an old boatman, said she had heard the name. It lay in the Manding, south of the Joliba River, beyond the highlands of the Futa Jallon.

No trading routes led directly to that region now. Marco considered what he knew of the people further inland and what he heard from the American. And he thought of gold.

Village: photo taken in Guinea in 2005.
The modern structure is intended to suggest the headquarters of the Commandant

CHAPTER II

GAOUSSOU CONDÉ FACED PROBLEMS on many fronts.

The first was that of power in Kri Koro. The Condé lineage no longer ruled as they had done for centuries. The *nasrani* had come, with soldiers and new authority. He was not sure what they wanted. Kri had been conquered before. The Songhai came when they invaded the remains of the empire of Mali, but that was a distant event remembered only for its destruction. In his lifetime, Kri Koro had paid tribute to Samori. He and his brother had joined the forces of Mori-Ule who had resisted the rise of Samori. They were defeated. It was a short and embarrassing battle. The *sofa*s of Samori's army simply overran the poorly armed militia of Mori-Ule. His brother Cejan...Cejan had distinguished himself. With his sword he killed several *sofa*s before being knocked to the ground. Then Samori arrived and halted the slaughter, saving Cejan's life. Samori usually put a defeated lineage to the sword and named one of his *sofa*s the ruler of the town. But after a short exchange of words with Cejan, Samori made an exception: he only imposed tribute of cattle, millet, and slaves. There must have been some other element in the terms, but what?

Cejan represented the second concern.

His older brother was the titular head of the lineage, although his incapacity made him irrelevant for all daily affairs.

Still, he had not passed on their lineage secrets. Those secrets had real effects, as Gaoussou realized after that disastrous battle. Cejan had maintainted the Condé lineage in power even after they had sipped the *dege*.

When would Cejan acknowledge that his death was inevitable and imminent and reveal the secrets to his brother and heir? Cejan clearly understood that his secret knowledge ensured him the care and comforts he enjoyed. Gaoussou didn't know what would happen if his older brother died without passing on the deepest elements of the family lore. It must have happened before. But for the moment, he had no approach to the question of Cejan's knowledge, and so he had to deal with purely worldly affairs. These now included men from far distant countries.

The *nasrani* had different rules. They hadn't yet demanded tribute, although exactions (taxes, forced labor) would surely come. They came with other Africans, *farafin*, men who belonged to his world. Most of the score of soldiers who served the new *nasrani* master were Wolof.

The soldiers, however, were less important than their leaders. He quickly learned there were two men to consider: the interpreter, Mady Sisibé and the lieutenant of the soldiers, Samba Ly.

A cough sounded outside his door. His *jeli*, Fadigi Kuyate, came in.

Here was a trusted adviser, one whose observation and understanding of events were second to none. The two men exchanged greetings, and as a mark of encouragement and intimacy, Gaoussou offered the *jeli* a kola. The two chewed for a time.

"Times are changing," advanced Kuyate, after some

moments of silence.

"Tinye don," answered Gaoussou. Then, after another silence, "What have you learned of this *nasrani*?"

"Very little," admitted Kuyate, with unusual frankness. "He is new to our land, he has no friends."

"He has two principal assistants," observed Gaoussou.

"I cannot tell which of them he might favor," answered Kuyate. "The interpreter, Sisibé, must have some influence, for the *nasrani* speaks no Maninka. But the Fula leader of the soldiers also speaks his tongue."

"And you think he is lonely?" Gaoussou put the query with some hesitation, for loneliness was not a part of his usual experience. People were never lonely unless they were hunters lost in the bush. There was always someone within calling distance, and all too often someone asking him for something. He was considering the possibility that this new *komanda,* the only *nasrani* for miles around, might feel isolated.

"He has no intimates," answered Kuyate. "I haven't heard of any woman called to his bed; he eats alone."

"Women?" The tone was delicate. Some men didn't enjoy women, although the topic was rarely admitted. With a *nasrani,* all aspects must be considered.

"There is no sign of other inclinations."

"He should have a household." Gaoussou left the observation hanging.

Kuyate's eyes glanced up to him with understanding. "Indeed. He needs attendants."

"Through whom should we deal? The interpreter or the Fula?"

"I shall make inquiries." Kuyate shook his head.

* * *

In the *campement* Samba Ly had come to a decision. Advancement required the support of the new *nasrani*. The region had been pacified; the wars with Samori had given the people a distaste for fighting, so military actions were unlikely. Now the *komanda* dealt most often with Sisibé, the interpreter. How could he establish his credit and influence with the *nasrani*? In the most direct and intimate way: he would provide him with a woman. The man was alone in a strange country; surely he would be susceptible?

Samba had tested the waters. He sent Assya walking across the compound at times when he knew the *komanda* was present; he observed the *komanda*'s reaction to this most beautiful of women. Her graceful walk, her outline, her youthful figure. The *komanda* was not the only man who watched her, sometimes greedily.

Samba would have to give her up. He didn't expect to share a bedmate with the *nasrani*. What did he lose? She was barren. After three years she had borne no child. She shared nothing of herself. He could only guess at her past. She had been a concubine in Kumi which implied experience. At times he thought she had seen too many men and nothing about them could surprise her. He never discovered what might excite her. She responded obediently but distantly to his passion. She was an enigma. She also had other useful skills. She spoke several languages—Maninka, Fula, Soninke, at least—although he didn't know which was her mother tongue. So she could be a teacher to this *nasrani*.

And her beauty would bring him power.

* * *

Marco and his American, Tristan Harcourt, were on their way. Marco had circulated madly among his acquaintance, had wrung them dry of every drop of consideration they might offer, and so had a small stock of tradegoods, some food, and the services of a young porter. They left Geba early in the morning before the heat arrived. They were chewing dried mangoes.

Marco chose to travel south before turning east towards the interior. He had heard of conflict involving Musa Molo, a Fula whose realm straddled the boundaries of French and English territories to the northeast; such troubles were best avoided, especially when travelers had no official documents. They came to Boke with their young porter and found men of his family, so they could send him back in safety.

From Boke they would turn east to ascend the escarpment into the lush highlands of the Futa Jallon. They could expect perils. The Futanke were devout Muslims. Marco was scarcely a Christian, and the American was certainly a stranger. In the old days the Fula would have slaughtered them on sight. Marco trusted that they would not dare kill a *nasrani* in these times.

Tristan Harcourt walked in bewilderment. He was accustomed to semi-tropical heat and humidity; his home near St. Augustine prepared him for such conditions. He had found his way to Geba, the town where his grandfather traded in the old way-back days, before the war. Grandpaw had all sorts of stories, but few listened to him. Times then were hard.

The Harcourts prospered before the war. They had their own ship. Grandpaw traded through Geba. The Portuguese in Geba didn't care if the English had forbidden slave trading. The local middlemen could supply slaves of all sorts: smiths and rice farmers and tanners and nubile girls. The rice farmers brought a very good price when slipped past the coast guard.

The Yankees burned their ship. They freed the slaves who now lived miserably as sharecroppers and house servants. Grandpaw remembered his travels and his dreams. He had told Tristan. Grandpaw had learned some Mandenka and enough Portuguese not to be robbed entirely blind by the Kristons of Geba. When selling the slaves through his networks in Florida, it helped to be able to describe their abilities. During the ocean crossing he spent time talking to his commodities.

One of them offered a story that Grandpaw remembered. It was offered, of course, as a plea for freedom: 'There will be a ransom,' 'You will be rich.' He'd heard many such pleas, and believed no promise of facile wealth. But this man offered a secret: a throne of gold, hidden in a cave. The land of the serpent's head, he said, a black serpent, the Bida, in a kingdom called Kri.

So Tristan adventured across the wide ocean and came to Geba in quest of this golden throne that was the head of a serpent. He was grateful to have found Marco. He was also lost in wonder. At first he felt shock. No experience of the sharecropper hovels had prepared him for the poverty he found in Geba. Nothing of the industrial age had yet reached this small town at the end of a long and winding river. All was handmade, all was bartered or traded. Bridges were merely fords guarded by men who watched for crocodiles. There were no stores; people came to market with goods they had grown or made or acquired or perhaps stolen, and throngs milled around as seekers located sellers and sellers summoned seekers.

Marco listened and embraced his cause, and now the two of them were embarked on an adventure. Tristan had the inspiration; Marco, he trusted, would have the means to bring it about.

* * *

In the *campement,* Ramata was scolding Gorkel, the semi-adopted son that Samba Ly brought back from some expedition beyond Mopti. Gorkel was a young Fula with a very high opinion of himself—he claimed to be the son of a chief. His father sent him with Samba Ly, also a Fula, because he saw wisdom in placing a son with the *nasrani* power, much as a cuckoo spreads its eggs among many nests.

Gorkel could be charming. He had a certain art with words and he loved stories. He also loved gossip.

Ramata considered him a valuable resource when she could believe him. On this occasion he was stretching her belief.

"But *neen'am*!" he protested, "The *nasrani* have the sort of wealth that comes from the spirits. They have tools and weapons...They produce goods unlike anything our craftsmen can create. They have the color of dead flesh."

She paused. This part of his argument she could almost believe. The *nasrani* were the color of ghosts. It was the sequel that she found excessive. "The *nasrani* are human. They have flesh. They speak and think and eat and sleep and..." She paused, remembering Gorkel's reasoning. Her thoughts would have led elsewhere.

"Yes, they eat." Gorkel leapt on the opening. "So they are like men in some ways. But in other ways, they are more like spirits. So the question is what happens to the food they eat?"

"You shouldn't need to ask," answered Ramata dryly.

"Is their shit the same as ours?" continued Gorkel,

disregarding her. "That is what I want to find out."

"Gorkel," began Ramata, with little hope of convincing him, "men are men. Men and women come in all shapes and colors. The Fula are red. The Maninka are brown. The Wolof have blacker skins than the Maninka. Beneath the skin they are the same. A Fula man and a Wolof woman will produce a child. No matter what they say about the Fula, no one has yet seen a heifer with the head of a woman or a man with the head of a bull. The *nasrani* are men, from a far land. You might as well compare them with the *serifu* of the Muslims. The *serifu* set themselves up as teachers and diviners because of their ancestry. Have you ever wondered about their shit?"

"I have never been close to a *serifu*," admitted Gorkel.

"You would do better to observe what comes out of their mouths, rather than the other end," she suggested, referring either to *nasrani* or to *serifu*.

Tea pot:
Drinking tea is a major social ceremony, especially among Muslims who do not drink *dolo*.

CHAPTER III

RAMATA REMAINED TROUBLED. SAMBA was planning something involving his domestic arrangements. She had been his companion for long enough to identify moods and intentions. Recently, he would sit thinking in the morning before he put on his uniform and heavy boots. He was undecided about some matter. He never needed to reflect on any question involving his duties. He was intelligent and well-informed; solutions presented themselves more quickly to him than to others; he had acquired the skill of convincing his listeners. Uncertainty meant this problem was personal, and as he hadn't discussed the question with her... it must be a matter of the bedchamber, the *suudu*, as the Fula called it. And if not her, then it must involve the other woman, the Soninke enchantress. She was not a witch, Ramata was sure; she didn't practice sorcery, she didn't consume the *nyama* or the souls of people around her. But she caught the attention of men quite easily, and she was far more skilled than Samba at manipulating people.

Right now Ramata needed various leaves for her sauces. The staples such as millet and an allocation of rice would come from the company stores. But dressing up the basics was her function, and, she had to admit, her pleasure. With Samba, food was easily available; she was grateful for that security, having seen too many starving villages. So her first errand today was a visit to the market.

When she reached the little square in which the women gathered to offer the produce of their gardens, the fish from their husband's nets, the pots they had turned, she saw little that she wanted. She continued her walk. She hadn't yet seen all the town. She headed west, past courtyards, under the shadow of mango trees and the sparser shade of acacia or palms. She had seen the weavers and leather workers in the eastern quarter. She didn't know what she might find on this new path.

She left the last clustered houses and trees and found herself in open space, some sort of marshy brush. Not far before her a small hut, ill-kept and dilapidated, rose from the reeds. Curiosity caught her so she approached. She was sure it was not the place where women with their monthlies withdrew for privacy and seclusion. A small fire burned before the hut in a space littered with all sorts of trash. *Does no one sweep here?*

"*Nhnh,*" came a voice at her elbow. There was an old woman, her thin hair white, face and skin wrinkled and flaccid, the breasts thin folds of skin over a visible rib-cage, the waist wrapped with a filthy dark cloth.

"*N'ba.*" Startled, Ramata greeted her. "My mother, how are you this day?"

"A foreigner," commented the old woman. "And one with man troubles. Come, sit." She walked past Ramata. Beyond the fire along the wall of the hut a length of tree-trunk lay on the ground and served as a bench. Ramata stood for a moment, and then joined her.

"Women are always foreigners," observed the old woman. "They leave their homes to follow their men, they establish themselves in new households. They face their in-laws. But this," and she gave Ramata a sidelong smile, "is not something you must do. You are the woman of the *keletigi*." It was the Maninka word for a war leader. "His family is far from here, and they mean nothing to you. What might they mean to him? Now you wonder what he is planning." This was a definite statement. It had nothing of the hesitancy that Ramata recognized in the diviners she had occasionally consulted because she was childless. She understood their hemming was a strategy to gain information. This woman had no doubts about Ramata's situation.

"My mother," said Ramata, "I did not come for consultation. I was walking in the town, and I saw this hut..."

"But you are welcome, and you should return," said the old woman. She stood and entered the hut. There was the sound of rustling. She emerged with two ears of corn. She laid them over the fire. Then she went around the back of the hut and returned with two small coconut shells filled with water. Ramata drank gratefully. When the corn had roasted they ate the ears. Ramata insisted on sweeping the little courtyard before she returned to the town.

* * *

The gathering beneath the mango tree in the Condé courtyard was not unobserved. Everyone paid attention to Gaoussou Condé. When he had a visitor in a uniform and red cap, many feet found themselves on the path that allowed them to glimpse the parties in the shade. Some even envied Ataya, the slave serving the tea, for he certainly knew what they were talking about. But Ataya had learned silence. Soon after Gaoussou took him into service they visited an outlying village, one of the many that paid a collective tribute to the Condé. There they were served tea by a man who had lost his tongue; he gargled in answer to their greetings. Ataya had stared, then realized his master was watching him; when their eyes met, Gaoussou shifted his gaze to the servant. Ataya realized he faced the consequences of indiscretion.

After the gathering finished their second glass of tea, Gaoussou moved past the generalities of health and good wishes. He and Kuyate had considered his approach. They could not decide which of the two, the interpreter or the lieutenant, would be the better avenue to the *komanda*. The obvious step was to meet both and to offer inducements to each.

Samba had almost expected the invitation. He represented access to authority, and so should be cultivated. As yet he knew little about Kri Koro. The town had been ruled by the Condé lineage, but their eldest was incapacitated. A younger brother spoke for him; this was the accepted protocol for such situations. Others—brothers, kin, aspiring rivals—might challenge the Condé claims.

After the first words, Samba decided there were no challenges. Gaoussou spoke with confidence and an authority that proclaimed his supremacy. Still, Samba sensed there were unanswered questions. When they discussed the town's history, Gaoussou was vague on the status under Samori's rule. He couldn't explain why the Almamy spared him and Cejan in their battle. Samba inferred that Gaoussou was not yet master of all the lineage secrets.

The discussion also confirmed one point for Samba: he must establish some ascendancy over the interpreter; he must establish an unbreakable relation with the *komanda*.

* * *

"*Yereñ ko haala*!" Marco put as much emphasis as he could into the statement. He did not speak Fula well. The statement that 'silence is speech' was intended to deflect questions he didn't want to answer.

Marco and Tristan had made their way from Boké into the lush highlands of the Futa Jallon. Marco hadn't expected the passage to be simple, but he was threading a course between perils: avoiding Musa Molo and other warlords in the north, yet not going far enough south to enounter the Baga along the coast. The Kristons of Geba had encouraged slave-taking raids in that region; the Baga were noted rice growers and their skills were in demand across the ocean. The Baga remembered and hated Kristons.

The climb had been tiring; they rose from sea level to some greater altitude as if they had been climbing stairs, passing through a jungle where apes hooted in the distance and every step might reveal a serpent. The trail ran across the slopes as it climbed, then looped around outcrops. Occasionally the path allowed them a view over the lands below. Marco took comfort in their ever-increasing elevation above the sea of green tree tops. This climb was only the first hurdle. Reaching the crest, they entered the Futa Jallon. The Fula had settled here in the time of Mari Jata, and now had established a Muslim state, buffeted by past wars.

From the crest their achievement was visible. No more mountains lay before them to the east. The temperatures were pleasant and the path ran flat. In the morning, mists hung over all the lowlands, softening the contours. It was a beautiful land.

Near Labe they were stopped. The Fula were wary of strangers, jealous of competing traders, and hostile (when not violent) to anyone who didn't share their Muslim faith. Now

Marco had to answer questions.

"From you, silence is a lie," came the retort from the leader of the guards who was questioning them.

"Your ignorance makes everything seem a lie," retorted Marco. "I have told you I may not speak of our mission. I'm accompanying a foreigner, a *nasrani* of a sort you have never seen, for purposes that cannot be shouted in the market. Have you no knowledge of the world outside your village?" He paused. Not to leave the opportunity to speak would have suggested an intention to deceive. No reply came. He continued. "The Fula trade north and the Fula trade south, with the *anglizi*. The Fula didn't trade with the Sussu. But now the Fula obey a new sort of *nasrani*, the *franzawi*, who come from the land of the Sussu. Will these new *nasrani* allow the old trade with the *anglizi*?" Again he paused. Again no reply.

"I'll share with *you* part of a secret." He looked around at the other men in the room, and then back to the leader who understood his tacit message and motioned to the other men to leave. Marco suspected they would keep their ears glued to the walls, but that didn't matter. The point was to establish, in the leader's mind, the privilege of intimately offered knowledge. "The *anglizi* profited from their trade, as did the Fula. Trade spreads benefits in two directions; both parties profit. But the *anglizi* are not always friends with the *franzawi*, just as the Fula and the Mandinka are sometimes in contention, or the Fula and the Sussu. So the *anglizi* are concerned that the *franzawi* may now interrupt the trade."

"But why are you in Labe?"

"We are in Labe because you brought us here. We should not be here. Our mission—and the profits of the Fula traders—is in peril should the *franzawi* learn of our presence." Here he was guessing, but he had also noted on a hill overlooking the broad valley a house of clearly European style. He suspected the French had put an administrator in the territory. So was this warrior a servant of the French? Was he connected with the trading networks outside Labe? Marco was counting on knowledge two steps up from ignorance: the man should recognize the players he identified, but not really understand the specifics. He should fear to draw attention to himself in the wrong way.

To Marco's relief, the Fula's face showed worry and uncertainty. The man had gone beyond his depth. All foreigners and unbelievers were to be mistrusted on principle. But he knew the great men he served dealt peacefully with foreigners and unbelievers. This foreigner was probably lying, but there was still a risk...The big men kept their secrets, and they were not happy with men who revealed them.

"*Wonaa andi piiw haali piiw,*" advanced Marco. One must not tell all that one knows. A truism, perhaps useful, but it might serve at this point. The Fula respected anyone with some knowledge of their language. The remark tipped the scales.

"We shall send you on your way," said the guard. "You shall have an escort to the limit of the territory of Labe."

"Is this for our protection? Or as punishment?" Marco challenged him. "You have caused us delay and taken us out of our path. If you wish to assist our mission, you should do more than send a guard. You should provide us with food, some chickens and some millet would be good."

When they left Labe, he carried several pounds of millet. A guard was carrying a small cage with half-a-dozen chickens. The millet was heavier than the chickens, but Marco knew what the guard's shirt would be like after a day of carrying chickens in an open-fret cage.

* * *

Among the routine circulars from Dakar, Dumont found an interesting item in his mail: a German ethnographer had requested permission to travel to Kri Koro to investigate and record local traditions. Under other circumstances, the request would have been refused outright: no German could have any interest save spying in a newly-settled French colony. But *this* German was a recognized ethnographer, and Paris was currently accommodating the Germans, hoping to settle certain boundary questions between their adjacent colonies of Dahomey and Togo. So the visit had been approved.

Ethnography was a new discipline, born from the comparative observations of travelers and the conundrums of colonial administrators. Its speculative origins, such as Montaigne's essay on cannibals that Dumont read in the *lycée,* had now acquired a functional orientation intended to help rule alien peoples according to their customs. The French were oriented in a different way: the conquered were to assume the identity of the conquerors. Gaul, once divided into three, became all Roman save for one irreductible village. The French had overthrown their kings and emperors, but still sought the principle of unity. Dumont's charge was to make his district French in spirit, not to encourage separatism. Still, the thought of a European visitor, familiar with concepts such as newspapers and opera and electricity, was pleasing.

He left his office and took his supper by the light of a small oil lamp, alone, on the porch overlooking the town. He stood for a while looking down over the roofs, invisible in the dark, but limned here and there by the light of a fire. He wondered about the quarters, what defined the neighborhoods? He had known the quarters of Bourges, the principal town in Berry where he grew up, almost to the cobblestone, and had gained a good knowledge of the much greater city of Paris when he went off to study. But he did not yet have a sense of this place or this people.

He took the oil lamp and made his way through his office to his bedchamber. He placed the lamp on a small stand near the bed—not too close because he used a mosquito net that might catch fire. He removed his jacket and hung it over the stand, then turned to the light to unlace his boots.

He realized suddenly that he was not alone in the room. At the edge of the shadows, just inside the door that led back past the watercloset to the servants' quarters, a woman was kneeling on the floor. She was dressed in a dark blue wrap, a *pagne,* that left her shoulders bare, and she had no cloth on her hair. Her hands rested on her thighs. Her neck was slender, but the features of her face were obscured by the shadows, save for the gleam from the whites of her eyes. She was watching him and waiting for a reaction or a sign.

He paused, but already instinctive reactions were taking over. There was only one possible reason for a woman to be in his room. It certainly involved intrigues for influence. But why should he resist temptation? He could see she was shapely, and the edges of the face caught by the lamp's flame were finely traced. He took off his boots and walked over to the waiting woman. When he came close enough her arms rose and her hands clasped his hips.

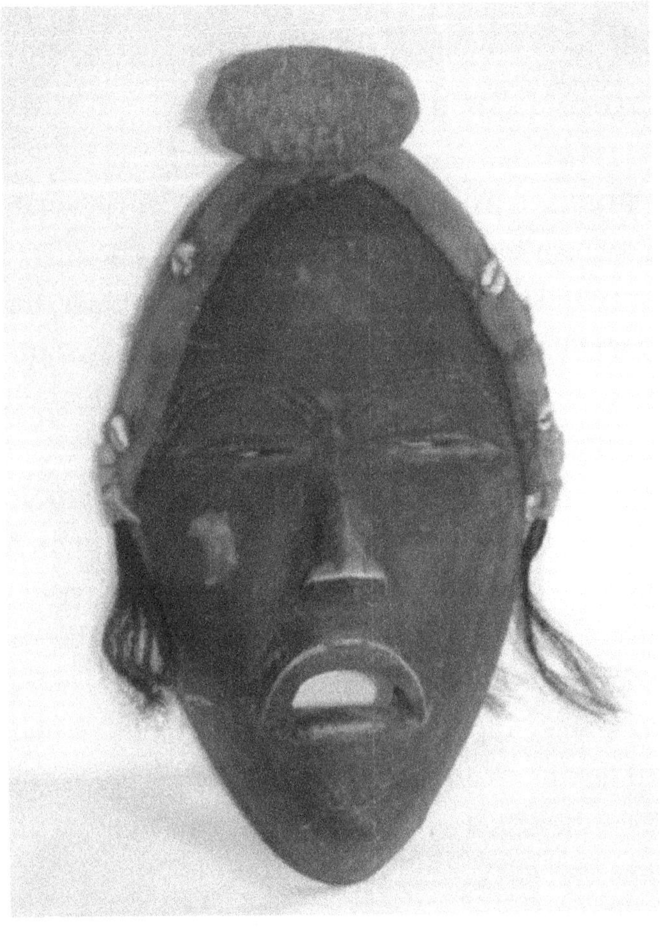

Female Mask
Purchased by author in Nzerekore, Guinea, in 2005.

CHAPTER IV

AT THE MORNING MEAL, Gorkel imparted the news that the Soninke woman had left Samba Ly's quarters. Ramata found Gorkel's attention to the other woman healthier than his curiosity about the *nasrani*'s excrement. Still, she was troubled. Change was afoot. She went about her chores then decided to take some food to the old woman who had comforted her with understanding. The old woman had shared her corn. Ramata filled a small calabash with *to*—after several years in the land of millet, she still longed for rice—and covered the paste with a meat sauce, a dish from her home in Thiès. She had been able to find the right spices and to recognize the right tufts of leaves in the market. She wrapped the calabash in a cloth, put it on her head, and left the small cantonment.

"*N'ba*!" she called as she approached the hut.

"Come behind!"

Ramata circled the hut. The old woman was sitting on a small stool, smoking a pipe and staring at some figures drawn into the sand.

"I hope I find you well," she said, and they exchanged the conventional greetings. Then Ramata offered her bowl of food. The old woman nodded thanks, and went off. She returned with a small basin of water. Ramata rinsed her hands and then held the bowl up to the old woman in turn. Then the woman placed the dish of food between them and muttered something inaudible and incomprehensible. Her fingers neatly shaped a small ball that she dipped in the sauce. She brought it slowly to her mouth; her thin lips parted just enough to allow entry to the food, as though she wished to prolong the sensation of its passage into her body. She chewed very slowly before she swallowed. Ramata waited for her to finish this first taste before she dipped her own hand into the dish and took a much smaller morsel. While her fingers were shaping the ball of millet, the old woman spoke.

"You used *ngoyo* instead of the tomatoes that they grow in Senegal."

This was true; tomatoes had not yet reached this region, but Ramata felt that the *ngoyo* she found in the market was a reasonable substitute. "*Tinye don*." How did this woman know about tomatoes?

Then they said nothing more until the dish was empty. It is bad manners to talk while eating; it suggests a lack of appreciation for the food, and food, however cooked, stands between humans and the slow pain of starvation. When the dish was empty, the woman brought a gourd of water and each of them drank. At her first swallow Ramata felt a burst of freshness expanding from her gullet throughout her body. She had not known she was so parched, to be so refreshed by this simple, clear drink.

The old woman filled her small pipe and lit it with an ember from the fire. The smoke she exhaled swirled around her and then streamed away, even though the air was still. "I thank you, my child," said the old woman. "You cook well."

Ramata nodded to acknowledge the compliment.

"Are you happy here?" Her tone changed; this was a direct

and challenging question.

"My mother, I do not know the Manding well," she began hesitantly, and the old woman scoffed. The Manding was not the issue. Ramata admitted the truth. "I find my circumstances uncomfortable."

"Indeed," agreed the old woman. "But circumstances may change. Wasn't your grandmother a *signare*?"

This question startled Ramata. Yes, her grandmother on the mother's side had been a *signare,* one of the Wolof woman traders who had integrated closely with the *nasrani*. It was a point of unspoken pride with her; her family had learned to blend worlds and to prosper. The old woman's question suddenly made her wonder. Had the thought of her grandmother's competence given her the courage to follow Samba Ly in his red fez?

"Are you a seer?" she asked.

"Hah!" the old woman dismissed the question. "A matter of deduction. An adventurous Wolof woman... But my question had a point. Kri Koro offers opportunity. The town has resources and can offer wealth to those who seek it."

"My mother, I will soon need resources, if not wealth," answered Ramata.

"Then return tomorrow."

* * *

Dumont passed a sleepless, delightful night. He recalled his first sight of this woman in the cantonment, and the suspicion that she was being paraded before him. He later learned to whom she was attached. He would settle the question in time, and on his own terms.

He had wondered if he would need the interpreter. But she spoke French, halting with disuse at first, and curiously archaic. Perhaps it was just an unfamiliar dialect. The French language, like the nation's cheeses, came in many flavors. Had she learned it from a wandering poet? At one point she murmured to herself *"Assavoir mon se ces fillettes ... Ne furent-elles femmes honnêtes?" Honnête* certainly did not apply to their most recent activity. He was sure he had read or heard the words, but couldn't remember where. When he asked her name she gave no answer. She did answer other questions: she was not from Kri Koro by birth, she had come from the north, she was Soninke. She quickly began to echo his accent.

He sent her off before dawn to wherever she wished to go in the dark. He offered her a coin, a silver five-franc piece. She stared at it, and then muttered, *"S'ils n'aiment fors que pour l'argent, on ne les aime que pour l'heure."* She looked up at him, and then her hand clasped his, closed it round the coin, and pushed it back to his chest. *"Tana si te,"* she muttered. He was surprised and puzzled by the response. Surely she had come to his bed on terms of compensation; there had been no flirtatious encounters, no courtship, no prior acquiescence, although he could not complain of her responsiveness. He laid the coin by and took her hand. *"Tu reviendras?"* he asked.

She smiled, nodded, and vanished in the shadows.

* * *

The Fula guard readily agreed to an extra day of portage with the prospect of a roast fowl. In the next village Marco enlisted a small boy, and another the day after. He put off killing the last chicken. Their path led them across plains, from village to village, and coursed around the occasional hill or mountain. No matter what its size, the hill was always called *kuru*: the stone mountain, the black mountain, the big mountain. They crossed one large river and many smaller ones. Occasionally they heard the roar of a lion or the cackles of hyenas; more often they heard the hooting of monkeys in the trees. Leaving the broad grasslands of the Futa Jallon, they saw fewer and fewer cattle. The evenings were cool, and for Marco the contrast with the sweltering heat of coastal Geba was a delight.

Tristan gazed at everything in wonder: the peculiar plants by the side of the path, the crystal chameleons crossing the path with deliberation, the people in strange dress and their implements. When offered water in a ladle made from a gourd he would examine the ladle; he would finger the haft and blade of the *daba*, the short-handled hoe; he ran his hands over the clay water pots that stood outside huts. He even held a pestle and mimed the action of pounding in a mortar which caused the onlooking women to chortle. He stared back at the innumerable children who swarmed out of villages to see the strange white men.

Marco had brought a small stock of glass beads and paper to ensure shelter and food. If there were Muslims about, the paper was a precious rarity; if the village was pagan, the glass beads were a welcome and recognized commodity. Curiosity served them. Men didn't question a *nasrani*, yet they certainly wished to know what they might learn. Marco took care to ask his own questions as well, as they sat with their hosts in the evenings.

The hosts were always happy to talk about themselves and their uneasy relations with other villages. The Sangalanka had a history of territorial conflict with their Fula neighbors, complicated by their own lack of unity. Different lineages claimed power—the Keita, the Kamara, the Nyakhasso. Uneasy alliances collapsed at the first test. Marco listened carefully and tried to remember the lineage names. These, he knew, were a key to understanding the people, and with understanding came opportunity.

* * *

Nyelle was almost in tears when she came to Cejan for what she thought might be the last time. Her hand shook slightly as she raised the spoon toward his lips.

The old man noticed and pulled his head back, the sign to stop. His eyes met hers and his lips framed the question, "What is it?"

"They wish to give me away," she told him while considering how she could explain the situation.

"*Furu*?" he asked. Was she to be married?

That was the crux of her problem. "I don't know," she answered honestly. "I don't think so. There is a new *nasrani*, the *komanda* of the town. They wish me to go serve him, and I'm sure they mean in bed." This was franker talk than she would ever have dared with another elder, for she had absorbed the lessons of humility and deference to seniority. But her pride and the value of her lineage were involved. The *bemba* had a stake in the placement of the clan's daughters. She was sure Gaoussou hadn't shared this plan with his brother. But the eldest should know.

"*Ahha,*" he replied, clearly pondering her problem.

She waited.

He reached a decision.

"Go," he said. "Say...monthly." She understood: she was to use menstruation as a reason to withdraw from the compound. "Village edge...west?" He stared at her to make sure she understood, she nodded. "Old woman...Say this to her." He muttered some lines and she repeated them twice for him. "She will advise. I...helpless, you see."

"No, *bemba,*" she answered, "you have helped already!" He had understood, he had cared and was concerned, and best of all, he had a possible solution. Her hand did not shake as she fed him the rest of the gruel. Then she laid him back in bed and rolled him over, so she could wash and oil his skin on either side. His back, against the cloths and skins on his bed, often became dry and brittle. His behind was slightly soiled; she wiped it and took the cloth outside to rinse it.

"Gaoussou," he said as she was leaving. He wished to talk with his brother.

Chicken
Photographed in 1989 in
Selibaby, Mauritania.

CHAPTER V

NYELLE WENT FIRST TO her mother. Her ear took in Nyelle's indignation and Cejan's solution, and she undertook to communicate Cejan's request to Gaoussou. By mid-morning Nyelle was on her way to the hut of seclusion. The Condé women usually went to the east. There was a hut not too far from the sacred spring in the hills. Nyelle instead followed the path to the west. There she found the hut Cejan had described.

An old woman was sitting on a section of log smoking a pipe. This was rare; to Nyelle's experience tobacco was costly. The smoke, coiling around the head and rising in suggestive but indistinct shapes, held her eyes for a moment. She remembered her purpose. She drew in her breath, and in her best imitation of a *jelimuso,* she declaimed the words Cejan had taught her:

Condé muso!
Tuma ni Bagi moden!
Jonmakan ni Bagi moden!
Sigi ma diya!
Sigi ni gundo! Kunsigi ni sanu!

The old woman removed the pipe from her mouth and sat up. She glared at the young woman. "*Eeeh*!" she protested. "You are no *jelimuso* to go singing praises! You should be ashamed!

You are a Condé, of the lineage of kings and princes! Mari Diata was born of your lineage! You *receive* praises! What do you think you are doing?"

Cejan was clearly sure the invocation would open the door. Nyelle decided that deference to age was appropriate; it did not matter that the old woman was apparently poor and an outcast. "*N'ba,*" she answered, "my great-grandfather told me to come to you for help. It was he who told me how to greet you. I trust I have not misunderstood his instructions." She paused. The old woman's expression softened slightly at the mention of the great-grandfather. "I hope I find you well."

"Is your great-grandfather Cejan the elder?"

"It is he who sent me."

"Did he explain the words to you?" asked the old woman.

"No," answered Nyelle frankly. "He shared with me what he thought might help against the trouble that has come to me."

"And what is this trouble?"

"The elders wish me to serve in the house of the *nasrani,* to lie in his bed, but not to be married." That seemed the simplest summary of the welter of possibilities. "I spoke to the great-grandfather, and he sent me to you."

"With the excuse of your monthlies?"

"*Anh-anh,*" agreed Nyelle.

"How well do you know the *bemba*?"

Nyelle explained how she had been assigned to bring him his food and clean him up, and how they had talked and sometimes joked together. She recalled his nickname, *kumboro-tigi,* master of the bees.

"Very well. You shall stay a few days. You must make yourself useful!"

"Of course, my grandmother. I have some food."

"That can wait. First, sweep up this courtyard."

Then she was sent to cut reeds; they would need more bedding, and to gather firewood. When the day reached its hottest, they sat down in a bit of shade to share the food she brought. The old woman ate most of it. After a rest, Nyelle was sent for firewood and water.

In the late afternoon Ramata came down from the cantonment with some porridge. She listened to Nyelle's description of her situation without comment, but intense thought. The three of them ate quietly in the dusk, then Ramata left them for the night. The old woman sat on her log, smoking her pipe and sent Nyelle to sleep.

* * *

Gaoussou didn't visit Cejan immediately. First he and his *baramuso* settled on a girl to replace Nyelle: Djanka, about Nyelle's age, a daughter of his third wife. In the afternoon he approached the older man's hut.

Cejan was dozing, but reacted immediately to Gaoussou's step at the threshold. His eyes opened, his head turned, his hands reached down to support the torso as it stiffened and rose. Their eyes met. Gaoussou was surprised at the strength of Cejan's gaze. They exchanged greetings. Cejan's speech was halting, but clear. He asked no questions about the town or the family.

Gaoussou was sure Nyelle was one reason for his brother's summons, and hoped Djanka would prove adequate; Cejan was losing a trusted attendant. Might there be something else? Did Cejan know of the plan to place Nyelle with the *nasrani komanda*? Did he understand that her status would be...exceptional? The lineage was offering a woman in exchange for access, for influence, and eventually for power. They had done so many times before. Family alliances were the mortar that held the various bricks of power in a stable structure. Women should be pliant, conformable. The lineage faced new powers, they needed new adaptations to ensure an avenue to influence.

"Nyelle's mother told my first wife that you wished to see me," he began. "We have found a girl to replace Nyelle. We wish Nyelle to..." He hesitated on Nyelle's status.

Cejan muttered. Gaoussou leaned closer to hear. "Nyelle... *komanda*?"

Evasion was inappropriate; Gaoussou respected Cejan as his elder brother. "*Tinyè don*. We seek access to the *nasrani komanda*. He has men to serve him. He does not have women."

"Not marriage?"

"He is a foreigner; let him determine the status..." Gaoussou hesitated again. Cejan nodded and closed his eyes. Just as Gaoussou was beginning to worry, the eyes opened as bright as before. The lids had shuttered to concentrate the thought.

"Better path to power."

Gaoussou had to control his reaction tightly; if Cejan saw a path unknown to him, he must be drawing on the lineage's secrets that he had so far refused to share. "Women have helped before," said Gaoussou. The list of kings in the Manding who were defeated through a woman was very long. It began with the usurper, Sumanguru, seduced by Mari Diata's sister into revealing the secrets of his power.

"*Nasrani* power not power of *farafin*," observed Cejan. "Not kinship, tradition, passion. *Nasrani* work with wealth." Gaoussou accepted this.

"Kri Koro...has wealth," continued Cejan. "Wealth...gold."

Gaoussou stared at his brother. Never had he heard of gold in this region. How could the town possess a resource that no one had discovered or exploited?

Cejan shaped a half-smile at his brother's surprise. *"Tinyè don."* I am old. The implication, Gaoussou understood clearly, was that Cejan felt it might be time to pass on the secrets of the lineage. But the statement was not absolute; Cejan offered it as a warrior playing *warri* advancing a piece on the board.

"But still alive. In spite of Samori's *sofa*." This reminder of their shared past was a peace offering; Gaoussou knew there was rivalry of a sort between them. Even when the father was gone, the spirit of *fadenya*, the competition of half-brothers over power in the lineage, persisted. But the two of them had been friends in years past.

Cejan nodded. After a moment of silence, he said, "Nyelle."

"She is a sweet girl," said Gaoussou. "What do you wish for her?"

"Marriage." The word came sharply. "Not *komanda*. But soldier."

"The *komanda*'s captain has two women. We did inquire." Gaoussou smiled. Cejan would have expected investigations of the possibilities.

"Marriage... old," said Cejan. Then, as he saw Gaoussou's face shaping itself into thought, he bridged the gaps. "Soldier will come for marriage." So the secret of the gold was not the price for Nyelle's marriage. "Gold to *komanda*. Power to Condé."

Gaoussou understood the implied timeframe. Once Nyelle was honorably disposed, they could address the question of the gold. Not a question, but questions. "Is there a source of gold? Or is there a golden object?"

Cejan closed his eyes. Gaoussou considered it a sign the discussion was ended. Then Cejan opened them again. "Both."

* * *

After his breakfast, which today included two cups of precious coffee, Dumont sat gazing over the town. The countless cones of thatch breaking above the foliage had overnight become less alien. They marked the living spaces of complex lineages. Under or around them people carried on their lives much as had the peasants, the bourgeoisie, and the elite of Bourges. Bourges was governed by a prefect, appointed by the central administration in Paris. During his school days, the prefect was actually a Breton who had great difficulty adapting to local usages. Bécassin, they had called him, because of his prominent nose. Now Dumont was the Bécassin of Kri Koro, without the nose. He finished his coffee, rose to move over to his office, and told the servant to summon Mady Sisibé, the interpreter.

Sisibé came quickly. The hierarchy of the cantonment was centered on the *nasrani komanda,* and those with direct access to authority responded immediately. It was unusual for the *commandant* (Sisibé was proud to know the actual French word) to call him so early.

Dumont considered approaches. Foremost in his mind was the woman. He was certain Sisibé wasn't involved. But what might Sisibé know? Was it common knowledge in the cantonment that...the *komanda* was susceptible? He was sure it was common knowledge that he had not slept alone. He put that topic aside.

So Dumont began by announcing the arrival of the German ethnographer as an assignment or burden placed on them by the central administration. Sisibé, standing at the other side of the desk, listened with interest. Dumont didn't know how much the interpreter might have learned of the history of French and German interactions. Questions of lodging were easily disposed of—there were many empty spaces around the town in which the ethnographer might set up camp, if he had tents.

More interesting was the subject of his research. The ethnographer wished to learn of the history and practices of the people: who could inform him? Here Dumont waited curiously for Sisibé's answer, for he knew the interpreter, like himself, was a stranger in this town. But Sisibé smiled.

"If he wishes to learn the history of the region, he must speak with the Kuyates of Jelikoro. They are the *griots* of this region, they are the ones who know the families and the stories. They send their sons to serve the kings and princes of the region, but the heart of their knowledge is preserved in their village by the *belentigi*, the supreme loremaster, who owes allegiance to no lord. But," he admitted, "like any *griot* or *jeli* he will accept presents."

Griot was an unfamiliar word to Dumont, although he had heard it explained repeatedly during his orientation in Dakar. It meant something like a singer, a bard, perhaps a lore-master.

Sisibé noted his hesitation and amplified. "The *griot* speaks for the nobles and sings their praises. It's always useful for a ruler to have a spokesman to announce decrees and commands. Then, if some problem arises, the ruler may say the spokesman has made a mistake. Some noble lineages are associated with lineages of *griots*, sharing origins and history. The noble Traore and the *griot* Diabate were once brothers. They were hunters seeking to kill a magical buffalo. When they met the beast, one brother was brave while the other was stricken with fear, so the brave brother became the noble and the fearful one sang his praises. Now Traore and Diabate are united. The Kuyate are bound to the lineage of Mari Diata Keita, the founder of the empire."

Sisibé's tone showed more enthusiasm than Dumont had yet observed in him. "How do you know this? You are not from this region."

"I am a child of the Manding. We share a history, we share practices. Our peoples throughout the old kingdom of Mari Diata are linked because he brought us together. In this region the Kuyate of Jelikoro are renowned for their knowledge."

Dumont smiled. "Then we can easily help this German," he acknowledged. "You will have no troubles with the Kuyate of Jelikoro?"

"If the German will pay, they will speak, they will sing, they will fill his ears," agreed the interpreter with a grin.

"Excellent." Dumont paused. "I would like to discuss another matter." Sisibé straightened himself and his brows rose just enough to signify interest and sympathy. "A woman of the cantonment has come to me," he stated. Sisibé's expression didn't change. Dumont continued, "A beautiful woman. I have seen her in the company of Samba Ly. But she is not listed as a spouse or a daughter. Indeed, Samba Ly has no dependents of record."

Sisibé would certainly see here a door to intimacy and influence. How would he react? To Dumont's satisfaction, he responded not with innuendo, but with information.

"He lists no dependents, because he has no children. Because he has no children, he does not count his women as wives. It is a matter of some delicacy with him," that Dumont could easily believe, "for fatherhood is expected of any man.

Samba Ly has had many opportunities, but still has no sons. In the same way, motherhood is expected of all women, and those who have no children are considered inferior, if not worthless. For Samba Ly, a soldier on assignment, some ordinary expectations are suspended. Still, those around him do not talk of family matters when he is present. His women count as servants, although Ramata, the Wolof woman, has earned respect."

"And what do you know of the other woman?"

"She is a mystery. No one knows her origin. It is said she came from the household of Diosse Traore of Kumi." Dumont nodded recognition of the name; it figured in Samba Ly's file. Sisibé continued, "When I first met her I addressed her in Maninka. She answered in the purest Soninke, my mother tongue. On another occasion I heard her speaking with Gorkel, Samba Ly's fosterling, and she spoke perfect Fula. When she speaks with the other women of the cantonment she speaks excellent Wolof. She never speaks of herself."

"Thank you," Dumont nodded, and Sisibé withdrew.

* * *

Marco had half-expected their current situation. They were in a Sangalan village of the Uyukha grouping, detained by the chief. The chief was a Camara and that line was unfathomable. The name was Maninka or Sosso or Sangalanka. He couldn't count on words alone to move them through this town.

They were not imprisoned. The chief was chary of inconveniencing *nasrani*, even suspicious ones without papers or soldiers. But he had placed two watchmen in front of their hut. Still, there was a way out. Marco had examined the structure of the hut and noted the latticework supporting the thatched roof was not firmly embedded in the clay of the walls. With Tristan's help, he slowly and carefully raised the back of the roof until there was enough of a gap for him to slip out. They wedged the gap with a water pot. He took their last chicken, a gray hen torpid in the dark, wrapped it in a cloth to keep it quiet and peered out under the roof. Was there someone out there wondering at the strange movements? He saw and heard no one. He slipped through the gap.

A partial moon and starry sky gave enough light for guidance. He made his way to the edge of the village, far from houses, and there he killed the chicken, cutting off its head. He wanted no sounds. He had considered using the chicken before the chief as an oracle. It was a familiar method. Cut the chicken's throat and let it stagger and thrash about: if it came to rest on its back, the answer was favorable for the chicken faced the sky-god and was honest. If it lay on its belly, it was dishonest. Marco had devised an alternative.

He returned to the center of the village and the walls of the chief's compound. He circled to the rear and found the midden, where waste was deposited. He hid the carcass under some half-rotted palm fronds, saving the head and some feathers. Then he returned to the front. When he could see the entryway he paused and quietly tossed the chicken's head over the wall into an open space. Along the path between the chief's compound and the hut in which he and Tristan were being lodged he dropped the feathers. Then he ducked into an alley and rejoined Tristan.

Affairs went quite easily the next day. Marco was outraged—they had been robbed of their chicken in spite of the guards courteously placed in front of their lodging. He demanded an immediate audience with the chief. On the way to the chief's compound he identified some of the feathers of their gray hen. In the compound he found its severed head.

A pair of confused guards stood by as Marco expressed his indignation. The chief listened, bewildered, as Marco detailed their loss and the curious, indeed suspicious, indications of a trail leading into the chief's compound. Marco hinted that the chief was practicing sorcery, seeking to influence the *nasrani* who would soon be appointing a *komanda,* or perhaps to kill him! Was this chief playing games with the different powers? Throughout this performance, Tristan sat silent, as befuddled as the chief. But Marco had briefed him on how to behave. Tristan maintained a stern expression, occasionally fingering the large knife he wore at his belt (they had not been disarmed: that would have been too obvious a slight on the authority of the *nasrani*). No doubt the chief realized the *nasrani* now ruled the land. Did the chief think that he could use their chicken to create some *korte,* some *dalilu,* that would bring them under his sway?

The chief had no explanation for the lost chicken. He had no confidence in his authority to detain a pair of *nasrani* when they assailed him in this way. He sent them on their way with a guide and also three sheep to make up for the lost chicken and the affront.

Food at a road-side stand. Photographed in Guinea 2005.

CHAPTER VI

NYELLE SPENT FOUR DAYS with the old woman. To her, it seemed more like eight. From the earliest morning, when it was light and cool, to the end of the day, when heat and dust settled over the valley, she was busy at one chore or another. Water and firewood—after the first day she realized the old woman knew exactly how long it *should* take her to walk to the spring and back, and whether she was dawdling in the bush. Sweeping the area around the hut with a short besom broom, in a pattern that the old woman prescribed quite strictly, circling one way in the morning from the door away from the fireplace and then around, and then in the afternoon from the east towards the sun in the west, around the fireplace, to the door, and then across to the rubbish pile. Her back ached from the bending and her head was at times dizzy. Scrubbing the few dishes, mostly of wood. Watering and weeding an unkempt garden behind the hut where she recognized onions and *ngoyo* but little else. Washing filthy rags...

Water especially was the never-ending chore, for besides what they needed for drinking, washing, and the garden, the old woman insisted every day in the mid-afternoon that she should take a basin of water and sprinkle it about the dusty space in front of the hut. Nyelle understood the logic: the moisture kept down the dust after the hottest time of day. Still, it was one more load of water to fetch from the spring. The basin itself was a curiously ornamented calabash bowl whose outer side was a rich red from the rubbing of hands. Around the outer rim a serpentine figure was carved, undulating between lines. Nyelle could never make out a head to the figure. The old woman was also curiously careful with the tuft of leaves she gave Nyelle for the sprinkling; she would vanish into the bush behind the house and return with a fresh handful each day. She watched Nyelle carefully as the young woman dipped the leaves in the water and then whisked them through the air.

On the second day Nyelle earned a nod of approval, and for some reason this pleased her greatly. Without being told, she had swept the ashes into a piece of broken pot and spread them over the garden, at the roots of the plants. The old woman grunted, "Good idea."

But the compliment came with a price: she was told to watch for cow-droppings when looking for firewood to put in the garden. She did find some, dry and flat, so the task wasn't too messy. When the droppings were watered they dissolved into the earth.

Ramata provided a respite from the chores. She came each day as the afternoon waned and after Nyelle had sprinkled water over the dust. They would share her porridge, and then the old woman would sit on her log with her pipe. As the light faded, the glow of the burning tobacco highlighted her brows and made her eyes pools of darkness while the swirls of smoke shaped themselves into the suggestions of dreams and the stuff of visions. Ramata always left before full dark.

* * *

Curious, Sisibé watched Gorkel. The boy was prowling around the *komanda*'s residence near the latrine behind the *komanda*'s bedchamber. The residence stood on pillars for ventilation and cooling. The space under the latrine, where a pit had been dug, was sealed off with a wall of *banco* bricks. For some reason, this enclosure fascinated Gorkel. Sisibé had seen him there several times acting with artificial and unconvincing nonchalance.

He had instructions: to prepare for the arrival of a new *nasrani*. From Dumont's information, this *nasrani* brought his own housing, tents, no doubt. But he would require space, access to water...At home in Bondu, Sisibé would have summoned a *griot* from his father's retinue and sent the man to make overtures. In Kri Koro, he had no *griots* at his service. In fact—a strange and uncomfortable thought—he himself had become a *griot*, the spokesman for the *nasrani komanda*. In that light, his status was lowered.

But the world was changing, and so were the conditions for status. Sisibé left the cantonment.

The walk down to the compound of the Condé lineage was not long. When he arrived at the *bolon* he was immediately recognized and a servant invited him to take a seat in the shade while they informed the master of his arrival. There was no suggestion that his arrival was inopportune.

A young woman brought him a cup of water; he it drank gratefully. A youth appeared near him at a small fireplace with a pot of coals and began to prepare tea.

Gaoussou then strode into view. Sisibé admired the man: no longer young, his body was still straight, his bearing powerful. He knew Gaoussou was not the senior of the lineage. Gaoussou was respected: a proven warrior, a faithful brother. He wondered about the elder brother.

They exchanged civilities while the youth finished preparing the tea. Gaoussou asked about Sisibé's family, so he elaborated: son of a chief in Bondu, sent to the school 'for the sons of chiefs.' The implications were that his father was powerful enough for the *nasrani* to want a measure of control, and that he was valued by his father. He hoped Gaoussou would appreciate these points. A secondary consequence was that Sisibé had now mastered the language of the *nasrani*, and perhaps had access to their power. Sisibé was well aware that everyone—Gorkel, for instance—assumed they possessed magical powers. Gaoussou, however, clearly considered the *nasrani* a human power with which he could deal on the usual terms of advantage, prestige, and profit.

They quickly agreed on a campsite for the transient ethnographer: a small hill at the north end of town, close to a spring. Gaoussou could also provide servants, as needed, and other necessities such as food and firewood.

The ethnographer's interests were a more delicate issue. How would the Condé elder understand this inquiry? To ask about origins was often to question them. Was there any question or doubt about the Condé legitimacy in this region? But when he mentioned the past to Gaoussou, the older man smiled briefly.

"This branch of the Condé lineage is among the oldest in the Manding," he stated proudly. "We have been kings since the time before Mari Diata, although his mother Sogolon Condé, was not of our lineage. In her father's place we would not have incurred the wrath of Du Kamisa."

Sisibé thought he understood the reference, but to be sure he inquired, "Was she the old woman who became...?" Before he finished the question, Gaoussou nodded.

"Yes. She was denied by her kinsmen and became a witch. As a wild buffalo, she slaughtered the people of Do."

"Then, to learn this history..." began Sisibé, and Gaoussou again finished the thought for him.

"We shall call on the *jelilu* of Jelikoro. One of the Kuyate will come to sing for this German and tell him of the past. He will bring the heroes to life again; he will speak their words and describe their deeds. The German will be satisfied." And they both knew, with satisfaction comes rewards.

Not far from them, Cejan was far from satisfied. The new girl—what was her name? Djanka had none of Nyelle's skill and tenderness. Djanka was not his great-grandchild, she came from Gaoussou's line. She wasn't happy with her task.

She fed him decently, but that was all. She didn't clean him as carefully or as gently as Nyelle, and he knew that he stank. It shamed him as his weakness did not. Cleanliness was easier than healing. He remembered his youth, the days spent in the fields…

He was a noble, but because of the wars men were few. He and others of his age group moved across the fields plying their short-handled hoes as a singer followed them, providing rhythm and spirit to their movements. There had been several singers over the years, but one in particular came to mind. "He who would farm, let him farm!" was the refrain of the tune. What was the *griot's* name? Fadigi...Those days in the field left Cejan with long, thin, steely muscles that served him well when it came to warfare. He didn't like rifles; he found confidence with a sword. His greatest, and last, fight came at the end of their campaign with Mori-Ule. It was stopped by the Almamy, by Samori himself, who called back the *sofa* Cejan had been fighting. Cejan's valor had saved his life, and Gaoussou's. It earned him the time for Samori to learn of Kri Koro's resources and to perceive that conciliation would be better than bloodshed. Memory of that fight was a balm to his pride.

Now he lay, scarcely able to move on his own. Djanka was absorbed in other thoughts, most probably of herself. She didn't understand her tasks, and so they were not properly completed (again, unlike Nyelle). He didn't think she was in love, for in his observation that led to a distracted dreaminess, not the awkward and occasionally graceless movements he observed in her. He missed Nyelle's care.

* * *

Tristan could not understand why they had the sheep. He did understand that the chief, a Camara, had at first been very suspicious, and that somehow Marco had made the chief ashamed of having detained them and then eager to make up for the fault. Now, instead of the chicken, they had three sheep on one tether that Marco handed to him. He had to haul the sheep. They wanted to return to their home, they wanted to wander off in the rich grass—he could understand those urges. He himself wondered if his quest for gold had taken him too far. No, nothing was too far from the life of bitter, backward-looking poverty and resentment that had been the daily fare in that hamlet near St. Augustine. So he hauled the sheep, trusting that Marco knew where they were going.

Marco knew their destination. He was less sure of their course, for they didn't follow trade routes along which distances and stages were common knowledge, as well as the hazards ranging from rivers to venal chiefs or skilled brew-wives (these last might be considered attractions, although they often caused a delay). Kri Koro was not a known crossroads of trade. He imagined the town as the center of a cluster of five or six villages, fed by their wares and produce. From Kri Koro, larger currents might carry those goods to distant ports and bring back a varied array of the useful, the ornamental, the lethal (weapons were always a choice item of trade) and the incomprehensible. He remembered a shipment of glass bells from Lisbon to Geba: they were intended to keep flies off the food. They didn't sell. Still...There was the load of gaudy parasols—utterly unacceptable on the sober streets of Lisbon. They flew out of the merchant's warehouse to bedeck wives and mistresses, shielding them from the sun and proclaiming their status.

They were now making their way from the watershed of the Bafing to the greater valleys of the Niger, that godlike waterway coursing through forests and swamps and deserts and plains and gorges…also through time, through kingdoms, empires and legends. The gold of Kri Koro was also the gold of that past, traded north across the desert sands. That gold had brought the Portuguese down the coasts and into places like Geba.

Marco was content to let Tristan haul the sheep. He considered himself a man of words and people. He was now challenged. Around him Marco heard the cries of birds and the occasional startling whoop of monkeys, not the murmur of people. Once, as the path led across a small stream they startled a family of warthogs that snorted loudly, then ran off, their short, straight tails raised in the air. They reminded him of pigs in Geba, but warthogs were much uglier and swifter. He and Tristan were in the bush, the world of nature that surrounds and threatens the world of man. He didn't know how far to the next village, although the tenuous trail, trampled through the grasses and bushes, reassured him that it lay somewhere ahead.

He looked up at the trees and saw fruit bats beginning their evening flight to their sticky and sweet meals. The evening brought an increased chattering of birds arguing over perching sites. If they waited too long they would find no firewood. It was time to make camp. Curiously, this was the first time in their peregrination from Geba that they hadn't found a village in which to lodge.

Tristan made no complaint.

They found a clear space under a tree and tethered the sheep. They easily started a fire. For food they had pieces of roast yam. They laid up firewood to last through the night, agreed on who would take first watch, and settled down for the night.

Sheep
Photographed in 1989 in Selibaby
Mauritania

CHAPTER VII

"NEIN, NEIN," **BELLOWED LÖWENSTEIN.** "We may not talk of savages! The peoples of Africa have a history, no matter what the sainted Hegel may say. It reaches deep in time, it joins our own!"

The German ethnographer had arrived the day before, announced by a runner who reached the cantonment just in time for the noon meal. Sisibé went to meet the expedition accompanied by a soldier and by Fadigi Kuyate, the *griot* of Gaoussou Condé. The party was small: perhaps a score of porters carrying an assortment of oddly shaped and well-wrapped bundles in canvas and other water-resistant materials. Far fewer than French military columns. Sisibé noted that the *nasrani* was walking. He had not hired litter bearers to carry him along the path as some of the *nasrani* did.

They exchanged greetings. The German was accompanied by a guide, one who Sisibé would have considered a *siratigi* in the case of a trading caravan: a man from the Manding who knew the protocols. He seemed quite young to be handling such unusual affairs as a German ethnographer in a French colony, but something inclined Sisibé towards respect. The guide treated Sisibé as an honorary kinsman, representing a *jatigi*, who would benefit from the visit. His tone, suggesting cooperation, was quite a change from the exchanges among the French military which were governed by rank, precedence, and frequently by hostility and rivalry. *Fadenya*, the competition for advancement among the sons and heirs born of different wives, was mild in comparison to the meetings of rival French officers.

After the introductions, he invited the German *nasrani* to stay in the *komanda*'s residence while his camp was being set up. The German accepted. Sisibé and Kuyate led the party to the site that Gaoussou suggested, then told the *siratigi* where the market was held. Gaoussou had promised to deliver firewood and water. At this point, Fadigi Kuyate nudged him, and Sidibé stepped aside. Kuyate informed the party that his master Gaoussou Condé, whose praises he briefly intoned, would provide their dinner as a welcome for their arrival, and that he would lead them to the Condé compound when they were ready. The German listened to the proclamation, and then to Sisibé's translation, and exclaimed, "*Ach! Dort soll ich fressen*!"

But the German came and dined on spicy chicken with the *komanda*.The next morning, the two white men shared breakfast on the veranda. Biscuits, brought in tins from Europe, fresh fruit from the market, and Dumont's treasure: coffee. The conversation the night before had covered careers. This morning they were turning to aspects of local interest. Dumont began by inquiring what the current view of African indigenes might be in the German sphere, explaining that in France one current of opinion held that the effort involved in pacification and exploitation of the colonies was not worth the possible rewards. Many considered Africans incapable of civilization. Dumont himself had wondered when he applied for his job, but his observations since his arrival in St. Louis and on the trail down to Kri Koro, had long since erased the question. Still, he asked what the Germans thought. They too had colonies in Africa;

what was their experience?

Löwenstein exploded. Objecting to the word 'savage,' he explained his developing theory of regional cultures. He mentioned languages that Dumont had never heard of: Swahili and N'debele and Chichewa and Masai and Ge'ez, and then moved on to regions. "River basins!" insisted Löwenstein. "The roots of our own civilization lie in Mesopotamia, the land between the rivers. For Africa, we begin with the Nile, the rival of Mesopotamia. But between the Nile and this part of Africa, around us," he gestured expansively, "there is the Sahara. A desert, a dry wasteland. Was it always so? We have the Niger River running through the Sahara and then to the ocean. Was the basin of the Niger a cradle of kingdoms? In the south, there is the Congo. It runs through impassable jungle, but in the headwaters, in the savannas, we find kingdoms and distinct cultures. I have visited the Kasai. Their refinements of culture are considerable. Would you believe that in that region a principal element of their mythic history was the Tower of Babel?"

Dumont stared.

"Indeed! The story was altered, but the structure," he snorted at his pun, "was the same. Men tried to raise a tower to heaven and were punished. The inference is clear. The peoples of Africa share the roots of our culture!"

"I've heard of nothing similar in this region," objected Dumont, not because he disagreed but because he wished to learn how this advocate might answer. He did not mention that he was a new-comer.

"*Ja*! There we have the circles, there we have the basins, there we have the rivers dividing the peoples!" answered Löwenstein. "Here we have a culture that has grown up around the Niger. What do they owe to peoples outside? In this region, I don't look for Egyptian influence—the river basins are too widely separated. I look for a connection north, across the Sahara. I consider the Garamantians, described by Herodotus. And we find there is indeed trade north and south across the sands. And do you remember what was the basis of that trade?"

This answer Dumont knew quite well. It had been drummed in during his training. "Gold," he answered.

Löwenstein smiled. "Exactly. Gold created kingdoms. And where there are kingdoms, there is history, no matter how it is recorded. The rulers keep track of their dominion. And where there is history, there are stories," he paused and smiled, for he had reproduced a German subtlety in French: *'où il y a de l'histoire, il y a des histoires,'* to match *'wo man findet Geschichte findet man auch Geschichten.'* "I have come to learn the stories. The gold I leave to you."

"If I could find gold," admitted Dumont, "my duties would be considered fulfilled."

* * *

Ramata came early to the old woman's hut while Nyelle was fetching firewood. Ramata had learned why the younger woman was staying there, and she was discontent. She guessed the intentions of the Condé elders. They wanted to buy influence in the cantonment using the girl. With the *komanda*? with the interpreter, Sisibé? or with Samba Ly? The *nasrani* would of course be the first choice. He held the power. But she knew he now had a woman, a woman far more desirable and skilled than young Nyelle. Would he take a second? From what she had observed, the *komanda* was not a man driven by physical desires. And his intimacy with Assya was recent—he would still be infatuated.

The interpreter? She knew little of Sisibé except that he seemed considerate and observant. She had also learned that he had noble origins. That nobility worked against her understanding of his present function: an interpreter was a *gewel* (she still used the Wolof word for *griot*), and therefore outside the class of nobles. Sisibé's position was equivocal. In the matter of Nyelle, though, she was sure the Condé would underestimate the power of language and knowledge, they would misunderstand the question of status. The interpreter wouldn't be considered.

So the most likely target of Condé ambitions, failing the *komanda*, would be Samba. As the soldiers' leader, he represented the form of power with which they were most familiar. He counted as a *keletigi* (this time her mind offered the Maninka word). He had the ear of the *komanda*, he commanded the soldiers of the *nasrani*. He would certainly appreciate the offer of a woman.

She liked Nyelle. The girl's attentive obedience, spiced with the spark of intelligence and character, deserved appreciation. Nyelle also performed her chores with grace. Men would consider her very attractive. Still, the Condé elders intended to use her to win favor with the *nasrani komanda*, most probably through the chief of the guards, Samba Ly. Nyelle was being sent to replace her. This was the last day of Nyelle's stay. In the morning she would return to her family. No doubt, she would be in the cantonment by evening.

She put the bowl of food down by the door and sat. The old woman was tracing designs in the sand before her with a twig. There was a pattern, a progression to them, although Ramata could identify none of the figures. It was neither *nasrani* lettering nor Arabic script. The old woman was working through some sequence or problem. Her pipe was laid to one side. It was dull, and Ramata inferred that the old woman had been working her problem for some time.

The old woman looked up and greeted her, the warmest response she had yet received. Then the white hairs turned down again to the designs in the sand.

"What I see is the *yere-yere,* the spinning of winds and threads," she said. "I don't see the message." She sat up and relit her pipe with an ember from the fireplace. When it was smoking again, she continued. "You're concerned because the Condé men wish to give our Nyelle to your man." Ramata was not surprised at such a direct observation; she had long since decided that the old woman was a *gisaankat*.

"They seek power." The old woman's tone was meditative. "Between families, the easiest path to influence is through women. A bride creates a link, especially if she has been taught obedience and loyalty. Men may think they rule, but it is women who weave the texture of our communities." She paused again, the smoke swirling above her face. "Be kind to Nyelle. She will do you no harm. She will not serve the Condé as they hope. Besides," and her eyes turned directly on Ramata, "you will not stay much longer in that bed."

The direct comment perturbed Ramata. She hadn't yet formulated such thoughts. Then Nyelle returned with firewood.

Later, Ramata commented to Nyelle, "You return to your family tomorrow." Nyelle looked at the old woman, and then nodded to Ramata.

"Let me see if I can't do something with your hair," suggested Ramata. She had brought her combs and some beads and some oil. She had thoughts about what might be done with the young woman's mat. Nyelle hadn't learned much about styling her hair. Ramata had traveled more widely and learned from the other women following their own soldiers. Styling hair was a pleasant and social pastime.

As the afternoon faded to dusk, Ramata combed and cleared knots, smoothed curls, then began to part and shape it into tresses, highlighting the braids she created with red and blue beads from her precious stock. When she had finished she sat back. The old woman grunted approvingly. Nyelle filled a calabash with water so she could see herself; curiosity and vanity overcame her normal submissiveness. What she saw made her thank Ramata enthusiastically. The oval of her face was now framed above and on the sides with ringlets bedecked with colored beads. No such fashion had yet been seen on the ways of Kri Koro.

"My child, you are very pretty," said the old woman. "Be grateful to Ramata for her gift. It is far more attractive than what I have prepared for you." She reached behind her stool and pulled out a packet tied with a leather thong. Ramata recognized it immediately as a protective charm. The old woman tied it loosely about Nyelle's neck; the thong was long enough so the amulet hung down below the top of Nyelle's shirt, against her flesh.

"We send you home with gifts. May they serve you as you have served me." In those last words Ramata saw a true judgment, and also a grandmotherly smile.

* * *

It was time to talk again with Cejan. Gaoussou was sure that

Djanka, the new attendant, would be a topic. He had chosen Djanka mostly for her looks. He understood there was some level of physical intimacy involved in the care for the aged and feeble body. He suspected his brother enjoyed a nubile attendant, and so he provided to the imagined needs. He summoned Kuyate, the *griot,* for he desired both a witness and a separate perspective for interpretation. Kuyate in turn motioned to a servant, and the boy assembled the materials for tea.

Kuyate preceded Gaoussou into Cejan's hut, intoning Condé lineage praises. The old man was lying, half-propped against the wall. A cotton cloth, blue with lines of red and black, covered his body from the navel to the knees. The feet protruded, broad, flattened and hardened with use. Cejan seemed to be contemplating them in wonder as they entered. The feet still belonged to the functional body of past years; age had not withered them. His eyes turned first to the noisy *griot* and then to Gaoussou. He nodded slightly as his glance moved to a small bench and a chair. Goussou took the chair. The *griot* placed himself on the bench and stopped his chant. The boy stayed outside the hut to brew the tea.

Gaoussou had come on his own, not at Cejan's request. Greetings were formal. Affection between the brothers varied with mood, but there was at least a common understanding: they represented an ancient line, and they owed it to their ancestors and their descendents to ensure its continued prosperity.

Cejan came to the point immediately, forestalling Gaoussou's possible questions. *"Condé gundo fila,"* he began. There are two Condé secrets. Gaoussou and the *griot* both leaned closer to make sure they heard his words, for his speech was no longer clear. Nyelle had the gift of understanding, acquired through practice and, Cejan believed, affectionate interest, but these two men did not. He would have to be as clear as he could.

"The first...the village. Sènètèla." His listeners nodded. That village lay to the north; the inhabitants were not farmers. This was most unusual in a region where famine was a frequent visitor. They were fed by the Condé slave villages which farmed the fields around the town. Gaoussou had never understood the cause of this arrangement.

"They give gold." That statement explained it all. Gold ensured Condé influence and power well beyond the limits of Kri Koro. The producers of gold were entitled to certain protections and privileges. But who were the intermediaries, the agents? Gaoussou needed to know names. Cejan gave them, enunciating carefully: the village chief, the earthmaster, the leader of the miners. He explained the protocols by which the commerce operated in secret. The need for secrecy was obvious to Gaoussou: gold on the table captured the attention of all, and too often that of the more powerful. No one could force the earthmaster to produce when he was unwilling—that was an established fact, proven time and again by failed attempts—but neither could one count on the earthmaster's allegiance. He would sell where it benefited his people.

"The second secret. A cavern. A throne of gold." Gaoussou nodded. He knew that past kings had claimed great nuggets which might be fashioned into a seat of power. Cejan continued. "Stolen. Not delivered. Kept for wealth. Hidden." Gaoussou wasn't surprised. How many rulers would set aside a source of wealth to honor a distant obligation? "A guardian." Gaoussou expected as much. And as a Condé he had a suspicion what form the guardian might take.

* * *

The sheep woke Marco. They were bleating in terror. Their cries went beyond the belling protests of an unhappy animal being dragged to an unknown (usually bloody) fate. He sat up. Tristan had already roused himself.

A lion stood at the edge of the clearing. It had just emerged from the bush, drawn by the smell of the sheep (or so Marco hoped). It was male, with a full and tawny mane lit by the moonlight. It was unsure of the space it had entered, or else it would long since have leapt onto the sheep and wrought bloody havoc. The unfamiliar smells of humans and smoke and fire gave it pause. It observed its prey and the environs as the sheep protested.

To Marco's wonderment and admiration, Tristan acted without hesitation or fear. From somewhere he produced a gun. Marco did not recognize it as a Colt revolver. As the lion raised its head to roar, Tristan knelt and aimed, steadying his right hand with the left arm braced on his knee, and fired twice. The bullets apparently went through the lion's mouth and into its head. The roar ended abruptly, as the lion's head jerked back, and then the whole body sank to one side like a slow wave rolling over the sand. Tristan waited a moment, until the beast had collapsed, and then he rose.

The sheep continued to bleat. The gunshots terrified them as much as the lion.

Beads aquired here and there in Africa by the author.
Beads were a major trading commodity, especially in the time before the Colonial Administrations introduced money.

CHAPTER VIII

RAMATA AWOKE ALONE, HER thoughts in turmoil. She had arranged Nyelle's hair because she had become fond of the child and wished to make a gesture. At the same time she felt a conflict—what woman would willingly adorn a rival? But sweet Nyelle—she didn't think the child had the instinct for self-advancement that other women might employ. She had watched Nyelle's service to the old woman; the girl obeyed through an innocent desire for approval and a respect for her elders. She was lovely, but lacked the selfishness that leads to advancement. Marriage with Samba was very unlikely, and if not that, what would be her fate? When Samba had finished with her, what then? Might she become nothing more than a camp follower, the plaything of the *nasrani*'s soldiers?

That question brought Ramata back to herself. She had followed Samba Ly because she fell in love with him. She had loved the man. She had no thought of advancement, for herself or her family.

Their union had not been blessed with children, although this was the expected seal and confirmation of any alliance of man and woman. The nature of the relationship was open to question in the eyes of others. The challenges of Samba's professional life had distracted her, and she found satisfaction in the business of supplementing the military needs. It was some comfort that the Soninke woman also was childless.

Did she still love Samba? He was no longer the gallant soldier of Thiès. His new visions of promotion and advancement in the world of the *nasrani* had changed him. The Soninke woman he had acquired was less of an issue; she was willing to admit that parallel intimate relations might exist, that a man might love his different wives, perhaps as a mother loves her different children: true to each of them in his fashion, in his own way. But she didn't think Samba cared for either of the women in his household. He had become selfish, she admitted. It went beyond the intrinsic masculine condition that she viewed as a form of social blindness. He now cared only about himself.

Besides love, the incomprehensible force that draws two humans together, there was the question of...was it status? Security? A form of coupled commonwealth? She no longer trusted Samba Ly to plan for her as well as for himself. She had made best use of the opportunities that arose, to their mutual benefit. What reward was there at the downfall of that Bamana warlord, Diossi? Samba acquired those women and disposed of them of profitably, saving one. Ramata had received some fine robes and beads as an afterthought.

Perhaps her path no longer lay with his. It was a strange thought for a woman reared to the belief that men and women are incomplete until they are coupled, but it was one that had been pressing on her for some time. Visiting the old woman, who lived alone and without kin, made her consider her own future.

* * *

Some time later, Nyelle retraced the path Ramata had followed the previous evening, with less perplexity. She stayed to sweep the old woman's forespace and to fetch firewood. Now she was moving into an unpredictable future. Her refuge with the old woman had bought time, encouragement, and confidence. Now she would have to obey the elders and face the tribulations they imposed.

"Nyelle!" It was Kandia Traore, a friend. Her father had lands and villages south of Kri Koro. "What have you done with your hair?"

Nyelle, absorbed in thought, had forgotten Ramata's work. Kandia's admiration reminded her how pleased she had been at the reflected image, and then of stares she had draw from men along her path.

"Traore!" she greeted her friend. "You are well?" They exchanged more polite greetings, then Nyelle explained how Ramata had done her hair. Kandia talked for a bit longer about inconsequentialities, then confirmed the name of the stylist, Ramata, and the connection with the *nasrani* cantonment.

Nyelle was far more cheerful when she reached the Condé compound; the encounter heartened her. Her mother welcomed her with a hug, and then held her at arm's length to admire her appearance. She went to greet her *bemba,* Cejan, and he approved her looks with a smile. He also noticed the leather cord around her neck and pointed to it. She pulled the amulet from under her shirt and laid it in his outstretched hand. His fingers closed over it, he smiled.

"*Condé gundo.* A Condé secret," he commented.

She was reassured. She had protection that the *bemba* recognized. That must have been the reason he sent her to the demanding old woman.

* * *

Meanwhile, Sisibé was trying to keep up with torrents of words from both sides. He had spent a day circulating through the town before he found the *griot* he sought. It would have been simplest to enlist Kuyate who served Gaoussou Condé, but he did not want a simple solution. He'd been asked to find a man of knowledge to meet a *nasrani* and talk of the past. He wanted to find one who would do justice to the heritage he shared with the Condé, the Traore, the Keita. Each notable he approached would name some *griot* who advanced their own interests, by song or praise or representation, and then would mention Korongo Kuyate of Dafama as a *griot's griot*: a man of vast and detailed knowledge, of considerable skill in music, who followed some other goal than advancement and influence. By good fortune, he found Korongo in Kri Koro; he had come to visit his kinsman Fadigi (Gaoussou's *griot*) for the naming ceremony of a child. The man agreed to come and talk with the German *nasrani*.

Now he was faced with the challenge of translating two voluble, eager, and excited speakers. Faced with a *nasrani*, the *jeli* had much to say about his skills and knowledge. The German, although clearly accustomed to working with interpreters (he paused, at least every second paragraph or so), had many requirements and specifications to detail. Sisibé was translating the first sentence of each utterance, and then finding himself flooded by an answer that interrupted the second sentence. The conversation was foundering when the young man, the *siratigi*, intervened. To Sisibé's surprise, he spoke in German.

"Bitte, hören sie erst den djeli, *um zu lernen was er sagt. Sicher*

können wir uns einverstehen über das Arbeit. Aber hier in Afrika soll man immer der Sprecher beenden lassen."

"Er hat nicht den Speer," commented the German.

The guide answered in French, for his master and for Sisibé. "The Soninke pass the spear from speaker to speaker in councils. We are in the Manding, where the master *griot*, the *belentigi*, carries the spear that gives authority to speech."

"And is this man the *belentigi*?" The German seized on the Maninka word.

"No." The *siratigi* answered flatly. "From the *belentigi* you will get only the accepted, simplest, least disputed versions of events." He glanced at Sisibé. "This man has been chosen for his knowledge and because he is one who can explain questions, who can report differences." The German nodded.

The conversation went much more smoothly after that. The German was able to explain his interest in the traditions of the kings and rulers of the region, and in old customs and beliefs. The *jeli* took such an interest for granted: the past was glorious. He was willing to let the German record his words in some manner.

As the different parties separated, Sisibé thanked the *siratigi* and asked his name. To his surprise, the young man answered, "I have lost my name. The *wokòlò* took it."

* * *

Still far from Kri Koro, Marco and Tristan were learning the fame that comes to the killer of a lion. Marco congratulated Tristan on his skill; Tristan said nothing but reloaded his revolver and secreted it again in whatever pocket he carried it. They examined the carcass. Then Tristan suggested breakfast.

They were warming water for tea when a man appeared. His gait suggested caution, the pace of a man aware of strange activities and unsure of danger or oddity. He looked around at the strangers, their sheep, and then saw the dead lion. His jaw dropped.

Which was more astonishing to him: two *nasrani* in the middle of the bush, or the dead lion? The lion was the more familiar peril, perhaps one he had expected or feared. But it was dead! The man bowed to the two strangers, then examined the carcass. Both of Tristan's bullets had passed through the open mouth and lodged within the skull, leaving no external marks of violence. The man was perplexed. Had it been killed by *nasrani* magic?

Marco intervened. "See, here?" he opened the lion's maw, to show the bullets' path. The head was heavy. "*Marfa*." He used the Mandinga word for rifle. The man pointed to him, and Marco pointed to Tristan.

"*Jarafaga ngana*!" The man hailed Tristan, the lion-slaying hero. Then he withdrew, not turning his back on them. Marco and Tristan resumed their breakfast.

After they finished their tea and grilled yam, a party of men arrived. Some carried poles with which they quickly constructed a stretcher for the lion's carcass. One was a singer, who stood in the middle of the clearing, bellowing words that Marco interpreted as praises for the lion-killer or perhaps the lion. Another took the leads of the sheep, and another, after Marco nodded consent, wrapped up their other belongings and raised them onto his head. The man who had first discovered them approached them.

Their village wished to honor the killer of the lion. There would be a feast, so all might share in the flesh of the beast. Was this acceptable to the *nasrani*?

Marco agreed quickly.

Later, he began to wonder. He couldn't understand much of the praise-songs that the *jeli* was intoning in a fluent and nasal stream of Maninka. The words he did grasp seemed addressed to the lion rather than to the lion-slayer. Almost every male of the village came in a procession to observe the carcass, to touch it, to feel the claws. Many bowed. Some were speechless with gaping awe.

Marco knew that almost every lineage of the Manding and the areas around had a special relationship with some animal; they would not eat its flesh. He knew that many villages had great snakes or lizards they honored, and sometimes fed with sacrifices because they were taken to be spirits from the underworld, representatives of the ancestors who (everyone hoped) were watching over their descendents to protect and guide them. Had they come upon a village whose *tènè*, their guardian animal, might be the lion? Would they honor the men who had killed a dangerous animal? Or would they punish a sacrilege? Would it matter that he and Tristan were *nasrani*, and so outside the normal limits of society? He watched and listened and waited…

After the men had paraded past the lion, all the women and children of the town came as well, or so it seemed: an endless stream of jabbering and chattering females of all ages and shapes and sizes, almost all the women carrying an infant or small child and towing two or three others. They passed by the lion and touched its paws or its tail and shrieked in wonder and fear. Some mothers tenderly raised their children's hands to the paws, moving limbs that hesitated in fear or uncertainty.

Finally there came a team of capable-looking men. They

erected a screen of woven palm-fronds around their work area and began to skin the carcass and dismember the joints.

The village leader (Marco could not identify his title) invited them to his home. A woman soon appeared to offer them *dolo*. It was surprisingly good.

After the beer came questions, delicate but deliberate. They were familiar, so Marco could offer careful answers. Yes, this was a *nasrani* from a far land, not from Faransi. He himself was a trader from Geba. They didn't choose to declare the purpose of their trip. Marco felt the statement that it was a '*nasrani* affair' should settle the matter for casual inquiry. Then, directly, ***the*** question: how did they come to kill the lion?

This was the crux. Was the lion sacred to this town? Or was it a perilous beast to be overcome?

He did not answer directly. "We have traveled from the coast. Our path has not been easy. The land is difficult, the paths are bad, the rivers are dangerous, the bush is full of perils. There are beasts and brigands. We have persevered, because my companion, the *nasrani* from the distant land—not that of the Faransi whom you may have met, but another group—has a purpose that is honorable," Marco gestured very relieved to see that Tristan was sitting up straight and alert, listening to the conversation as though he could follow it. "This matter pertains to the relations of the *nasrani* groups. We have encountered obstacles. In the Futa Jallon we met men who wished to detain us, but when they realized their error they set us on our way, and to make amends they offered us some chickens. You laugh," this was not true of the chief, but some chuckles in the audience justified the comment, "but for travelers any assistance is good. We came to a village of the Sangalan. Their chief seized the last of our chickens, for he believed it was some sort of *nasrani dalilu* (magic). But we exposed his theft, and so he gave us some sheep in compensation for the chicken. We were traveling with the sheep when the lion came upon us this morning." Here Marco paused, because any reaction might give him a clue. But his audience was listening intently, and their faces showed no indication of skepticism.

"We called to the lion. We asked him to leave our sheep. We told him how the sheep had been given to us in compensation for our troubles. We explained that these sheep were needed to allow my companion to fulfill his journey and his great purpose. But the lion would not listen. He said humans existed only to feed lions, and that after he had eaten the sheep he would eat us." Marco paused again, but no one seemed ready to challenge his account. "So my companion, the *nasrani* from the far land, said that he could not allow the lion to take these sheep, so necessary to his purpose on a journey that had brought him across more miles of open water than you can imagine, that had brought him to Geba, that had brought him through the Futa Jallon, that had brought him through the land of the Sangalan and now into the Manding! But the lion refused and roared. So my companion killed him. He has the powers of the *nasrani* of far lands, equal those of the Faransi who defeated the Almami Samori," Marco paused to see if this name was known here, and was relieved to see nods of acknowledgement, "and so the lion fell dead."

Marco took a deep breath and examined the audience. "Had this lion been troubling your village? We have heard of towns where a *wara* ravened on the folk, killing all who ventured out into their fields. If so, through the power of my *nasrani* companion, it is no more—*a bana*. It is dead. We do not know your customs in relation to this king of beasts, but if you wish to hold a feast for the village," again a pause, and around the circle of listeners a wave of nodding heads, "we are happy to be able to join you in this occasion."

Lion
Photographed in 1967 in Tanzania

CHAPTER IX

NYELLE HAD NEVER IMAGINED herself being delivered like a package, a basket of rice or a coil of cloth, yet she could not help seeing herself in that way. In the mid-morning of the day after her return, Fadigi Kuyate, Gaoussou's *jeli,* appeared at her mother's chamber. Nyelle had done no packing but her mother had prepared a bundle of necessities. Nyelle had expected formalities. But the *griot* came and seized her; his urgency and the absence of any discussion shocked her. Clearly, the elders, specifically Gaoussou, had begrudged her absence.

Kuyate led her through the town. He did not hold her hand, but his bearing and the slight advance he had on her steps showed clearly she was being taken somewhere. She disliked his behavior. She couldn't help thinking of a real marriage: the pomp, the music, the noise, the crowds of people come to admire her finery. Now she was being dragged down the streets with no time for greetings or other amenities.

At the cantonment she was taken to the quarters of Samba Ly. He appeared and showed her a sleeping chamber that would be hers. He showed her where the other women of the cantonment were occupied, and suggested that she spend some time with them. Ramata was nowhere around. Nyelle had wondered if she would see the older woman whom she now considered a friend. She didn't dare ask about her.

She tried to hide her nervousness as she approached the other women. To her relief they showed no surprise at her appearance and even seemed pleased with her offer to help. She was soon slicing onions. Her knife was a *nasrani* tool, its blade dark with a silvery cutting edge, white where whetting had polished it. It worked well on the onions—a far larger pile than any in her experience. They were cooking for a crowd.

The seasonings simmered in palm oil, the meat was cooking, the onions and other greens were tossed in. The women settled down to wait. They chatted, but Nyelle could understand nothing. They spoke in Wolof. Occasionally one of them looked at her and smiled, but Nyelle couldn't be sure what the smile meant.

After the soldiers were served their meal, the day wore on until finally the moment came that she had anticipated and feared: Samba Ly came to her after the evening meal and led her not to the chamber she had been assigned, but to his own. She followed, for she had no choice. He was much larger and stronger. His manner was brusque, or worse: something had made him very angry. She later learned that Ramata had broken with him that afternoon and taken her belongings.

"You are Nyelle, a woman of the Condé," he said when they reached his room. He spoke Maninka with a strong accent, but she could understand him. "Your lineage, your elders, have sent you to this cantonment to serve us, and thus to ensure good relations between our establishments. Do you understand this?"

She nodded.

"I am the leader of the soldiers. In Maninka, you would say I am the *keletigi*, under the *Faama*, who here is the *nasrani komanda*. I shall decide how you serve us in this cantonment. Do you understand?"

She nodded again, but more slowly. The direction of his thought was clear.

"The *nasrani,* the *faama,* now has a woman from my household. I am now without a woman. You understand how that diminishes a man in our lands." He left a slight interrogation on the last phrase. She didn't respond.

"Therefore, for now, you will serve me. You shall replace the woman I sent to the *komanda.* You shall do this to serve your lineage and to ensure our good relations. Do you understand?"

Nyelle understood quite clearly. But she refused his terms. "I shall serve you," she answered. Then her courage grew allowing her to continue, "But unless the kola nuts pass from you to the lineage and the terms are accepted I shall *not* come to your bed." Ten kola nuts were the accepted and recognized sign of the first step in negotiating a marriage alliance between families.

Samba sat silent for a moment, erect on his seat, his white shirt shining. His chest was broad and powerful. Though seated, he was still a tall and impressive man. "Do you understand," he began, and she could see that he was making an effort to control himself, "that conditions in this cantonment, between the people of the town and the power of the *nasrani,* are not as you have seen before? Kri Koro is under a new power. Those responsible for the town seek an arrangement. Your role is one that women have played through the ages: to establish the alliance, to join the powers. You must accept what is asked of you."

She said nothing. She would not accept. The powers of the town asked for something against honor and decency. It was not a sacrifice for the community. The secrecy alone proved that. She had heard of human sacrifices: the princess paraded through a town to be fed to a monster. The public nature of that event made it legitimate. All were informed, all had consented. There was the value.

Here there was no public knowledge, no recognition. She was a bribe from Gaoussou Condé to Samba Ly. She would not accept that role. "I am a *horon*, a noble woman of the Condé lineage," she answered him. "I will not give my body outside of marriage."

Instantly, his fist shot out, swinging to knock her from her seat. But to the surprise and amazement of both of them—for Nyelle expected the blow to land—his fist stopped two handspans from her cheek. He was the one to recoil and fall back off his seat. Nyelle felt nothing but a movement of air by her cheek. Samba Ly picked himself up. He shook his fists and glowered at her. "What have you done?" he roared, and again he struck at her, this time with both fists coming together in a roundhouse. Again, he was repelled; his fists and arms swung back and again he fell back. He rose and tried to kick her: his foot bounced back and he tipped over.

After this last attempt at violence, he stopped. He glared at her. "I have heard stories of Condé woman witchery," he said. "I shall consider you as such. Since you cannot serve me as I need, I shall send you to one who needs a servant and who can probably deal with your sorcery."

* * *

Marco talked with Sylla, the *garanke*, discussing the preparation of the skin. It would be five days for the proper preparation. This gave them time to talk about cusoms and history. The name Sylla was not Maninka; his clan claimed Soninke origins. Marco knew little of the Soninke; in the region north of Geba the term signified an unbeliever. To his surprise Sylla claimed to be a Muslim and denied that the term Soninke meant a pagan.

"No, no," Sylla insisted. "The Soninke dispersed from Wagadu in times long gone." He sighed. "It is said that the kingdom was rich because of gold that came from a serpent of the earth. The serpent was slain, and that ended the rains of gold. The head of the serpent flew into the air, to the south. It brought gold where it landed. But no man has found the serpent's head." He shrugged. "I travelled north once, into Bondu. Their land is parched and baked. Further north, beyond the river, it is desert. Here," Sylla gestured around them to the green trees and grasses, "water is not usually a problem, although the farmers always complain about the rains. I believe the Soninke moved south to escape the desert." Thus, perhaps, Sylla's ancestors had settled in the heart of the Manding. Marco noted the association of the Soninke and of gold, and wondered about the tale Tristan's grandfather had heard.

Marco and Tristan waited the five days until Sylla, as the master *garanke,* declared that the lion's hide was ready. Marco knew nothing of the details of the work after the lion's carcass was butchered for the feast. The tanners worked in privacy, scraping the skin and soaking it in various mixtures (a potash liquid, a brew made from acacia pods) to ensure that corruptible flesh became enduring leather, and further, that the leather was not some stiff and brittle dried stuff, but soft and pliant as it had been while the lion lived. With some ceremony, Sylla's group of workers brought out their bundle. No one made a speech; the *garankelu* were not *griots.* They expected their work to speak for their skills.

Sylla laid their bundle on the ground before the two *nasrani.* A crowd had followed the leather workers and now spread around them, elbowing each other to ensure a good view. Slowly, Sylla unfolded the skin and spread it out, the tawny fur golden against the red earth of the village ways, the head laid before them. The mane was dark, and the *garankelu* had preserved as much as they could of the lion's mask, so that a snout lay before Tristan's feet. The tail stretched out into the crowd. The eye-holes were empty. Marco tried to remember if he had noticed the lion's eyes. He couldn't.

Sylla then presented to each *nasrani* a small leather pouch. Marco cupped his hand under the leather and felt many hard, small objects; he opened it and found, as he half-expected, the teeth of the lion. Tristan's bag contained the lion's claws.

"These will make significant gifts. We should reward those who have helped us," said Marco, speaking in French. Tristan agreed immediately and handed him the bag of claws.

Marco turned to Sylla. "We do not know your customs, or the traditional division of the animal in this part of the Manding." He had heard that when a hunter killed an animal, there was a specific division of its limbs and organs that observed local alliances and obligations. He had no idea what claims might be advanced here, especially with such a special beast as the lion.

He thought over the village's response to their arrival. The feast of the lion's flesh, a small portion distributed into pots in every compound leading to a full night of dancing, a wild procession through town. Geba had no such celebrations. That night had been spent in dance and song, following the drum-leader playing the high-pitched *jembe* that spoke to the heart and the marrow, following also the hands of young women from the village who danced from hand to hand of the men in the parade, singing some hymn of praise, and then weaving back into the throng. All of them made sure they were wearing their finest cloths, and many scented themselves with aromatic smokes and oils. He would never have dreamed the village contained so many attractive young women. He danced with them and lost himself in dreams, and occasionally remembered to look at Tristan. The American was trying to follow the steps of the dance, clumsy but clearly good-natured and well-intentioned, and several times a young woman would come to him and try to lead him through the steps. The village had made the two strangers their own that night.

Now was the time to offer a return for that warm hospitality. Five assistants had helped Sylla to tan the lion's hide and escorted him in its delivery. Marco reached into Tristan's pouch and counted out five claws. These he offered to the tanners. Each took the claw in both hands, bowed slightly, and drew back, muttering thanks. To Sylla, Marco offered a claw and a tooth, searching his pouch to find an incisor. Then he reached into his own store of goods, the little bag of beads, and pulled out two red glass cylinders that he laid on either side of the tooth in the man's hands. Sylla grunted in satisfaction; clearly he could envision an arrangement of beads and tooth that would bring him prestige or profit.

Other teeth and beads went to the village leader, a portly man with a wisp of a beard. He later said he would provide them with an escort to the next village, and that from there they would be only two days' march from Kri Koro, which he understood to be their destination, since there was another *nasrani* there. He hoped they would bring good report of this village if they chose to mention their passage to the *nasrani komanda*.

* * *

Ramata decided to depart quietly. She didn't want a confrontation with Samba Ly. Visiting the market, talking with the women, she learned who might have space to share. She went to a Sanogo woman who traded in spices and quickly came to an arrangement. Then she stopped by the potters to commission one or two specially designed pots. It was simple to bring her belongings from the cantonment to her new quarters: she recruited two Sanogo boys as porters. She quickly packed her clothing and other possessions in a leather trunk. After her nomadic life with Samba Ly, it was a familiar routine. More painful was the new task of sorting her own belongings from his. Before they left her chamber she paused, hesitant, and then told the boys to wait. She went out and approached Binta Dieng, a *jambur* with whom she had always been on good terms.

"My sister," she began. Binta immediately led her to a quiet space away from the bustle of the cantonment's kitchen. Ramata smiled.

"My time in this cantonment is done," she announced. "I do not know what path..." she paused. She didn't want to speak the name of Samba Ly. Binta laid her hand on Ramata's arm and then squeezed. "I think I have some useful skills, and there are opportunities in this town." Binta nodded agreement. All Wolof, female and male, were enterprising. She suspected how Ramata might start. Ramata had often done their hair.

"I shall be happy to tell a possible customer where to go," she answered. "Should an angry man inquire, my knowledge will vanish."

Ramata embraced her. "There is a Sanogo woman in the market," she said, and the other woman nodded.

"Spices?"

"Yes. She will know where to find me."

"*Ba beneen nyom.*"

That evening Kandia Traore came by the Sanogo compound to inquire if Ramata could style her hair in a way...yes, like Nyelle's, but more impressive, more stylish. Ramata considered her face and its proportions. Kandia's cheeks were rounder than Nyelle's. Her brows were good. Ramata described possible coiffures. Kandia listened, tried to imagine effects, and soon agreed to one of Ramata's ideas.

With a first customer, Ramata's concerns for the future eased. She had dressed the hair of Nyelle of the Condé lineage; she would now dress the hair of a Traore girl. She was dealing with the elite of Kri Koro. So long as she could vary the styles and the accessories, she would be able to support herself. She needed more beads. They were so useful in highlighting and profiling the braids of hair. She had not yet found a bead merchant in the market, although she knew such men must pass through the town: there was enough glass and porcelain and amber and coral and shell around the necks or on the ears of the local women to prove there was a good trade in the commodity. She wondered what else she might be able to use. Threads? Wool? Feathers?

* * *

"*Yamari yo*!" Korongo Kuyate began his performance.

He arrived before the noon meal, and after that there was much talk. Löwenstein wished to record as much as possible, using some new form of *nasrani* machine, but the cylinders needed to be replaced at intervals. So there must be pauses.

Kuyate required a comfortable seat, for himself and for his accompanist, and reviewed the terms of payment. After the meal came tea, and then a certain amount of what Löwenstein considered fidgeting as the singer settled himself and tuned his *kora*. The *kora* was unexpected. It was an instrument, something like the arm of a catapult: a long curved wooden stem rising from a great skin-covered bowl, its arc transected by harp-like strings attached on either side of the stem and fastened to a bridge across the bowl. The fastenings on the stem needed repeated minute adjustments. Löwenstein couldn't help thinking of a lutenist adjusting his mobile frets. He wondered, having observed many performers, if this habitual activity was intended to induce a performance trance—that state of mind that allows the storyteller to enter the story world.

Seated near Löwenstein, Sisibé felt a thrill. Ordinary stories told around the hearth began with ordinary words, or with their name: "*Talen*! a story," someone would say, and then introduce some new adventure of the hare or the little orphan boy or girl. But *yamari yo!* moved the story into a higher and nobler realm. The implicit claim was that the subsequent delivery would be a matter of history and past lore, not the inventions of a singer aiming to please. Those songs almost always started by reciting the names of the person from whom the singer desired a reward.

> *Yamari yo!*
> *N'ye Mari Jata le ma!*
> *N'ye Nare Magan Konate le ma!*
> *I la jelilu bara i kan bo!*
> *N'ye Manding maana le ma!*

Korongo Kuyate was singing of Mari Jata who founded the

empire of Mali. Löwenstein had asked him to sing of the great kings of the region, so the starting point was obvious. He didn't consider the early history of the land. He began instead with a conflict: when two co-wives gave birth at almost the same time, but the first messenger stopped to join in a meal. So the second-born was the first acknowledged. The stage was set for rivalry. The Berte woman felt a visceral hatred for her co-wife. That hatred moved her to enlist sorcerers, the *kortekèlu,* who hexed the son of Sogolon Condé so that his legs were crippled and he crawled on four limbs like a dog. His infirmity left the path clear for her son Dankaran Tuman to become king in time.

Though crippled in body, the child Mari Jata had abilities, perhaps from his mother. His age group soon reached the time of circumcision, when hair began to appear around their *foto.* Mari Jata's father would not allow his crippled son to undergo the ritual. On the day appointed for the master of the knife to do his cutting, Mari Jata wielded his powers. That morning the *numu,* the smith who was to perform the circumcision, came to his ruler, Nare Magan Cenyi to confess that he could no longer perform the ceremony. His penis had regained its hood; he was no better than a *bilakoro,* an immature boy. Nare Magan Cenyi heard the man and then reached into his own trousers. His face changed as his hands found their mark. He summoned his *jeli,* Jankuma Doka, and asked him whether he was still an adult man. The *jeli* was surprised at the question, but bent to make the necessary examination. He was faint when he turned back.

Inquiries were made. The trail led to the son of Sogolon who had announced that if he was not to be circumcized then no one should be. Many had heard him. Very quickly, Nare Magan Cenyi agreed that his son Mari Jata should be allowed to participate in the ceremony.

At this point Löwenstein stopped the story to change the cylinders on his recording machine. Sisibé and the nameless *siratigi* had been whispering comments to him that allowed him to follow the tale.

Following the circumcision ceremony, the new young adult men withdrew to a secluded camp where they healed, hobbled around, were instructed in traditions, lore, and decorum, and finally were released. To mark their return, there was a traditional meal, a dish with a sauce flavored with the leaves of the baobab tree: a condiment easily available, for baobab trees were often planted in the center of a village. The young men needed only to climb up on the roots, or perhaps to shinny up a rope thrown over a branch, to pick some leaves for their mothers.

But Mari Jata couldn't perform this task. The Berte woman, rejoicing in the way she had protected her own son, couldn't help taunting Sogolon Condé about her son's inability, and Sogolon Condé, humiliated, couldn't control her tears. Mari Jata asked the cause, although he knew quite well why her cheeks were wet.

"*Nare Magan, I te wilila?* Will you not rise!" she cried, and then covered her face, ashamed at the outburst.

His response was to crawl to her hut, in whose shade he rested, and to raise his hands against the ochre walls of clay. His muscles stiffened; his arms pushed, his body went rigid, and his bent legs straightened slightly. He raised his hands further up the wall, and a spasm went down from the forearms to the legs, lifting him slightly higher. Again and again he pushed, rising ever higher against the wall as his mother watched agasp, until finally the legs beneath his body had straightened completely and he was standing erect against the wall of the hut, his head brushing against the overhanging thatch. For a moment he stood, and his head turned from the wall of the hut into the courtyard. Then he dropped his hands from the wall and his body turned, supported only by his feet. His eyes did not meet his mother's, but as she watched in wonder, his legs began to move. Step by step he advanced, past the hearth, past the limit of the compound, into the paths of the town.

"People of Manding!" screamed his mother. "Today is a great day! Never have I seen a day like this one!" and at the sound of her voice the household gathered, as well as neighbors and passers-by. All could appreciate the marvel before them, for the infirmity of Sogolon's son was well-known.

Step by step he advanced until he reached the nearest baobab. He did not try to climb it. Instead, he spread his arms and somehow they enfolded the vast circumference of the trunk. He braced himself, flexed his legs and stood taller. The tree shuddered and came loose from the ground. Several boys up in the branches fell down.

Deliberately he carried the tree back to his mother's hut. "Mother," he said, "they will now come to you for their flavorings." Then he laid it down, while she and the other people of the town cried themselves hoarse singing his praises and acclaiming his deed.

Kuyate had clearly worked himself to a climax of the performance at this point; his speech became almost incomprehensible as he uttered snatches of praise-songs in a declamatory mode. His cadenced narrative, flowing with the notes from the strings of his *kora,* dissolved into evocative fragments of recalled songs and odes.

The *siratigi* looked at Sisibé. "We shall have trouble translating those fragments of the *faasa,*" he commented. The *faasa* is the praise-song attached to any great lineage. Sisibé was mildly comforted by the implied promise that the *siratigi* would help him with the translations, for already he was feeling inadequate to the task of explaining the nuances of the *jeli*'s phrasing to a *nasrani* who had no knowledge of life in this region.

Löwenstein was unaffected by such reactions. "*Das is sehr gut!*" he exclaimed. "*Hier haben wir ein Meisterspielman!*" And he pressed a small gift upon Kuyate before then becoming more businesslike and inquiring what the next part of the story would cover.

Balafon
A wooden xylophone associated with the Epic of Sunjata. The performer in this case is a Kuyate from Niagassola, in Guinea; they are the traditional guardians of what is said to have been the balafon of Sumanguru. The photo was taken in 2002 at a conference in Leiden, The Netherlands

CHAPTER X

SAMBA LY'S ANGER WAS righteous. He had offered an eminently desirable woman, expecting access, influence, and eventually power. In exchange, he would be compensated by a young and nubile woman of good family who would enhance his status in this close-knit town. And now he was also denied his desires. He couldn't understand how the girl, promised and delivered, had resisted him.

Now he was alone. Ramata had disappeared. He would not go looking for her. His status as war leader for the *nasrani* cantonment didn't admit domestic squabbles. Knowing Ramata, he could be sure that if he found her, everyone within one hundred yards would hear her views. On reflection, the loss was not great. Ramata was aging. Had he not been a soldier following the *nasrani* assignments, he would long since have given her two or three co-wives with whom to share chores and over whom she would have ruled as the senior wife. Besides, she had given him no sons.

His plans for influence with the *nasrani komanda* weren't advancing smoothly. He blamed the German ethnographer who had arrived and bellowed, mixing French and German expletives, preaching an understanding of the African past. Sisibé had become more important to the *komanda* than his officer. Rivalry fueled his anger.

He needed information on their discussions. He left his dark chambers and called for Gorkel. The lad appeared quickly. Samba laid his hand on Gorkel's shoulder. "*Ngar* [come]," he said. "Let us find some food." He assumed the boy was fully aware of Ramata's departure.

There was a woman who grilled fish in the evenings not too far from the cantonment. They loaded their bowls with *to* and fish and began to eat by the light of the glowing embers. Carefully, Samba Ly inquired about the extent of the boy's explorations of the cantonment and what he might be able to hear.

Proudly, Gorkel claimed he knew every inch of the space and that he was sure he would soon be learning the secrets of the *nasrani* magic. "If," he qualified the answer, "this *nasrani* shares in them." He still had doubts about the status of *komanda* Dumont. No one had ever seen him with a weapon; no one had been executed by the knife or the rifle.

Samba Ly reassured Gorkel that this was an authentic *nasrani*. "The *nasrani* no longer need to blast the *farafin* with cannon; the *farafin* leaders have drunk the *degue*. Now the *nasrani* seek wealth. There are opportunities for those who serve them." He paused, and Gorkel nodded eagerly. "So keep your ears open, and keep me informed what you may hear."

* * *

Before noon Marco, Tristan, the lion's skin, a porter, and an honor guard of hunters arrived at the outskirts of Kri Koro. Marco and Tristan had been accompanied every step of the way, over two days and through many villages. The excitement of a lion skin and a *nasrani* lion-slayer preceded them faster than they walked. Everywhere they were greeted by screams from children and praise from adults. Their path inevitably led to the village center where a leader greeted them and sometimes a singer chanted something. Neither understood the words, but Marco knew the conventions. He slipped each singer some small present, cowries or perhaps a glass bead if the audience's attitude signalled that the singer was a master. They would then unfold the skin to be admired by all who wished, often in a procession. Their former escort would bow to them and back off while a new crew arrived: a stalwart youth to carry the skin, and hunters in their ocher shirts, often studded with charms. Marco had more respect for the older hunters with fewer charms; they were more business-like and efficient.

The small caravan paused at the sight of Kri Koro. The path led down through fields and then into the town, hidden by a canopy of trees that obscured the thatched roofs. On a hill to the south they saw a bungalow and other buildings, clearly European, marked by angles and straight planes rather than curves and contours.

Tristan voiced the doubts Marco felt. "The more quietly we enter this town, the better our chances of finding..." he left the gold unspoken. Marco agreed. He thanked their escort and dismissed them. Then he took the lion skin on his own head, becoming Tristan's bearer. It was a tacit acknowledgement of a rebalancing of their statuses. Until the lion, Marco had really been in charge, although their quest was driven by Tristan's knowledge. Tristan had established an ascendancy, for the moment; every village honored Tristan as the lion-killer.

Marco and Tristan followed the red trail down towards the town, through scrub and into fields. The path led them past a hovel at some distance from the line of palms and mango trees that marked the edge of town. It was a poor and inadequate dwelling made of palm-fronds and branches and bits of mud.

An old woman was sitting on a piece of log in front of the house smoking a pipe. The smoke swirled around her in tendrils.

"*Nasrani-kelu*!" she called as they came level with her home.

"Our mother," answered Marco, politely. "I hope you are well."

"You have come," she stated. "You," she looked at Tristan, "have come across the waters. And you," this time at Marco, "have accompanied him. You were detained by the Fula, who gave you chickens." Marco realized she was speaking the Mandinga of Geba, not the Maninka of this region. "You were troubled in Sangalan, and the chief gave you sheep to replace the chicken you lost." She paused and grinned at Marco. Marco was unsettled. He knew gossip preceded them, but only he should know about the chicken. "The lion prepared to assault your sheep, and the far-land *nasrani* killed him. You have taken the lion's skin. And now you have come to Kri Koro to seek wealth. Is it not so?"

"*Tinye don* [true]," he answered, amazed at her description of their venture. "You are a woman of knowledge, our mother."

"Then sit with me," she invited them. "You need a *jatigi* in this town, and I know a person who can help you. She will be coming soon. There is water in the pot."

* * *

"No, the only rifle I have is the standard issue Lebel," said Dumont. He and Löwenstein were discussing hunting equipment. Löwenstein had brought a long-barreled Mauser and on the recommendation of a white hunter he had met in southeastern Africa he also had a Martini repeater. Past expeditions included well-armed zoologists hoping for some as yet unnamed species of antilope or larger beast, but Löwenstein no longer included this category of collector when he traveled. He thought of the passenger pigeon of North America that once darkened the skies and whose last survivor now lived in a zoo, and the blaubok of southern Africa, and the dodo.

Hunting was a noble sport: a sport for nobles, reserved in Europe for the elite who could maintain their preserves with deer and boar and bear. But the opportunities on the African continent were superb and enviable: fearsome predators such as lions, leopards, crocodiles; massive and dangerous prey such as elephants, rhinos, hippos; and all the edible herbivores ranging from the great eland to the dainty dik-dik. Still, the game in West Africa could not rival the masses of wildebeest, gazelles, and impala that spread over the savannas of eastern Africa. The forests might teem with life, but understanding of that life lay in the realms of botany and entomology and probably also mycology. The forests offered not so much macrofauna such as elephants or antelope, but what he might term macroflora: enormous trees that supported a parasitic or symbiotic population from all the families of the animal kingdom. Associated with them were mesofauna in the form of insects, frogs and tiny rodents.

"We should go out," said Löwenstein. "I hear there are elephants in the region. Even an antelope would be useful. My porters prefer what they call bush-meat to any other food. They say it has greater savor."

"Then let us go tomorrow," agreed Dumont politely. "I

have not yet gone north of the town. There are few villages, but fewer people may mean more game. Sisibé will find us guides." He glanced over. The intepreter's attention was divided. Dumont had been invited to observe how Löwenstein recorded a performance; the German had been delighted with the first occasion. On impulse, Dumont suggested to Assya that she too might come. Assya brought Nyelle. Sisibé clearly found Nyelle most attractive.

Dumont had no idea where Nyelle had come from. He knew she was not being paid from the cantonment accounts. He examined those very carefully. She appeared and now accompanied Assya, to whom he was offering a small stipend 'for living expenses' he explained. He had never tried to keep a woman and was unsure of the proprieties. He was quite sure of the improprieties. They were why he kept the woman. He wasn't in love, although perhaps—certainly?—he was infatuated. She kept her distance; while she yielded her body with delightful ardor, she hadn't yielded her heart. He didn't care. He could never bring her back to his home in Berry; he could never formalize a relationship. White men didn't marry black women. This was almost a spoken rule of the colonial service he had entered. The only exception might apply to the French *départements d'outre-mer* in the Caribbean. Dumas, for instance, whose sagas of the French past had inspired in Dumont the urge to great deeds, had been of mixed ancestry. But as yet Africa offered no respectability to such couples.

The mixed party was waiting for Korongo Kuyate to arrive to continue his commissioned performances of the *Manding maana*. The *jeli* arrived and quickly settled himself and his *naamu*-sayer in their appointed positions. The *naamu*-sayer was an apprentice who sat facing him as he played and sang, and the apprentice marked the rhythmic cadences of the master with responses, echoing the phrases from the lead or simply punctuating the sequence with the agreement, *naamu*.

Today, Korongo was describing the consequences of Mari Jatas's miraculous recovery from the crippling sorcery practiced upon him by his mother's co-wife. Mari Jata became a hunter, feeding entire villages with the game he slaughtered. His half-brother, Dankaran Tuman, felt threatened by the growing popularity of Mari Jata. Dankaran Touman enlisted further occult powers against his *fa-den*, stronger than those Mari Jata had already overcome: the nine witches of the Manding. For the price of a bull the witches agreed to do away with Mari Jata. Mari Jata learned of the plot. He came to the witches alone and almost naked. He stood before them and bargained: for his life, he would offer not one bull, but nine buffaloes. The witch-women listened and pondered. They admired his courage. Some admired his body. All weighed the bargain and acknowledged that he offered far more than his half-brother. They spared him, and he paid them.

But the signs were clear to him, to his mother, to his far-sighted sister. They were not safe in this region; they must depart and find refuge elsewhere.

Bara kala ta le, Simbon!
Pick up your bow, Simbon,
Pick up your bow and go!
Pick up your bow!

That was the song chanted as the small family party (a mother, her sons, her daughter) went off on their road.

At this point Löwenstein intervened. There was a delay

between utterance and understanding. Two interpreters worked next to him, whispering a running translation. Two more took notes. To the side, another assistant was minding a new machine, a phonograph that recorded the sounds in squiggly lines on a wax cylinder. Löwenstein didn't trust the wax, given the heat of the region. He interrupted with a question, taking the story back a moment.

"These nine witches!" he barked. "Who are they? What are their names?"

The question was translated; Korongo had paused at the sound of Löwenstein's voice and lowered the kora before him. "The witches of Manding...are a delicate matter. Mari Jata alone could meet them as an equal. Other men have not his power. Some names have been remembered. Sititi and Sototo, they were the leaders. Miniamba and Muruni-Pembele were the enforcers; one took the form of a serpent to strike from the path, the other wielded a blade to strike heads from shoulders. Sungana and Kulutugubaga were the healers. There was Tumu Maniya, but I have not heard her powers, and then..."

Korongo was interrupted. From the side, Assya spoke up, her clear voice carrying through the crowd. "*Jeli-kè*!" she called. "You should remember that Tumu Maniya was no witch. She was a *jeli-muso*, the greatest of her time, with a voice that thrilled the heart. She composed that song of the bow you were just singing. No *jeli-kè* should forget her contribution to your art." Assya paused. No one protested her intervention so she continued. "The last three witches are Jimbi-Jamba, who learned the secrets of the night, Dagani, who cleaned up after her sisters, and Kamisa."

Korongo stared in shock at such contradiction. As Assya continued, he registered agreement and then a startled pleasure, the delight of a specialist discovering new information. He nodded. *"Tinye don,"* he acknowledged. "Your knowledge is greater than mine in this matter." This situation was embarrassing for a *jeli*: to be corrected publicly? And by a stranger—even more surprisingly, by a beautiful young woman, the sort who normally stays silent, content to attract admiration? He was not sure how to respond. This maiden possessed knowledge he didn't (and how could that be?), but her correction rang true; he had always wondered about Tumu Maniyan.

Then his eyes caught sight of Nyelle, sitting beside Assya. He might be uncertain about one woman, but he recognized a daughter of the ruling lineage. He could assert his traditional role and mastery. "Ah! Condé-*muso!*" he cried, and then launched into the *faasa*, the traditional praise:

Tira Magan ni Kanke jan!
Suu saare jon!
Tuma ni Bagi moden!
Jonmakan ni Bagi moden!
Bari ni Kanijo moden!
Fele ngana kulun bali Tunkara!

"What is this?" Löwenstein's question was quiet, but it carried. All knew who paid them. Korongo stopped his song. Sisibé and the two translators glanced at each other to see who would tackle the intricate explanations required. The translators waited on him: he was the local. Sisibé noted they also glanced at the *siratigi*. Their silence was his cue.

"The woman with the *komanda,*" Sisibé began delicately, "corrected the *jeli* when he was naming the witches of the

Manding. She said that Tumu Maniyan was not a witch, but a singer who composed the *Song of the Bow*, the song that marks Mari Jata's departure into exile. Then the *jeli*," and he nodded to Korongo Kuyate, who would surely note the word, "saw a noble-woman of the Condé clan and praised her in terms of her ancestry."

"Can you explain his praises?" demanded Löwenstein.

"No." Sisibé was definite. "The language of the *faasa*, the clan praise song, is ancient and obscure. You must ask Kuyate for his interpretation."

Löwenstein stared at him then said, just loud enough to be heard, "*Ach! Hier haben wir etwas echtes*!" He smiled at this encounter with deep-rooted tradition. He turned to the *jeli*, nudging the assistant on his right hand to translate. "Your tale of Mari Jata has been interrupted. Perhaps you will now tell me of the *faasa* that you sang, and how you understand it?"

The *jeli* nodded agreement. A *jeli* always accommodates the patron.

As the session devolved into explication and interpretation, Dumont thanked Löwenstein and departed, followed by Assya and Nyelle. Sisibé was struck by the intense gaze that the *siratigi* focused on Assya.

Rifles
Photo taken in Atar, Mauritania, in 1987

CHAPTER XI

ASSYA AND DUMONT DINED on a chicken dish with onions and olives brought from N'Daar. She tried to explain the import of the *faasa*. He understood the question of lineages and names, *siya* and *jamu*, and quickly grasped the relations of noble lineages and their associated *jeli* families.

"So a Kuyate will serve a Keita, a Jabaate will serve a Traore?"

"With local variations."

"We have local variations in France," he admitted. "How did these relations come about?"

"The first Kuyate was Jankuma Doka, who served Mari Jata, the first Keita. Two Traore brothers faced a beast; the younger proved braver and slew it. The elder became the first Jabaate and sang his praises."

"The instrument this *jeli* played..."

"The kora."

"Is he a master?" His voice was tinged with a wistfulness, a memory of lost musics and dying strains.

"Kuyate is a master of knowledge and lore. He plays well, but he is not the most skilled I've heard. Shall we find you a *griot?*"

Dumont considered the offer. Should he establish himself as a *seigneur*, a feudal lord with his own minstrel? Status was not the appeal. He yearned for the enchanting music.

"Please do."

Assya didn't talk with Nyelle until the next morning. After Dumont had bathed, Nyelle came to help Assya clean and dress herself. Nyelle overflowed with questions, she was still discovering the ways of the cantonment and wasn't at all sure of her status. That concern reminded her that on the previous afternoon they had departed without leaving a gift for the *jeli* who praised her.

Such neglect was almost unforgiveable. But was she now entitled to praises?

Assya found herself delighted by Nyelle, entertained by her questions and curiosity. She treated her not as a servant, but as a younger sister from whom she expected deference and assistance, but who was otherwise not unequal to her.

"We shall send a gift to Kuyate," she reassured Nyelle. "He will learn the value of the franc." She explained coinage to Nyelle and showed examples: the centimes, the francs.

"It's curious," commented Nyelle, recalled that moment when the *jeli* had praised her before the crowd. "My *bemba* taught me a verse that was a bit like the *jeli*'s, but still not the same."

"Was it an ordinary family verse, or was it for a special occasion?"

"I sang it for the old woman at the edge of town," explained Nyelle, "when I didn't want to be given to Samba Ly." She hesitated at the name.

Assya considered her memory of Condé praises. "What was the verse?"

Nyelle recalled the verse with effort. Much had happened since she learned it.

Condé muso!
Tuma ni Bagi moden!
Jonmakan ni Bagi moden!
Sigi ma diya!
Sigi ni gundo! Kunsigi ni sanu!

Assya listened with idle curiosity, and then with astonishment. She made Nyelle repeat the verse three times and explain where she had found the old woman.

In the crawlspace under the floorboards Gorkel listened. He hoped constantly to learn something intimate about the *nasrani*'s power. He also now found himself fascinated by Assya. Moving from the bed of Samba Ly to that of the *komanda* had transformed her in his eyes. Her beauty was enhanced by the mystique of some arcane knowledge that allowed her such easy intercourse. He noted Nyelle mentioned Samba Ly. Surely he must inform Samba Ly of this conversation?

* * *

A bit later that day Ramata went to visit the old woman. She had not gone the day before. Kandia Traore had come to her, full of admiration for the coiffure she had observed on Nyelle and eager to outdo it. She wanted a style to mark her as a Traore, of the lineage of kings (to be respected and honored) while also showing her to be an attractive and nubile woman (to be appreciated and approached). She kept changing her mind as Ramata proposed little curls before the ears or dropping down her forehead. Kandia left three chickens.

One of those chickens, stewed in a pot with rice, came with Ramata as she took the path out of the village. She almost turned back when she saw two strange men seated in front of the hut. The old woman sat with them, smoking her small clay pipe. One of the men—a *nasrani,* but not a soldier and not an official—was also smoking. Just as she stopped to wonder at their presence he blew a smoke ring that rose and floated over his companion's head. His companion was a *métis,* half-African and half-*nasrani,* more familiar to Ramata.

The old woman saw her and raised her pipe in greeting and perhaps also a summons. The two men followed her gaze and saw Ramata on the path. She could not turn back now. She advanced and put down her pot near the smouldering fire. They exchanged greetings.

"N'ba,"

"Ah! den-muso! I ni bara ?"

The question about work cut the sequence of greetings short. Normally, the old woman would have asked about her family members, their health, and the conditions at her home, although the old woman knew, of course, that Ramata's family was non-existent and that her home was not a place of comfort. If the old woman mentioned work, she knew somehow of the new enterprise Ramata had undertaken.

"There is work," she answered, which was not the conventional response (all is fine, thanks). "I have found clients."

"That is good," approved the old woman. "As you see, I have *luntan* [strangers] here. They have come from different places, but now they travel together. Here you see Marco," and she pointed with the stem of her pipe, "who comes from the coastlands south of N'daar. This other," the pipe-stem swiveled, "comes from beyond the far salt-waters, where his own *bemba* told him of Kri Koro. We must count him a *ngana,* a hero, for he has slain a lion."

Ramata examined Marco and Tristan. Marco, a handsome young man, was examining her. Tristan clearly couldn't follow the conversation, but also inspected the visitor. His eyes went from Marco to the old woman to Ramata and back again. He pretended calm, but his evident confusion amused Ramata. She smiled at the two men.

"You are welcome in Kri Koro," she began, "although I am not a child of this town."

"Ramata comes from the world of *signares*," interrupted the old woman. Marco would understand this term. It evoked that world of traders, brokers, intermediaries, facilitators, agents…factors that swarmed the port of N'daar in Senegal, bridging the worlds of the *nasrani* and the *farafin* and promoting profit. In this description, Marco and Ramata overlapped in their experience and knowledge. Marco nodded. Tristan didn't. Turning to Marco, the old woman continued, "You need lodging in this town. You seek a source of wealth—that's what drew your fellow over the salt waters. I don't think you will find what he seeks, but you may still find wealth. Ramata may choose to help you." She turned to Ramata. "Can you find lodging for this glorious lion-slayer" (she used the hunter's honorific title, *simbon*) "and his associate? I think that you too may profit from their presence."

Ramata considered. There was space within the compound in which she now lived. The owners would be astounded at the thought of a *nasrani* living among them, and delighted. And a *nasrani* who had killed a lion! Ramata now realized what the folded bundle of leather lying before the two men must be.

"I can offer lodging," she answered. "And if..." She paused, remembering the client of the morning and her demands. "If by any chance they have a store of beads, the glass-ware, *verroterie*, not necessarily items of value, then we may have an opportunity to realize some profits."

She looked at the two men for their response to her implied offer. Marco was smiling broadly. Tristan, taking his cue from Marco's smile, was nodding.

* * *

Korongo Kuyate was lodged with kinsmen not far from the market. Sisibé found him easily. Passing through the market he made a purchase wrapped in a broad banana leaf. The *jeli* was resting when Sisibé arrived, but rose and greeted him warmly. The normal delicacies of status (a *jeli* counted as inferior) and age (the *jeli* was older, and due respect) were set aside. Besides, Korongo had learned that Sisibé had selected him among the many *jelilu* claiming mastery and knowledge. A connection with the cantonment should lead to profit, or at least enhanced status. The days were long gone in which a *jeli* who pleased a king might expect the reward of a hundred goats and a hundred sheep and a hundred cows and maybe even a hundred slaves.

He called out, and almost before they had finished the extensive exchange of greetings a young boy appeared with tea.

Sisibé brought the Condé name into the conversation. Korongo nodded and offered some information on their past: their royal antecedents and more recently how Cejan and Gaoussou had fought against Samori, but survived.

Sisibé recalled Korongo's praise of the Condé lineage the day before which he had uttered when he saw a young woman. The *jeli* suppressed a grin; he grasped the import of this visit and was delighted. He knew all about Nyelle: she had cared for

Cejan, whom he respected, and was being pawned off by Gaoussou, for whom he had less respect but who now held power. The mystery was why she was not in the bed of Samba Ly, for all the signs pointed clearly to that outcome. Still, he didn't wish to see a Maninka princess sent without ceremony to the bed of some *nasrani* or his surrogate, which clearly had been Gaoussou's plan.

Korongo answered Sisibé's gambit. He thought the young woman would make an excellent bride for such a worthy servant of the new authority. Her kinship connections were valuable, and even better, she was an intelligent and diligent young woman. Sisibé broke into a chuckle.

"*Jeli-ke*! I infer that you approve my intentions. Are you willing to carry some kola nuts for me to the Condé elders?"

"It will be an honor, and you may trust me to bring back a favorable response." The older man bowed slightly. Sisibé handed him the nuts he had just purchased in the market.

* * *

Dumont returned to Löwenstein's camp in the early afternoon. The German was overseeing his assistants who were transcribing and collating the different recordings from the previous day. The praises that so often appeared in the narrative left him baffled and frustrated. He quickly agreed to Dumont's suggestion that they leave the town and walk up into the wooded hills to see what game they might encounter.

They went north through the town to the slopes of the hills on the east side of the valley and quickly found a trail that led up along the slope of the hill, threading among the large trees. They walked several miles and came to a small cliff that allowed them a view of the valley; they paused to enjoy the breeze and the sunlight. Looking down, Dumont saw an oddity and pointed it out: not far from the foot of the cliff another ledge of rock showed through the lush vegetation. Just in front of the ledge were dark spots.

"What can those be?" he asked. No one answered. The question deserved investigation. The hunter led them down the steep slope adjoining the cliff, beating the bushes in front of his feet to scare off any snakes.

There were three holes, each about eighty centimeters across, cut down into what seemed to be rock, although not the hardest of rocks. They were spaced some three meters apart. They peered down into the holes, into darkness. They could see nothing. "The holes are man-made," observed Löwenstein. "No natural process produces such holes in rock."

"Why dig holes in rock?"

Their eyes met, and both spoke: "Mines."

Dumont put the question on all their minds, "What would draw men to mine such rock?"

The answer was obvious. Gold! They thought no more of hunting but returned to Kri Koro. They would come back later to pursue this new quarry.

Gold Mine
For an in color view & more details of this & all pictures in this book – make sure to visit the author's FaceBook page: https://www.facebook.com/stephen.belcher.7370/

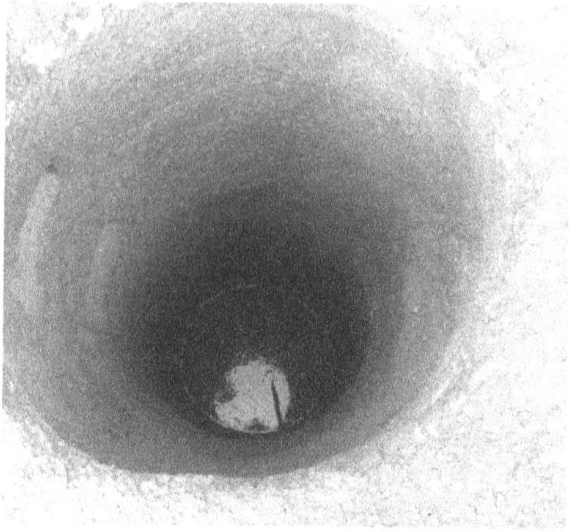

CHAPTER XII

THE SANOGO COURTYARD WAS unusually busy with unexpected visitors, their real purpose was to glimpse the two *nasrani* and the lion skin spread before them. The Sanogo clan leader sat in the shade of the mango tree considering how he might turn this notoriety to use.

Marco and Tristan were each caught in their own thoughts. Tristan had reached a place of legend, but he could see no path towards his goal. This town of *banco* and thatch offered no palaces, no great temples to house a treasure. The largest building was the cantonment of the French commandant, and it represented a threat. The French might imprison foreigners without proper papers. He was lost.

Marco, not forgetting the gold, considered the commercial possibilities of a prosperous town. The children were healthy, noisy, and active. Their hair showed none of the reddish tint that marked hunger and want. Clothing was scanty and of local weave. Very few sported imported *nasrani* cloth. The utensils in the kitchen area of the compound were also local—earthen pots or wooden ladles. There was a market here.

Apart from them and visible from the street, Ramata was at work, surrounded by the paraphernalia of her new trade: calabashes of water and little clay pots of karite-butter and palm oil, and on a leather cloth an array of beads and strands of cotton and wool. She had spent a day finding providers and materials. From the Fula herdsmen she arranged a supply of carded wool from the goats and sheep in their charge. From a woodcarver she acquired a graded series of combs, from hard and stiff to fine. Best of all Marco, observing her preparations, offered her a pouch of colored glass beads.

Kandia Traore had come two days before. No doubt she now regretted having missed the opportunity to have her hair done in the presence of the *nasrani*. Today Ramata was working on the head of a Camara, the daughter of a rich smith with six apprentices. An aunt chaperoned her while two friends watched. The occasion was an imminent offer of marriage from a young man, a Condé of a collateral line (not one of the rulers of the town), she met while going to the well for water. He had called out, "You are as sweet and clear as the water you carry." The friends were sure this was a song. Ramata didn't know Maninka songs. She carefully oiled and combed the hair, pulling out the tight curls into strands she would be able to braid. She worked by thumb-breadths, slowly but steadily…And she listened.

Tristan was watching Ramata's clients and her companions with particular interest. They were pretty and lively.

* * *

Gorkel knew he should have gone immediately to Samba Ly, but (quite unusually) he met the son of a Fula herder in the market. They went off on a lark, then he ate with the herder's family. They had many questions about the cantonment and the *nasrani*. He didn't see Samba Ly until after the morning drills. Samba spotted him and waved him over after he dismissed the squad.

Gorkel began hesitantly. "I was listening to the Soninke woman and her companion. They talked about a song, part of the Condé *faasa*." Samba Ly nodded encouragingly. This was exactly why he had assigned Gorkel to that surveillance. "The Condé girl said her *bemba* had taught her a verse to sing to an old woman who lives at the edge of town. It was a Condé praise, but different from the one the *jeli* sang yesterday."

Samba Ly leaned forward. "This is how it went, when she recited it. She said it several times, because the Soninke woman suddenly became very interested and asked her to repeat it." Gorkel recited a close approximation of the verse.

"What was that last line?" asked Samba Ly.

"*Sigi ni gundo! Kunsigi ni sanu!* " repeated Gorkel. He was sure of this line because he recognized it as something other than the name of an ancestor.

"You are sure the word was *sanu*?"

"*Ko goonga*!"

"And you know that *sanu* means gold?"

Gorkel nodded.

* * *

Korongo Kuyate shook the little sack. He knew it contained ten kola nuts. That number announced that the sender was interested in marriage. Sisibé's influence had already profited him: he was now engaged with the loud *nasrani* who wished to learn the stories of the Manding's past. Sisibé also worked with the *nasrani komanda*, which meant influence. He readily accepted the interpreter's claim of noble origins in Bondu. Besides, a *jeli* never refused a profitable commission.

At the Condé compound he requested a meeting with Gaoussou Condé. Cejan might be the titular head, but Gaoussou had assigned the campground on which the German *nasrani* was settled. He was now the manager. Gaoussou received him quickly, which Korongo took as a good sign. As he approached the lineage elder, seated on a mat in the shade, Korongo straightened his back and called out a praise, "*Murulu Faganda*! *Murumurulu Faganda*!"

Gaoussou smiled acknowledgement. Korongo approached, then at a sign, seated himself on the mat. Gaoussou waved to a servant, and tea quickly appeared. They sat and sipped the first serving, the strongest and most bitter, but also the most quenching to thirst. When Gaoussou put his cup aside, Korongo did the same, and placed the sack with the kola nuts in front of himself, in sight but not yet in reach of the other man.

"*Jeli-ba*," Gaoussou greeted him. "I see you have come as an envoy. Do I know the one who sent you?"

"I come at the request of Sisibé, the interpreter at the *nasrani* cantonment. He comes of good family in Bondu. His father was chief in Fateconda. His father sent him to a *nasrani* school for the sons of chiefs. Now he serves the *nasrani komanda* as a trusted assistant."

"I have heard of him," admitted Gaoussou and looked at his *jeli*, Fadigi, seated beside him.

"The Sisibé are noble," proclaimed Fadigi. "This young man is known for his skill and his promise. He serves his *komanda* well." He skirted a delicate issue here; in Maninka society service implied lower status. The *nasrani* establishment stood outside normal conceptions of service, respecting no local protocols.

"He has met a daughter of this house," said Korongo,

moving to the point. "She serves in the cantonment of the *nasrani*." This point answered the delicacy of Fadigi's statement. Within the *nasrani* establishment, the daughter was certainly not as important as Sisibé, and both now lived outside the norms. But the offer he brought restored the traditional rules.

Korongo could not know that Gaoussou saw this offer not only as a face-saving link to the governor (a Condé woman should not be a concubine), but also as a valuable counter in his dealings with Cejan. Cejan hadn't yet delivered all the clan secrets, and he suspected that those most closely guarded were the ones most closely concerning wealth. If the promise of marriage for Nyelle might sway him, then the offer should be considered.

"You speak of Nyelle," said Gaoussou. "She is a dear child, and now is becoming a woman."

"She now attends the *komanda*'s woman," said Korongo. "And naturally her path has crossed that of Mady Sisibé. He was most favorably impressed, and so he has sent me to inquire whether you might consider an alliance with his lineage." At this point, he pushed the kola nuts across to Gaoussou. "He is modest, and has not proclaimed to me the glories of his family. I have not traveled in Bondu. I can see that he stands high in the cantonment. He is young, he is talented, he is sure to rise in this new world of the *nasrani*."

"We shall take the kola nuts," said Gaoussou, reaching for the bag. He did not open it. "We consider ourself honored by his request. But as he is a stranger in this town, we do ask for a larger token, greater than kola nuts."

Korongo nodded. The agreement came far more easily than he expected. He was not surprised Gaoussou wanted more. "I'm sure he can find a gift that matches his intentions and the worth of the girl."

* * *

Sisibé stopped in Dumont's office before going down to the German's camp. The *komanda* was looking through papers for some geologist's report. He found mostly military evaluations of communication lines, along with a good deal of imaginative speculation about the local culture. He remembered reading of a gold trade across the Sahara. How far south did it extend? If he could find gold mines in this area...Sisibé had one piece of information to pass on. A foreign *nasrani* had come to the town. They knew nothing of him. Dumont considered this question briefly. The dangers of espionage seemed minimal; no European power seemed likely to risk an incident. They were being friendly to each other. He had welcomed the German Löwenstein. He told Sibibé to document the *nasrani*'s status.

Sisibé left Dumont and went down to the German's camp. He arrived shortly after Korongo, who returned to his host family for the noon meal before going to the German *nasrani*. Korongo took a moment in his preparations to inform Sisibé that he had delivered the kola nuts and the answer was favorable, but the Condés expected some extra gift. Sisibé heard this and reflected. He was still stunned by the effect Nyelle had upon him. He constantly recalled his observations: her posture and form, her eyes and their movements, her smiles and the shape of her lips. Somehow, all these details translated into the woman of his dreams. He sent the kolas almost without conscious deliberation. Normally, he would have communicated with his own family (whatever the time required for the messages back and forth) for their opinion before sending the kolas, considering his means and her status and prospects for advancement. None of that crossed his mind. He had seen Nyelle smile—and she had smiled at him, he was sure—and that was enough.

In the midst of Löwenstein's recording equipment, Korongo finished tuning his instrument and settled himself. His apprentice sat on a stool nearby. They would continue with the story of Mari Jata, who had gone into exile. Resuming the strain that had been interrupted, the *Song of the Bow* of the *jelimuso* Tumu Maniyan, he recounted how Mari Jata and his family—curiously, not wife and children, but his mother and his siblings—had traveled from court to court, in each place being received and welcomed until a messenger came from the new king of the Manding, Dankaran Touman, with threats or bribes, demanding their death or their exile. Their welcome was then cut short. They ended up far from the Manding in the sandy desert kingdom of Mema. There Mari Jata quickly became a noted war-leader.

Then Dankaran Touman came to grief. A king from the north, Sumanguru, invaded and conquered the Manding. He did this even after accepting a bride sent from the Manding; he took the woman and the *griot* who accompanied her. Then he brought his armies and seized the land. His rule made the people very unhappy. He was not a noble, but a smith. He was not generous, but greedy and cruel. The story went about that he took the wife of his nephew because she could somehow feed ten times as many people with one pot of *to* or rice than any other woman. And this was not just any nephew: this was the son of the very sister whom he had offered to the spirits in exchange for the *balafon*, the musical instrument that had captured his soul.

So the people of the Manding resolved to call back the other son of their king who had departed to some unknown place. Their messengers took with them plants that flavored the characteristic dishes of Manding cooking. The messengers wandered far, finally they came to Mema. It was a market day. They laid out their assortment of condiments.

Soon Mari Jata's sister came by. Their mother was infirm; the sister saw to the marketing. At the Mande condiments her nose twitched. She recognized a smell. She leaned closer to examine the plants and powders. "Oh!" she exclaimed. "These are spices from the Manding! Have you come from there? Can you give us news?"

The messengers identified themselves and learned that she was the sister of the man they sought. Elated, the party accompanied her to the compound where Mari Jata resided. He and his brother were out hunting. They had each killed an antelope. Sogolon, their sister, had no food to offer these welcome guests. Yet she was a Condé woman, gifted with sight and other powers. She summoned the hearts and livers out of the carcasses of her brothers' kills so she could prepare a worthy meal for her guests. When Mari Jata was dressing his kill, he guessed from the absence of vital organs that his sister must have met a need. He chuckled. His brother was resentful and furious; he had planned to grill the liver and eat it there in the bush by himself. On their return, the brother cursed his sister, so that her wrap fell from her hips and she stood almost naked before her siblings and her guests. With a spell, she called back the wrap. Again he cursed her. Again she called it back. Mari Jata stopped the quarrel. "My brother," he judged, "your sons shall never become kings."

Korongo paused there and Löwenstein, after the translators

finished their summaries, had questions. Was Mari Jata's sister a witch? How did she come by her powers?

Sisibé sat beside the *siratigi*. The other man fixed him with a look, and then an engaging smile. "They should ask you about the powers of the Condé women," he commented. "You seemed quite taken with the maiden who came the other day."

"You had eyes for another," retorted Sisibé. Then he admitted, "*Tinyè don*. I have sent Kuyate," he nodded towards Korongo, "with the kolas to the Condé clan."

"You did well. Act when your heart moves you! What was their answer?"

"They are willing, but they wish for some signal gift to mark my interest."

"I've heard that two strange *nasrani* have come to the town, and that one of them killed a lion on the road."

"I too have heard this. I have been asked to make inquiries."

"*Ah*! They did not inform the *komanda* of their arrival?"

"No. We do not know where they are from."

"Then you should inquire about their papers. If they lack authorization..." The *siratigi* had no need to complete the sentence. If the foreign *nasrani* lacked papers that Sisibé could provide, he had leverage. The *siratigi* saw the understanding in Sisibé's eyes and continued, "I can show you the papers that were issued to this German *nasrani* as he entered the territory."

Kola Nuts
Kola nuts are chewed as a mild & bitter stimulant and they are part of social rituals through much of west Africa.
Photo taken in Atar, Mauritania, 1987

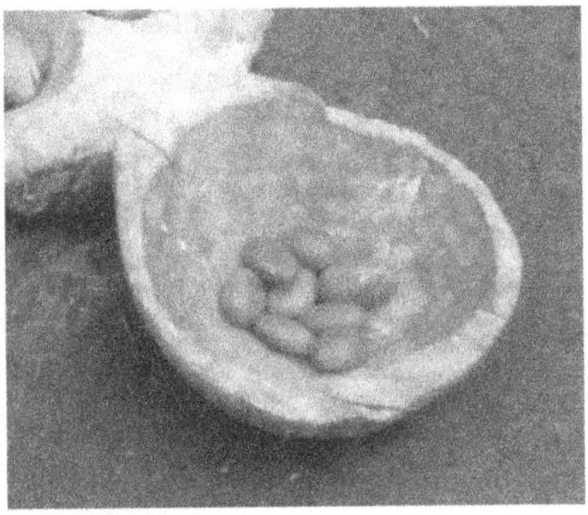

CHAPTER XIII

GAOUSSOU WAITED UNTIL THE morning after Korongo Kuyate brought the kola nuts to visit Cejan. He was still concerned about the new girl whose reports on the older man were vacuous. Still, there was no one else he considered eligible for the task. He called out before entering the hut, then moved from the bright sunlight to the gloom of the chamber. Cejan struggled to raise himself but the pillow behind his back was out of place. Gaoussou assisted him. He wanted his brother to be comfortable and well-disposed in this conversation. He didn't notice the grimace of pain that flitted over Cejan's face as his back rubbed against the fabric beneath him.

Cejan thanked him hoarsely. Gaoussou examined his brother: his eyes were bright and the mouth had the subtle motions of an alert intelligence. Cejan knew that Gaoussou desired the secrets and understood they had struck a bargain that Gaoussou would have to fulfill. Cejan wanted marriage for Nyelle.

"We have received kola nuts," began Gaoussou. "The interpreter in the cantonment, Sisibé, enlisted the help of Korongo Kuyate." He decided to gossip a bit. "You have heard that Korongo is working with the German *nasrani* who has come to learn old stories. We have lodged the German beyond the market." Cejan nodded; he knew the spot. "Korongo goes there every day or two to tell his stories, and the German *nasrani* notes them down. The *komanda* has gone down there, and certainly the *komanda* sends his interpreter to help the other *nasrani*. I think that is how he met Nyelle."

Cejan nodded. "Korongo is a master of lore."

"Yes. So this Sisibé sent the kolas. I've come to you to ask your decision." That last word was deliberately chosen, promising that Gaoussou would respect the choice of the clan elder.

"Marry her," said Cejan. "Do not worry about the bride-price. I am sure this Sisibé is a good man." Gaoussou waited a moment before nodding his acquiescence, inviting justification. Cejan understood him perfectly and showed that he remembered their last meeting and the terms laid out. He spoke more clearly than he had done in years.

"You know of the tribute of the village of Sènètela. The royal stool made of gold is hidden," he began. "I think it carries a curse. It came to earth in the time of our *bembas*, even before the time of Mari Jata. The *soma* who examined it called it the head of a serpent and said that it should be cast into a well or our sacred spring, and then it would ensure our wealth. But our distant *bemba* was enthralled by the mass of gold. This ancestor disregarded the words of the seer. He kept the golden stool as a tool of power. After the stool came, the Condé found the mines; a *soma* explained that gold had called to gold. Troubled times came to the Manding." Gaoussou nodded; he knew their history during this time. "The stool was hidden in a cavern." He paused, coughing slightly, and Gaoussou offered him some water. "The cavern is protected by powerful *dalilu* and *bolilu*."

Haltingly he continued, "This golden stool was guarded by blood. The *bilakorow* who carried it to the cave were killed. Their skulls watch over the cave to wake the guardian created by Condé magic. At the entrance to the cavern they cut the throat of a maiden of the royal line. Her spirit protects the stool. But she will answer to a rightful Condé who approaches the cave. This is how you must sing to her." And he taught Gaoussou a short verse, the same he had taught Nyelle some weeks past.

Gaoussou repeated it and departed. He might have noticed a smell, but the chamber was redolent with the odors of human occupation. On Cejan's lower back, where Djanka had neglected to wash and oil him, the bedsores had become infected.

* * *

Sisibé had no trouble finding Marco and Tristan: all knew where the *nasrani* of the lion skin throned in the Sanogo compound. He had to make his way through a crowd to enter the compound. He approached the two *nasrani* with caution. He had instructions from the *komanda* to inquire about their status. He planned to ask much more. He represented the temporal authority in this town. Still, he hesitated to pit that prestige against the immanent stature of two white foreigners, one a lion-killer. Still, he needed something from them. He introduced himself and explained that the *komanda* had asked him to verify their legal status. It was curious that they had not already presented themselves to the *komanda*. Times were delicate. Foreigners should expect attention, and for *nasrani*, of course, respect. The authorities didn't worry about the movement of villagers and townsfolk to and from the centers.

Marco tensed as he saw the interpreter making his way through the courtyard. He had expected their presence would draw attention from authorities. With that attention would come uncomfortable questions. He had mentioned the issue to Tristan. Tristan had no understanding of identity papers or travel authorizations, any more than he understood the shifting and jealous powers through which he wandered.

Marco had a story. Yes, they had papers issued in Ziguinchor by the French authorities authorizing a trading venture to the interior. While crossing the Bafing their pirogue overturned, they lost many important parts of their baggage. Sisibé nodded with sympathy. They had continued on their path. His own family had long cultivated connections over the waters and over the lands. His companion's family had partnered in past commercial activity over the waters. Marco was sure Sisibé would understand the trade had been in slaves. Circumstances had changed, and now the family sought new trading partners.

Sisibé admired their determination to overcome obstacles. Still, with great apologies, he did need to have some form of documentation to report to his *komanda*. The *mot d'ordre* from N'daar was definite. Without papers, they might be required to reside at the cantonment for a period, until their situation had been clarified and rectified. Marco grasped that they would not be treated as guests of the *komanda*.

Marco asked immediately if there might not be some method of expediting the process to replace the lost papers?

That would require extra effort on Sisibé's part, and there might be questions. Why had they not presented themselves to the *komanda*? The situation was most unusual. But he would help them in any way he could.

Sisibé left the compound with the lion skin wrapped in a brown cloth and carried on the head of a Sanogo *bilakoro*. The lad, rewareded with sugarcane, walked in awe of his load.

Dumont walked down to Löwenstein's camp. He never used the sedan chair. He associated it with the presumption of imperial status, colored also by a vision of Oriental monarchs of exceptional splendor and obesity. The Berrichon farmer in his background warned him that such pretensions were perilous, despite the glory of his uniform. It was a straight path, along well-trodden ways. The town had many shade trees, most often mangoes. A great baobab stood near the market offering little shade but serving as a hub around which vendors arranged themselves.

The *jeli* was settling himself with his apprentices while Löwenstein and his own assistants busied themselves with their own preparations involving the large cornucopia (so Dumont saw it) of their recording apparatus, the black blossom of a trumpet vine, curved to capture sounds. One assistant turned a crank to wind up the machine like a clock. Sisibé immediately joined him. He was distracted; his eyes kept slipping past Dumont to the two women who accompanied him. Löwenstein came to greet him. Dumont wondered if the German saw his presence as interference, but Korongo Kuyate's account of the past had fascinated him, and the music of the kora had enchanted him. He hoped Assya could find him a personal musician.

"When this story is done, we must go back to the hills," barked Löwenstein as he released Dumont's hand. "Have you sorted out the question of those mines?"

Dumont smiled wryly. "In confidence, the reports I have were drawn up by soldiers who worried more about Islamic rebellions and prophets. They understood angles and trajectories" (both men understood he was talking about artillery) "but were not well-informed in matters of geology."

"Then let us go out again."

Dumont smiled agreement. "And what will this singer tell us today?"

"I think this will be the end of the story," answered Löwenstein. "Mari Jata has been summoned from exile to return and lead his people. Can he do anything but conquer?"

As Korongo sang the story, Mari Jata failed to conquer! He assembled an army made up of those discontented with the rule of Sumanguru the sorcerer smith, those faithful to the house of his father. The armies met—Mari Jata was defeated. As Korongo phrased it: "The laughter went to the Sosso, the weeping went to the Mande." This happened nine times. Korongo did not enumerate each and every battle, but he had a refrain that seemed to recall these defeats: *Nyani-nyani, Kambasiga...*

While Korongo sang, Assya's eyes swept the gathering and paused on the *siratigi*; their eyes met with recognition. Further glances conveyed questions and assurances.

A different set of exchanges was less articulate. Those involved hadn't been touched by the spirits and were moved by purely human emotions. Nyelle had heard about the kola nuts. She sat near the man who had sent them. Each had been watching the other, until their eyes finally met. The eyes, it is said, are the first line of love, the first meeting of the minds and hearts.

Korongo narrated on. Mari Jata's sister understood that her brother was being defeated by magic. She undertook to overcome that obstacle. Korongo's voice shifted from the martial and elegiac tones in which he had recounted the battles and the defeats and took on a more intimate note. The sister went to Sumanguru bedecked in beauty by all her arts and wiles, and there she lured him into intimacy. He was warned against this strange women—his own mother came and protested! But he overrode the objections, he silenced his mother, and he admitted the secret of his magic powers to the alluring woman of the night. The secret was known! Counteractions were quickly accomplished. At the next battle, Sumanguru saw his forces repelled, defeated, driven into the bush. He turned and rode away with his favored wife behind him. They were pursued by Mari Jata and his cohort. Just as Sumanguru had spurred his horse into a great leap over the river Joliba, a magic arrow fired from the bow of the Simbon, the great huntsman Mari Jata, struck him and he was turned to stone with his wife and his steed.

"*Aha*! I knew he would conquer!" exclaimed Löwenstein as the translation trickled through to his ears.

Dumont had a far different reaction as the details of the story were delivered. Women were the key to revealing...secrets, weaknesses. Was he different from Sumanguru? Had he given himself over to a woman of whom he knew nothing? Suddenly he felt doubts and anxieties. He had wondered before why she had come, and had suspicions. He hadn't expected love under conditions of wide social and cultural difference. Now he had just been reminded that for the woman to offer herself in such a way must be a ploy, a strategy aimed at influence and power. It was one of the local strategies.

Brothers

CHAPTER XIV

KORONGO SUMMONED A DRUMMER for his delivery of the lion's skin to the Condé compound. Such a rare gift required special notice. He considered asking the *tabala* master to come, but the interpreter was not a chief, despite his influence. A *jeli* is a master in the fine judgment of status and perquisites. He settled for a *jenbé*, sure that the high-pitched and staccato tones of the instrument would bring to his mission the attention he desired. Besides, the *jenbé*, like the interpreter, was not considered a native to these parts. No legend told how it had been acquired from the spirits.

The noise served to alert Gaoussou to the ceremonious arrival of the *jeli*. He listened as Korongo intoned praises of the Sisibé clan and of the accomplishments of their scion in the town of Kri Koro. He was impressed as the *jeli*'s assistants unrolled the lion skin before him. He admired its quality. Korongo didn't explain its source, although he was sure Gaoussou might know it.

Gaoussou rose. "We must show this to the elder," he said. They brought the skin into Cejan's hut.

Cejan wasn't well; he seemed feverish. At the name of Nyelle he roused himself somwhat, and then when the assistants spread the lion skin before him, over his knees, he seemed to waken. His hands, bony and almost fleshless, the skin over the knuckles whitened with age, passed over the lion's mask and on to the mane, thick and tawny. His fingers lost themselves for a moment under the coarse long hairs.

"For Nyelle?" he asked. Gaoussou, crouched before him on the other side of the lion skin, nodded.

"*Nin ka di* [it is well]," he responded. "Let the marriage come quickly." He smiled and his hands fell back on his coverlet. Gaoussou assented loud enough for his brother to hear, then the party withdrew.

* * *

Some miles from there, Dumont and Löwenstein had retraced their path to the gold pit, guided by the same hunter. Their bearers carried tools such as hammers and chisels, as well as water-skins and food. Dumont had a *tirailleur*, this time armed; Löwenstein also had the *siratigi* with him.

Their course took them up the valley and then east into the trees up the slopes. They moved through the lowland shade of acacias and the *karité* of oily nuts to enter a world of forest giants, trees with huge trunks that towered over them. For some reason, on this second passage through the forest, Dumont began to see shapes within the trunks and their mighty branches above. The wrinkled bark seemed the skin of ancient creatures; above, in the gloom under the leaves, the branches suggested limbs and bodies and occasionally a face. From the leaves under the unseen sky, a bird called out: *Wuutuutuu!* It had an ominous sound, unlike the chirping and skreeking he usually heard around the cantonment. This bird spoke to the soul. It announced that he was entering a primal space.

A steep slope led to the ledge where they had found the

pits. He dismissed thoughts of the soul. He was too breathless. From the ledge he was actually looking over the treetops that had seemed so numinous. He saw butterflies of all colors, and now he heard birds in their normal song. The sunlight warmed and comforted him, especially after a cool draft of water.

Löwenstein seemed insensitive to the emotional affect of the landscape. He examined the soils on which he trod, the stones on which he stepped. He was appraising facts beyond Dumont's appreciation. Löwenstein walked under the trees on the upper slope examining the earth that lapped over the stone, then returned.

"We have two options," he stated. "We might stay here and try to empty these pits of the water that has filled them, but that seems idle. We know the pits are here; we – or you," he acknowledged the authority of Dumont and the French, "may empty them at leisure to see if there is anything worth exploiting beneath. But to increase our knowledge, there are two courses: to move up the slope and seek outcrops of the auriferous rock, or to move down the slope and seek points where the rocks' erosion may have brought gold in alluvial form."

"We passed near a village," answered Dumont. He didn't know its name; it was, in fact, Sènètela, which paid a tribute to the Condé lineage. "They will know of any gold washing from the hills. I shall make inquiries." Here he spoke as a colonial administrator aware of the powers of his office. "We should move up the hill and explore the geology of the region."

Löwenstein nodded agreement. He was at heart romantic and believed that the quest required movement towards the unknown. He had spent his life on travels in Africa: through the mountainous fastnesses of Ethiopia and Kordofan, across the broad savannas and veldts of southern Africa, into the great jungles of the Congo basin. Everywhere he had been tantalized with the thought that he might encounter some pristine and primeval site, a suggestion of mythic Eden. He didn't believe in an historic Eden; he was rational and educated. Still, he found in Africa something primordial, fundamental to humanity. So of course they should pursue the unknown.

They went north where the rock of the ledge subsided into the overlayer of composite soils and clays and the vegetation reclaimed its sun-given right to growth and exuberance. It was very difficult to determine the contours of the terrain. The *tirailleur* took the lead, perhaps remembering childhood romps through the bush. Dumont nodded approval. Löwenstein's eye would be more educated in matters of geology. He was sure the German would speak up if something caught his notice. Besides geology, they might also encounter snakes. If so, the *tirailleur*'s thick boots offered better protection than his own walking shoes. He didn't notice Löwenstein's *siratigi* suddenly looked up and around them, as though seeing something invisible to the rest.

They passed around a dip filled with bushes and were about to enter the shade of the great trees when the ground shook with the impact of great blows. In Europe, Dumont would have compared it to the passage of a great freight train. Here, he could think of no explanation.

A great, dark form emerged from the trees with extraordinary speed, charging them! Its shape was indistinct but massive, swathed in the gloom of shadows. Dumont caught a glimpse of a glittering bar at the top and glowing red lights—eyes? it seemed impossible—and then the rush overthrew their column. The *tirailleur* and the hunter at the front were trampled to the ground. The others were buffeted and tossed aside into the bushes. He thought he saw a spark of red light as the *siritigi* ahead of him dove to the side. Dumont was knocked down by a great blow. As he fell, he rolled a bit and caught a glimpse of the creature's rear. The tail shone silver.

He was picking himself up when he felt himself pushed back down. Löwenstein's *siratigi* was the only man of the party standing. He had turned to face the creature. Almost absent-mindedly he had pushed Dumont back off the trail and out of sight. The man was looking back along the line of the creature's charge, and perceived an imminent danger; his stance proclaimed the dynamic poise of a warrior in battle. Whatever had just assailed them was turning to renew its attack. Behind him, the others were also in the bushes, save for two bodies lying still and limp on the earth.

* * *

Sisibé ventured into forbidden territory. The *komanda* had gone off with the German *nasrani*. This was an ideal opportunity to find the forms for a *laissez-passer* that would serve the two foreign *nasrani*. A Wolof or a Sosso would have taken their bribe and then denounced them, but he was of noble Soninké blood and he acknowledged obligations. He would find them the form they required, matching the one the *siratigi* had shown him issued to the German *nasrani*.

He started his search at the *komanda*'s desk with the bottom drawer on the left; there, he intuited, would be the forms least required in ordinary business. He knew already that the *komanda* kept the usual forms for the weekly accounts of the cantonment management and salaries in the top right drawer.

His intuition was quickly rewarded. There were several folders made of colored *papier kraft*. Each folder had a different administrative form. The third contained the printed form for the *laissez-passer*.

He was reading through the instructions when he heard a step behind him. It came from the door leading from the *komanda*'s office to his private quarters. He turned.

Nyelle stood there, looking at him curiously. He never forgot that picture of her in the doorway: an indigo-blue pagne, a brown top, her feet bare, one hand against the door jamb. And her eyes! They sparkled with mischievous delight at her discovery. Her mouth was bowed into a half-smile which she was trying to hide behind concern at an intruder in the *komanda*'s space. He hoped she greeted him as a welcome suitor.

"Condé-*muso*," he greeted her, then paused. Such a meeting was highly improper. But they stood in the very epicenter of new authority and rules: the office of the *komanda*. He disregarded the old rules. "Nyelle, I am Mady Sisibé. Do you know that I have sent kola nuts to your *bemba*?" She met his gaze and took a half-step forward, into the room. "I saw you in the camp of the German *nasrani*. I had no hesitation." He now took a step towards her, still holding the paper. "I have sent kola nuts and another gift to your family, and they are agreeable. But since we meet here, let me ask you too whether this idea seems sweet to you as well?"

Nyelle's answer was to move yet one more step closer and he reacted instinctively: they met in an embrace. He had not been the only person smitten at the German's camp.

Nyelle had mentioned the interpreter to Assya after they returned to Assya's chamber, trying to sound casual. Assya fixed Nyelle with her dark eyes for a long moment, and then smiled. "He is a Sisibé," she commented. "He comes of Soninké lineage, and I think he will go far and rise high."

Sisibé broke from the embrace very reluctantly. It was against all custom. In the world of the *nasrani* rules had to change somewhat, but certain measures of value remained. He was sure, from the brightness of her eyes, that Nyelle would quickly learn to adjust to the new world, but he also felt it necessary she have the approval of the old one.

And he remembered his debt. He owed the two strange *nasrani* the right sort of papers.

* * *

Assya was not in the cantonment. She had been pondering Nyelle's version of the Condé song her grandfather taught her as well as Nyelle's account of the old woman. She had to meet this old woman herself.

The cantonment was still in the absence of the *komanda*. Assya didn't notice Gorkel sitting behind the stairs leading up to the *komanda*'s headquarters. But he noticed her, and when she left the cantonment he followed, trying to be discreet. She wasn't paying attention to followers. She was intent on her path, if not certain of its course. She stopped at a crossroads to reflect. She did not ask directions.

She chose a course to the west on a path that led out of the town. When she reached the beginning of the open sunlit fields she paused again, searching out something in the distance. Then, with visible confidence, she strode forward along the beaten earth of the path. Gorkel waited in the shade until she had moved on, then followed. Samba Ly's instructions justified his conduct, but he feared the anger of this strange and beautiful woman.

She went only a few hundred meters and then she came to a ramshackle and decrepit hut in a small clearing among the fields, just off the path. She turned into its courtyard and paused. Gorkel stooped and hurried up, hoping the cover of the bushes would disguise his approach.

Assya had come to the old woman's hut following a thread, a hope, a glimmer of recognition. The fire in the front had died down. She stepped up to the doorway and stared into the darkness within. After a moment, her eyes adjusted and the few furnishings appeared: a few pots, a pile of cloth, a low bed. On the bed lay an aged woman, apparently unconscious. By her right hand lay a polished piece of stone—a mirror of the old sort.

Assya examined the old woman. She didn't notice the approach of Gorkel. She moved closer and examined the woman's wrinkled face. The woman lay half-naked, which was not unusual; the cloth wrapped about her hips was a dingy piece of cotton weave, grayish brown in the poor light. On her wrists were bracelets and charms.

When the Soninke woman entered the hut, Gorkel decided he should inform Samba Ly. He didn't dare spy on women's secrets. Samba Ly might have the courage or the strength to withstand the potent magic within the hut. That there was magic was, for Gorkel, a certainty. He turned and made his way back into town.

Assya looked around and found the earthen pot that held the drinking water. She dipped the calabash cup and then sprayed the water over the unconscious older woman.

"Kamisa!" she called. "Kamisa, wake up!"

The old woman's head rolled to one side and then jerked

itself erect. Her eyes opened, bleary and unfocussed, but after a moment their gaze sharpened and took in the elegant figure before her.

"You must tell me, Kamisa," began Assya. "Are you the *kun-sigi* of the buffalo, or the *kun-sigi* that marks where the serpent's head fell to rest? Or is it both?"

Buffalo
Photo taken in 1970 in Tanzania

CHAPTER XV

DUMONT STARED AT THE one man still standing, and then followed his gaze to see glitters of golden rays embedded in a shadow vanish like a lost rainbow. The man, Löwenstein's assistant, was looking back along their trail, his expression one of puzzlement. Clearly he expected to see some trace of their assailant. Dumont began to pick himself up and this time the man offered a hand to lift him up. Dumont realized that the earlier movement had been protective, to keep him out of harm's way.

Löwenstein also had been pushed into the bushes. He stood up. The two bearers were clearly terrified to the point of impotence. They squatted in the trail moaning and wrapping their arms around their chests as their heads bobbed up and down.

Beyond them, on the ground, lay the soldier and the hunter. They were motionless; certainly dead. Their bodies seemed to have been pressed into the ground, although oddly not crushed.

The *siratigi* walked warily back along the path, apparently looking for their attacker. Dumont wondered at the man's nerve, to seek out such a malevolent force. But after some twenty paces the man turned back. He passed between the survivors to examine the dead men. Apparently he no longer feared another attack.

"*Ah!*" he exclaimed softly to himself. Löwenstein barked questions. Dumont approached. Hesitantly, Löwenstein's *siratigi* said they had been attacked by a protective spirit. It had killed only those who carried offensive weapons—the soldier with his rifle and the hunter with his bow. This was merciful behavior. Other spirits would have slain them all.

"Spirits!" cried Dumont, yet in this case, against all rational disbelief, he had to place his personal experience: the blow that had knocked him over, two corpses on the trail. This was not a fantasy.

"An *ancient* spirit," answered the *siratigi*. "I think I saw a buffalo with golden horns and a silver tail." He paused and looked at the faces around the group for confirmation or denial; none challenged his observation. "We must ask the master *jeli*, Kuyate, to tell us of this creature."

Then he turned to the grim business of constructing stretchers for the two corpses. He sent one of the bearers down to the village in the valley to fetch help. It was unthinkable that the *nasrani* should act as bearers.

* * *

Gorkel found Samba Ly drilling the soldiers. There was little else to do. The *komanda* had gone off without him. As soon as he spied Gorkel, he dismissed the men.

Hurriedly, Gorkel explained how he had seen the Soninké woman leave the cantonment and go out of town to the strange hut. Gorkel remembered that Nyelle had spoken of 'the old woman' when telling the Soninke woman of the song she had learned. He thought this place might be where the old woman lived. He hadn't stayed to spy on the meeting.

Samba Ly considered inferences, strategies, actions. His gambit for power with the Soninké woman had failed. She was the intimate of the *komanda*'s bedchamber, but her access didn't translate into influence for him as hoped. Now the little Condé girl served her. The Condé family possessed the secret knowledge of the land and its wealth. The girl had taken refuge in this hut, and then returned with *basi* that defeated him. The connection was curious and tantalizing.

He thanked Gorkel and dismissed him. Then Samba Ly returned to his chamber and quickly removed the symbolic outer layers of his uniform. He decided not to take any weapon. He didn't think he could threaten this strange old woman. He had no real experience of the arcana of women's magic, although he understood it was potent. All his adult life he had been immersed in the world of the new-come *nasrani*. Serving the *nasrani* was good insulation from the female currents of power and belief, for the *nasrani*'s world was grounded in tangible materials. Most effectively in the lead and steel of their firearms and blades. And those were the tools with which he had been trained. He had long since put aside much consideration for the beliefs and practices of the *farafinya*. But Nyelle had resisted him, and that memory cautioned him. It was a quiet voice, though, drowned out by his masculine self-confidence.

Following Gorkel's directions, he headed straight for the western edge of town. He easily spotted the weather-worn and airy hut out in the fields. He could see no one around. He approached quietly and crossed the courtyard. He stood to one side of the doorway and listened.

He could hear Assya's voice: she seemed to be tending to another person. She offered water; there were the sounds of cloth rustling at body movements. The other person spoke, but it was a low murmur. He couldn't distinguish the words. Assya answered, "I understand what you were doing, my mother," and then she was interrupted by some exclamation. "Age has nothing to do with it. You have progressed further than I…" and again she was interrupted. She was quiet for a time, listening to the murmur. Try as he might, Samba Ly could make out nothing of the other person's remarks.

"But I am asking about the head of the great *bida*, the golden pledge."

That he could understand, and it was was exactly the sort of information he'd hoped to overhear.

"It's not only a Condé secret. You know my stake..." More murmuring.

"So the guardian dwells in the cave?"

Samba Ly's mind raced. A golden pledge? He knew the *nasrani* were eager to learn of any wealth that might be exploited.

* * *

Ramata had spotted Assya walking. Assya hadn't noticed her. Ramata had situated her workplace where it would be visible; she counted on curiosity and vanity to bring her business. The location also allowed her, when not intent on the scalp before her, to see those who went by. Assya passed. Immediately afterwards Ramata saw Gorkel and guessed: Gorkel was spying on Assya for Samba Ly.

She quickly filled in the unknowns. Assya never went to the market; that had been a point of dissension when Ramata was buying and cooking for three. Samba never required of Assya the domestic duties he expected of Ramata. Assya was now served by Nyelle. She wasn't on her way to the Condé compound. What might she be seeking? Ramata left it at that for a time. She didn't want to make Assya her business. But as she finished plaiting a tight braid and capped it with one of Marco's beads, a thought came to her. The chain of connections led to the old woman in the hut.

Twenty minutes later her inferences were confirmed. Samba Ly came walking on the path Gorkel had taken. He *wasn't* in uniform. He still stood out because he was tall and because he wore a bleached white *nasrani* shirt that shone brightly in the sun. She had finished with her client. Quickly, she packed up her small bag of tools and ornaments and took the bag with the two stools back into the compound.

"Ramata, you are worried," commented Marco. She nodded but offered no explanation. The *nasrani* had become, in an odd sense, partners in her business. The fame of the speechless *nasrani* from Amriki, the one who had killed the lion but never talked, drew clients. Marco had provided a valuable stock of beads. Taking tea in the afternoon, she and Marco had discussed the commercial possibilities of the town. As the descendant of a *signare*, she approved his vision.

Quickly, she left the compound and headed to the old woman's hut. As she had half-expected, she saw Samba Ly standing outside the hut, clearly trying to hear to a conversation inside.

For an instant, she wavered on a knife's edge of conflicting emotions. In past days she might have laughed at him. But now he was following the other woman, a woman he had hoped to use for influence (in the cantonment, perhaps only Ramata understood what it meant for the Soninke woman to become the concubine of the *komanda*). Now Samba had invaded a space and a relationship that she considered hers, and moreover one that had brought her solace in her unvoiced griefs. The scale tipped to fury.

Her first shrieked words were Wolof invective. He was worse than a donkey's pizzle or a dog pissing on the road. He became a goat, and passed rapidly through the caprine digestive tract.

Samba Ly turned and recognized Ramata. She saw that he too had suffered a momentary hesitation, the sharp choice of courses. He also had anger within him. He chose to strike out at her. His large fist swung out in a thoughtless roundhouse. She avoided him; she was thinking unusually clearly and violently.

Against the hut wall rested a mortar and a pestle, both looking peculiarly new and unused. Certainly, she did not remember ever seeing such ordinary domestic tools in the old woman's space before. But her course was obvious. She took two steps, seized the pestle, and swung it around just in time to catch Samba Ly on the ribcage as he followed her, having recovered from the first missed swing.

He staggered back. Her backswing caught him on the thighs, and he fell to the ground. The pestle swirled over her head and then came down almost on his: somehow, her eye caught the exact angle so that the force of the blow landed in the dirt just beyond his head, and his brow caught only the blunted side impact. It would still be enough to stun and bruise him.

Samba Ly lay limp on the ground. Ramata dropped the pestle and turned, numb, towards the door of the hut, trying to understand the violence she had just committed. Was it Ramata who had seized the pestle, who had known where and how to swing it, where to strike, who had not cared about the injury she would cause? Or was it another? She knew she felt anger—no, fury—towards Samba Ly, but did that fury require his destruction?

The Soninke woman stood there. Ramata had never seen her more alive, more present in this world. In the three years they had shared the man lying between them, the Soninke woman had always remained abstract: a physical presence whose beauty had real effects on the men around her, but whose mind was uninvolved with the occurrences of daily life. Now she had found the path to her goal; she glowed with the force of her purpose.

Behind the Soninke woman, the old woman leaned against the door. She, by contrast, seemed weak and faint, as though she had risen from a sickbed against her will. But as her eyes took in the tableau before her—the triumphant Ramata brandishing her pestle, the fallen soldier by the overturned mortar—a smile flickered across her thin dark lips.

"Men are not millet," she murmured, this time loud enough to be heard.

"I didn't put him in the mortar," answered Ramata. The Soninke woman grasped the joke immediately and laughed. Her eyes met Ramata's. The two of them had once served as mortar to his pestle, in a common understanding of the symbols.

* * *

Late that afternoon, Dumont returned to the cantonment accompanied by the *siratigi* and several bearers carrying the body of the soldier; they had left the hunter with his kin. The shock had worn off. He was still mystified by the creature that had attacked them. He mourned the dead soldier. This humane consideration also raised an administrative concern: how should he describe the death? 'Supernatural causes' would have him summoned immediately to Dakar for a medical examination.

The answer would depend on the consequences. He must make inquiries. If there were dependents, he would try to provide for them. The justification for a 'line of duty' entry was clear: they had been looking for a source of gold that would enrich the colony.

Assya didn't greet him as he entered his chambers. Her absence was confusing and troubling. Since hearing the tale of how Mari Jata's sister had seduced her brother's enemy, he had been musing on the obvious purpose behind Assya's placement in his bedchamber. She was beautiful and desirable, and she had depths (her knowledge of French! her correction of the master bard) that he had not suspected. But he knew she was not his, in the sense that a woman belongs with the man she loves. He didn't know what useful secrets he might have revealed to her that others might covet. Certainly, he was mortal and could be killed by all sorts of means simpler than the spur of a cock fastened to an arrow.

What did Assya's absence signify? Would she be coming back? He did not know.

Large Pestle

PART III

Sacred Spring
This spring is named Dafra, it rises not far from Bobo-Dioulasso in Burkina Faso; it contained very large catfish, and the bank was covered with feathers and bones from sacrifices made to the fish.
Photo taken in 1980

CHAPTER I

I WILL SPARE THE tale of my wanderings between Bougouni and Kri Koro. Diawara decided to send me west on the routes down to the English *nasrani* port of Freetown. I mean down quite literally: the paths from Kissidougou to the coast were precipitous. They led us to a narrow plain and a town set about with mangroves and fever-trees. My third voyage there led to employment with the German ethnographer whose interest in the past traditions of *farafinya*, the African lands, brought him to Kri Koro. During that time I had little direct involvement with the *wokòlò*, although one welcome fruit of my exposure was a preternatural skill with languages. The *wokòlò* opened my ears, loosened my tongue, and preserved my memory for words. I wondered what price I would eventually pay.

I came to Kri Koro with Löwenstein. I was amazed to find Assya there. It was not her status, mistress to the *komanda*, but her very presence that astonished me. Her beauty could have carried her to N'daar or to Paris, the distant metropole of the *nasrani*. She was in Kri Koro, by choice or by accident. Our brief conversation in Bougouni had marked her place in my heart. It also showed a woman adrift, flotsam on the swell of the river of time.

She was in Kri Koro! Our eyes met during the performance by Korongo Kuyate. She knew me at sight and cared. That was the message of her eyes, and I found myself full of the thought, although unsure where it might lead. So often, dreams are not fulfilled.

Our sad party returned from the ill-fated excursion in search of gold mines. The hunter's body was delivered to his kin; the soldier was taken to the cantonment. Löwenstein and I returned to his camp. He retired to his tent. The evening meal came; silence settled over the camp. I was dozing when I felt a hand on my shoulder, a gentle touch intended not to startle, but to lure the wandering mind to wakefulness. I sat up.

"*Bamana-ké*," came a remembered voice. "Do you remember our meeting in Bougouni?" I turned to face the woman. Only the glow of the fire lit the camp. She was mostly lost in shadow.

"I could never forget it."

"Will you help me?"

This question is one of those that require consideration before the answer. Almost always, it is answered on the basis of emotion rather than reason, and the purpose is comfort to the questioner.

"As I can," I answered. The implied reserve reflected not unwillingness, but caution in the matter of spirit-dealings. But she was Assya, and I was I, so I added, "How?"

Her half-smile acknowledged my caution. "I think you have been appointed to help me. Did you not meet spirits in Bougouni?" My silent nod must have been visible against the firelight. "I need your abilities. I seek a treasure. I think you can lead me to it. Did you not meet a buffalo today? A buffalo with horns of gold and a tail of silver?"

I hadn't described the beast that assaulted us to anyone. I suspected the *komanda* might have seen something. His eyes, as I raised him from the path, were those of a man who has seen visions. How did she know of the buffalo? Was it through the *komanda*? That thought was painful.

She explained. "I may have saved your lives. The buffalo had a master. I awoke the person who was guiding it before it could turn to trample all of you."

"I am grateful."

"So could you see the trail of the buffalo?" This was the question that mattered to her. A small tremor in her voice revealed its importance. I was relieved, for now I did believe I could help her.

"Yes. It followed a spirit trail. I don't know how long it will last, but I have crossed such trails before."

At 'yes' she released her breath and relaxed visibly. Her hand fell on my shoulder again.

"Will you take me to it?"

"Now?"

"Yes."

"What tools or weapons should I bring?"

"Do you think weapons will be of use against this buffalo?"

"There might be other obstacles?"

She shrugged. I decided to bring a cutlass and a staff. I didn't want to go wandering unarmed in the night. I hung the blade in a sheath over my shoulder and returned to her.

Our passage through the town was silent and swift. I chose the path through the valley and the fields before turning into the forest. I had followed that path more than once. I trusted my memory to alert me to the turns.

As we walked, I ventured questions. "Can you tell me what we are looking for? And what we need to do?"

"First let us find the trail of the beast."

We walked together easily, matching our pace and our

stride. After some miles, the reflected light of household fires on treetops showed where we should turn away from the valley and towards the hills. We found the trail that circled around the village and advanced, oriented by the glimmers of the village lights. I was wary. The lights occasionally turned the leaves to spearpoints in ambush. Assya was not worried. What dangers she expected lay further ahead.

The trail began to rise. We came out on the ledge with the mining pits and its open view. Below us lay the village: an irregular pattern of lighted spaces stenciled by occluding trees. Above us, the night sky was brilliant with stars, a luminous deep blue.

I led the way off the ledge. "Here we went," I told Assya. "The *nasrani* were following the line of the rock." We followed the path I had taken that morning, the great trunks of the trees looming up in the dark on my right, while a clearing filled with smaller growth spread out to the left. We had been attacked just beyond the clearing. We came to the trampled space where two men had died.

"Here the buffalo attacked us."

Assya stepped up beside me to examine the trail, looking forward and back. "It was a spirit being," she said. "Can you not see the paths of spirits?"

I paused to collect myself and to recall the period after my first meeting with the *wokòlò*. The spirits left a trail of heat, of invisible power and energy. I could perceive the trail when...It involved a peculiar perspective, an oblique angle on the scene that revealed dimensions otherwise invisible, that my mind translated into a visible aura. As I remembered that aura, the darkness before us diffused; I was no longer trying to see the light, but to find that other angle. Hints of a glow passed before my eyes like the spots behind the eyelids when one prepares to sleep that recalls the last glowing lights they have beheld. But these spots endured and settled and began to acquire some fixity and even a suggestion of form: there, the line of prints left by the incorporeal, silvery hooves of the murderous beast. Behind us, I could see where it had stopped; no tracks returned. Looking forward, I could see two darker spots where the hooves flattened the hunter and the *tirailleur* and the line of its attack.

I took her hand. "Come," I said, unnecessarily. She had already grasped that I could see a trail.

The marks of the beast began to dim a short distance later, as though it had only adopted material being as it approached its attack. Faint as they were, they still glimmered before us. We moved forward, confident in our course, however ignorant of its perils.

The beast's prints led into a glowing track and were lost. I could see no particular sign of them beyond. I stopped and squeezed Assya's hand slightly, signalling a problem.

"The trail of the beast has joined a spirit trail," I told her. "I cannot tell in which direction it may have gone. I see no marks beyond the trail."

"Trace the line of the trail for me," she ordered, and I did so. She thought for a moment, considering angles perhaps, or some other geometry of the mind and memory, and then came to a decision. It was, perhaps, the obvious one.

"This direction leads away from the town. Let us follow it."

I had encountered such paths running across human routes before. I had even seen spirits moving along them; the memory marked the space as perilous for mortals. I had never thought to follow one. I didn't question Assya's command. Still holding her hand, I moved forward.

I half-expected our surroundings to change: I thought we would enter the spirit world and that the forest about us would be transformed into an ethereal network of entities and elements and forces that I attributed to the spirit world. But the earth beneath my feet was still solid as we advanced, and the darkness around us was undiminished. Step by step, we progressed; not as a blind man lost in the market, but as a blind man in his home, where the spatial relations of objects and landmarks are known.

Before us the glow of a spirit presence appeared. All too quickly it took form: a great crocodile, its head as high as a man's shoulders, the girth of its flattened belly sprawling well beyond the width of the trail. Its jaws were agape and its many teeth glistened against a threatening red glow from within its maw.

Without thinking, I stepped off of the trail, pulling Assya with me. I moved several paces away to the shelter of a great tree. I feared not only the jaws, designed to bite and to catch and to hold, but also the flailsome tail used to topple prey. The tree might protect us. I failed to wonder whether Assya might have had the skills or mastery to overcome it.

"What?" began Assya's question, but I quickly covered her mouth with my hand. I wished no sound to divert this monster from its course. It passed us, and for a moment I was relieved. Then I perceived the consequences of its passage: the swaying tail erased the glow of the spirit trail. Looking forward, I could no longer see our path. Looking back, I could see only darkness in the wake of the incorporeal and glowing reptile.

When it was out of sight, I ventured an explanation. "There was a great crocodile on the trail. I pulled you away to escape it." I waited a moment for an objection or a comment. "It has erased the trail we followed. The path is dark." This, I knew, was to her the gravest news. I was not mistaken. She uttered a choked groan, and then collapsed against my chest. Her shoulders began to shake with silent sobbing. She was no longer the woman filled with hope and anticipation who had brought me into this forest.

I held her up and hoped the circle of my arms could comfort her grief. Her own arms, after a moment, embraced me, her hands against my shoulderblades. But I still felt the cool trail of her tears on my skin. For a time she shook, and then she began to regain her composure. She broke free of my arms and stepped back around the tree that had sheltered us. For a moment, she stared wildly left and right. She turned back to me.

"Where did the path lead?"

I still had my orientation in the dark. I led her to the space of the spirit trail and pointed her in the direction we had been following, placing my hands on her shoulders from behind to orient her. "This was our course."

She stared into the darkness. Apparently she saw nothing to guide her, for she turned back to me. "Our trail is lost," she said. "You cannot see any trace that we might follow?" It was not hope speaking, but confirmation of a tragic fact.

"Not now," I answered, "but perhaps the dawn will bring better sight."

"So near," she murmured. "So near...And yet, I am sure this is the place." She turned away from me, and again her shoulders shook in her grief.

I began to realize that I had held her in my arms, that the warmth of her skin had been pressed to mine, that she had rested against me. I could still feel the impression of the different parts of her body that had touched my thighs, my belly, my chest, my shoulder. Seeing her, I had dreamed, of course; now I could add the sense of touch to my inventory of our contacts. But I didn't know why she was so close to me. She required service and assistance, I knew, and I was more than willing to give what help I might. But might that lead to something deeper? With this particular woman I would await her decision.

"Let us rest until the dawn," I offered. "Then we can resume our search. The spirits will not be so active."

"You speak sense," she acknowledged. "Let us rest." She stepped back towards the tree behind which I had sheltered us. The ground around its trunk was soft and clear, as comfortable as any resting place we were likely to find in the night. Her hand took mine, pulling me with her as she settled down upon the ground. I removed the knife from my belt and laid it next to my staff, close at hand. Then I leaned back onto the ground, my body inches from her own.

"Can you tell me now what we are seeking?" I asked. "I will help you in any way I can, but it would be good to know our goal."

She turned onto her side, facing me. Her kneecaps met my thighs. A hand reached out and rested on my upper arm.

"I seek to end a curse," she said. Her voice took on a distant quality. I couldn't tell if this was a story many-times told to others, or perhaps rehearsed only to herself. "You named me Assya, and said it was for the maiden in the kingdom of Wagadu. You remember, perhaps, the legend of her beauty. But you didn't understand the doom that came upon her." She paused, and her hand pressed more firmly upon my arm. "I told you this, when we met in Bougouni."

"I remember clearly." My voice was firm.

"The maiden was the seal upon a pact, a pact made many generations before her birth. The first king, the Khaya Maga of Wagadu, reached an agreement with his half-brother, the spirit of the earth in Koumbi: the serpent-spirit provided wealth, and the kingdom offered a maiden every seven years. The pact balanced the worlds. It brought concord to the men and the land upon which they lived. It was a model for the many settlements of humans through *farafinya*, or perhaps it was an echo of the great primordial pact. Everywhere, humans must reach an accord with the forces around them: the spirits of fire and of the waters, of the living and of the dead. But in Wagadu, that pact was broken. An arrogant man proved more greedy and lustful than we believed possible, and he slew the serpent. And since that time..." She paused.

"There are other pacts," I commented. "The Manding houses many earthmasters who link the worlds of men and of the spirits."

"This was a royal pact. It governed the kingdom, the entire people. It was not a local arrangement between neighbors, but a principle of honor and mutual respect. It promised to fulfill the needs of men. Those needs are not fulfilled in this land. I have seen wars and famines and plagues...Worst of all were the famines." Her voice trembled and she pause. "Hunger has stalked these lands. The people have suffered, but they endure." That last intonation was more positive. "I was the token of the pact that was broken. I have sought a way to restore the balance or to atone for the breach. The key, I was sure, was the head of the Bida-Serpent, the head that flew into the air after that hero's blade cut its neck." Venom marked her voice at the word 'hero.'

"But I didn't know where to find it. I wandered. I went north, to Muslim lands. At that time they held power, so I thought that perhaps the head had granted it. I crossed the sea to the land of the *nasrani,* the Franks. I found no sign of the serpent's head. I returned south, across the great sands with the Moroccans who destroyed the Songhay. The times that followed were unpleasant." She fell silent; clearly the last word was an understatement and she wished to move past those years. "I wandered after that, not by choice or direction, but according to the fortunes of war and capture. Warriors and horsemen swarmed over the savannas in those times. I was beautiful, but barren, so men treasured me briefly. Too often I was desired, and then later despised, courted and then cursed. I found some revenge; I brought doom upon some princes. But that wasn't my goal. I sought signs of the serpent wherever I went. I followed hints, often obstructed by princes and their war-leaders." Her hand tightened on my arm.

"In Bougouni, when you greeted me, I felt some hope: surely, I thought, if a man recognizes me, then my quest is coming to an end. But nothing came of it. I lost you. Now, here in Kri Koro, for the first time I've heard words and seen signs that made me believe I might find the treasure, that I might fulfill my quest. And you have reappeared. The man who recognized me and whom the spirits marked. So I hope and wonder. The buffalo that attacked you is not the venerable protector of a hallowed treasure. It is the vicious guardian of ill-gotten goods. I think the serpent's head fell here, so many years ago, and people understood what they *should* have done. But they were bewildered and dazzled by the gold and the prospect of riches. They hid it away." She paused, composing her thoughts. "The *nasrani* and the Muslims both believe that humans fell from paradise because they ate of the fruit of knowledge. But I don't think knowledge is the root of evil. I think it is greed and selfishness."

I placed my hand over hers as it lay on my arm. She made no motion in response, but her fingers relaxed beneath my own and her breath began to slow down. Soon I was sure she was asleep.

Crocodile
This was a small animal kept in a basin at the center of the courtyard of the University Hotel in Kankan. Photo taken in 2004.

CHAPTER II

DUMONT BATHED ON HIS return. The activity reminded him of Assya's absence; several times in the past days she had come at such moments, with pleasant enhancements. This morning he decided to wash again. He rang his bell; the servants brought the water, and he began to sponge himself off in the privy area. When he finished, he raised the half-empty tub of water over his head—he could have asked the servants to stay and do this for him, but he hadn't learned to disregard the servants. Nudity was private. Slowly he poured the water down onto his hair and over his shoulders, along both legs, and then through the slatted floor beneath him.

He was quite surprised to hear a gasp—a human voice, surely! It was followed by the sounds of slippage and then the splash of a body landing in a viscous pool. Had someone been lurking under the privy to spy on him? Dumont saw no reason for anyone to spy on a young colonial officer, but he could easily imagine interest in Assya. He quickly wrapped a towel around his waist and knelt down to peek through the lattice. In the gloom he could make out a head against the earthen tones: someone was wallowing in the liquid filth beneath the privy. He inferred the sequence: his second bath had made the ground more slippery than usual. Slick clay, the force of gravity, and perhaps a lack of caution had done the rest.

A face looked up. He thought he recognized the lad.

Dumont withdrew to his dressing room, pulled on a robe, then summoned one of the house-boys. "Someone has fallen into the hole below the privy," he said quietly. "I think it may be that boy who is attached to Samba Ly. Go and tell Samba Ly of this occurrence. But first send the watchman beneath the bath-space with a rope to get this person out of the muck. When he is washed—thoroughly—I wish to question him."

The servant, engaged in St. Louis and trained to *nasrani* service, heard these instructions impassively. He withdrew and indulged in a chortle. It deserved more than a chuckle. That brat Gorkel! His obsession with the secret of *nasrani* powers had just taken him too far. Then the servant summoned the watchman who complained bitterly until the servant observed that he need only throw a rope and then help pull it. He could throw a rope?...Yes, of course the watchman could manage that.

The servant then went to Samba Ly and told him what had happened and that the *komanda* expected some explanation. He was surprised by Samba Ly's appearance.

So was Dumont when Samba Ly appeared before him. The man had clearly been beaten: he was marked with a livid bruise on his head and he limped.

"What happened to you?" asked Dumont. "Were you attacked?" The thought of an insurrection against French rule crossed his mind, but more likely was a disagreement about a bribe or a wager. So far the burden of French rule had lain very lightly on this town, although he knew his plans to requisition a labor force to build roads north to Kita and west to Kankan would be resisted. That plan was an imperative from the government in Dakar and he would not shirk this duty. Besides, he firmly believed that open roads promoted commerce and thus prosperity.

"A family matter," admitted Samba Ly, most reluctantly. "I would request that we not pursue it."

"There is, in fact, another family matter before us," answered Dumont drily. "Your adopted lad, Gorkel, was spying on me in the bathroom, below the floor boards, and he slipped into the pit below the privy. I have told people to fetch him out and clean him. Can you tell me why he was doing this?"

Samba Ly cleared his throat. He was not sure he could explain Gorkel's fascination with the excretions of the *nasrani*, or if he should. Denial was probably safest. "No, *mon komanda,*" he replied. "The boy has curiosities he does not explain to me." That opened the possibility that the boy might have been looking for the woman. Dumont grasped the hint, for he stared at his subordinate intently for a moment before looking down at the papers on his desk. Samba Ly was sure the *komanda* was considering the fact that they had shared the same woman.

"Do you know where the women have gone?" asked Dumont, unexpectedly.

Samba Ly stared. "*Mon komanda...*" he began, and halted. He did not know what to answer.

"I understand there is to be a marriage," continued Dumont. "The serving girl is betrothed to Sisibé." Samba Ly didn't pause to wonder where he might have learned this item. "I presume she is away with the preparations for the ceremony. But the other woman also has disappeared and I wonder if you have heard anything?"

Samba Ly decided to voice his wilder guesses, reached as he followed Assya's trail and overheard the parts of the conversation that he could understand. This information might restore the favor that he had just lost through Gorkel's effrontery and clumsiness. "There is a rumor the Condé lineage possesses a treasure of gold. The Soninke woman may have learned of it; it is a matter that has preoccupied her." He admitted his knowledge of the woman, hoping the other information would be a distraction. "If she has learned where it lies, she is seeking it."

"Is it not kept in the compound of the lineage head?"

"I have not heard so. Such matters are not freely spoken of."

Dumont nodded. "Go and see how the boy is doing. And send Sisibé to me."

* * *

Cejan was dying. The infection from the bedsores had spread quickly through his aged and withered body, bringing a fever that Djanka's desultory wiping didn't abate. His eyes were crusted over. She dabbed ineffectually at them, not daring to press hard. As she removed her hand, the eyes opened, bleary at first, then lucid and fixed on her. His voice was faint. "Gaoussou," he ordered. The intonation was unmistakable.

Djanka went straight to Gaoussou, bypassing the hierarchy of the compound. She was afraid. Gaoussou was surprised to see the girl and immediately sensed the urgency. He hastened to Cejan's side and found his older brother gasping. His eyes were open, but they had begun to wander in the sphere of the Otherworld; his mind was clearly ready to drift away.

"Cejan!" Gaoussou barked, hoping the noise would bring his brother back for a moment. The eyes wandered a few seconds more and then settled on Gaoussou's face.

Slowly, Cejan's intelligence returned to them. "Old woman in the west," he murmured. "Guardian. Intruders." Gaoussou nodded slowly. He thought he understood what Cejan was talking about. He would verify it.

Cejan's body twitched, a grimace of pain shaped his mouth. Gaoussou reached out to lift his brother into a more comfortable position. As his hand slipped behind his brother's ribs, it encountered moisture and a creamy substance; when he withdrew the hand, it dripped with pus. Slowly, he turned his brother over so he could see the sore. Almost tenderly, he wiped it over with a loose cloth. He laid the cloth on the ground by the door, and then moved a pillow under Cejan's head, where the older man lay on his side. Slowly, he left the hut. He did not speak to Djanka, waiting outside, but pointed inside to the soiled cloth. He crossed the courtyard and called his first wife, and she in turn summoned a helper. They went to wash Cejan's body and to change his bedding. But all knew that it was too late to change the outcome.

* * *

Ramata was still deeply furious after her encounter with Samba Ly, although some calm had returned. She, Assya, and the old woman had shared tea and conversation. Ramata saw that Assya and the old woman had some bond, although she was certain they had never met before that day. They joked about men and foods, however never about children. It occurred to Ramata that the old woman was in the company of two barren females. And might that make three? Surely, if the old woman had children, they would care for her, they would have brought her to live in their households. But she was on the edge of the town, so far outcast that to go further would make her a creature of the wild. Perhaps it was a knowledge of the wild that linked the other two women? Certainly it was not some matter within Ramata's sphere.

Returning from the old woman's home, she bought a grilled fish from an acquaintance in the darkened evening market, the empty space was lit by the red light of charcoal embers. The contrast between the daytime bustle and the evening void struck her emotions for some reason. She sat in the glow and picked the flesh from the fish's ribs, still feeling the void, perhaps because she had been thinking of the loneliness of the outcast. When she returned to the Sanogo compound, all was still.

The next morning, she rose at dawn by habit. As a lodger, she wasn't expected to join in the morning chores, but she found she couldn't lie or sit idle when so many familiar and essential activities were underway. No one was fetching water—it was brought from a well by donkey cart, an innovation. But the women of the household were sweeping or assembling the laundry or cooking; one of their commercial activities was the sale of fritters in the market place. Breakfast required very little preparation; it usually only involved finishing the porridge left over from the night before. Later meals demanded more effort. Although, Ramata had to admit, the senior Sanogo wife managed the establishment very capably, assigning tasks according to ability and ordering food according to availability. These were ordinary lessons of household economy, the very ones she herself had acquired in her travels with Samba Ly. Still, she was impressed.

She swept out her own area and drew some water from the common water pots. She would start the day with tea. As the water boiled, she sat observing the part of the compound in which the strangers were housed. She suddenly noticed an absence: the lion skin that had covered the ground before the sleeping space of the the *nasrani* was gone. It might have been put away. Yet she suspected something more serious, so when Marco emerged yawning, she invited him with a raised cup of tea and then proceeded, gently, with her inquiries.

She quickly learned how the lion skin had been traded for administrative documents, and to whom. She knew enough of the story to understand why Sisibé sought such an item of prestige. The arrangement seemed an opportunity.

"What documents are required for trade?" she asked Marco.

He sipped his tea, then looked her in the eye. "All sorts of documents are required," he answered drily. "It depends upon the direction and the merchandise. To bring goods into the territory of the Franzawi requires permission because they prefer to receive Franzawi goods. But to take merchandise out requires far less trouble. And the one document that allows passage in all directions, of course, is currency."

They both chuckled at that obvious point. Their eyes met with understanding and a certain delight at future projects. "Gold," said Ramata carefully, "can be found in many ways."

"There is wealth in this land," agreed Marco. "I would not try to trade fish over a great distance, but I have seen products that don't rot and are desired in other parts."

They both looked across the compound. Ramata was watching the women preparing the fritters. Marco was looking at the piles of *karité* nuts to be shelled, pounded, and turned into the creamy paste that had so many uses. They looked back at each other.

Tristan came out to join them. He always let Marco get up first because then Marco would do more of the necessary chores.

* * *

Nyelle was not in the cantonment. She didn't wonder at Assya's absence until the morning, and then a lad, one of the many fosterlings sent by country cousins to seek advancement in the Condé compound, came from her mother. His news was bad. Without hesitation Njelle left, outpacing her escort.

Her mother greeted her with an embrace and led her to Cejan's chamber. Gaoussou's chief wife and her assistants had finished their messy business. Cejan lay on clean cloth; a bandage over a wad of floss covered the abcess. Nyelle's eyes saw that his skin was gray and lifeless. She had never seen his hands quite so limp, even in sleep. She understood immediately that his *nya* was dissolving its bonds with his body, having reached its term. Still, he was her grandfather, the *bumboro tigi* of honeyed treats, and more recently the only one who had helped her avoid shame. For her, he was the embodiment of Condé family pride.

She wondered briefly if the *nasrani komanda*'s medicine chest might have something to help her grandfather. She had watched while Assya opened the chest and scanned the contents. Assya had seemed to understand the medicines she examined. She seemed only a year or so older than Nyelle, but her knowledge was immeasurably deeper. She wondered if Assya or the old woman—suddenly, she linked them in her mind, both bearers of knowledge and power—might have some recourse. Then she corrected herself. Cejan was very old, weakened by bedsores and infection. She could do nothing.

His limp hands bothered her. She got some *karité* butter from her mother and rubbed it over Cejan's hands. And because she remembered he had enjoyed the smell, she also rubbed some on his cheeks and lips. Her mother found her sitting, holding Cejan's hands between her own. Nyelle had not noticed that they had lost their warmth, and that the body was slowly stiffening.

Soninke Painted Wall

CHAPTER III

GAOUSSOU STOOD PERPLEXED IN the center of the compound. His thoughts were in turmoil. He and Cejan were *faden,* step-brothers, and that was normally a relationship of rivalry and tension. He'd never resented his elder. Their service in the wars had bonded them; Cejan had earned his respect, and that was one reason why the older man was still alive: Gaoussou had ordered good care for him. Many such elders didn't live so long, and some died much sooner.

Cejan's eyes had demanded urgency. Not about his death—that had been long expected. Cejan feared or sensed some other crisis. The old woman was linked with the hidden treasure. Might it be at risk? Gaoussou wavered, wondering whether to sit a wake by his brother or to try to forestall the danger. He stood immobile long enough to worry the women watching him. They attributed his distraction to concern and grief for his brother. His meals over the next weeks were exceptionally good.

He would find the old woman. He needed to know what she might tell. He quickly assembled a squad of men. Under *nasrani* rule private households were not allowed armed retainers, but the habits of past generations argued for safeguards. The Condé compound had a staff of able-bodied male servants. Gaoussou led them quickly out and through the town. It was a small troop, it bore few visible weapons—staves, long knives—but because of the man who led it people noticed.

Gaoussou soon found the hut…looking unusually dilapidated as though the owner had wrought artistic destruction to create an effect. There were gaps in the walls and the thatch; debris was strewn over the front area. The old woman sat on a trunk of wood smoking her pipe. The sunlight caught the wisps of smoke and Gaoussou thought for a moment he saw shaped forms: houses and trees and beasts. He waved his men back with a gesture, then approached the old woman.

"Condé *muso*," he greeted her, with respect and also a certain measure of authority, even arrogance. He might already be the patriarch. "Cejan is dying. He told me of you, and I understood that there might be some urgency."

"*Ah*! Gaoussou! *Tuma ni Bagi moden*!" the woman answered with a praise that acknowledged his authority. "Truly, he was right to send you. I fear the time is late. The treasure that the Condé retained is in peril. One with an older and stronger claim has come, and she seeks to correct—I do not say to avenge—a wrong that our ancestors committed."

"Who is this person?" demanded Gaoussou.

"A long-lost princess."

"And where...what is her path?"

"The hidden cavern lies above the village of Sènètela," she answered. "What the path beyond that may be, I don't know. Our ancestors certainly knew where the treasure should have been placed, but their greed misled them. They didn't fulfill their obligation."

"Explain," requested Gaoussou. Quietly, without mannerisms or tropes, the woman told him of the failed sacrifice, the flying head, and its appropriation by long-dead Condé ancestors.

"I must still try to retain it, for the good of the lineage," pronounced Gaoussou. The old woman nodded. "Beyond Sènètela, you said?"

"She will seek to return it to the spirits of the earth," answered the old woman.

Gaoussou thanked her. He consulted quickly with his men and then set off on the path through the fields that led north to Sènètela.

* * *

Ramata observed Gaoussou's departure. She went to Marco and Tristan and roused them.

"You came to seek a treasure!" she reminded them, unnecessarily. Both looked up, Marco at her words and Tristan at her tone. "You risk losing it. Others now seek the same treasure." Marco stared; Tristan sat up. "The Condé elder has departed to learn of this secret from its keeper. If you follow him, you may have a chance to obtain what you seek."

The two men looked at each other and rose at once. Marco voiced the necessary question: "Where is he?"

"He set off on the path to the house of the old woman." Ramata didn't need to say more. Marco would certainly remember the path to the home of the woman of uncanny knowledge. Marco seized a water skin as they strode out of the Sanogo courtyard. Tristan presumably still carried his weapon.

Marco and Tristan retraced the path to the western edge of town and out into the fields. He explained their purpose on the way. As they approached the old woman's hut, Marco looked north. A line of men was visible following a trail through the middle of the fields.

Marco pointed. Tristan followed his finger, nodded, then shrugged. Children or goats might pass unremarked, but a *nasrani* and his companion—all too likely to be surrounded by children, if not goats—would find concealment more difficult.

* * *

Samba Ly and Sisibé almost collided at the door to Dumont's office. Samba Ly was reporting that Gaoussou Condé had left the town in haste with a party of men, almost certainly armed. Sisibé was reporting that the two *nasrani* had suddenly left their residence and were on the path leading west of town. Dumont heard each and hardly hesitated.

"Lieutenant," he ordered Samba Ly, "assemble a squad for a rapid pursuit of the Condé group." He carefully avoided looking at Samba Ly's bruises. "You should remain here. Tell Thiam to lead the group." He turned to Sisibé. "You shall inquire among our sources," (a polite term for their network of informants) "what they have heard." The sequence of events in which white men found old gold workings, began to explore them, were attacked by a strange force, and then important local people suddenly began to rush around did not seem unrelated incidents.

As before, he passed up the sedan chair. He made sure that two soldiers carried water skins. The group set off through the town and into the fields. They didn't worry about being seen.

When they reached the fields and turned north, Dumont thought he could make out human figures far to the north. He thought of his field-glasses, the only pair in Kri Koro, unless Löwenstein had some...A tool is useful only when it is at hand. Once again he had left them hanging in his office. He shaded his eyes and stared. He could see a few figures before him and far beyond them a larger group. The distances reflected differing times of departure. He was seeing the human equivalent of the new astronomy in which the observations of the most distant objects were also an observation of the most distant past. It occurred to him idly that humans might also do the same: the peoples most distant are presumed to be the most primitive, the closest to the ancestors. He'd often heard colleagues comparing the various peoples of Africa to the many tribes of Gaul. Some Europeans encountered (or sought?) their inner primordial savage in Africa. He didn't, and he missed his binoculars.

* * *

In the cantonment, Sisibé happened to spot Gorkel sitting miserably in a corner, well-scrubbed but still very smelly. The story of the privy had spread quickly. Gorkel was now almost a by-word across the town of Kri. Blacksmiths were rehearsing jokes and jibes to release when they next saw a Fula. The Wolof women were chortling. Sisibé felt a certain compassion for the boy. Curiosity and a willingness to investigate, even under unpleasant conditions, were traits not to be despised.

He walked over. "Pullo!" he called. Gorkel looked up at him, still shamed. "I understand you wish to understand the secrets of the *nasrani*," he began. "Many in *farafinya* share that desire and hope to learn their power." Gorkel shifted slightly out of his corner. "I don't believe it's through *korte* or *dalilu* or *boli* that they achieve power. They are human. They have learned more than we. They know secrets of iron that our smiths have not discovered. They have devices to make cloth that are more efficient than the most skilled *maabo*." He intentionally used the Fula word for a weaver. The gambit was successful. Gorkel turned fully out of his corner to face Sisibé.

"To learn the secrets of the *nasrani*," he suggested, "you should learn their language and their customs. You've been interested in their bodily by-products." This was a nuanced statement. The smells were still strong. "You thought they used the same sort of magic that we practice here." He stopped, because he needed to think about his next propositions; he was trying to articulate thoughts that had been simmering in his own mind as he studied and as he worked with the various officers and administrators of his career. "You wonder at *nasrani* power. You think it resides in the *nasrani* body, and so you look at the body's products." Gorkel half-nodded. "Consider not what comes out, but what goes in. Do you understand the words that the *nasrani* use? Do you know how they understand the world? Their shit proves only that they are as human as the rest of us."

Gorkel knew Sisibé mainly as an important figure attached to the *nasrani*, but not accessible. He began to smile in gratitude.

"You might attend their school," offered Sisibé. "They wish to train officials. You can learn their language and something of their skills."

Gorkel moved to embraced Sisibé. The older man stepped back.

Kamisa
Photo from a painted mural of the story of Sunjata that was in the library at the University of Kankan, but has now been destroyed (there were student riots some years after the author took this photo was there).

CHAPTER IV

I AWOKE WHEN ASSYA'S body moved away from mine. Green light, the softened sunlight that passes through leaves, shone from above. She had moved gently, and I allowed myself to lie and think over recent events and our current situation. For the immediate present—we needed to find the trail. I had suggested that dawn would bring new paths, but hope, not confidence, uttered those words.

Voices sounded, softened by distance. One was was Assya's. My eyes opened fully and I sat up.

Assya stood some thirty paces away. She faced a great hyena, its head level with her chest. It was seated on its haunches: not ready to pounce, but the posture of an animal considering the world around it. Much of its fur was tinged with grey and white. Dark spots shone against tawny fur along the flanks, but around the jowls and the dark mask of its face the fur was clearly lighter. This was an old, even an ancient, animal. My gaze finally reached its eyes. I found not the dark and dangerous focus of a meat-eating animal, but the sort of reflective and receding perspective that I had seen in the *wokòlò*.

In many tales hyenas are the monster that seizes a child. In others, they are the buffoons outwitted by the hare or the tortoise. They have their place in cults: as the earthly eaters of carrion, they are the gatekeepers of death. We respect and fear them. I recalled this lore as I watched Assya.

Assya was speaking in Soninke. I couldn't hear her first remarks. I did hear its answer, which was chanted.

"Xusu balanbale, xusu kanyante

Xusu Wage..."

I later learned the creature spoke of her beauty and said she was headstrong.

Assya answered. "You know me, then, *Turunu*? Are you then the *Namaninga*, the master of the cults, the watcher on the ways, the one who collects knowledge from the passing spirits?"

"I am of the lineage of that beast that guided Jabe son of Dinga to Koumbi. Always we recognize the royal blood of Wagadu. You are the long-lost princess." There was a hesitation in its voice, a reluctance to speak the rest of the identification.

"I am the sacrifice that was not fulfilled. That is true."

"And what is your purpose?"

"I seek to fulfill my obligation."

"You seek a path?"

"Last night I followed a path. A beast destroyed it."

"Daughter of the line of Dinga, do you remember the story of Jabe?"

She was thinking. I did not step forward. This was her affair, not mine. She understood the implications of the hyena's question and was searching for an answer.

"Mama Turunnun, Tunka Turunnun. I come to you as you see me. I cannot strengthen you with the livers of white horses. I have no wealth."

"You are not alone."

Something in the tone of the ancient predator sent a chill through me. Suddenly I wondered why I had been brought on this venture; I remembered that this woman had told me the night before that she had betrayed princes; I remembered the passion with which she had described her goal. For her this quest outweighed individual human lives. Was I an offering brought to the altar?

"I can ask nothing of my companion. He has no part in this business." I heard that answer also with a chill. She wouldn't give me up to the beast as a sacrifice, and that was reassuring. But...I had followed her because she held my heart. I would do anything I could to further her progress. I had dreamed that she understood that intent. Was she denying me? Was she cutting me off?

"He may act on his own. Should you not invite him?" These words from the beast were spoken in Maninka, loud enough for me to hear. Assya looked over her shoulder. I construed this as an invitation.

The hyena examined me carefully. In its gaze I saw not the focused intent of a predator on the hunt, but the interrogative assessment of a wise human. It also observed dimensions unknown to me. "*Bamana-kè*, I see you are connected with the *wokòlò*. How did this come about?"

I glanced at Assya and she tossed her head slightly: this was my question, not hers. Yet she smiled, and her hand reached out to mine.

"My father was poisoned by his brother. My mother told me to flee, and I obeyed her. Leaving my village, I encountered a *wokòlò* who took me into service, although he didn't specify my tasks. My *wokòlò* took my name from me."

"Did you meet the *wokòlò* again?"

"I met the spirits again in the waters by Bougouni." I wasn't sure that creatures such as this one recognized the human names of places, but perhaps they acknowledged the living communities of those spaces. "This came after my first meeting with the princess of the Wague."

The hyena considered and nodded. "Your paths are linked. Will you help her in her search?"

"I am here," I answered simply. I assumed the fact spoke for itself and clearly the hyena understood my meaning.

The hyena turned again to Assya. "Your companion has a stake in this matter. Will you accept his assistance?"

"I will not give up his life," she answered flatly. "Take mine, rather." At that statement, my heart leapt.

"No life is required in this matter," said the hyena, somewhat drily. "However blood must be offered. You know that is the measure of value of the stake." Assya nodded shortly. The hyena turned to me. "You wish to help the woman." The statement suggested a curious scorn for the mating practices of bipedal primates and the complications they introduced to a simple process.

"I do," I answered.

"Will you give your right hand?"

I stretched it out. With a glance up at Assya, the hyena leaned forward, opened its mouth, and took my hand in its jaws. The whole hand fit neatly into its mouth. I felt my fingers sliding over the tongue down to the throat for a short second. Then it bit down on my wrist, its teeth piercing the jointure between hand and forearm. I had anticipated a sudden and sharp pain, the slicing of a part from the whole; what came instead was extended agony. The entire hand was being destroyed in its various parts: I could feel a corrosion that devoured the skin and the softer flesh beneath with the pain of acid burns, the burning of the nerves as they were consumed, and then below them my bones, from the first phalanges back towards the nubbly carpal pieces, were all crushed by the powerful jaws of the animal.

Despite myself, my legs gave out and I fell to my knees. I was furious at this weakness: I had felt pain before, and had been sure I could resist it. The occasion most similar to this one was my circumcision ceremony when I squatted over a log and the smith reached out and pulled the foreskin of my member for the quick sharp cut; I included in that memory the days of delicate torture as the wound healed while I still required the use of its orifice. The challenge then was not to scream and to rise without assistance. I had achieved both goals. But this pain defeated me. I don't know how long it lasted, nor what time elapsed between the first damage to the the fingertips to the final consumption of the last bits of bone; somehow, I went numb, feeling the pain but unable to react. Even had I wished to, I couldn't have summoned the muscular control to pull my hand away; everything was blurred with the pain.

I was on my knees. Assya's hand was on my shoulder, offering comfort. The ordeal ended. The hyena opened its mouth and sat back. I looked down, expecting to see a mangled stump pumping blood from severed arteries. But my hand was whole, unharmed. Every finger, complete. Amazed I moved them and saw them wriggle.

Assya and I stared at the ancient beast. It smiled, not quite laughing. "It is a matter of intent and determination," it explained. "The sacrifice is not the flesh or the blood, but the pain." It looked directly at me. "You were willing to make the sacrifice, and you proved that point. It is enough. Now let me show you your path."

It turned, its low haunches moved away from us into the gloom under the trees. I quickly picked up my staff; Assya was already following the beast, clearly fearing to lose this guide to her heart's desire. We had difficulty following the hyena. Its facial fur may have been hoary with age, but its hindquarters were still dark and mottled and they blended easily with the sprottled and spotted shadows. Assya and I hurried along, trying to shorten the gap. As though to frustrate us, the hyena would step up its pace when we were too close, vanishing briefly into the dark before turning its head to give us a glimpse of the whitened fur.

I scarcely noticed the dense forest about us. Usually I was keenly aware of threats from the tiny, unseen scorpion under a leaf to the hissing serpent of lethal fangs or constricting coils: I had once seen a python consume a warthog in a terrifying and ineluctable tragedy of compression and slow swallowing. Ants, leopards—none of these perils crossed my mind, intent upon the woman before me and upon her focus, the elusive haunches of the hyena before her. I don't think we actually went very far: a kilometer, perhaps, but little more.

Once again we found ourselves confronted with rock. It rose before us, black and silvery, out of the shadow of the trees. In a gap before which the hyena finally seated itself, allowing us to catch up, I observed a greater darkness. The rock was the reflective black of slate, catching and returning light. Here the light vanished. Darkness visible, I might have said, or perhaps it was that light that continues beyond the range of human vision. I didn't try to assess its qualities. The hyena had stopped; Assya came up to it, and I was close behind.

"Mama Turunnun, Namaninga," said Assya. I knew she believed those names exercised some power over the creature. I was less sure. I existed without a name. As I observed our guide and tried to infer its purposes, I sensed principally an amused

acquiescence, a curious participation in some almost idle exercise. The creature didn't exist only to guide us. I couldn't guess its true calling yet. Perhaps that notion was a human conceit. This being was content to exist. Its needs were not those of a fleshly animal.

"I can offer you no further help," the hyena stated before she phrased her question.

"You have guided us; I ask no more," answered Assya confidently. "You may still have knowledge we need. You know that the...treasure was not delivered to its proper home. I'm not sure I know the destination."

"Princess of the Wage, if you achieve your first goal the path will be shown before you. I act on instructions. I am only one among many servants."

Assya smiled. "Then please accept my thanks and deliver them also to the *Muso Koronin* who assists me."

The hyena vanished. Assya and I looked at each other, then turned to face the darkness in the rock wall. I became aware of a deep and unhappy bourdon: the humming of countless bees. Raising my eyes I saw that upon the rocks and in crannies above there were hives about which swarmed a multitude of black-bodied and silver-winged bees. Their bodies danced and waggled, there seemed no pattern to their movement. The deep thrum of their noise was discordant. I knew little of bee-keeping, yet it was clear these hives had lost the ruler or governor that guided their work and operations. Fortunately for us, the consequence was confusion and indecision rather than riotous rage. Later, I thought to connect these hives—placed to guard an entrance—with the Condé rulers of the town and to link this confusion with the death of an elder, with the passage of power from one master to another.

Assya and I joined our hands and stepped forward into the darkness. At the threshold of the cave our feet encountered smooth bumps in the clay. Across the entrance we could see four rounded protrusions rising above the ochre clay in a line across the entrance. Their color was a pallid tone between green and yellow, the patina of aged bone, and through each ran a seam of darker color.

"*Ah*," observed Assya. "These are boys, the *bilakorolu*. They died by violence. I presume they were involved in delivering the treasure to this site. They are not the principal guardians." She released my hand. "Step to the side."

Then she cried out a song:

Condé muso!
Tuma ni Bagi moden!
Jonmakan ni Bagi moden!
Sigi ma diya!
Sigi ni gundo! Kunsigi ni sanu!

I sensed motion within the cave. As we entered, a form started coalescing within the darkness: the ponderous shape of a buffalo with glistening horns. I had seen that shape before and had dodged its charge only by luck. As Assya sang, the shape faded back into a liminal space between its world and our own, where its substance became ethereal. It still threatened assault and destruction upon our plane should we make a false step. Assya again led me forward. Beyond the skulls of the four hapless boys who had been led to slaughter, a skull sat on a flat stone. A phantom rose: a pallid and translucent maiden. She was simply dressed, a cotton cloth wrapped about her hips, a darker blouse covering her chest. She was not armed, but her presence was menacing. She raised a hand against us.

Assya repeated the first lines of the song. Then her tone become conversational and she greeted the maiden in Maninka, "*I ka kènè*?" This is the ordinary greeting exchanged by friends who meet on the street. I was astonished by its banality. To my surprise I saw the maiden's lips move, but I couldn't hear or understand her response. Assya spoke again, words I could not hear. An exchange occurred: the communion of a woman denied her sacrifice with another on whom it had been imposed. After a moment, the phantom faded and Assya turned to me.

"This is the Condé maiden who was sacrificed to seal the cave," explained Assya. "Her spirit takes the form of a great buffalo to attack intruders. This is one way in which Condé women show their power."

I remembered her intervention when Kuyate was talking of the witches of Manding. "Kamisa?"

"Kamisa for one, Sogolon and her daughters as well." Assya smiled slightly. I learned later that she was reflecting on Sogolon's magical power which manifested when men tried to sleep with her.

I had heard the story. I began to believe that Assya might overcome the protections on the cave.

We stepped past the fifth skull. I held my staff before me like a blind man testing the unseen ground. Before us the dark was broken by a thousand points of light grouped in close-set pairs: eyes that captured the dim light from the entrance and returned it with a baleful and hostile glow. They kept their distance. I was sure they were spiders: the large and hairy forest spiders that wander like miniature lions, savage in attack, ravening on their prey. I shuddered.

What else was glittering in this cave? We stepped out of the light from the entrance, then tentatively, foot by foot, advanced. I didn't know what to expect, what sorceries besides the spirit of the maiden protected this space, what earthly creatures besides the horde of spiders might await us. I was more sure than ever that those pairs of eyes rising from the dark were evidence of spiders large enough to fill a drinking calabash, the width of two hands. For now they remained on the walls, staring down at us.

The tip of my staff, swinging gently before me, struck some dark object with a muffled knock. Expecting gold, I had been looking for reflections; it occurred to me now that the object might be wrapped and covered. Assya also heard the sound and joined me. Together, we reached out, bending low to the ground. Our hands met leather: a hide of some kind. It was stiff and cool, not the living skin of some unseen and frightful creature. The object was placed somewhat away from the wall, for which I was grateful: as we touched it, the pairs of eyes shifted over the walls and began to move towards us, so that soon the wall behind the object was a mass of hostile eyes.

Assya knelt, paying no attention to the threat on the wall. Her hands ran swiftly over the object, judging its size and contours, testing where the cover yielded, whether there were cords or other fastenings. I rose to stand behind her, grasping my staff in its middle in case I needed to use it as a weapon.

I heard a rustle. Assya was lifting the cover from the object, and the crinkled leather whispered as it folded back, brittle and in places crumbly. As it was lifted, a glow appeared. Assya became impatient and tore the cover off, throwing it back against the wall where it knocked several spiders to the ground. To my relief, they scurried back up to a safe elevation

Assya had revealed a royal throne—a stool, we would call

it in Africa. It presented a flat seat whose plane ended in scrollwork on either side. Four pillars supported the plane, ending at the ground in paw-like forms. Between the pillars hung a filigreed lattice, burnished, embossed with the sculpted figures of animals and men. Principal among them were hippopotamus and catfish.

The glow blinded me; my eyes had been adjusting to the dark.

"My sign!" cried Assya embracing the stool. She lay over it for a moment while I looked around, expecting that this revelation would bring some reaction from the forces that guarded the cave. I was relieved that removing the cover hadn't brought down the horde of glittery-eyed creatures upon us; in fact, they seemed to have retreated from the light to the darker recesses and their shadows.

Assya rose and turned to me. "We must take this. It fell here long ago. It should have been returned to the under-earth. But it was stolen out of greed and hidden here. We must return it to its intended destination."

I began to understand why she had asked for my help. It had been a relief, earlier, to learn that I hadn't been brought as a sacrificial offering, a sop to hostile powers. Now there was a task at which I had some experience. But I could immediately perceive a problem. "Assya, such a weight of gold is too great for one man." I was ashamed to admit this, yet it was true: the stool before me must have weighed as much as eight of the bars of salt I had carried.

"You're looking with your human eyes," she answered. "The *wokòlò* gave you another sight. See it as they might, as you saw the path last night."

I closed my eyes to recall the spirit path and to allow my

mind to settle in whatever pattern allowed it to observe such a reality, and then opened them again. I could still see a glow in the shape of the golden stool. Within the glow sat another object: the head of a monstrous serpent. Not a snake such as one finds in the fields, sleek and streamlined, but a dragon's head with a great brow projecting over a broad snout with spikes and tusks bristling out in all directions: from the ridge over the brow forth from below the eye-sockets, along the lines of the upper and lower jaws. It was black, blacker than ebony or jet, the color of a chthonian being brought impiously to light. The glow of gold died as it met the surface of this relic; the light vanished, swallowed and destroyed. Its eyes were shut, to my relief; I wouldn't have wanted to look into the eyes of such a creature. I realized that Assya must have looked into those eyes. She had faced the *Bida* as it rose from the well to consume the sacrifice. She must also have seen the change as the hero's blade met the flesh of the neck and parted the head from the body. Life had remained in the head: it had pronounced a curse upon the land of Wagadu.

Assya sensed my understanding. "Come," she ordered, "let us be on our way." She retrieved the cover and we slipped it back over the treasure. Then she took the end of the snout; I moved and reached for the place where the jawbones met the skull. Together we raised it—heavy, ponderous, massive in dimensions I couldn't imagine, yet still mobile in our world. I slipped under it to carry the weight upon my head. Then we walked quickly toward the light at the entrance of the cave. Behind me I heard a susurrus of motion—the spiders, no doubt, responding to the removal of the radiant glow, or perhaps the removal of the treasure. We reached the entrance stepping quickly into sunlight before they caught us, if indeed they were in pursuit.

Assya and I both paused, blinking. We were in the deep shade of the forest trees and the light had the green tinge of the world beneath the canopy.

What was our path now?

Hyena: a small brass statuette in author's collection.

CHAPTER V

APPROACHING THE VILLAGE of Sènètela, Gaoussou observed men coming from the village. When they were close enough, he recognized the two oldest men, the chief and the earthmaster of Sènètela with an escort of young men.

"Condé *ba*!" the chief greeted him as soon as they were close enough for speech. He didn't pause for courtesies. "It is well you have come. We have serious news." His escort, save for the earthmaster, withdrew. Gaoussou gestured; his men also stepped back, leaving three old men standing in the middle of the millet fields. Gaoussou was still tall and imposing; the other two had wizened skins and very sparse white hair. Their clothing was poor: plain cotton, now a dirty grey, and some leather straps.

"The secret of the cave has been breached," announced the chief. "In the night, the earthmaster felt a disturbance: humans followed the *sira gbana*, the hot trail," (he meant the spirit path) "and the earthmaster felt the presence of a guardian. Not the wild buffalo that was roused two days ago when the *nasrani* men came, but the *bama-jinu*, the crocodile that sweeps the paths."

Gaoussou nodded. Cejan hadn't provided such details, but Cejan might not know all the secrets.

The chief continued. "The crocodile swept the path and

returned to its lair. But it didn't destroy the intruders. We fear they may discover the cavern of the secret."

"Did anyone see them?" asked Gaoussou.

"No."

Gaoussou thought of the old woman's words. The thieves did not seek profit, only restitution. What might the chief know of the history behind the treasure?

"Do you know the source of the treasure?" he asked.

The chief shook his head, but the earthmaster nodded slightly, so Gaoussou turned to him.

"Tell me what you have heard."

The man shuddered slightly, as though in fear of the secrets he was ordered to reveal. His voice whistled, "The treasure came from the sky. It was destined for a certain place. It was not delivered. The ancestors saw it as a golden treasure and kept it for themselves, hiding it in their own secret place."

"Have you seen it? How did it appear to you?"

The old man covered his face. "Every earthmaster is taken to the cavern when he is learning the secrets. The treasure is covered and guarded. Each may see something different. I saw the head of a great *karana*, a serpent or a dragon."

"And do you know where it should have been placed?"

The chief answered, "That was a Condé secret. We know nothing with certainty."

"If it was the head of a *karana*," added the earthmaster, "then it needed to be returned to the waters of the earth. And only one place in this region would serve."

All three knew where Gaoussou must go: Kri Kulun, the well of Kri that lay in the hills above the town, a deep pool formed by a spring that rose in a cleft of the hills. It was a very sacred place. Hunters avoided it, although otherwise they usually used springs and water sources as prime stalking grounds. That area, though, brought bad luck to hunters.

Gaoussou thanked the chief and the earthmaster, then turned back to his men. "We must change our course," he told them, indicating the direction they would follow.

Looking back, he saw people behind him. He would not meet them. A short way back, a cross-trail led through the fields to a path that ran north of the town and back to the sacred well.

Marco and Tristan were dismayed to see Gaoussou's party suddenly turn back. They withdrew into the millet stalks until they saw Gaoussou turn aside. Then they ran to make up the lost time.

Behind them, Dumont observed the meetings, cursing himself again for forgetting his binoculars. When he saw how Gaoussou changed his course, he followed immediately.

* * *

In Kri Koro, Löwenstein was cursing the absence of his manager. No one could say where he might be. In the night a woman had come. The two of them departed. Löwenstein wasn't concerned. Men sought women everywhere. He suspected his porters traded on the prestige of the white man's expedition to persuade the gullible.

As the morning passed his forbearance diminished. He wanted the man who had said the *jeli* Kuyate could offer information on the strange, violent, and evanescent beast he had encountered and escaped the day before.

He didn't know the dead bearer. He did try to know the men who worked with him, but couldn't always learn about the bearers. They hired on for a day or two, from one village to the next, perhaps at the limit of their worldly horizon.

He was often struck by the similarity in outlook between these villagers and those in Germany: any place more than a day's walk (or a cart ride) from their home was foreign and untrustworthy, the likely home of witches (in Germany) or cannibals (in Africa). Men came and went. Men who had information he desired belonged to a different category.

After the noon meal, he sent a messenger to the cantonment to request the assistance of the official interpreter.

Sisibé accompanied the messenger on his return. Sisibé had heard all sorts of rumors the day before when the exploration party returned with two corpses. His exchanges with the *komanda* about the strange *nasrani* shed no further light on the matter, nor had Gorkel provided information. He had suspicions that he didn't voice, and he was eager to hear what a loremaster might offer.

Korongo Kuyate arrived later. After tea and greetings and exchanges of pleasantries, they reached the point of discussing the matters he would recount this day. The *jeli* gave no sign he might have heard of peculiar and distressing events. Löwenstein took Sisibé aside at that point and asked him to inquire carefully about buffaloes marked with gold and silver, and especially buffaloes that killed men.

"*Jeli-ba*," began Sisibé, "the *nasrani* has a question separate from the *maana* of Mari Jata. Yet I have heard that this matter may pertain to the *maana*. You may have heard that yesterday our *nasrani* went with the *nasrani komanda*, the *franzawi*, and they were attacked by a *jinu*. The spirit took the form of a buffalo with horns of gold and a tail of silver. Our *nasrani* here," he pointed back to Löwenstein, "wishes to know if you have heard of such a beast."

The *jeli* listened quietly. His gaze met Sisibé's with understanding. He paused for drama, then answered, "Indeed, such a buffalo lies at the source of the story of Mari Jata. I have not yet spoken of his mother. She was a Condé woman, known as Sogolon Kuduma, Sogolon of the Warts, because she was so ugly. She became the wife of Mari Jata's father by a curious sequence of events. Shall I tell it?" That question was the mark that he would then perform and expect payment at an appropriate rate.

Sisibé didn't need to translate the answer. *"Ja! sicher! Das muss ich hören!"* came the bellow.

So the singer recounted the ancient tale of the monstrous buffalo, the shape taken by Du Kamisa, the old Condé woman.

After her nephew denied her kinship and her share in a family feast, she became a monster and ravaged the fields and slew all who rose against her. The land of Du suffered and word went out that they desired help. Many hunters and warriors came and were slain, crushed by thundering hooves or pierced by shining horns. After some time, two brothers answered the call. They were guided by the words of a diviner, and they came without pride or swagger. At the edge of the fields of Du they found an old woman living in misery. They helped her: they brought firewood and water, and one of them even cooked for her. For a man to cook was extraordinary, and the meal was not the worst she had tasted, as the old woman admitted. They stayed with her for some days assisting her. On the third day, she gave them the secret to their quest: they couldn't kill the magic buffalo with an ordinary weapon. Only a spindle, shot from a bow, could bring down that monster.

The brothers went forth on their hunt. The monster appeared, as it always did when armed hunters walked through the fields of Du. It was a great buffalo, darkness incarnate, save for the horns that gleamed golden as the sun and for the tail that shone silver as the moon.

At this description, Sisibé gasped slightly, and so too, after the translation, did Löwenstein.

The brothers evaded the beast for a time. The older brother set the spindle to the cord of his bow, but when the beast appeared he panicked and the spindle fell to the ground. The younger brother quickly seized it and sent the shaft into the heart of the beast as it thundered towards them. The buffalo fell and dissolved, leaving only its horns and tail, the gold and the silver, behind.

The brothers took these tokens to the king of Du, he who had denied kinship with the old woman, and he offered them their choice of any maiden from the kingdom. This was the reward announced for the killer of the monster. The brothers had been advised by the old woman; they took the ugliest maiden, the one disfigured with warts: Sogolon Kuduma, the Condé maiden.

Kuyate noted the surprise in his audience. He then told how they brought the maiden (they had tried to sleep with her, but she defeated them) to the king of Narena. He too had been advised by a diviner, and so he rewarded them with compliant women and took this strange being to his marriage bed. Peculiar stories are told about the conjugal coupling: she resisted him in many ways. Her pubic hair became as stiff and straight and sharp as porcupine quills. He found himself manless. But he overcame her resistance. An iron knife passed over her body and her warts and other deformities vanished. Her attempts to deflate him failed.

After she yielded her maidenhead, she wished to observe

the celebrations outside their nuptial chamber and so her neck extended like the body of a serpent, and her head flitted out to watch the drumming and the dancing.

Kuyate was almost disappointed. Usually, the audience gasped and trembled as he described the sorceries of the bride Sogolon. They took the killing of the monster in stride, for in many ways that story was ordinary.

This audience had thrilled more to the buffalo than to the quills. Truly, the *nasrani* were strange.

Grassland: outside Kankan in 2004

CHAPTER VI

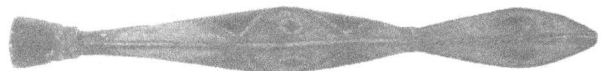

ALONG THE PATH TO the sacred spring of Kri Kulun stood a small shelter. It protected a guardian and a variety of sacred implements. It was unobtrusive and easily missed in the lush vegetation that grew along the stream that rippled and babbled down from the sacred waters. The guardian was alternately a Magasuba, considered the earthmasters of Kri Koro, or a Condé from a collateral line. Rulers long ago learned to align themselves with popular faith.

It was a simple shelter, not a shrine, not a site for rituals or ceremonies. Such activities always took place at the water's edge. Still, it contained a secret: it housed a python. The snake linked the world of men to the underworld from which the spring emerged. The guardians fed it milk and occasionally a chick brought by a supplicant. This snake was not yet large enough to devour a chicken.

The guardian of the day, a Magasuba, arrived and poured out the milk into a small calabash dish. He called out to the python, coiled in the shadows among the leather cases containing ritual objects, knowing it would expect the milk. The python began to uncoil itself and to move toward the bowl of milk. The guardian watched with fear and awe. All snakes were considered lethal. Yet the colored geometry of the scales presented such beauty to the eyes, and the motion was so smooth and graceful that peril could be overcome.

Normally, the snake coiled itself near the bowl and lapped at the offering. Today it ignored the calabash. Its head turned away, towards the spring; the body coiled beneath it, and with a smooth and graceful motion, it launched itself in a ballistic arc into the air. The black and white patterns of its body registered on the guardian's eyes as a glowing missile, the arrow of death perhaps. Then it vanished.

The Magasuba stared. The calabash and the milk were still there. He saw no snake. He walked around the hut, still finding no trace of the guardian python. He began to follow the path that led along the stream up to the spring, and suddenly felt himself halted. He could see no obstacle, he could feel nothing before him, but he couldn't move forward.

He turned back. He needed to consult with his peers in Kri Koro.

* * *

Gaoussou knew the paths around Kri Koro as well as anyone. He couldn't be sure how much advance the thieves might have, but if they were heading to the well of Kri Kulun, he should be able to cut them off.

"Duga ba!" cried a man at the front of the column. He had glimpsed a great vulture, its wings briefly a black bar against the sky and then lost in the trees.

All stopped and stared, but the bird—if a bird—was no longer visible. The man who cried out was already wondering if his eyes might have deceived him. Gaoussou said nothing, but trusted the man's perception. Vultures belonged to the realm of occult powers and he was sure that his path led him into that realm.

They rounded the lower slope of the northern hill and descended into the vale. They crossed the stream of water from the sacred spring and found the path that led up to the spring, past the guardian's hut.

They didn't find the guardian.

Gaoussou paused at the empty shelter. An absent guardian was a sign of trouble. Where might the man have gone? He saw no blood, nothing overturned from a fight. He noted a small calabash with milk—what sort of creature were they feeding? He had skilled trackers among his men, yet they could tell him nothing. They moved on past the shelter with caution.

One of the trackers led the column. He was stopped by an invisible barrier. Gaoussou and the others quickly joined him. But no one could advance along the path.

* * *

Not far behind Gaoussou, Dumont consulted his compass (he always carried it in a pants pocket). He could orient himself, although he didn't fear getting lost.

Striding amidst the *tirailleurs*, he was thinking of geology and hydrology. The curious excavations, suggesting artisanal gold mines, lay to the north. The Condé group headed first in that direction.

Why had they turned away? They must be pursuing something else—a treasure? Something stolen? He remembered, unhappily, what Samba Ly had said about the Soninké woman seeking a treasure. Her absence wounded him, although he had done his best to consider the relationship purely physical. Her qualities were not only physical: she possessed exceptional intelligence and knowledge, she showed empathy and warm affection. This thought of a stolen treasure immediately dissolved the protective partitions in his mind.

Crossing the stream through rippling water distracted him and returned his mind to thoughts of hydrology, and thence to alluvial gold. Then from gold to a vivid and still disturbing memory: the spirit attack of the day before. If spirits guarded the gold workings, what might watch this path? As a rational Frenchman, he didn't believe in demons and spirits, although he didn't question aloud possible miracles such as the vision at Lourdes to avoid unpleasant disputes with the fervent faithful. His skepticism was now frayed. He couldn't explain the buffalo.

The forest blocked his view of the landscape. He gazed up toward the path, trying to understand the terrain. He and his men were surprised by an extraordinary flash of light. It appeared several hundred yards ahead in a place lost in the greenery, but it lit up the underlying leaves of the great forest trees and reflected back strongly enough to make him blink. Some elemental force must have been released. Again he thought of spirits. The hue of color in that explosion of light was golden.

"Quick!" he ordered. "We must catch them!" So he and his troop charged forth to meet the Condé party and demand answers. Dumont was now prepared to apply his colonial authority. He didn't fear causing social turbulence; he required information, and he would force Gaoussou Condé to reveal it. He was backed with *tirailleurs* carrying reliable and loaded weapons. What more might he need at this place and time?

* * *

Tristan and Marco were caught in the middle. They had been following the Condé group closely when the explosion of light half-blinded them. They stood blinking and astounded, then heard the unwelcome sound of heavy military boots behind them. The *komanda* must be close—it must be the French authority pursuing Gaoussou. They ducked off the trail to the left, bursting through the bushes into the stream. Marco lay flat in the waters. Tristan crouched. Marco guessed he was protecting his weapon from the wet.

They waited. They heard the *komanda*'s party pass by. Soon after, they heard voices: a babble of indistinguishable sounds in different tones, according to the languages. The first murmur was cut short when a sharp voice—French, thought Marco—asserted itself. A second polyphonic murmur began, interpreting, exploring, suggesting possibilities.

Their attention then was divided. Marco listened to the voices, trying to guess the conversation from intonations. He couldn't distinguish languages, much less meaning. He heard peremptory challenges, polite and lower responses, the extended murmur of apologies or explanations. The stronger voices he attributed to the *komanda* who would have the weapons and the colonial authority to enforce his demands.

There was an extended silence. He couldn't see how Dumont accompanied Gaoussou up to the point of the invisible barrier, tried to pass, and then admitted to the Condé elder that there were powers beyond understanding at work.

The conversation then resumed, with fewer sharp exclamations and much more quiet interchange.

Tristan waited, wondering if action would be needed. He trusted Marco to interpret the human aspects of the situation. His gaze wandered around the stream and the plants at the edge. He noted the shapes of leaves, the angle of stems, the movement of insects. His eyes kept returning to the gravel bed at the stream's edge. The pebbles seemed a mosaic that required understanding: what was the picture they composed? He examined the shades of ocher and yellow and black. Some few stones were red, many were white, suggesting perhaps crystals or chalk. He found himself staring at them.

Shadows fell over the two of them. In the shadows, several of the white pebbles began to glow, as though they had preserved the sun's light and were now returning it. They weren't bright, they were very small, yet they stood out from the mass of other pebbles. Curiously, Tristan reached out and collected a dozen of them.

Shrine

CHAPTER VII

THE HYENA HAD VANISHED. We needed a new guide. I wondered if my red-skinned and knock-kneed *wokòlò* might appear, but I was disappointed. Assya cast her eyes all around, then closed them and stood, her hands folded beneath her breasts, the line of her neck rising clean out of her gown, her face in sharp profile: the embodiment of stillness and concentration. I stood silent beside her. I have never lost the image of her loveliness at that moment. Bride of a long-past time, hardly unravished (by her own admission), yet still somehow immaculate and pure. I was sure that I saw her then as the *Bida* had seen her a thousand years before.

The quiet was broken by a hoarse call from above. I immediately glanced around so I didn't see Assya awaken from whatever state she had entered. I still regret not having shared that moment in which her prayer was answered.

The clearing before the cavern was larger than when we had entered: the trees seemed to have moved back. I recalled overhanging and threatening boughs whose shadows merged with the darkness of the cavern's mouth. Now we faced a lighted space. At the end of the clearing stood a dead tree, its trunk and limbs white against the dark green foliage. On the topmost limb sat a dark bird with a red head, a vulture, greater than any white-ruffed scrambling scavenger I had so often observed on the midden-heaps of the villages. This vulture was larger than an eagle, and at that moment even more noble. Its glossy feathers, darker than ebony, the poise of its head, not slung low but erect and commanding, and finally the sharpness of its gaze: this creature was not a carrion-hunting parasite, rather it was the visible symbol of that greater process through which living tissue grows, dies, is consumed and so is renewed and reborn.

Assya apparently saw it more intimately, for she cried out immediately, "*Janban ngana*! *Douga koro*!"

Again the bird called out, raucous and inarticulate, clearly a summons. It spread its great wings and swooped off its perch to soar over us. The arc of its flight took it briefly over our heads. As our eyes turned to follow it, it spiraled back up to rise above the trees and out of sight. Again we heard its harsh call.

Assya took my hand; the path lay plain before us. We followed it under the trees, around the bulwark of rock that housed the cavern, then up a slope. The load I carried was heavier than any bars of salt. I trod carefully and slowly, following the more lightfooted Assya. We climbed until we reached at least the height of the rock face; from there, the path led us back towards the hills east of Kri Koro.

After a kilometer or two, we came to a clearing overlooking Kri Koro. We again glimpsed the vulture, perched on a limb stretched out beyond the canopy. We paused there, enjoying the fresh air and looked down. The town lay before us; to the right were the fields in the valley flatlands. Coming through the fields were parties of men! One group was quite close, cutting through the fields back towards Kri Koro. Far behind them a second large party hastened on their trail. We watched them for a minute. Assya announced, "Gaoussou Condé seeks to recover the family treasure. And behind him comes the *nasrani komanda* who wishes to acquire treasure for his masters."

"Do they know we are here?"

"I fear that Gaoussou may know where we must go."

"Then we must move on." We moved on below the vulture into the shadows, led by its hoarse call.

Our path now descended the slope. After a mile, we reached a vale marking the limit between the mountain that housed the cavern and its neighbor. My feet were steady; still, I hoped fervently that our course lay not up to the next mountain's peak, but towards its feet where (from what I knew of caves and wells and pits) we were more likely to find the place where Assya hoped to return the serpent's head.

We came to a clearing. Assya looked up, saw the vulture, and her hand pressed on my arm in reassurance. She led me on. The path descended, crossed a stream, a trickle running through a wider gravel bed. As we were crossing, Assya stopped me. She dipped water into her cupped hands for me to drink: clean, clear, and refreshing beyond expectation. *Tu taro ji*...Water of the spring, the words of the song came to me.

We were again moving around a hill. After climbing a gentle slope the path leveled off: we were circling the mountain, away from the town, into the fastnesses of the hills, the stream not far off to our left. The trail rose again, and at the top we paused and looked back. Assya gasped. I turned carefully to follow her gaze. The Condé group was close behind us. As we descended hills, they had traversed, and they were now not far behind. I wasn't surprised: with my load I moved more slowly than as usual. We would have to increase our pace.

Assya clearly shared my thought. "*Bamana-kè,* let us make what speed we can." Her soft hand passed under my elbow and her fingers ran down my forearm.

We came to another larger stream, still marked by wide gravel banks and wide enough to create a break in the canopy above us. The sun shone brightly down on us, glittering on the water and the pebbles. On the far side I could see an ordinary human trail.To our right, it led back towards Kri Koro. The left led into the hills.

The water was cool on our feet as we waded across, but this time Assya didn't stop to refresh us. Urgency impelled her: the excitement at a possible fulfillment of her millennial quest, worry about the men chasing us who were certainly on the path from Kri Koro and headed right for us. How far behind?

After the bright sunlight of the streambed, the path under the trees seemed unusually dark, although Assya seemed not to be bothered. The path was well-trodden and clear. In fact, more than clear: it glowed to my sight. Humans might have trod the soil, but beings of another sort also used and marked it, leaving no traces for humans to discern. I thought of telling Assya, for the spirit trace confirmed our course, but she needed no such assurance. She led me on eagerly.

Some hundreds of meters further I noticed a greater light approaching us on the trail. Assya stopped and reached her hand back to touch my arm.

"*Bamana-ké*," she asked, worried, "do you see what I see? Is this the spirit that drove us off our trail last night?"

I looked past her and recognized the shape. The spirit-crocodile was lumbering down the trail, its jaws level with our chests, slightly agape, clearly capable of swallowing either of us, or perhaps both, in one bite. I could see little other than its maw, with a hint of the great bulk behind it. The tail I had observed swinging the night before was invisible behind the body.

"It is the crocodile," I agreed. I have sometimes pondered how I might have tried to oppose it and clear a path for her. I had no weapon that might mark or harm it, no *dalilu* or *basi* or names to control it. I knew, though, that we could not escape by leaving the trail. The spirit would not be put off twice by the same trick.

Assya decided for us. Our only hope of repelling that beast was to confront it with the power of the *bida*'s head.

"*Bamana-kè,*" she said, "lower your load. You are too tall." I kneeled placing the *bida* head level with her shoulders.

"Close your eyes, but reach up so you can touch your burden," she ordered. I understood she was going to lift the cover. The crocodile was very close now.

Smoothly, she pulled the cover off, lifting it from the back of the head. For a moment, I thought she should have pulled it from the front, but then realized she was avoiding the horns on the snout that might have snagged the cover. She moved quickly, but I could still sense a rush...not air, but whatever ether is disturbed by the passage of spirit beings. The crocodile was opening its jaws to attack us. I was briefly thankful that it didn't charge us; I knew how quickly a crocodile can sprint even out of water. Then Assya finished pulling the cover away and let it drop, placing one hand against my arm where it met the burden so that her palm touched me while her fingers lay against the scales.

Through my tightly-closed eyelids I sensed an explosion of light. It shone with the radiance of the sun whose color it had captured; it glowed not with heat (or we would have been cooked) but with some other potency. For an instant, I felt myself caught in a primordial force of nature, fed by the actions of water and earth and wind and fire, nourished to govern the space around me and to create or destroy

The moment passed. We had not been devoured by the crocodile. I kept my eyes shut as I felt Assya restoring the cover to the *bida's* head. After she tucked the leather down against my chest, I opened my eyes. My vision was disturbed by blots of color, swelling, shrinking, drifting across my field of view, but there was no longer a gigantic and threatening spirit-crocodile, and we were alive and unharmed.

"It passed us by," explained Assya, with mischievous laughter in her voice. "It may meet the men who pursue us." She said no more, but our eyes met. I wondered what *dalilu* the Condé might have to overcome the crocodile, then dismissed the worry. I owed them no loyalty or consideration. I raised my burden back up onto my head. We walked with less urgency.

The trail followed the stream up into the hills. The slope was not steep. My body and my burden had come to terms; I was sure that later I would feel the aches I remembered from my first day in the salt caravan, but for now I was moving easily.

The water's noise increased: the stream was running faster. The slope also rose. Then we faced a rock wall, the meeting of cliffs that rose on either side, creating a narrow gorge through which the stream tumbled and fell with noisy cheer. The stone on either side and under foot was dark. Assya drew a deep breath and moved forward to explore the passage we must make.

It wasn't physically difficult: the path narrowed beside the water tumbling through the cleft of rock, and twisted around great boulders. But I felt sapped and weakened as soon as I set foot on the dark stone: it resisted my passage and sought to attack me. Assya, before me, also slowed. A croak came from above: the vulture had rejoined us to mark the passage. Our steps became lighter, our movement easier.

We came to a small round valley, a secluded paradise. The air was rich with the smells of flowers in bloom and the humid processes of life. A few large trees rose, their trunks towering above us and their foliage shading the area. There was also an exuberance of other plant life smothering our sight in greenery.

We found our entry blocked. A great lustrous body marked with ebon lozenges and silver streaks lay across the stream, letting water flow beneath its bulk, too great for us to step over. We stopped and stared.

A monstrous hiss greeted us. The markings proclaimed a snake, but I could not admit that any snake could grow so large, its body thicker than a man is tall.

I looked again, this time with the sight of the *wòkòlò*, and perceived infinity. This was the serpent that girdled the world whose body steadied the brittle crusts of land floating on the fluid elements of eternal chaos: Da of Dahomey, who stabilizes the earth.

Assya seemed unconcerned. She stepped forward, laid a hand on the shimmering and beauteous scaly body, and began to sing.

Saa ba! Saa ba! N'y'i dondo!
Saa ba! Saa ba! N'y'i dondo!
Saa ba! Saa ba! I y'an dondo!
Saa ba! Saa ba! I y'an dondo!

She explained later that this was the ancient song she had heard sung in the court of Wagadu, an invocation of the great serpent to which she was to be sacrificed. The singers were the escort who wished to be spared.

As she sang, a great blunt-nosed head rose above the body. A long forked tongue flicked out, almost touching us. The nose angled down, revealing the eyes far above; eyes that glittered a brilliant bluish-black, suggesting the endless reaches of the night sky. To my unthinking relief, its mouth was not open and prepared to strike.

Above our heads the vulture again called out. Too quickly for certainty, I apprehended a glance of those deep eyes up to the vulture and back down to us. A deeper hiss came from slightly parted lips. Somehow this sound contained meaning where the first one had simply offered a threat.

Assya didn't speak. Her arm rose and pointed back to the load on my head. I adjusted my stance for better balance and raised my hands to the bottom of the cover in case she wished me to lift it up.

The head moved over the barricading coil of its colossal body until it almost touched the snout of the *bida*'s head. The shadow chilled my raised hands, my body shivered. The python exhaled, its breath as cold as its shadow, suggesting the nothingness from which life strives to rise and against which the warmth of living beings is our ephemeral bulwark. It had no smell: neither the fetid panting of a dog nor the fertile aroma of a cow.

Assya's hand grasped my arm and her touch restored warmth to my body. I almost removed my hand from the load it steadied to take her hand.

For a long moment the python's head hung over us as we awaited its decision. Then it swung low, its eyes level with our own and focussed on Assya. She stepped forward.

"I have come to fulfill an obligation," she stated clearly. "Is this not the place where the *bida* must be delivered?" Suddenly I had the thought that the fulfillment of the obligation might also be termed a consummation. A thousand years ago Assya hadn't been swallowed by the serpent. Had she stepped forward to her death?

The python's tongue flicked out again, making only the slightest contact with her brow. She didn't flinch. The head withdrew as the neck straightened and towered high above us. There was a motion, a rearrangement of its position that traveled wave-like down its body, and when it was concluded the coil before us, across the stream, had arched just high enough to allow us passage.

Assya's hand moved from my arm to my waist and she led us forward. I thought I might have to duck as we passed under the serpentine arch; I did not. Perhaps the guardian serpent raised its body or perhaps the two otherworldly bodies yielded each to the other in some unfathomable interaction of being and ether.

Before us lay a circular pool in a ring of stony cliffs, the waters clear and deep and shadowed. High above us the walls rose to a height over which the sun might shine and breezes move. Here, in this crater, all was still. The air was fresh and cool. The water's depths contained the spring that was our goal.

Assya's hand pulled on my arm, and I lowered the *bida*. Again, she carefully removed the cover. It did not blaze incandescent this time. It glowed more softly and warmly: a familiar and welcoming light, that of a hearth or a lantern by the home gate.

Her hand led me: we walked forward into the water. Almost immediately, we sank towards the depths; this was indeed a well, not a shallow puddle. We didn't drown. Very quickly we were floating in a bluish world that I remembered visiting once before. As we sank other colors and flavors met us and permeated our bodies. Eventually, we attained some point of stasis. Assya's hand held my arm: not a clutch, nor the desperate grip of a drowning victim, but the intentional link of one who seeks to maintain a bond.

The blue haze around us cleared. We had entered the world of the water-spirits. Not the great hall of Faro, the master of waters. This was a dedicated entrance…we were waiting outside, floating at the threshold. We sensed three beings approaching us. I had seen them before: Jangana Boro, the mother of the great *bida* serpent of Wagadu, and her sisters Katana Boro and Sune Karo. They were shrouded in misty and midnight draperies, their shapes were impossible to define. The eyes of Jangana Boro lit with a golden glow that obscured all behind her. She moved forward and stretched out her limbs. Together Assya and I laid the head of the *bida* in her grasp.

From her sisters rose a wail that transformed gently into a rhythmic chant. An incantation or a dirge? I couldn't tell. Their tones communicated no human emotions.

"*Muso*," the spirit addressed Assya; I was included in the silent communication. "You have paid your debt. You are released. But remember that the pact was broken, and it has not been restored. You humans cannot count on help from the spirits." It paused to observe us. "But as a mother, I thank you for the return of my son's remains. You may go."

The figures dissolved into the waters. Assya and I rose swiftly out of the vaporous world and quickly found ourselves splashing through the waters to the bank of the pool. We climbed onto the bank and I began to look around for pursuers. I was quickly interrupted. Assya gave a low whoop of delight and triumph and then seized me in a fierce and powerful embrace. Her lips rose to mine; my arms enfolded her, and for me a long-held dream came true.

Some time later, I began to think again of our pursuers. They could no longer frustrate Assya's quest; it had been accomplished.

They could still cause trouble.

I mentioned this idea to Assya. She laughed quietly, unconcerned by such a detail. But she agreed we should move on, and she also agreed it would probably be best not to return to Kri Koro.

"Where will you take me, *Bamana-kè*?" she asked.

"We shall go to the village of my master, Diawara, and there I can resume my work for him in his trading. I'm sure he will greet us hospitably."

She acquiesced with the sweetest smile. We left the little valley, circling around the hill away from Kri Koro and wandering through the forest on the mountainside until, many kilometers later, we came to another trail. We found a place to sleep then, and in the morning we rose to continue our path.

Before we set off, Assya took my hand. She was smiling, a look of deep and soft satisfaction.

"*Bamana-kè*," she announced, "you are going to be a father."

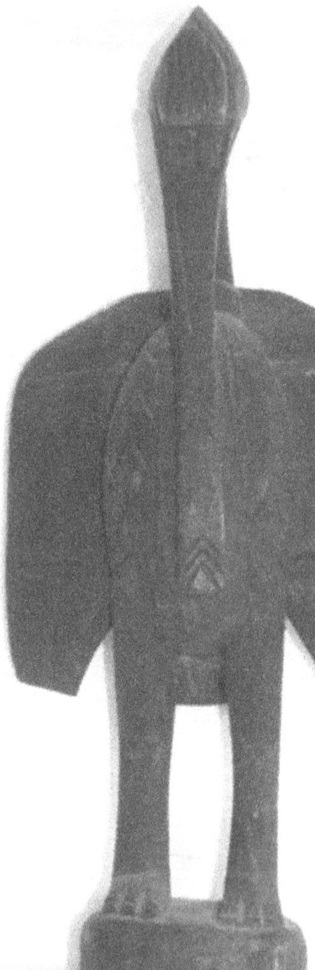

Bird of the Komo
Vulture statuette purchased in
Kankan, Guinea
circa 2005

(Suggests the sacred status of
vultures in several west African
cultures)

And what happened to ?

The crocodile spirit didn't encounter or destroy the group led by Gaoussou Condé. No one saw what happened to it after the cover was lifted from the long-lost head of the *Bida*-serpent when Assya was making her way to the well of Kri.

* * *

The conversation (or negotiation) between Dumont and Gaoussou Condé was unbalanced; Dumont was prepared to exert his authority quite unpleasantly if need be. Gaoussou had stopped thinking clearly some kilometers before. He had responded to the threat to the occult ancestral power. He followed the trail of the thieves, because it was the obvious thing to do. Then he was blocked by powers he didn't understand: the flash of light that half-blinded everyone, and then an impenetrable, invisible obstacle. He feared an end to Condé power, and this thought was deeply unsettling. Such doubts were reserved for the eldest of the lineage: this he grasped in a moment of insight, thinking of Cejan his senior. That flickering thought of Cejan also defined the unpleasant moment as he faced an angry and intransigeant *komanda*. He remembered how he and Cejan had faced the *almamy* Samory: they survived through submission.

Dumont examined Gaoussou's face carefully: they had met on his arrival in the area when the notables of the town greeted the new authority and on a few other occasions. He saw a man caught in a crux of his understanding, not one who controlled spirits. Dumont was sure he had the upper hand.

So when Dumont demanded answers, Gaoussou yielded them. The tangible treasure, the throne of gold, was apparently lost. There was still wealth in the gold deposits. It was better to offer this knowledge than to face the shiny steel circles at the end of the *nasrani*'s guns.

As a result of this forcible exchange, Dumont won the favor of the authorities down on the sweltering coast, who then dispatched parties of geologists and engineers. Dumont himself profited, inevitably, but he found himself less and less preoccupied with administration. He became more interested in the languages and the lore of the peoples, wishing he had the gift of languages that he once found in a certain woman. Somehow, in the history he encountered everywhere in the Manding, he found reflections of her presence and the knowledge she had shared. His enduring memory of her came not from their intimate moments, but from the look on her face when she had challenged Korongo Kuyate on the witches of the Manding: an expression of assurance and confidence in her knowledge. He saw the peoples he ruled caught between the customs of the past that had ensured their livelihoods and the new situations with which they were confronted. Only rarely did he see the courage and defiance that Assya had demonstrated.

Gaoussou and the Condé lineage had to give up the secret of the gold mines and watch as strangers came to develop them. They didn't really suffer. Gaoussou soon realized that in a gold rush, profit came to those selling food, shelter, and other necessities, not to the desperate and obsessed men seeking wealth in the streams and in perilous undergound shafts. The

Condé lineage could easily provide those services. They maintained their wealth.

* * *

Marco and Tristan eventually rose from their cool position in the stream. The other groups had withdrawn. They pushed through the bushes to the path.

"Someone must have found the treasure," admitted Tristan mournfully.

Marco nodded.

"But what others have found, one might still obtain," suggested Tristan. Marco disagreed. The treasure that was being pursued was beyond the reach of the local chief and even the French commander. If *they* had abandoned the search, it must be lost.

They returned, disconsolate, to Kri Koro. Ramata divined their distress and did what she could to console them and help formulate their next plans. Tristan eventually showed Marco his glowing pebbles from the brook and Marco, curious, ran one against the little tea-glass he was holding. He stared in amazement at the scratch it made. He knew of only one stone that cut glass: diamond!

Tristan and Marco remained in Kri Koro, forming a partnership with Ramata and trading through the good offices of Sisibé (who could provide them with all the necessary papers) down to Freetown in Sierra Leone, where the diamonds brought them a good stock of desirable merchandise. The paths they had traced from Geba were too complex.

Sisibé and Nyelle were married very soon after these events, although the wedding was delayed by the funeral ceremonies for Cejan Condé. Sisibé chose to make his career in Kri Koro rather than following the vagaries of colonial administrative placements across the colonies; his preference was accepted higher up in the hierarchy because his efficacy was undisputed. They found themselves very happy together.

* * *

Löwenstein, following a discussion with Sisibé, planned an expedition to Nioro at the edge of the Sahel where he was able to record a rich hoard of heroic stories.

* * *

Samba Ly, still bruised, chose to be reassigned to another district where he served with distinction. He helped to pacify the militant Muslim Fula in the green-pastured region of Macina, and at the end of his career was named king of Sandingsan, a medium-sized town along the Joliba River, or, as it was becoming better known, the Niger River. Sandingsan had never had a king, but they and their ruler adjusted to the new situation.

* * *

Djanka learned how Nyelle had served the old woman, and so she also made her way there. But Djanka found the chores expected of her excessive, and rarely completed them. She spent her time flouncing around the messy compound. The old woman sent her out for firewood and water too often, she demanded that the front space be swept several times—and surely the first time had been enough for such a hovel? But Djanka was confident she was fulfilling her obligations.

After five days, she asked to be allowed to go home, expecting to be rewarded. The old woman, puffing on her pipe, gazed at her face, and then agreed that she might leave. She reached behind her small bench and pulled out a little gourd, its opening closed with a thick tuft of grass.

"My child, I know that you desire the beauty that shall bring you the most desirable husband," she said. "This potion may help you to that goal. Be sure to open the gourd only when you have reached your home and are alone. Otherwise, the magic may go wrong."

Djanka almost snatched the gourd and set off with only a mumbled thanks. Her impatience overcame her. She found a space behind a hut, away from the path, and with trembling hands she pulled the grass stopper from the gourd. A vapor arose, smelling of oxen and rotted leaves. She dimly saw a fog that emerged and then condensed on her face.

When she reached the Condé compound, her face was covered with warts.

ABOUT THE AUTHOR

Stephen Belcher is the son of a Foreign Service officer, and spent much of his childhood in different parts of Africa (Egypt,Nigeria, Benin/Dahomey, Tanzania, with a year at a boarding school in Kenya) and in France and Italy. This background compelled him, in college and graduate school, to include Africa in his research interests.

It also gave him the language skills in French to serve as a contract interpreter with the U.S. State Department accompanying African visitors around the US. This connection led to work accompanying American performing arts groups to countries he could never have visited otherwise, in Africa, Asia, the Near-East, and Latin America.

He has a doctorate in Comparative Literature from Brown University. He has taught at the University of Noukchott in Mauritania as a Peace Corps volunteer, the Pennsylvania State University, and the University of Kankan in Guinea on a Fulbright grant.

He is the author of *Epic Traditions of Africa* (Indiana UP) and *African Myths of Origin* (Penguin Classics), and now lives in Vermont. He is working on a family history that includes two woman artists, and continues his involvement with African studies. He has completed two translations of books on Guinean history by Lansine Kaba (one recently published), and is working with a colleague, Stephen Bulman, on a corpus of colonial-era accounts of the story of Sunjata that has been accepted for publication by the British Academy.

GLOSSARY

A kamane no rini, a wo dangini 'This world comes into being, it will pass.' A phrase from a Soninke epic.

Almami from the Arabic *al-imam*, the religious leader. A title used by the leaders of the Futa Jallon and later claimed by Samori Ture. (Arabic, Maninka and Fula)

ba mother or, with a different intonation, big (Bamana/Maninka)

ba beneen nyom a farewell expression (Wolof)

badenya the bond between the children of the same mother in a polygamous household; opposed to *fadenya*, the rivalry that marks the relations between children of different mothers in their competition for family resources (Bamana/Maninka)

Bagamoyo is a personal name, so no italics (it is also the name of a town inTanzania.

balafon a xylophone, quite literally: wooden slats on a frame over resonant gourds (Maninka/Bamana).

balanza acacia tree (Bamana)

Bamana-kè Bamana man. (Bamana/Maninka).

bangala the male member

banko mud bricks, that Americans would call adobe (Bamana/Maninka)

belentigi a master griot and loremaster (Maninka).

bemba grandfather; more generally, the ancestor of a lineage (Bamana/Maninka)

bida a great serpent (Soninke)

bilakoro uncircumcized boy (Bamana/Maninka)

boli a magical object, an object of occult power. Often translated as 'fetish'. (Bamana/Maninka)

bolon the entrance space before an enclosed compound (Bamana)

buru ba mother horn (Bamana/Maninka)

canari earthen water pot (French).

ce-bolon the man's hut; the sleeping quarters of the leader of the household, that is also the place where the magical or sacred objects of the household are stored (Bamana/Maninka).

chi-wara the antilope mask, used in fertility ceremonies (Bamana/Maninka)

commandant de cercle district administrator (French)

daba the short-handled west African hoe, used to till the earth (Bamana/Maninka)

dali, pl. *dalilu* methods or means, often occult; sorcery, spells (Maninka).

dege a gruel made from millet; in the time of Samori Toure chiefs who were submitting to the warlord would drink his *dege*, that was presumed to contain magical potions that would ensure their obedience. It may simply have been a sign of trust.

diji honey-beer, mead (Bamana/Maninka)

dina from the Arabic for 'religious faith.' The name of a Muslim state founded in the middle delta of the Niger river in the 19th century. (Arabic/Fula)

dloki A shirt. The simplest are made of several strips of cloth sewn together, with a hole cut out for the head and thin bands of cloth holding them together under the arms, leaving the sides open for ventilation; more complex shirts will have sleeves and pockets. (Bamana/Maninka)

dogo small, young (Bamana/Maninka)

dolo millet beer (Bamana/Maninka, and other languages)

dudun a form of drum (Bamana/Maninka)

duga vulture (Bamana/Maninka)

dugu town (Bamana/Maninka).

dugutigi leader/chief of a town (Bamana/Maninka)

dyoburu a form of horn (Bamana/Maninka)

faasa the praise-song of a lineage (Bamana/Maninka)

fa-den step-sibling, joined through the father but not the mother; a proverbial relationship of hostility and rivaly in the Manding (Bamana/Maninka)

fadenya the relationship of children sharing a father, one of rivalry (Bamana/Maninka)

Fama the title of the kings of Segou (Bamana).

fanga power, force; used among the Bamana to signify the royal authority based on their military might (Bamana/Maninka)

farafin black skin, i.e. African as opposed to European (Bamana/Maninka).

Faranse France (general)

faranse-kan the French language (Bamana/Maninka)

fitiri the evening prayer-time (Arabic)

flanton age-group, united by the experience of circumcision or excision at the start of puberty; young men or women within a few years of each other's age who form an association (*ton*) and assume a progression of responsibilities and tasks in the town as they grow older (Bamana/Maninka).

foto penis (Maninka)

franzawi French (Arabic/Bamana/Maninka)

furu marriage (Bamana/Maninka)

garanke leather-worker (Bamana/Maninka)

gesere a praise-singer and lore-master, like the *jeli*/griot. (Soninke)

gewel a praise-singer and loremaster, a griot (Wolof)

gisaankat diviner (Wolof)

Guro an ethnic group/language in Côte d'Ivoire.

hoddu a three-stringed instrument (Fula)

horon noble or free, as opposed to slave/captive (Bamana/Maninka)

horonya the quality of being *horon* (Bamana/Maninka).

Ilo Dadie the primordial herder of the Fula, founder of their way of life in that aspect.

jamana-tigi the leader of a district (Maninka)

jambur a class among the Wolof, neither noble nor slave. (Wolof)
jamu family or lineage name. (Bamana/Maninka)
jara wild beast (often a lion) (Bamana/Maninka)
jarafaga lion-slayer (Bamana/Maninka)
jatigi the local host (and trading partner) of a traveling merchant; the institution works across ethnic lines.
jeli a praise-singer, a musician. Also often called a 'griot.' A social category among many peoples of western Africa, going by different names according to the people. (Bamana/Maninka)
jeli-ke a male griot.
jeli-muso a female griot
jenbe a high-pitched drum, held between the thighs in performance, associated with spirit-cults and passionate events.
joliba the Niger River (Bamana/Maninka).
juguya evil (Bamana/Maninka).
kafu a territorial or political unit; a polity (Maninka).
kamalen a young man in the period between initiation (at puberty) and the responsibilities of family life; in this period the young man is usually working for his father or other relatives (Bamana/Maninka)
karité shea-butter; the oil or cream produced from the nuts (Bamana/Maninka)
ké man (Bamana/Maninka)
keletigi a war-leader, a general (*kele* is war, *tigi* is leader or master). (Bamana/Maninka)
ko goonga 'that is the truth.' (Fula)
kokotla a measure of bar-salt, based on the width of the hand (Maninka).
komo an initiation society associated with hidden knowledge and maintaining social order (Bamana/Maninka)
koro elder, senior (Bamana/Maninka)
korte a hex or magical poison (Bamana/Maninka)
kortekè, –lu sorcerer(s), masters of harmful powers (Bamana/Maninka)
kumboro bees (Maninka)
La 'illa ila 'illahi wa Muhamad rasul ... 'There is no God but God and Mohamad is his Prophet, Praise to the Lord of the world.' The *shahada*, or statement of faith in Islam, used often as a sort of exclamation or commentary. (Arabic)
langue du terroir local idiom or dialect (French)
luntan stranger (Maninka)
maabo, maabube the Fula jeli/griot, but also weavers. (Fula)
mansa king. n.b. The titles for rulers vary; the king of Segou was called a '*fama*,' from the word for power, and many other leaders such as Samory took their titles from Islamic words. The word *mansa* suggests an authentic, indigenous ruler along the lines of Mari-Jata. (Maninka)
marfa or *marifa* a rifle, a gun (Bamana/Maninka).
marigot a watercourse formed in the rainy season when the flood-

waters leave the river beds; also the dry watercourse when the waters have receded. (French)

mogofaga 'person-killer.' A title taken from hunters' associations, but with less positive connotations. (Bamana/Maninka)

Mpaari a game played by warriors in their idle time (Bamana).

muso woman (Bamana/Maninka)

N' (preceding a word): my (Bamana/Maninka).

nasrani literally, Nazarene, Christian, but more generally used to mean 'white man.' An Arabic word adopted in west African languages; nowadays the general term for a white man is *tubabu.*

N'Daar Dakar (Wolof and other)

neene mother. *neen'am* my mother (Fula)

nègè iron (Bamana/Maninka).

nègè da a cannon (obs. Bamana/Maninka)

ngana hero (Bamana/Maninka)

ngar come (imperative) (Fula)

ngaringa a ridged metal bar that serves as instrument; the sound is evoked by drawing a bar across the ridges (Bamana/Maninka)

ngoni a three stringed-instrument used to accompany the singing of epics (Bamana)

nin ka di 'it is well.' (Bamana/Maninka)

N'koro My elder. A title of respect, widely used. (Bamana/Maninka)

n'tomo a youthful initiation group (Bamana/Maninka)

numu Blacksmith (Bamana/Maninka).

nyama the vital spirit of a person or animal; the magical energy released through certain actions, most notably through killing. (Bamana/Maninka)

nyancho a warrior class of the western Manding, in the Gambia (Mandinka)

papier kraft Construction paper (French)

patois local dialect or speech, a somewhat derogatory term (French)

perepereperepere an onomatopoeic phrase indicating speed (Bamana/Maninka).

pulaaku the quality of being Fula; the precise definition will of course vary with the context and the intention of the person invoking this ethnic trait (Fula)

saa serpent (Bamana/Maninka

samafaga 'Elephant-killer.' A title in the hierarchy of the hunters' societies (Bamana/Maninka)

san yelema the turning of the year (Bamana/Maninka)

sanu gold (Bamana/Maninka)

senankuya a joking relationship established between clans, peoples, and social categories that allows gross insults, but not offense at those insults.

serifu the Shaarif, that claim descent from the prophet Muhammad (Arabic and other).

service colonial colonial service (French)

Shaitan Satan (Arabic)
sigi a word of many senses. It may refer to a game played by warriors (including Mari Jata); it also means a seat or throne; it also means the wild buffalo. (Bamana/Maninka).
signare one of the trading women of Dakar and St. Louis (Portuguese *senhora*, French and Wolof)
siratigi the master of the path, i.e. the leader of a caravan or an expedition (Bamana/Maninka)
siya lineage (Bamana/Maninka)
sofa warrior, soldier; the term is associated particularly with the mounted soldiers who followed Samori Toure in the period 1860-90 (*so* means horse in Maninka/Bamana). (Bamana/Maninka)
soma a seer, a diviner (Bamana/Maninka)
subaga muso Witch woman (Bamana/Maninka)
suudu bedchamber (Fula)
tabala a kind of drum, louder and deeper than the *jenbe*.
talen a story (folk-tale) Maninka/Mandinka
talibe from the Arabic, student at a Koranic school. At the time of the story, the term referred also to the followers of al-Hajj Umar Tal, the Tukolor leader who had conquered much of the Manding in the time before Samori. (Arabic/Fula).
tènè a taboo, most usually the avoidance of some foodstuff by some clan, but applying in other areas as well. (Bamana/Maninka)
tinye don 'it is true.' (Bamana/Maninka)
tirailleur sharpshooter; the name of the African army corps of the French colonial service. they were mostly Senegalese and accomplished the colonial conquests under the command of French officers (French)
tirayé see *tirailleur*, above (Bamana/Maninka and other).
to steamed millet paste, the starch eaten with a sauce at the main meal of the day. (Bamana/ Maninka)
ton association, brotherhood (Bamana/Maninka)
tonjon 'slave of the *ton'*. A word that usually denotes the warriors of the kingdom of Segou, who were sworn members of an association. (Bamana/Maninka)
waraba lit. great beast, the name of a masked figure (Bamana/Maninka)
wokòlò a spirit of the bush (Bamana/Maninka).
worodugu land (*dugu*) of the kola nut (*woro*); also used generally as a term for the forest areas lying south of the desert. (Bamana/Maninka)
wyrd a prayer of the Sufi Muslims (Arabic)

CPSIA information can be obtained
at www.ICGtesting.com
Printed in the USA
LVHW030856051221
705331LV00002B/142

9 781954 253063